IN T  F THE NG

Fulk, Earl of Stafford—the bravest warrior and one of the most powerful barons in England. Envy would drive his foes to barbaric acts.

Prince Henry—he was so young, yet his learning and brilliance amazed the barons.

Alys of Dol—her gypsy red hair and her reckless spirit had seduced more than one lord. Yet when a man she once loved was brutally murdered, she would have revenge.

Rannulf, Lord of Ledgefield—Fulk's son, a nobleman more suited to the clergy than to the battlefield, who deplored his father's rough ways, and the strategies of power and survival.

Thierry—England's tournament champion who nursed a bitter blood feud with Fulk at a time when murder was an acceptable means of settling disputes.

Books by Cecelia Holland

The Death of Attila
The Earl

Published by POCKET BOOKS

THE EARL

Cecelia Holland

POCKET BOOKS, a Simon & Schuster division of
GULF & WESTERN CORPORATION
1230 Avenue of the Americas, New York, N.Y. 10020

"Oh, where are you going?"
Said the Knight on the road.
"I go to meet my God,"
Said the Child as he stood.

INTRODUCTION

In 1120, THE ONLY LEGITIMATE son of King Henry I of England drowned in the wreck of the White Ship. The king married again, but as it became evident that this union would not produce another heir, Henry's attention turned toward his remaining legitimate child, his daughter Matilda (or Maud), who because of her marriage to the German Emperor Henry V is called the empress.

Her husband the emperor having died in 1125, Matilda (or Maud) made her way back to England. In 1127, her father forced his tenants-in-chief in both England and Normandy (which he had taken from his brother Robert Curthose in 1106) to swear homage to Matilda as his heiress and successor.

The barons were not happy. They demanded the right to counsel and consent when the king married off his daughter a second time. No one doubted that he would; the nature of the Anglo-Norman kingship required a king, not a queen.

Henry was an unscrupulous, crabby, suspicious man.

The husband he chose for the heiress of England and Normandy was the son of the Count of Anjou—Normandy's ancient blood-enemy. The wisdom of this choice was not immediately apparent, especially to the Norman barons, and foreseeing this, the king arranged the marriage in secret so that they would have no chance to object. In 1128 Matilda married Geoffrey, heir to Anjou.

The barons were furious, and the bride and groom disliked each other, but in 1133 Henry was presented with his first lawful grandson, who was named for him. The king, now in his sixties, hastened to extract another oath from his barons, securing the succession firmly on Matilda and her heirs. Late in the following year, Henry I ate a dish of lampreys, always chancy in those times, and died of acute indigestion.

Matilda was in Anjou. Her obvious rivals—the grandsons of William the Conqueror—were in Normandy. Her half brother, Robert, Earl of Gloucester, was a bastard, but William the Conqueror had been a bastard, and Gloucester was able and respected. Her cousins, the sons of the Conqueror's daughter Adela and Stephen of Blois, were wealthy, powerful, admired men. In fact, the eldest of them, Theobald, Count of Blois, was the choice of the Norman barons to become their duke.

Theobald's younger brother Stephen was quicker or, more likely, had been planning longer. He raced across the Channel to London, where the people acclaimed him king, and sped on to Winchester. Another brother, Henry, was, happily, Bishop of Winchester, and he was waiting there, with the head of Henry I's administration and the keeper of Henry I's treasury, to greet Stephen and give him the old king's money and seals and their own support.

Stephen had, of course, sworn the oath to Matilda, twice, and so had the Archbishop of Canterbury, whose duty it was to anoint England's king. Who should now conveniently appear but Hugh Bigod, a baron who had attended the king on his deathbed, and who swore that

Henry with his dying breath had repudiated his daughter and named Stephen as his heir. Freed of the oath, the archbishop anointed Stephen king of England. When the news reached Normandy, Theobald reluctantly gave up the duchy to his brother. The entire operation had taken only three weeks from the death of the old king.

The two men who had engineered this coup, Stephen of Blois and Henry, Bishop of Winchester, were sons of Stephen of Blois, who had distinguished himself during the First Crusade by climbing down the wall of besieged Antioch on a rope and fleeing back to Europe with the news that the Crusade had failed. Their mother was an iron-willed and influential daughter of the Conqueror. Henry was raised in the monastery of Cluny and trained in that tradition of co-operation between ecclesiastical and lay rulers. Stephen himself grew up at the court of his uncle King Henry, who treated him as a son, giving him precedence, in fact, over Robert of Gloucester, his real though illegitimate son.

At first, the other barons accepted Stephen as their king. His personal holdings, in England and in Normandy, were extensive, he was rich, he was a courageous and chivalrous knight, and he was extravagantly generous. Even Gloucester, after some hesitation, did him homage as king. Robert Beaumont, Earl of Leicester, and Waleran of Meulan, the twin brothers who were heads of the great House of Beaumont, became Stephen's chief advisers. Matilda appealed to the Roman Curia for justice, but Winchester seemed able to deal with that.

Stephen's most splendid moment, however, was the coup that made him king. Before long, he had managed to alienate his brother Winchester, who was passed over in his absence in the election of a new Archbishop of Canterbury, and the Earl of Chester, whose interests Stephen ignored in a settlement with the king of Scots. Finally, in 1139, Stephen made the error of attacking the Bishop of Salisbury and the bishop's son and nephews—the Bishops of Lincoln and Ely.

This action lost him the support of the Church, and Robert of Gloucester took the opportunity to make his formal defiance and revolt against the Crown. The empress landed in England to raise the banners of her cause, and immediately a half dozen other, smaller rebellions broke out.

The pattern for the next fourteen years was quickly set. The empress's center of support was in the west, with her base at Bristol. She had her supporters and their armies and the occasional help of her husband, the Count of Anjou, who was spending most of his attention and men on the conquest of Normandy. King Stephen controlled London and the east. Along with his feudal levy (under the circumstances not very reliable), he had an army of Flemish mercenaries under the command of William of Ypres, one of the few competent generals in the whole civil war.

The heaviest fighting took place in the Midlands, along the frontier between the two centers of power in England—Wallingford was besieged so often because it controlled the entrance into the upper Thames Valley and the heart of the empress's holdings. Neither side was strong enough to defeat the other. In their attempts to gain the decisive edge, both the king and the empress rewarded their supporters with lavish grants of power and authority. In 1135, there were seven earls in England. In the eighteen years he was king, Stephen created nineteen more, and the empress appointed eight.

This generosity allowed certain of the barons to fatten at the expense of both rivals. The civil war itself masked the existence of many smaller conflicts fought between baron and baron or baron and people, and in their endless pursuit of each other, the two royal rivals lost their control over local authority and jurisdictions. Therefore, a man like Rannulf, Earl of Chester, would put together a great mass of land—gifts from both king and empress, as well as his family's holdings—and rule it like a little kingdom. In recent years it has become

fashionable to make light of the Anarchy, and indeed
the reports of some of the chroniclers reflect extreme
local conditions rather than the condition of the whole
kingdom. Yet in some areas the authority of the Crown
was forgotten, and order was maintained by the personal power of local men, or by mere inertia—or order
disappeared altogether.

In 1141, the rebellion of the Earl of Chester against
King Stephen led to the confrontation at Lincoln,
where the king graciously surrendered the advantage
of the terrain so that the battle would start on even
terms. He was gloriously beaten and taken prisoner. At
first he was treated well, but soon he was seen bound
in chains.

The empress entered London in triumph. Before she
was even crowned, her arrogance and the fondness of
the City of London (whose burgesses were barons) for
the king sent her scurrying for the safety of Winchester.
Stephen's queen, who for the sake of confusion was
also named Matilda, led the pursuit with an army of
mercenaries under William of Ypres. The empress and
her friends retreated from Winchester, and the retreat
became a headlong flight. The empress narrowly escaped, and her brother Gloucester was captured.

Gloucester was exchanged for the king, and, leaving
his sister in Oxford, he went to Anjou to ask the help
of her husband. The count was conquering Normandy
and pressed Gloucester into service there. When he
finally got back to England, he found the situation
desperate. Stephen had attacked the empress in Oxford and seized the city and besieged her in the castle.
Before Gloucester could rescue her, she escaped in the
middle of the night and ran through the ice and winter
snow to Wallingford.

Gloucester quickly defeated the rampaging king, who
in his turn barely avoided capture, and brought the
west of England somewhat under his control again.
England lapsed into an unaccustomed calm. A number
of the more warlike barons went on Crusade in 1146,

including Leicester's brother Waleran. The country was exhausted. Even when the empress's fourteen-year-old son, Henry, came to England, general enthusiasm could not be mustered. Henry, who had brought along some Flemish mercenaries, soon found himself without the money to pay them. He appealed to his cousin Stephen for help, and the king paid off the rioting troops and sent the boy home. In 1148, Gloucester died and the empress left England for Anjou. She never returned.

King Stephen was left with the problem of bringing under control a number of men and communities that had been ignoring him for years. The great earls were building castles without his permission, making treaties between themselves, fighting private wars and in some cases minting money, all without any regard for the rights and prerogatives of the Crown. The ordinary business of the kingdom—collecting taxes, holding courts of justice—had apparently all but ceased. Through the generosity and ineptitude of the two rivals, some of his own supporters had become a match for the king when he tried to bring them under control. Certain towns defied him as well.

While Stephen went about straightening up his kingdom, the decisive action of the civil war was taking place neither on a battlefield nor in England. The empress had put her case before the Pope as early as 1138. Under the direction of his brother the Bishop of Winchester, Stephen's envoys were responding to her charges. The Bishop of Winchester was a Cluniac —a monk of Cluny. This alone made him the enemy of the influential and fanatic monk Saint Bernard, who was a Cistercian—a monk of the new order of Cîteaux. But Winchester and the House of Blois also represented the Cluniac tradition of compromise and co-operation between the ecclesiastical and secular rulers; Saint Bernard therefore considered Winchester a compromising, worldly, unreformed, and wicked monk and his brother a usurper.

When a Cistercian was elected Pope in 1144, the

Cluniacs in power in England fell into disfavor, the empress's case was heard more sympathetically, and, in 1148, King Stephen was excommunicated. Two years later, the Pope refused to allow the Archbishop of Canterbury to anoint Stephen's son Eustace as heir to England.

In that same year, 1151, the Count of Anjou died. He left a will that gave Normandy to his elder son, Henry, who also fell heir to his mother's claim to England. Anjou went to the younger son, Geoffrey. Henry overturned his father's will and seized Anjou. He was not yet twenty, but he had ruled Normandy since his sixteenth birthday and his father had trained him carefully. Only a few months later he doubled his territories by marrying Eleanor, the heiress to Aquitaine, former queen of France. This marriage involved Henry in a war with the French king, and he was forced to a settlement that was less than glorious. But in January of the following year, 1153, Henry invaded England to answer the appeal of the city of Wallingford for aid against King Stephen.

The Earl of Chester came to his support, and the Earl of Leicester quickly joined them. Henry with their help consolidated his position in the west, moved through the Midlands gathering supporters and bringing towns and castles under his control, and laid siege to Tutbury, the seat of the House of Ferrers, earls of Derby. It is here that the story begins.

With the exception of the family of the Earl of Stafford, his attendants, and some minor figures, the characters are drawn from history. The castle, borough, and earldom of Stafford actually belonged to the Earl of Chester. The Earl of Pembroke, Gilbert Fitz Richard de Clare, died in 1148, and there are doubtless other such errors. Readers interested in the period will find A. L. Poole's *From Domesday Book to Magna Carta* (Oxford) a good overview of the century and H. A. Cronne's *The Reign of Stephen* (London) an interesting closer look at the Anarchy itself. People who like old chronicles will find the *Gesta Stephani,* now complete, among Nelson's Medieval Texts. The ballad herein called *The Song of the White Ship* is, of course, a free version of *Sir Patrick Spens.*

THE EARL

ONE

"ARE YOU AWAKE, MY LORD?"

"Yes," Fulk said. "Light a candle, will you." He could not remember the name of the page, who was one of Derby's household. Sitting up in his bed, he put his feet on the floor and stood up. In the darkness, a candle began to gleam, shielded by the page's body. The rustling sound of the rain filled the whole room.

"Send Sir Roger to me," Fulk said. He took the candle and put it on the table. "Thank you, I'll dress myself, get Sir Roger."

The page stepped back and cleared his throat. "Sir Roger—is he the—"

"The tall blond knight who commands my escort."

"Yes, my lord." The page dashed off.

Fulk had been sleeping in his shirt. He sat down on the bed and groped for his clothes. The candle lit only a small circle of the floor, showing him his boots and coat; his hose lay half under the bed. He put them on, fumbling in the dark.

"My lord," Roger said, and came in the door. The

page had brought another candle to light his way, and he put it down and came over to help Fulk dress. Roger said, "Are we going to Stafford?"

"Yes," Fulk said. "At last. Get the men ready. I want to go before my lady wakes up." Margaret was sick, his excuse for not sleeping with her, and would probably sleep until long after he had gone.

"My lord," the page said nervously, "my lady Countess is already awake. She says you must eat before you go, and she is waiting for you in the hall."

"God——" Fulk sat down, and the page bent to put on his boots. Over the boy's head Fulk and Roger stared at each other. Fulk shook his head. "Damned woman."

"Shall I order the men to get ready?" Roger said, expressionless.

"Yes."

Roger went out. Fulk stood, and the page brought him his coat and helped him into it. It was still completely dark outside. He buckled his belt, took his dagger from the floor by the bed and sheathed it, and, with the page before him holding a candle, went into the next room. People still lay sleeping here. The candlelight showed them bundled together in the beds, their feet toward him and their heads lost in the dark. The page held open the door, and Fulk went into the hall.

Except for a table near the hearth, a few benches, and one candle standard, the hall was bare of furnishing, and like a cave it echoed. The rain thundered on the roof overhead and roared along the eaves. Fulk's wife and the Earl of Derby were sitting at the table, eating by the light of the fire and six candles. Fulk crossed the hall toward them and sat down on the bench opposite Margaret.

"Good morning," Derby said, beside Margaret. "Did you sleep well?"

"Morning," Fulk said. "It's the middle of the night. What are you doing out of bed, my lady? I thought you were sick." A page set a dish of cold meat down in front of him, and he drew his dagger to cut it.

"I am," Margaret said placidly. She was tall for a woman, shapeless with fat, her wide, clear gray eyes almost lost in her round face. She had a cold; her nose shone red as a holly berry, and her voice was hoarse. "I would be a poor wife, would I not, if I let you go away without a farewell?"

Derby said, "Surely you don't want to go now anyway, Fulk. Not in the rain."

Fulk gave him a sideways look, and Derby went quickly back to his cold roast chicken. Margaret said, "I cannot see the need to go to Stafford at all, my lord."

"A dangerous outlaw has seized my castle, the seat of my family," Fulk said. "I suppose you wish me to—"

"You choose to interpret it that way," she said. A servant brought up a plate laden with warm bread; Fulk took a loaf the size of his hand and split it lengthwise. Margaret said, "I am sure you are needed more at Tutbury than at Stafford, my lord. You neglect your prince, going to Stafford."

Fulk chewed a mouthful of bread, swallowed it, and reached for the wine. If she could, she would keep him here arguing all day long. He had intended to go the morning before, but suddenly she had arrived, started a fight, and kept it up until he had to stay another day. "I'm not going to argue with you," he said.

Derby said uneasily, "I have to be back in Tutbury, anyway, of course. My lady, let me offer you a cake." He gave the page a bit of simnel cake spread with red jam, and the boy carried it the three steps to Margaret.

She accepted it absently, her eyes on Fulk. He made himself busy with his food. Servants moved around the table, on the edge of the light, taking away plates and bringing others. Fulk knew that Margaret was wondering why he and Derby were meeting here, a day's ride from Derby's castle of Tutbury, when Tutbury lay under siege by the army which Fulk in part com-

manded. He took a sip of light wine, rolled it around
his mouth, and spat it onto the floor.

"You still haven't told me how you knew I was
coming here," he said to Margaret. "Surely my com-
ings and goings aren't gossiped about all the way up
in Yorkshire?"

Margaret gave him a long, vacant stare. Turning to
Derby, she said, "I'm sure the rain will keep up all
day long, aren't you, my lord?"

"Oh, probably, yes."

"Not at all," Fulk said. "In this season, it will clear
before noon."

"Well," Derby said, "perhaps it will."

Fulk sat back and pushed his plate aside. He was
full; he tapped his foot impatiently on the floor. Margaret studied him. "See how eager he is. Poor Thierry."

"Poor Thierry," Fulk said. "Poor Thierry is a mur-
dering, whoring, swinish, worthless outlaw. God's bones.
You're always so worried about our honor—after
Thierry, we have none. It humiliates me that you defend him." He looked toward the door, wondering
where Roger was.

"He is of your own blood," she said.

"Precisely why I am responsible for him. I'm pleased
you take my point so readily, my lady."

Margaret sneezed, put her hand over her face, and
sneezed again. Fulk rapped his fingertips on the table.

"I wish you'd wait until the rain stops," Derby said.

"No."

"If he waited," Margaret said, and sneezed. Her
watering eyes glared at Fulk, but before she could finish speaking, another sneeze took her, and Roger came
up out of the darkness toward Fulk.

"Are they all ready, finally?" Fulk said.

"We can leave whenever you wish, my lord." Roger
bowed to Margaret, who muttered something at him.
A nervous smile on his face, Derby got up, and Fulk
took his cloak from the page who had wakened him.

"Allow me to attend you, Fulk," Derby said.

"Thank you, Robert. My lady, I shall expect you at

Stafford Castle directly the rain ends. See that you care for your health." He jammed his hands into his gloves.

"And you, my lord," Margaret said. "I shouldn't wish a humor like mine on you."

Fulk grunted. He stamped toward the door; a page led the way with a candle, but now the dawn was coming, and he could see the door, pale in the dark wall. He stopped before it to put his cloak on. Outside, he could see the courtyard streaming like a river in the rain, the knights waiting in their saddles, everything gray.

"Take the high road, at least," Derby said, clutching Fulk by the arm. "There are outlaws thick as cream in the forest, and what if Thierry has heard you're coming? If he tried to ambush you—oh, well." He smiled apologetically. "Your lady is upset that you're going to Stafford."

"She's in love with my uncle, like all the other women in the world." That was not why she was upset. He hated to talk about Margaret to anyone else, and he started toward the door.

"Well. Whatever. I have taken to heart what you told me, Fulk. You do well in the service of your prince."

Fulk made a noncommittal sound in his throat. The boom of the rain on the wooden roof distracted him; he had to think to remember what Derby had said. "The kingdom is a ruin, and I believe he can mend it." He put up his hood, the soft fur packed around his ears. Catching Derby's eye, he smiled. "You don't really want Tutbury, do you? With that midden stench around it?"

Startled, Derby laughed, and Fulk headed for the door. Derby came after him to the edge of the rain.

"I shall see you soon. Have no fears for your lady, we shall care for her lovingly."

"Thank you." Fulk went out into the rain.

Knights filled this courtyard, swathed in their cloaks, their lances at rest. A groom led forward Fulk's big bay horse, and Roger whisked the cloth from the saddle and in the same motion boosted Fulk up onto the horse's back, before the rain could wet it. Fulk stabbed his feet into the stirrups.

"We'll take the forest road."

Roger mounted. The knights were working their way out the gate in a double file. With Roger just behind him, Fulk pushed through the crowd to the gate and fell into the moving column two pairs from its head. The meadows around Derby's hunting lodge were misty and dim in the rain, and the mud of the road sucked at the horses' hoofs.

At Roger's shouted order, the column trotted into the left fork in the road, straight into the forest. Mud splashed up from the horses in front, and Fulk reined back a little. The bay horse snorted and shook its head, protesting, but it slowed obediently.

One thing that heeded him. Margaret had been spending the spring with their daughter and her children, far north of here, but as soon as she'd heard Fulk was going to Stafford she'd ridden to deflect him, catching cold on the way. All to save Thierry from him?

"We'll be there before dark," Roger said.

"We had damn well better be."

The column moved at a quick trot down the edge of the road, less muddy than the center. Fulk shifted his weight more comfortably in the saddle. Margaret wasn't concerned for his sake, certainly, and she wasn't much concerned for Thierry's sake. The only person who could have dragged her away from their daughter was Rannulf, their elder son. She had never mentioned his name, but she thought that Rannulf was with Thierry at Stafford, or she would not care if Fulk went there or not.

"Did you send a messenger to Ledgefield?" he said to Roger.

Roger looked around, surprised. Mud had splattered his long-nosed, fair face. "Of course, my lord. Yesterday, when you told me."

"Remember. I may need witnesses to my innocence."

"My lord," Roger said, blankly.

They rode deeper into the forest. The road wound downhill, slippery with mud and full of stones. Birch trees and the thick pine gave way to oaks, taller, muffling the sound of the rain. Ahead, the road pinched down to a trail, littered with half-buried boulders like uneven steps, and Roger formed the column into a single file. They slowed to a walk down a steep hillside. On either side of them, the forest stretched out into darkness.

"What did you think of Derby's hunting lodge?"

Roger looked at him and smiled. Fulk laughed. "Did you see much of it?"

"As much as I could, my lord. He builds more for comfort than for safety, I think."

"My lord Derby's always had a use for comfort." Derby was ready to join Prince Henry, one more necessary step toward a settlement of the long wars. Fulk stared into the forest to his right. The idea of peace seemed alien and exotic, like a word in another language. Dark green and pale green and brown, the forest resounded under the rain in a vast surrounding roar. Outlaws, poachers, stray English, the forest was tenanted with strange, dangerous people. No more dangerous and strange than your common Norman earl.

If he caught Thierry at Stafford, he meant to kill him. If Rannulf was there it would be difficult, perhaps impossible. Fulk could understand Margaret's protecting Thierry but the thought that Rannulf might angered him. It made no sense.

"Are you thirsty, my lord?"

He looked around and saw the wineskin Roger held out toward him, swaying with the strides of the horses.

"God's bones. From your brother's vineyard?" He snatched it, wrapped his rein around his wrist, and pulled out the stopper. The de Nef vineyards were superb. Roger smiled at him, and he took a long drink from the skin; strong, tart wine flowed warmly through him, until his head whirled.

"Thank you."

If Rannulf were silly enough to go to Stafford for

Thierry's sake, he deserved to be caught. Fulk gave the wineskin back to Roger, and they picked up a fast trot.

Long before they reached the river, they could hear it, overflowing its banks in the late, unseasonable rain, rumbling stones and tree branches along in its course. They crossed it shortly before noon and rode on deeper into the forest. The rain lessened. Twice Roger stopped the column to let the horses rest, and the men sat talking in their saddles, passing wineskins back and forth, the steam rising from the flanks and backs of their horses.

Fulk dismounted the second time they stopped and walked around to stretch his legs. The idea that Rannulf was at Stafford gnawed at him. He kicked up the mulch under his feet and watched white insects burrow away from the open air. There was still the mystery of how Thierry had gotten into Stafford in the first place. Roger was calling orders to the knights. Tearing up the floor of the forest with his heels, Fulk walked back to his horse and mounted.

They rode on. Fulk told Roger to move the men riding behind them up to the front, where they wouldn't have mud kicked up in their faces. They were all men from his army at Tutbury, and after the boredom of the siege this was pleasant for them; he heard them talking to each other about it. Thierry had only a few men with him besides the garrison of Stafford Castle, who were Fulk's and knew better than to support an outlaw against their lord. He remembered the adage about outlaws—the wolf's head, that any man might cut down. He had to shout to Roger twice before the big knight heard him.

"How long did it take us the last time we came this way?"

Roger scratched his nose. "Longer than now, I think. A few days longer, my lord."

"We had to wait for the knights to reach us from Ledgefield, though."

The last time they had come north he had brought four hundred men, knights and crossbowmen and a corps of engineers for siege work. They'd been going to meet the Earl of Chester to discuss a treaty, and Chester respected only overwhelming force. They had all gotten that way a little in the wars.

They rode into a crossroads, and Roger called orders in a crisp voice. The column slowed to a jog trot. In the middle of the junction stood an old stone cross covered with climbing blue flowers. Smoothly, without changing pace, the horsemen swung into the right branch of the road. Each of the men passing made the sign of the Cross, but Fulk merely bowed his head.

JUST BEFORE SUNDOWN, they rode up the steep path to Stafford Castle. Occasionally, through gaps in the pine trees that covered the hill, Fulk could see the town at its foot, surrounded by its wooden wall. The air smelled richly of pine. Above them, the castle, built of dark red stone, rose beyond the pines—on the road it was already darkening, but the last sunlight shone on the walls and roofs of the castle. From the tower and the gatehouse, Fulk's banners flew, and his garrison with their lances at salute stood all along the rampart on either side of the gate, which was open wide to welcome him.

At a smart trot, the knights moved up the last stretch of the slope toward the castle. Across the cloudy sky beyond, the red and orange of the sunset grew bright, mounting steadily into the peak of the sky. They rode into the shadow of the castle wall and Fulk reined to a stop.

"They knew we were coming," Roger said, frowning.

"Apparently."

The column of knights trotted briskly through the gate and into the wide outer court of the castle. On the inner wall and from every window facing them, people leaned, and when they saw Fulk they cheered. The knights lined up against the wall, their horses turned head in, and dipped their lances, and the people of the castle cheered again. Fulk rode into the middle of the courtyard. Gilbert, his bailiff, came forward to greet him.

"My lord, we had no word of your coming until your messenger arrived, or we would have—"

Roger dismounted and walked up to hold Fulk's horse. Fulk swung down from his saddle, and immediately a flock of pages and grooms surrounded them.

"I understand my uncle is here, Gilbert." He gave his cloak to a page.

"He was," Rannulf said. He came up quietly through the crowd of servants. His face wore no expression at all, but he'd clasped his hands behind him, like a small boy waiting to be scolded.

"I never sent a messenger," Fulk said to Gilbert. His face burned; his voice seemed tight and harsh. He had never really thought that Rannulf would be here— for all his thinking, he was not ready for it. He met Rannulf's eyes, and Rannulf squared his shoulders and took a deep breath.

"Roger." Fulk swung away from his son. "See that these men are cared for, fed and quartered. I trust that we have food enough for them, Gilbert?"

"Of course, my lord."

"Good. I thought perhaps Thierry had looted the pantry as well." He looked back at Rannulf, and his son's set, polite face brought his anger up again, sharp as pain.

"Come into the hall, my lord," Rannulf said. "You must be tired."

"How long have you been here?" Fulk said softly. "What are you doing here?" He took a step forward, and Rannulf moved hastily out of his way. Gilbert hung by his side.

"I'll eat and drink in my room. Ale. I'll talk to you there. Send someone to Sir Roger to tell him where I am." He strode toward the side door into the gatehouse; he didn't want to look around and see if Rannulf was coming after him.

"Gilbert, send the lord of Ledgefield to me."

"My lord," Gilbert said. His voice quivered with curiosity. A servant threw the door open, and Fulk went up the narrow stone stairs.

"Thierry Ironhand was here," Gilbert said. He followed close behind Fulk up the winding stairway. "I would not have let him in, my lord, but he had orders with your seals on them."

"My seals?" Fulk looked over his shoulder at him.

"Yes, my lord."

A page opened the door into Fulk's antechamber, smoky and warm from the fire burning on the hearth. Fulk went into the center of the room and shed his cloak. The page went around lighting candles.

"How long was he here?"

"Eight days," Gilbert said, at his side. "He left when the messenger came. My lord Ledgefield can tell you more than I, my lord. He spent much time with him."

Fulk grunted. Gilbert, in saying Rannulf's title, had gestured behind him, which meant Rannulf was right there, following. Gilbert rushed forward to help a page drag over a table for Fulk to eat at. Kitchen servants came in with covered trays and a ewer of ale. Fulk glanced around the room: there were clean rushes on the floor, and fresh candles set into their iron holders, everything looked newly polished. Thierry had probably slept and eaten here, in Fulk's own chambers. He went to the fire and held out his hands toward it, so that he would not have to acknowledge Rannulf's presence. The room was crowded with people.

"My lord," Gilbert said, and Fulk turned and sat down before the table, covered with platters and cups. Rannulf stood near the door, watching him.

"Sit down," Fulk said, and pointed to the far side of the table. There was no chair, but a page brought one, and Rannulf came over and sat.

"How did you know that Thierry was here?" Rannulf said.

"Innumerable ways. It's all over England. I thought he was in Spain, contentedly fighting Moors. How is Eleanor?"

"Very well. And the baby."

"Excellent. Now we come to difficult questions. How did Thierry get into my castle?"

Rannulf said nothing; his face tightened. A page was slipping fur-lined shoes onto Fulk's feet. Fulk leaned back, enjoying the dry warmth of the fire, and drank ale. "The ale is very good this year."

"Thank you." Rannulf stirred. "It's from Ledgefield."

"I'm glad you're of some use. How did Thierry get into my castle, child?"

At least Rannulf didn't look away. Those servants with nothing to do withdrew out of hearing, up against the tapestries on the far wall. Gilbert ushered in kitchen servants with more platters, meat, and bread. Fulk wiped foam from his upper lip and put down his cup.

"Gilbert says that Thierry brought orders sealed with my seals. My information is that he and his woman were at Ledgefield before they came here."

"How could I turn them away?" Rannulf said. "They are my own blood kin."

"Bad blood. And Peverel's niece is no kindred of yours that I know of. The orders were of course destroyed?" Gilbert nodded. "Were they my seals, Gilbert?"

"Yes, my lord." Gilbert shot forward, his white hands busy with the meal being laid out. "I was very—"

"Or were they Ledgefield's seals?"

In the little silence, Gilbert retreated back into a corner of the room. Fulk held out his cup again, and Rannulf mechanically got up and filled it. A page brought Fulk a dish of meat and bread, and Fulk gestured to him to leave it on the table in front of him. Rannulf sat down.

"They must have been mine. I never saw them, but he was at Ledgefield, and . . . you know how similar they are, your seals and mine."

"Yes. So does Thierry. Where do you keep your seals?"

"In my own bedroom." Rannulf cleared his throat. "In my personal chest, beside the bed."

Fulk took out his dagger and cut meat. "Reasonably inaccessible, one would think." He watched Rannulf blush, laid his dagger down, and ate the meat with his fingers. "To Thierry, at least."

Rannulf looked over at the fire. His hair, brown like Fulk's, shone with red lights. "Well, there was Alys, you know."

With a bit of bread, Fulk sopped up gravy. "His leman. Did she have the opportunity?"

Rannulf nodded once.

The pages were moving around the room, lighting more candles; they reached the high ones on the walls with an iron pole. Fulk ate more meat. Alys of Dol, William Peverel's niece, ran away from her husband to follow Thierry Ironhand: he was surprised that Thierry had brought her back with him from his foreign wanderings. He pushed his platter away.

"What does Eleanor say about that?"

"She doesn't know." Rannulf looked quickly up.

"Don't suppose that because she says nothing she doesn't know. So Alys took the seals. Are they back? Have you looked?"

"Oh, they're where they're supposed to be. I never missed them. I guessed, when Gilbert told me, but—" He bit off the words.

Fulk studied him a moment. Everyone said that Rannulf looked like him, but he could always see the traces of his mother on him, in his wide eyes, his soft small mouth. He thought, Now is the moment for a homily on the sins of the flesh. He drank more ale.

"Where did Thierry go?"

Rannulf shrugged. "I don't know. He spoke of leaving England."

"He's in and out of England like a bird with a new nest."

"He says he's tired of fighting you."

Rannulf was watching him intently. Fulk picked around the meat on his platter. "He'd be far more tired if he ever actually did fight me. What did you talk about, you and he?"

"Oh—" Rannulf shrugged. "The places he's been. Wars. You." He looked swiftly at Fulk. "He asked about you often. How you were, if you'd softened toward him."

"What did you say?"

"That people are always harshest with the people they've wronged."

"Thank you. Why did he go?"

"He knew he couldn't hold Stafford against you. It isn't Stafford he wants, anyway. He—"

"He has no right to Stafford," Fulk said. "He has no right to anything of the Honor of Bruyère."

"I'm not going to argue that. He left her here as surety?"

Fulk jerked his head around. "Her? Alys? She's here?"

"Yes. I think he was tired of her. She wanted to go with him."

"Where is she?"

"In the tower."

Rannulf's brown eyes were all but closed; clearly he was pleased with Fulk's reaction. Fulk frowned at him a moment, ate another slab of meat, and slowly spread butter on the crusty, golden bread.

"Isn't it kind of Thierry to leave his problems to me. Gilbert, send a page to the Lady Alys and ask her to attend me."

"My lord."

Rannulf smiled. "She won't be a problem to you, my lord. Everybody knows you're cold to women."

Fulk cocked his eyebrows at him. "She's a Peverel, and I'm on very bad terms with William Peverel. A tender problem."

"Have you seen Hugh?"

"He's with Pembroke's army at Stamford, I think." Hugh was his younger son, a squire with the Earl of Pembroke. "Madelaine's baby is doing well, your mother says."

"You've seen Mother? Where?"

"She met me on the way here. She'll be at Stafford in a few days."

"She's coming here?" Rannulf got up and moved around the table to another chair, where he could see the door and Fulk in the same glance. "She met you on the way? Whatever for?"

"For love of me, of course. I never sent a messenger saying I was coming here. I imagine she did. Is the messenger still here?"

Rannulf shook his head. "He left immediately. Have you captured Tutbury yet?"

"It's only a question of will, of which Prince Henry has a superabundance."

"What is he like? This prince."

"You'll find out soon, I hope."

"I've heard—"

The door opened, and Rannulf shot to his feet. Skirts rustled. A gaunt woman in middle years came through the door and withdrew to one side of the room. Behind her, Gilbert held the door wide, and the Lady Alys came in.

Fulk stood up. She was taller than he was, as tall as Rannulf; she wore her dark red hair uncovered, plaited in long braids down her back and woven with extra hair, a style that reminded Fulk of his mother. He thought she had probably been more beautiful when she was more innocent—her eyes, when they met his, shone feverishly, and her mouth was harsh—but he could see why Thierry had taken her beyond the sea and why Rannulf had let her seduce him with his young wife scarcely out of childbed. She looked from him to Rannulf and back to him and sat down.

"My lady," Rannulf said. "May I present my lord the Earl of Stafford."

She sat in the chair as if she might be attacked, her hands clenched in her lap. "The Earl of Stafford is Thierry Ironhand."

Fulk sat down again. "As you wish, my lady. Do you know where he is now?"

"No."

She did know; her answer was too quick to be true. Fulk looked at the waiting woman hovering in the corner. "Did she come with you?"

"Lady Maud has attended Lady Alys since childhood," Rannulf said.

"My, my." Fulk put his elbow on the arm of his chair and rested his chin on his fist. "I didn't ask you. If you want to talk, go somewhere else."

Rannulf flushed dark red. Alys gave him a scornful look that made her seem much younger— Fulk tried to remember how old she was and could not. But she was very young.

"I'm sending you back to your husband, lady."

Her eyes opened wide. "No. You can't do that."

"You can't stay here. I won't send you to Thierry. Where else can you go?"

"My husband won't take me back."

"We'll see what can be done."

Rannulf stood up, still ruddy-cheeked. "May I go, my lord?"

"You have my leave. I'd be pleased if you'd help Roger settle those knights."

"Yes, my lord." Rannulf bowed, exaggerating the courtesy, and strode out. Fulk stared after him. He hated his children to treat him formally, and they knew it. The door slammed.

"Thierry said you were full of small cruelties," Alys said. "Now I understand."

"You don't. If you had any understanding you wouldn't be here."

Hot color rushed into her face. A page in Rannulf's livery brought over a jug and a cup and poured wine for her, and she wrenched her gaze from Fulk and stared at the bright stream.

"I'll help you with your husband," Fulk said, "if you help me with my uncle."

Her head flew up; she gave him the same scornful look she'd given Rannulf. The flush had left her face, and her skin was white and fine as flax. "I assure you, my lord, that very shortly you'll need far more help than

I could give you against Thierry—more than you'll find in this kingdom."

Fulk leaned back, stretching his legs, and stared at her. That was curious—there was only one reason why she would say that, with Thierry an outlaw and Fulk an earl. He put his head to one side. "So Thierry has gone to make friends with Prince Henry."

Her shoulders hunched. "I didn't say that."

"You did indeed."

"Henry will be king, and when he is, Thierry will have back everything you stole from him. Thierry will be Earl of Stafford."

"That I never took from him. Prince Henry's mother the empress appointed me earl long after Thierry was outlawed. The only land Thierry ever held by right was Beck. Unfortunately for Thierry's pretensions, Prince Henry has already found me to be of more use than Thierry ever could. Do you think you'll be a countess?"

She said nothing; her mouth screwed up into a sullen pout, and he sat upright, irritated with her. "You should pack up what you brought here. I'll send you to Peverel tomorrow. Lady Maud, attend your mistress." He stood up.

Alys stayed in her chair. One of her braids hung over her shoulder into her lap, and she wound its end furiously around her forefinger. Her face was inscrutable. Abruptly, she said, her eyes on his face, "You can't send me back. I won't go. I'll run away again."

"Like Thierry."

"Thierry didn't run from you. Don't delude yourself that Thierry ran away from you."

Fulk poured himself ale. "Go away, or you'll tempt me to more of my small cruelties."

"Swine." Her maid was pulling at her sleeve, trying to draw her away. Alys rose. "I hope I am there when Thierry catches you."

Roger came in through the open door. Alys marched out past him, Maud at her heels, and Roger turned to watch her go. "Is that Red Alys?" he said.

Fulk stood in front of the fire warming his hands; he nodded and gestured toward the ale on the table. "Indeed. Thierry's loving cup, drunk to the lees."

Roger picked up the ewer. "She looks as if there's something sweet left in her."

Fulk got a poker and jabbed the fire with it. "Don't talk of her like that. Her grandfather was an earl."

"Yes, my lord," Roger said, surprised. "I'm sorry."

Fulk stabbed the fire; a log burst with a shower of sparks.

HE OPENED HIS eyes into the pitch dark; the nightlight on the table beside his bed had gone out. Lying still under the weight of covers, he tried to remember where he was and could not. He heard the breathing of the two pages sleeping at the foot of his bed; his ears strained, trying to hear the sound that had wakened him.

I am in Stafford. With the realization, the room settled itself around him, no longer alien, and he knew what he was listening for. Obligingly, it came almost at once: a low wail, like a sick animal or the wind, just beyond the window. He did not think it was the wind. He squirmed deeper into the close warmth of the covers. Nearly every night he'd slept here, he'd heard that cry. The first time he'd been sleeping in this bed with his grandparents, and it had wakened him then, too. His grandfather had told him to comfort him that no one but a lord of Stafford ever heard the cry.

It sounded again, seeming farther away, soft and lonely. It no longer frightened him, it only made him sad.

"Thierry will not have Stafford," his grandfather had said. Thierry from his early youth had gone out wandering and fighting. Back in the days of King Henry before the long wars started, Thierry like a stormy petrel had broken the peace and defied the law as if he knew that with the old king's death peace and law would both be gone, while Fulk tamely served the old lord. So when the old man died, he gave Fulk the Honor of Bruyère and Thierry only the manor of Beck, in Yorkshire. I was fifteen, I never meant to take his inheritance, and what should I have done, outmurdered him? He swung his legs over the side of the bed, into the chilly air. A dog was sleeping on the floor, and he nuzzled his toes into the coarse fur until in the dark a wet tongue came stroking his feet.

"Merry," he whispered. In the dark something thumped on the floor. "Merry, up. Up."

The dog moved, brushing against his legs, and a weight landed heavily on the bed beside him. Fulk put his arms around it. The dog squirmed, licking his face, and patted him with its forepaw. My grandfather whipped me once for having dogs in the bed. "Good boy. Good dog." The dog licked his ear, breathing with a roar.

"My lord?" a sleepy page's voice called.

"Go stir up the fire in the antechamber and bring me a gown." He rubbed his face into the dog's shaggy coat.

A candle came through the air toward him, a page barely lit behind it, and lowered to the wick of the nightlight. The flame was reflected in the dog's eyes. The page saw the dog on the bed and opened his mouth to order it down, and the dog pressed its shoulder against Fulk. The page went off briskly.

"Get down, Merry." The other page had come up with a gown. Fulk pushed the dog off the bed and stood up, and the pages hurried him into the gown and put shoes on his feet.

"Are you thirsty, my lord?"

"No. Go back to sleep." He cinched a belt around his waist and took the candle. "Is the fire going?"

"Yes, my lord."

He went into the antechamber; the dog followed, its nails clicking on the floor. Before he shut the door, he heard the pages talking softly, over near the bed. They were talking about him, they had nothing else to talk about. He shut the door and went over to the fire, where Gilbert had left the records of the estates. This room was warmer than his bedroom, facing the courtyard, away from the wind; the firelight glowed along the wood of the chairs, the table. He sat down, pushed aside the rolls of revenues and tenants' dues, and found parchment and got out a pen and ink. While he was trimming the pen, the dog wandered around the room, sniffing at corners.

"Merry. Lie down."

The dog came over to the hearth and flopped on its stomach, its head on its great paws, and sighed. Fulk unstopped the jar of ink and dipped in the pen.

"To the Earl of Leicester, from Fulk de Bruyère of Stafford, greeting."

The neat words moving across the page settled him, and the strangeness of waking up in the middle of the night left him.

"I have spoken to Earl Robert, as we agreed, and he listened with an eager ear. I believe that he will join the prince if the siege of Tutbury is pressed and if we approach him properly. He is concerned for the protection of his lands that lie close to those of the Earl of Chester and it is my opinion that he can be won through that concern."

He dipped the pen into the ink again, thinking; Derby had gone into revolt because the prince had granted certain Peverel lands to Chester, and Derby was a cousin of William Peverel. Derby seemed willing to overlook that now, but it had to be settled. "You should see that he agrees to the prince's grants of land to Chester when you treat with him, or he may use that later as an excuse to break the agreement."

Lifting his head, he listened for the cry that had wakened him, but in this room he had never heard it. Once when he'd been very young he had crawled out the bedroom window looking for its source and had nearly fallen forty feet to the ground. Leicester knew why he had come to Stafford and would want to know about Thierry. Fulk leaned back in the chair, shifting so that the fire warmed his other side. He wondered if Thierry had ever heard the cry.

"I reached Stafford today and the castle is again in my hands. However, my uncle escaped and has gone off with his outlaws, and I suspect that he may come next to Prince Henry's camp. For our old friendship, cousin, if he should, watch over my interests." It did no harm to remind a Beaumont of a blood kinship. "Sealed at Stafford, by my own hand."

The heat of the fire was scalding his right side, and he got up and moved his chair. Pentecost was coming; they would have to celebrate it, and of course the town would have its fair. In a shire of small villages and herders' cottages and wide forests, the occasional fair at Stafford was a great event, and even he enjoyed them. They would have to mend the bridge—that was the responsibility of the monks of Saint Jude, who, Gilbert had said, had run away from the monastery because of the outlaws and the Earl of Chester's raids, *I should go there and see what condition it's in.* If the buildings were fit to be lived in he could ask the White Monks to set up a chapter at Saint Jude. He put sand on the parchment and shook it back and forth.

"Father?" Rannulf slid through the door and shut it quietly. "What are you doing awake so late?"

Fulk put down the letter. "I couldn't sleep. Sit down —why are you up?"

Rannulf sank obediently into a chair too far from the fire, got up, moved it closer, and sat down again. The dog on the hearth whacked its tail on the floor a few times and groaned.

"I saw your light. Are you working?" Rannulf picked up one of the tally sticks on the table. "Did you put a guard over Alys?"

Fulk pulled the skirt of his gown over his bare calves. "Yes. I told Roger to."

"Why?"

"Because my knights are in the tower with her. And I don't trust her. She said she would run away."

"When are you sending her back?"

"Tomorrow."

Rannulf took a splinter from the wood piled beside the hearth and cleaned his nails. "Do you think there's hope for her?"

Alys's desperate, shining eyes came into Fulk's mind. "Hope. What do you mean? Either they will say she was taken against her will, in which case her husband will have her back, or they will put her in a nunnery."

Rannulf tossed the splinter into the fire. "What do you think of her?"

"Nothing. I want nothing to do with her, she's had enough to do with men of my family."

"Yes." Rannulf looked toward the window. "I suppose so. I feel sorry for her."

Fulk said nothing. Rannulf in a lofty mood always made him angry.

"Don't you?" Rannulf said.

"Feel sorry for her? No. I don't know her well enough."

Rannulf leaned his elbows on his knees, and his eyes glowed: he loved to argue moral questions. "Must you know someone well to pity him? Pity is most Christian —in no way does a man come nearer to Christ."

"Go see if there's anything to drink up here," Fulk said. "Why can't we ever talk about the things men usually talk about?"

Rannulf took a candle from the iron holder on the wall, fished a twig out of the fire, and lit it. "What should men talk about, except high issues of the Christian life?"

"Oh, well. Women, getting drunk—" Fulk slid down in his chair and put his head against the back. "War, and tournaments, tenants, enemies, and friends."

"Saccage, soccage, tillage, dotage." Rannulf with the candle in his hand walked out of the firelight and into the dark of the room; he held the light before him, and it shone golden over his shoulders and his head. "I've had enough of war."

Rannulf had never gotten involved in the wars— Margaret's influence; she had always favored King

Stephen over the empress and now the empress's son. "What do you mean?"

"Don't you remember Lincoln? I was in the tower with the other hostages, we could see most of the fighting. I saw how you attacked the king, and how you rode straight through his army."

Fulk nodded. Rannulf came back, cups gathered into one hand, the candle in the other. "I prepared myself for death—I was certain King Stephen would have me killed for your treachery. But he didn't kill me. Out of Christian love and pity he treated all us hostages well."

"He had no chance to kill you—we captured him in the battle."

"Before then. He knew you were in the army attacking him, he told me so. He was bitter—he added several words about you that I've never forgotten."

"Don't bother repeating them, I think he told me them himself."

"Does it mean nothing to you that he treated you honorably and you betrayed him?"

"Why did you bring cups and nothing to put in them?"

"Oh." Rannulf went back into the dark to the cupboard. Fulk raised his voice to reach him.

"I did not betray King Stephen. While King Henry was alive I swore an oath to support the empress, and I never broke it, not when everybody else was betraying her to make Stephen king. Is that treachery? The king caught me once in a tight place and required a hostage of me, and I gave him you. I knew he'd kill no children. He's a soft man."

"Soft? I call him chivalrous, my lord." Rannulf came back with a ewer half full of wine.

"You might also call him a man who held England and Normandy in his hands and spread his fingers and let them trickle away. I have no interest in this conversation. Let's talk about something else."

"Would you kill hostages?"

"I have killed hostages."

Rannulf blinked at him. "Whose?"

"Our friends the untamed Welsh." Leaning forward, Fulk poured pale wine into his cup. "Old Gruffyd gave me two of his sons at Bryn Crug and went on raiding. They weren't really his sons, as it turned out. I got them later. You'll notice he doesn't raid any more, the old pirate."

"I can't believe you would kill innocent children."

"Gruffyd was killing innocent children and their families every day. There are things I have to—"

"Morgan is Gruffyd's son—would you kill Morgan?" Rannulf cried, triumphant.

"Don't interrupt me. I want to talk—"

"Answer me," Rannulf said.

"Gruffyd isn't a problem any more. Are you going to listen to me?"

Rannulf looked disgusted; he gulped his wine and set the cup down with a thunk. "On what subject?"

"The condition of the kingdom of England. In particular, the recent career of Henry Plantagenet."

"Tell me about him."

Fulk shrugged. "I've been with him months now in England and I have attended him at his court in Normandy for years, but I know him no better than I know the king of Araby. The point is, we are going to make him king of England."

"Who is we. You and Leicester?"

"He has all the old support for his mother in the west, and he'll take Tutbury. Since he came to England last winter he has won every siege and battle he has fought, and he's been energetic. I met with Derby on my way here and talked to him, and he will join us. Chester, Pembroke, Leicester, and I all follow him. The Pope has refused to let the Archbishop of Canterbury crown Stephen's own son king, either now or after Stephen has died. Henry is our only choice."

"What do you intend to gain by this?"

The stony, yellow wine reminded Fulk of Bruyère, in Normandy, where it was grown. "Henry has confirmed all the lands I hold now on me and my heirs, he has restored Beck to us, he has promised to make me sheriff of Stafford, and he has given me lordship of the borough of Stafford, and he has recognized you as my heir."

Rannulf thrust his head forward. "I don't want Beck. Beck is Thierry's manor."

"It was Thierry's manor. If he had not contrived to be outlawed by both the king and the empress, he might still have it. Now it's part of the Honor of Bruyère again. You should be pleased."

"Are you trying to pretend that you do all this for my sake?"

"Pretend? Everything I do, I do for your sake, for Hugh's sake, and Madelaine's—what else should I work for except my family?"

Rannulf looked at the floor and said nothing. Confused, Fulk gestured with his left hand. "Why, what did your mother say?"

"You were working." Rannulf stood up. "I'm sorry I disturbed you."

He started toward the door, moving stiffly.

"Wait." Fulk thrust the conversation back into his memory, to think about later, and hunted for something to soften what he had said. "Will you take Alys to Radlow?"

"I? Of course. If you think it's a good idea."

"Yes. I'll write a letter saying I believe she was taken away by force—you might convince her that's the only way she'll stay out of a nunnery." Relieved, he drew a deep breath. "Peverel's in Nottingham, but you can give her to the bailiff at Radlow. No sense taking her any farther. Do you have any of your own men here?"

"Just my bodyguard. I'll take them."

"Take ten or fifteen of mine, too. You'll have to cross part of Cheshire." He picked up the letter he had written, folded it, and thrust it into a drawer. Rannulf and the dog on the hearth were watching him curiously.

"If you think it's best," Rannulf said. "I'll take her."

Fulk nodded. "She might heed you, she won't me."

All the high color had receded from Rannulf's face,

but he did not smile. "Yes, probably. Good night, Father."

"Good night."

Rannulf went off into the dark and opened the door, and Fulk heard him speak to the sentry on the stair landing. He found fresh parchment for his letter to William Peverel and dipped the pen into the ink, but he wrote nothing. Outside the window, clear light shone; the dog slept growling on the hearth. A log broke, and the dog leaped to its feet—it had been burned once by an ember when a log broke.

Margaret would explain everything to Rannulf. He listened to her, and she understood statecraft and the machinations of princes, a prince trapped in her woman's body, holding me at Derby's lodge while she sent off a message to Rannulf, outflanking me. But Rannulf had no sense to act on what she did. He believed Thierry—Thierry also spoke well on large, empty questions.

Fulk laughed. Thierry at the first word that he was coming had fled away—it exhilarated him that Thierry was afraid of him. Inking the pen, he began to write.

TWO

Margaret came to Stafford two days later, borne on a litter hung with rosettes of ribbon, surrounded by her knights and waiting women and pages. As soon as she was through the gate the courtyard filled up with people leading off horses and greeting friends among her party and waiting to help. Fulk wound his way through the crowd to the side of the litter. The sun had faded the ribbon flowers, and the streamers were studded with burrs and thorns. He bent to look inside.

"My lady. Welcome to Stafford."

The inside of the litter stank of dogs and sickness. She had worsened—her lips were covered with crusted sores, and her eyes leaked, she seemed bloated. Her companion Hawisse was busy helping her get herself together enough to climb out of the litter.

"Good day, my lord." She held out her hand, and Fulk took it.

"You should have stayed where you were until you got better, damn you."

27

She snorted. Fulk gripped her arm and with Hawisse disentangling her clothes and Margaret herself pushing managed to drag her out of the close confines of the litter. One of her tiny dogs yapped at him from the pillow. Hawisse scooped it up and ducked agilely out the other side.

"Derby left to go back to Tutbury, and it was boring past belief." Margaret leaned heavily on him. Even through the thick stuff of her gown he could feel her fevered skin. "Is Rannulf here?"

"Off on an errand of mine. He'll be back." He half carried her toward the door. Gilbert and his wife bustled forward, babbling greetings, and Margaret acknowledged them absent-mindedly. The porter rushed over to open the door. Hawisse carrying dogs and a bundle wrapped in a green scarf hurried on before them into the dark.

"It's your own fault that you're sick," Fulk said. "I should whip you for sending that messenger."

"What messenger?"

In her voice he heard her smile. He heaved her up the stairs, her great bulk pressed against him from shoulder to hip. Pages darted about, and a pair of serving girls rushed past, their arms full of spring flowers. Margaret said, "He wasn't here, was he? Thierry, I mean."

"No. He wasn't."

"What a shame. No choice familial meat for poor Fulk to dine on."

They crossed the antechamber; she was breathing hard, but she straightened, looking around, a hand taller than he was.

"You take advantage," Fulk said. "You know I can't beat you when you're sick."

She laughed her warm, deep laugh. He helped her through the door and onto the bed; she was breathing too hard for the short distance she had walked, and while he watched she shut her eyes and lay still a moment. Finally, she looked up and began to arrange herself on the pillows, pulling a fur coverlet over her.

"Who taught me to use advantages? Hawisse, where is—there he is." She dissolved into a torrent of baby talk, and Hawisse deposited a small dog on the bed. Fulk went to the window and sat down on the sill. Maids and waiting women rushed back and forth across his shadow on the floor.

Clusters of flowers appeared on every available surface, and bundles and boxes sprang open and were emptied of their contents. Chattering women filled the room. The door flew open, and the cook, beaming, marched in with a tray of fresh pastries. Hawisse snatched it away and took it to the bed. Three maids began to air out clothes near the cupboards.

"Stafford again," Hawisse said, looking down her bony nose. "Oh, my lady, don't you wish we had never left Arby?"

"But Stafford's so much nicer," one of the three maids by the cupboards piped up, and Hawisse gave her a poisonous look. Fulk laughed. Hawisse glanced at him through the corner of her eye and sniffed; her sour mouth thinned to a wrinkle. Fulk grunted at her.

More baggage appeared, and Hawisse, arms raised, ordered it about. "Bring them here—Gilbert, isn't it? Yes. Thank you. We shall require another tall cabinet for my lady's things. Kindly remove this chest. My lady will—oh! oh!"

The lapdog on the bed charged across the covers, yapping, and Merry, who had just come through the door, snarled and broke into deep-throated barks. The women rushed toward him, shooing him out in high voices, but the big dog set himself. He looked mildly surprised—after the first barks he ignored the lapdog. All along his spine, brindle hair stood up in a roach. Margaret grabbed the lapdog and was soothing it. From the safety of her enormous arms it squealed and yipped and made small lunges.

"Merry," Fulk said, and the dog dodged around the women to him. "Lie down. Good dog."

The lapdog raced up and down Margaret's body,

screaming. Hawisse glared at Merry, who had lain down at Fulk's feet. "My lord, that dog."

"He's doing nothing at all." Fulk crooked a finger at a page and sent him for one of the pastries Margaret was eating. "Get rid of the troublemaker."

Margaret said coolly, "Take him, Hawisse, he scratches." She gathered up the lapdog like a ball and gave it to one of her women. "Leave me, all of you. The noise tires me. Hawisse, send up honey and more butter for these. Go on, leave me."

The room emptied out immediately. Across a litter of boxes and furniture, Margaret met Fulk's eyes and smiled. "As usual I've disrupted your life, my lord. Forgive me." She sounded amused and tired.

Fulk brushed crumbs off his palms. "I see being sick hasn't spoiled your appetite."

"I wish you had kept Rannulf here until I came. Move this cushion for me."

"The errand was pressing." He slid off the window sill and went to the bed. The cushion lay half under her back, and he pulled it free and stuck it in behind her head. She sighed. Crumbs and bits of dried jam littered the front of her gown and the fur robe. This close to her, he saw how sick she was, and he sat down on the bed, worried.

"I am so weak," she said. "I can barely lift my head." She turned her head and coughed, deep out of her lungs, tearing and wet.

"The air is better here than at Arby," Fulk said.

"It will do me no good. Where is Thierry?"

"Gone to Prince Henry."

"What a fool he is, he always puts himself at your mercy. Have you been busy? Isn't that a silly question? You are never idle. Here's the honey."

A page with Hawisse like a drover just behind him set down a tray with a pot of honey and a jar of butter on it. Fulk stared at Hawisse until she left. It was unlike Margaret to make so much of being sick.

"I got from Derby what you talked about, you two,"

she said, when the door had shut. "You think a lot of this little prince, don't you."

"Damn you, you always have to know everything, don't you."

"Put honey on that bread for me. It's boring being a woman. Of course I meddle. I think you're making a mistake, Fulk."

"I don't."

"King Stephen is an easy man. The empress was not, and I can't suppose her son is much finer, particularly when I consider his sire. You have always had a weakness for treacherous men."

Fulk stabbed the bread at her. "We came through this reign well enough, didn't we? For all my weaknesses and—"

"Don't be angry, you betray yourself too much. As for coming through well, other families came through far better."

"If you admire the chimerical successes of, say, the Earl of Chester, my lady, I shall go out and murder and rampage and fight for cities I can't hold and gain enemies in high places."

Margaret grimaced. She was a Clare and had all their arrogant ambition—her brother was Earl of Pembroke. Fulk thrust the honey knife into the pot of butter and lay down crosswise on the bed, his head propped up on his crooked arm.

"Suppose we enjoy a moment's truce. How do you feel, sick?"

"Look at me," she said stonily. "Do I look well?"

"Not at all. You'll be better in a few days."

"You may believe so if you wish. I knew I should get no sympathy from you."

"That's what Hawisse is for. Myself, I am wondering how you mean to use what you found out from Derby. If you've done anything, Margaret, I'll be angry."

"If you think your temper frightens me you're very wrong." She stared at him a moment. "I think you are nourishing a viper in this prince of yours."

Fulk shrugged. "I doubt that."

"If he is all you told Derby, then certainly when he is king his first action will be to weaken all the powerful men around him."

"Not if he owes his throne to us."

Margaret chewed on bread and honey, her cheeks stuffed, and swallowed with difficulty. "I am beginning to fear that you will make just as base a bargain with this prince in England as you did with his father in Normandy."

"Come, now. That's talk I would expect from Rannulf. Henry and his father ruined nearly every great house in Normandy but ours. I thought I did well in Normandy."

"You made a merchant's bargain with the conquerors."

Fulk picked dog hairs out of the fur coverlet. This was an old argument, rehearsed a dozen times before. "When I was vicomte we were powerless. Now I am bailiff, and we control the whole region. Power isn't base."

"There's no sense in arguing with you, clearly. Only see: the prince is Duke of Normandy, and he has overthrown his own brother to make himself Count of Anjou, and with this new wife he holds Aquitaine—more and richer lands than England. Will he let his English barons rule him?"

"Your dog is shedding. I don't know what he will do. I don't know if we can control him. But these wars are destroying the kingdom."

She laid her limp hands in her lap. "No one listening to you would imagine you are such a great knight."

The back of Fulk's neck and his ears grew hot, and he plucked furiously at the coverlet. "I will take that as praise."

"It was intended so."

In the little silence that followed, he heard men call-in to each other on the walls; he smelled the fragrance of the flowers crowding the room. He was reluctant to break the good will between them, but there was something he had to get her to do.

"I want Rannulf to come with me when I go back to the prince's army."

"He never will. He is King Stephen's man."

"He will if you tell him to."

"I won't."

"You have to. He goes if I must drag him. I'd prefer him to come willingly. Wouldn't you?"

She said nothing; she blew her nose and lay still, her eyes elsewhere.

"You must see the reason in it."

"The king may yet deal with this prince. He has done so before. You make too little of the king."

"I doubt anybody could make too little of that king."

She coughed, and the harsh, ripping sound developed into a spasm. Fulk lay still, waiting for her to subside. Finally she lay back, her face blotched with red, and gasped for breath, and her eyes moved toward him.

"You have met Stephen only at court," Fulk said. "I've talked to him in councils, fought against him, and been his prisoner."

"I'm not going to argue."

"Good. Tell Rannulf to come with me."

She closed her eyes and lay still, inert on the bed, her graying brown hair scattered on the pillows. Fulk sat up; the rasp of her breath alarmed him.

"I have to see Rannulf," she said. "Could no one else have run his errand?"

She's dying, he thought, and a shock passed through him. This was no simple cold, when talking exhausted her so much. He picked up her fevered hand.

"He'll be back in a day at the most. You'll be better by then."

"Perhaps."

"Margaret, I'm sorry. I'll let you rest."

She looked at him without moving her head, and her mouth twitched upward into a smile. "Without finding out what I mean to tell him?"

"I'll send for a physician."

"Hawisse is capable. We have to talk later, I have some things to settle with you."

"When you're well," he said stubbornly.

"I'm not going to get well."

He said nothing; their eyes met, and he saw that she read on his face what he was thinking. She touched her lips with her tongue. He had never seen her frightened before. He realized he was gripping her hand and relaxed his fingers. "I'll go."

"Stay until I fall asleep."

"I will."

She turned her head a little and closed her eyes. Sliding off the bed, Fulk moved over near the window, into the sunlight's warmth. I have seen enough people die to . . . Through the window, beyond the yew thickets that the wind combed back, he saw the thatched roofs of the town at the foot of the hill.

"Where is Hawisse?"

"I'll get her," he said, turning.

"No. Stay."

She could be long in dying or she could die now. In her sleep. Before Rannulf came. She would live until Rannulf came, if she could. He'd seen men fight off death for days. What made her die? No wound, no gush of blood, nothing but a cold. That pierced into her body and attacked the organs, heart, spleen, lungs, belly, all those things I have laid open to the air with a sword. He remembered saying she took advantage of being sick, and heat washed over him. I am so clever, I deserve whipping. He heard her rough breathing and turned to see her lying there, her mouth gaping, her eyes shut. Get a physician. She should be bled. He went to the door and opened it, and Hawisse nearly fell through.

"Listening again? I'll find a leech."

Hawisse looked down her nose at him. "Better a priest, my lord." She passed him, moving toward the bed, her wooden heels clicking on the floor. Fulk went out into the antechamber. I should send for Hugh and

Madelaine. The bed in there had been his grandfather's deathbed, too.

He still had to go inspect the abandoned monastery. He and Roger could go today, it was still only mid-morning, and the monastery was not so far away. The thought of spending the rest of the day away from the castle and its air of dying lightened his spirits, and he went down the stairs into the courtyard, looking for Roger.

"THEY SAY THE forest is packed with outlaws," Roger said. He reined his horse around a small tree in their path. "None of the garrison has actually seen any, of course." He smiled.

Fulk grunted. Looking back, he could see the red stone mass of the castle on the hill behind them, the highest hill, the steepest. Sheep were grazing on the slope below the wall. "The rumor's always worse. It does more damage, at least." The air smelled of the wet ground and the yew woods. "Let's go down past the river."

They rode along the foot of a low hill and around it, single file where the trees grew thickly, and came to the river. Here, it ran swiftly between low banks, not very wide, but difficult to cross without a bridge. They followed it a while, looking for a ford. Once or twice they crossed footpaths leading down to the water—a few herders had their cottages nearby; once Fulk smelled pine smoke from a hearth. The trees grew thickly down to the river, so that they had to smash their way through thickets of thorny brush.

The river veered off around a hill, and when they rounded the bend, Fulk saw that a flat barge was tied up to the far bank, near a hut with a brush fence.

"Wulfric the Fisher," Roger said. "He's made a wall around his house."

"Not all he's made." Someone had tied ropes across the river, between two trees, to draw the barge back and forth. "It seems that Wulfric the Fisher is now Wulfric the Ferryman. Come on, let's see if he'll take us across." He kicked his horse into a trot and rode down toward the bank.

Whoever had built the ferry had used craft; the rope ran through a block and tackle hitched to the trunk of a tree. While Roger shouted across the river, Fulk investigated the workmanship. There was a similar arrangement on the drawbridge at Stafford Castle. Wulfric often brought river fish to the castle kitchens and he might have gotten the idea there.

A man had come out of the hut across the way and was unmooring the barge, shouting all the while. Roger turned to Fulk. "What is he saying?"

Fulk listened—Wulfric was speaking English. "Something about the horses. We can't take both across at once. We'll leave mine here and come back for it, but I'll go with you. I want to see what his toll is."

The barge swam empty across the river toward them. In Fulk's ear the rope groaned and shrilled through the pulleys. Roger stepped down the bank to haul the barge up against it, and Fulk called, "Don't—leave it out a little, we can take the horse into the water." The weight of the horse might ground the boat. He led Roger's horse into the knee-deep water. Pebbles crunched under his boots. The horse threw up its head and snorted, rolling its eyes at the barge, but when Roger took its bridle it followed him docilely onto the flat bottom. Fulk pushed the stern away from the bank and threw one leg across the gunwale, and Roger grabbed his arm and pulled him in. The barge wallowed slowly back toward the other side.

Wulfric was hauling with all his strength on the ropes. Fulk sat in the stern, watching him, impressed by the man's skill. When they were nearly to him, Wulfric looked up; apparently he recognized Fulk, because for a moment he stopped pulling and glanced around wildly. Roger reached up and took hold of the rope over his head and hauled them onto the bank.

"So, Wulfric," Fulk said. "You've become a ferryman in my absence." He walked carefully up to the bow of the barge and stepped onto dry land.

Wulfric bowed several times, displaying his bad teeth. "The bridge is gone, my lord, I thought it was my Christian duty to help travelers like yourself, my lord."

"Yes," Fulk said. "What is your charge for ferrying us across?"

"Nothing, my lord." Wulfric bowed; his black hair barely concealed a balding spot like a tonsure on the crown of his head.

"Surely you charge other people something?" Fulk glanced back—his horse was still hitched to the tree on the far side. "We have to get my horse across."

"Sometimes people give me something," Wulfric said. He went to the ropes, and Roger got back into the barge. "Just as—you know—a token." Wulfric showed his teeth again in Fulk's direction. "Just some of their produce, or something like that, but from my lord, I would take nothing."

"Of course not," Fulk said, looking around at Wulfric's hut and the area around it, which had been his garden once and now lay fallow. "Do you still fish?"

"Oh, well," Wulfric said, hauling ropes. "When I can, of course."

The barge had reached the far side; Fulk watched Roger coax and whip his horse on board. Wulfric leaned against the tree, an alder whose bark showed deep scars from the ropes. "We hear something of what goes on, south," Wulfric said. "In the war. The young prince, now, he seems to be doing somewhat better than last time."

Fulk said, "He'll be your king someday."

Wulfric's eyes widened; Fulk could see him imagining how he would report that to the next travelers. "My lord Stafford told me . . ." The barge was in midstream, with Fulk's horse braced on all four legs, rigid, while Roger tried to soothe it.

Fulk said, "My bailiff was remiss—he never told me about your ferry. I'll have to ask him about it."

Wulfric went gray. He paused at the ropes.

"For example," Fulk said, "what do you give me for your use of my river?"

"Oh, well," Wulfric said, "you must understand, my lord—"

"A tenth seems fair enough, doesn't it? A tenth for me and a tenth for the Church."

Wulfric hauled the barge in to the bank and stood, half turned away from Fulk, watching Roger lead off the trembling horse. His knotted, freckled shoulders glistened with sweat. Finally he looked at Fulk. "A tenth, my lord."

Fulk nodded. Roger stood nearby, with both horses, waiting. Fulk reached into his wallet and took out a halfpenny.

"For our passage." He wondered if it was enough and decided Wulfric would never dare charge anyone more than a farthing. "Give my tenth to Gilbert at Stafford. Good day."

"Good day," Wulfric said, woodenly, and poked the halfpenny into a pouch at his belt. "My lord."

Fulk mounted, and they rode off toward the monastery. After they had gone a little way, threading a path through a stand of alders and willows, Roger said, "God's blood, the sour look on that one's face deserves a blow."

"Maybe." It was difficult to enforce laws when people had grown used to ignoring them. He went over his talk with Wulfric in his mind, wondering if he'd played a tyrant, and decided he had not. Ahead, the ground rose steeply, covered with tangled berry patches and seeding grass. They rode up the hillside, avoiding the outcroppings of rock; a pheasant boomed up out of the high grass, almost under the hoofs of the horses, and they shied.

"It's hot," Roger called. "It's going to be a hot summer."

"It's always a hot summer."

They rode up onto the crest of the hill and looked

down into a pine wood, across a slope littered with
boulders and heavy brush.

"That old bee tree has fallen down," Roger said,
pointing.

A huge old hollow oak tree that every summer had
swarmed with bees and dripped honey lay now in a
heap of dust and chunks of rotten wood across the
slope, halfway to the edge of the forest. The bees were
gone. Fulk nudged his horse down toward it, leaning
back in his saddle—on this steep slope the horse
hobbled downhill, picking its way.

"Let's jump it," Roger called.

Fulk gathered his reins and rapped his heels on the
horse's ribs. His horse burst into a lope, straining at
the pull of the steep slope; behind him, Roger let out
a yell, and his horse thundered after Fulk's. Fulk
tightened his reins to give his horse something to lean
on. The broken trunk of the bee tree rose out of the
grass like a wall, and the ground all around it was
littered with branches. The horse gathered itself like
a bow bending and sailed over the trunk, its neck and
head reaching, reaching—Fulk clutched a handful of
mane and watched the bee tree fly beneath them. The
horse landed and stumbled and flung itself at a full
gallop downhill. Roger's horse pounded after them,
wild drumming hoofbeats. Fulk shouted. The wood
rushed toward them, thick and dark, full of low
branches. They swerved into the mouth of a narrow
deer trail. Birds screamed and fluttered in the trees
overhead. Fulk crouched in his saddle. He had lost a
stirrup when the horse stumbled, and he poked his foot
around, blindly hunting it—the iron stirrup cracked
him on the ankle and he gave up. The ground flattened
out and his horse lengthened its stride, pricking up its
ears. Glancing back, Fulk saw Roger crashing along
after them, ducking branches; his horse's nostrils were
red and wide, pumping.

A windfall appeared in the trail, and Fulk's horse
hurled itself over it almost without checking. Branches
scraped Fulk's back and the pommel of his saddle

struck him hard in the stomach. He put his head down
—let the horse find its way—and used his hands and
legs to steady it and urge it on. The shifting of the
horse's balance delighted him, its quick coordination.
A tree whacked his leg.

The horse crashed through a narrow place between
two clumps of yew and burst out onto the meadow
around the monastery. Behind them, Roger yelled, and
the sound of his horse's hoofs drew nearer. Fulk's
horse flattened its ears to its head and drove on, straining for more speed. Fulk headed it up toward the
monastery gate. Roger's horse was the faster and with
each stride crept closer. The monastery gate was gone,
leaving only a gap in the rock wall, just wide enough
for one horse.

The lean gray head of Roger's horse drew even with
Fulk's knee; sweat had stained it dark as armor.
Flecked with yellow stonecrop, the monastery wall
sailed toward them. Fulk pressed his rein against his
horse's neck, moving it over against Roger's gray, trying to keep the other horse behind him; the rein shaved
the thick lather from the horse's neck in plumes.

Roger shouted. His horse surged up head to head
with Fulk's, and in two strides, right before the gate,
the gray pulled out in front. Fulk sat back to stop his
horse. The two plunged headlong through the gate and
into the courtyard. Their hoofs rang on stone. Fulk
sawed on his reins. Skidding on the half-buried paving
stones, the gray tried to stop and could not and ran
into the oak tree beside the door of the chapel, and
Roger fell off into the branches. Fulk wrestled his
horse to a stop and burst out laughing.

The gray horse stood shaking its head and snorting.
Roger clawed his way out of the tree, his hair in his
eyes, and looked dazedly from side to side. Fulk bent
over his saddle pommel and sobbed with laughter.

"I won, at least," Roger called, and went toward his
horse. When Fulk looked up, he was laughing too. He
wiped his eyes on his sleeve and rode over to the well,
which still stood in one corner of the courtyard.

"That's a good horse," Roger said. "He tried hard enough."

Fulk slid down from the saddle. "He's stronger than yours." The gray was a famous racer; Roger was always winning races at fairs and tournaments with him. Roger hauled up a broken wooden bucket full of water from the well, and the horses thrust their heads forward, snorting.

"No," Fulk said, elbowing his horse away. "You're too hot." He dipped up a palm full of water, drank it, and scooped up more for his horse. The thick pink tongue scrubbed his hand.

"How long have the monks been gone?" Roger said, looking around.

"Some while, obviously."

The chapel and the two other buildings in the monastery were all falling down. They were made of wood, and holes gaped in their walls. Grass and gray-green weeds sprouted all over the courtyard, splitting the paving stones, and the wall was tumbling slowly to pieces. There was an old fire bed in one corner of the wall, a half-burned log and a heap of charred wood. The road west from Stafford ran just below this hill, and wayfarers caught on the road at night probably came up here for shelter. Fulk led his horse slowly around the courtyard to cool it down.

This place made him uneasy, as if someone were watching him. The wind roared through the pine woods all around it, with a distant, constant howl, and the wildflowers in the courtyard stirred, their blossoms swaying from side to side. It was beautiful, but he preferred the squat, homely buildings of Stafford, where people lived and worked.

Roger was giving his horse more water. Fulk slid his hand between the bay's forelegs. Roughened with sweat, the hide there felt dry and cool. Roger's horse was probably still overheated. Fulk walked his horse around behind the dormitory, looking in the windows where the shutters had broken. Dry brush had blown up against the building in deep, soft heaps; twigs crackled when he stepped on them. He went back to the well and let his horse drink its fill.

"I'm going inside. Those damned monks, God save us from them. The place is a ruin."

Roger nodded; he took Fulk's horse off to tether it. Fulk put his shoulder to the chapel door and forced it halfway open.

The narrow, vaulted room smelled musty and mildewed. Nothing movable remained in it—either the monks had taken everything with them, or people had stolen it. Even the altar was gone. On the wall over the dais where it had stood, there was a patch of discolored wood the shape of a cross, where the Crucifix had hung. The air was dusty and hard to breathe. Fulk went to the side door into the dormitory—the silence and emptiness made the back of his neck prickle.

Made of oak and bound in iron, this door stood half open, and he put his hand on it to push it wider. Part of the door around the latch had been recently broken off. Someone had forced his way through here. He stepped back, warned, and shifted to one side to see through into the corridor beyond.

In the dim light he could see only a little way past the door, but the thick dust on the floor was covered with footprints.

"Roger."

He kicked the door open and went through it, drawing his dagger. The corridor stretched away empty into the brown shadows. He thought, There is nothing here, I am acting like a child. He went cautiously down the corridor, glancing into the open doors on either side. These were monk's cells, so small he could see every corner in a quick glance through the door.

Something whispered in the dust behind him, and he whirled, so that the club smashed down across his raised arm instead of his head. The blow knocked him sprawling down the corridor. He rolled—the wash of pain in his arm froze his breath in his lungs and blinded him, and he flung himself to one side, unable to see what was attacking him. The club smashed into his side and he cried out. He could hear someone breathing hard. His eyes cleared, and he saw the club descending and tried to pull himself out of the way, and it struck him across the knee. A huge man loomed over him. His right side and his arm hurt so much he was sick; he got his feet up and kicked, slamming his bad side against the floor, but his feet struck the man with the club in the groin and knocked him back across the corridor.

He could not move, he felt pinned to the floor, and slowly, slowly the man with the club was getting to his feet and raising the shattered stump of wood in his hands. Fulk caught his breath. He still held his dagger in his hand, and he flexed his fingers around it, while the man with the club straightened up and lunged, his club raised like an extension of his long body.

From behind him Roger swung his sword, two-handed, and cut him almost in half at the waist. The big man's body bounced off the wall and Roger hit him again, so that blood sprayed across the floor and across Fulk—he tasted it wet on his lips. He struggled to sit up and could not; it hurt unbearably just to breathe. The taste and smell of blood made him sick. Roger was bracing him up. The corridor whirled around him, shot through with vivid streaks of color.

"I can't—my arm." His tongue felt like leather.

Roger lifted him up and carried him through the corridor and the whirling lights. Fulk thought of the ride home and swallowed a thickness in his throat. His right arm was numb as if with cold. Roger laid him down on the floor of a cell, with his feet in a patch of sunlight coming through the window, and went away.

Fulk shut his eyes and the floor seemed to lurch and spin around him. He opened them again. He was still clutching his dagger, and he put it down and felt along his right forearm. It was already swollen, stretching his wide sleeve taut.

Roger came back with an armload of brush and a

blanket, dropped the brush on the floor, and spread the blanket over it.

"There's no one else," he said. "I was afraid maybe there were others. Let me do it." He lifted Fulk onto the blanket.

"Aren't you glad I'm so small?" Fulk said. Roger mumbled something he didn't hear. "What?"

"I'll get some water."

Fulk nodded. He could still smell blood. His left hand lay half under him, and he drew it free and felt along his right arm; the least pressure hurt all the way to his shoulder.

"Is it broken?"

"I think so."

Roger had brought in the broken bucket from the well, full of cool water. Suddenly Fulk's mouth was parched; he squirmed around until he could dip up water with his cupped hand and drank. Roger watched him, his face lined with strain, and Fulk smiled.

"Don't look so harsh. Here, get rid of this sleeve."

Drawing his dagger, Roger slid the tip under the cuff of Fulk's coat. "Can you ride?"

"Oh, probably. Certainly." This should not cripple me, he thought, this should be nothing to me—a broken arm? When King Stephen had taken him prisoner, at Hornby, he had been covered with wounds, and once in his war with William Peverel he had broken his leg and ridden half the night with it. He heard the cloth tearing; the blade of the dagger touched his forearm, and he gasped at the pain.

"It's broken," Roger said. "We'll have to bind it up, somehow."

Fulk pushed himself up so that he could take off the rest of the coat and shirt. His right arm was swollen, immense, and black, the skin stretched taut and shiny over it. Dear Lord Jesus, he thought, if it heals straight and strong I shall go on a pilgrimage.

"I'll be right back," Roger said. "Will you be all right?"

"Yes," Fulk said. Roger's fussy concern embarrassed

him. He watched the tall knight stride out the door and sank back against the wall, listening to his own breath hiss between his teeth.

With the clarity of something seen by lightning, he remembered the raid on which he had broken his leg —the pain had burned it into his mind. For weeks he had been trying to drive Peverel's men from a village they both claimed, and on that night he had done too well—he and Roger and a dozen other knights had crowded a band of Peverel's up against the bank of a river, and in desperation Peverel's men had turned and charged back through Fulk's knights. We did that here, too—he knew that the big man had attacked him because Fulk had come between him and his line of escape.

The pain spurted like blood through his arm. Sweet Lord Jesus, he thought. Lady Mother, Holy Mary. His mouth tasted bitter. They would have to go home by the road, if they could cross over the bridge. He felt suddenly weak; with his eyes fixed on the wall, he saw the edges of his vision turn dirty brown and darken, until he could see only a tiny patch of wall—like looking through a hollow reed. He strained against the darkness, and it gave way, the light came back, and he shook his head. If I had stayed with Margaret as a Christian man ought, this would not have happened.

Footsteps sounded in the corridor, quick and coming nearer, and Roger came through the door and knelt beside him. He had cut a bundle of sticks. Putting them down, he pulled off his coat.

"How do you feel?"

"I'll be all right," Fulk said.

Roger folded his coat and Fulk's together, with sticks wrapped inside them to stiffen them, and laid them down neatly on the ground. "That man—the one who attacked you—he has only one hand."

"He needed only one."

Roger hacked a piece of rope into thirds. "Who do you think he was?"

"Just someone we frightened."

"Hunh." Roger took hold of Fulk's arm at the wrist and the elbow, pulled them strongly apart, and twisted. Fulk whined. He could feel the edges of the bone rubbing together; he could not catch his breath. Roger laid his arm down on the folded coat and tied the cloth and sticks into a bundle around it. The pain faded to a dull throb. Clammy with sweat, Fulk watched him bind it tighter with their belts. The splints held his arm stiff from elbow to wrist.

"Good."

"He must have been an outlaw," Roger said, "who lost his hand for thievery."

Fulk shook his head. "If strangers had cornered me here I would have attacked them."

Roger was making a sling from Fulk's ruined shirt. "What about your ribs?"

"Never mind." He put his good hand flat on the floor and pushed himself up, and with Roger beside him went out the door and into the corridor.

The dead man lay in a heap against the wall, his cudgel broken under him; his left arm ended just before the wrist. Fulk crossed himself uneasily. He had always thought it was bad luck to kill a crippled man.

"We can send someone here to bury him," he said. "Lay him out straight, Roger."

"I'll take his coat, too," Roger said. "You can't go back half-naked."

"No," Fulk said. He was shivering; he cradled his arm in its sling against his chest and watched Roger pull the dead man's legs and arms straight and push the body up against the wall.

"That should warn any other outlaws not to stay here, too," Roger said.

Fulk leaned against the cold stone wall, nauseated. He wondered who the dead man was—he suspected he came from Cheshire, where rebellious villagers sometimes got their left hands cut off. Roger stripped off the man's coat and brought it to him. Made of undyed, coarsely woven wool, it was less a coat than a shawl, and it hung on Fulk like a tent.

They went out into the courtyard. The sun was going down. A cold wind rustled the leaves up against the monastery wall. Roger led over Fulk's horse and held it, and Fulk mounted, stepping up into the cool air. He felt strange, as if he were dreaming, detached.

"We'll have to take the road back," he said, and nudged his horse forward.

Roger rode up alongside him. Fulk thought, He is waiting for me to fall off, so he can catch me. Abruptly he remembered why they had come here, to see if the place was safe again for monks, and laughed.

THEY HAD BROKEN up the bridge once themselves, when Chester was attacking Stafford, so that he would have to come by the main road. Fulk's men had mended it again hastily, to chase Chester north again, and it was that mended part that was broken now. The three stone piers still stood, but the slab of stone between this bank and the first pier had fallen into the river, and lay now in the rapids just beyond. Someone had laid a plank across the gap, so that people could cross on foot. Roger scratched his nose, staring at it.

"They'll take it," Fulk said, and patted his horse.

"Mine. Not yours. You must ride my horse over."

Fulk shook his head. "If I'm on him, he'll go anywhere—he just won't be led." He tapped his heels against his horse's sides, and the bay arched its neck and poked its head down, ears pricked, toward the bridge.

"He won't go," Roger said.

"He will, he has to." Fulk rapped the horse's ribs again. The bay took three tiny steps forward and stopped, its forehoofs on the plank, and backed up in a rush.

"Hah! Make a liar of me?" Fulk kicked the bay hard, turning his foot so that his spur hit. The bay stepped out onto the plank. The ringing of its own hoofs on the wood frightened it; it quickened stride, panicked, and bolted across. Fulk reined it down with difficulty—the pain in his joggled arm made him sweat.

Roger followed him across. "I wouldn't trust a horse like that," he called, and mounted, smiling. "As apt to leave you or throw you as obey, that one."

"You, perhaps, not me." Fulk pressed the bay over beside Roger's horse. Black specks swam across his vision. He was cold, but he was sweating; the harsh cloth of the dead man's coat rasped on his skin. He knew what this was, this sickness, and he strained against it, holding it away until they reached Stafford.

"When shall we go back to Tutbury?" Roger asked.

"Soon. I'm not sure. My lady is so sick, I can't leave her until she is better or—" He thought, How strange, that Margaret should be dying, and I almost died today, both of us at once. The road darkened ahead of him. The sun was setting. But when he looked, the sun still hung in the sky, over the trees on the horizon.

Roger was talking, but Fulk could barely hear the words. A vast humming filled his ears. The light seemed to be fading away, as if it were deep twilight. He clung to his saddle with his good hand, staring straight ahead. At the end of the road was Stafford Castle; all he had to do was keep going.

"My lord."

"Yes," Fulk said. "Yes."

THREE

FULK HELD OUT HIS GOOD ARM, and a page slipped the sleeve of his coat over it and draped the coat over his other shoulder and the sling on his right arm. They had bandaged him and braced him with splints so heavy he felt off balance; standing up still made him lightheaded. He reached for the ivy-wood cup on the table. With a crash, the door opened, and his younger son Hugh rushed in. He had come to Stafford while Fulk was sick, just before Margaret died.

"Chester's here," Hugh said. "God, he just got here, he's got forty men with him."

With the wine buzzing in his head Fulk turned so that a page could put on his belt. "Somebody tell the cook we need twenty more hams, ten for Chester and ten for his men." He settled the belt and picked up the winecup again.

Rannulf came in behind Hugh. His face was thinner than before, and shadows like old bruises lay under his eyes. "My lord, our guests are in the churchyard."

"I'm ready."

"Did you see Chester?" Hugh cried. He was tall and big-boned, like Margaret, and with his bushy hair always reminded Fulk of a bear. Rannulf sneered at him.

"Can't you ever keep your voice down? I saw Chester long before you did."

"I saw him when—"

"Oh, be quiet." Rannulf shoved Hugh to one side. "Do you need help, my lord?"

"Stay away from me." Fulk went to the door, trailed by pages, and his sons followed. Hugh in his great voice went on and on about Chester. Fulk had been staying in the room above the one in which Margaret had died, and the stairs were narrow and dark. He set his feet down carefully on each step and held onto the iron grips set into the wall. They said that he had nearly died, too. At the foot of the stairs, he had to stop and let his head settle.

His household was waiting in the courtyard just outside the door, all in mourning, and when he came out their faces turned toward him in unison. It was a bright, windy day, a vivid English summer day; he looked up at the brilliant blue sky, and his uncertain spirits lifted.

"Lean on me, Father," Hugh said, in a muffled voice. Fulk glared at him.

Rannulf, on his right, leaned around Fulk to see his brother and whispered, "Leave him alone. He's well enough."

Fulk made his strides longer. Hugh said, "He isn't. You saw—"

"Be quiet," Fulk said, between his teeth. With the household massed around them, they crossed this courtyard to the gate into the churchyard. Roger was standing beside the gate—like Fulk he wore all black.

"You look well, my lord," he said quietly.

"Not as well as I will."

"Look among Chester's knights." Roger stood to one side to let him pass.

With Hugh and Rannulf behind him, he walked into the churchyard, where a mass of Margaret's friends and relatives waited in their fine, somber clothes. Margaret had died while he was still unconscious, and the things left unfinished between them dragged at him like the weight of his bandages. Walking toward the chapel door, he wondered about what Roger had said and decided he knew what it meant.

Margaret had devoted much attention to this chapel of Saint Anne, endowing it every year of their marriage with rich gifts, and when she was dying she had told Rannulf she wanted to be buried here and was pleased she died at Stafford. Dying, she'd told much to Rannulf, including that Fulk should find a husband for Hawisse. Hawisse was standing near the door, grim-faced as ever. Fulk went past her and into the chapel.

It was too small to hold all the guests. Margaret lay behind the altar rail, her hands folded on her wide breast. Painted statues of the Holy Family, crowned with gold, stood in niches on either side of the altar. Through the gap in the curtain over the door to his right, Fulk could see Father Michael standing, talking to the monk and the two boys who assisted him. Fulk could not bear to look at Margaret and finally looked down at the floor. He went to stand before the altar, opposite her head, his heart beating unevenly. The shuffle of feet filing into the church went on for a long while, the only sound.

He began to wonder if he could stand all through the funeral Mass. He wished that he had seen her before she died. Probably she had felt the same as he did now, full of vain regret. Remorse. He listened to the sound of the guests filling up the church. With one of her children sick, Madelaine had not come, but her husband had, and Derby, and Leicester's son, monks from the Bishop of Lincoln and the Bishop of Winchester, whole packs of Clares, and even a knight of the Earl of York's. Tutbury had fallen the week before, and people had the leisure to go to funerals.

The doors swung shut, and the shuffling of feet stopped. All around the chapel people coughed and shifted their weight and talked. Fulk turned to look over his left shoulder into the back of the chapel. Chester stood almost directly behind him, his feet widespread and his great belly drooping over his belt, but his knights were lined up in two ranks at the back of the church. Fulk squinted to see in the dim light. The third man from the end in the second rank was Thierry. Fulk turned front again.

Chanting, the priest and his censers went around the chapel, and the sting of incense came into the air. Thierry was here. Everybody would think it so chivalric and noble that he came to Margaret's funeral in secret. Margaret herself would have known better. Fulk could take him prisoner. The priest turned and made the sign of the Cross and blessed them, and they all muttered and crossed themselves. The priest's vestments, stiff with gold and pearls, flashed in the light from the candles. If Thierry was with Chester he was in Prince Henry's favor. He could not take him prisoner. Rannulf's voice in his ear droned prayers, earnestly intoned.

The priest had a deep voice, good with the Latin, but he was slow. Fulk's knees began to quiver. Just before he would have had to sit, they all knelt, and he relaxed as much as he could. They said King Henry had chosen Roger of Salisbury because of the speed with which he said Mass, and there was something to be said for that after all. He spoke the prayers with the others, the words coming up from long memory, from long usage familiar to his lips.

They stood. Rannulf's voice wavered, and tears shone on his cheeks. Hugh prayed with his usual gusto. How different they are. Hugh had been raised in Pembroke's household, and Fulk rarely saw him. More a Clare than one of Fulk's blood. He fought down the desire to look at Thierry again—he could always say he hadn't seen him. The priest spoke of the justice and mercy of God and of the loneliness of each soul apart from Him.

Even death had its uses for Holy Church. He had told her power was not base. His head swam. Stay on my feet. Just to his left Rannulf was praying softly, in a quaking voice. He could lean on Rannulf. He gripped his hands together in an attitude of prayer and watched the altar dissolve into one long blur. A tremendous buzz sounded in his ears.

Kneel. He collapsed to his knees, and his head cleared; a rush of cool air filled his lungs. All through the chapel, voices rose in the Credo. He should think about her. He should be sorrowful. She was happier dead. Certainly hope so, he thought, since she is.

Unbidden the memory leaped into his mind of their wedding in the cathedral of Caen, and how then they had mouthed the things their elders had taught them to say, understanding almost nothing. Bewildered little boy and unhappy bewildered little girl. She'd wanted to become a nun. All girls did at her age. He did not remember what he had wanted. Certainly not Margaret; she had been fat as the Martinmas hog even then.

Twenty years since, he mouthed the things his elders had taught him to say and understood almost nothing. They had never come closer together than that day. They were strangers when she died. But he thought of times they'd been together, always fighting—on the day Rannulf was born they had fought over names and godparents and nurses; and regret and loneliness filled him, and tears burned in his eyes.

HIS HANDS RAMMED into his belt, Chester said, "Your lady's death is a sorrow to us all, Fulk. You have my grief attending yours."

"Thank you." Fulk waved off a page with a platter of cut fruit. "She was a great-hearted woman, you know. She kept faith with me, in her own way. I wish I'd listened to her more. You brought a strange guest to me."

Chester's bushy brows rose. His fleshy face was pocked with small deep scars, and he never blinked, so that his bulging pale eyes had a stony stare. "It was Leicester's idea. Thierry is a good drinking companion for the prince. Would you prefer I'd left him there?"

"Not at all." Two of the Clares came up, and Fulk took a step to one side to greet them. "Excuse me."

"My lord," the taller of the two said, clutching Fulk's good hand. "God be with you in your bereavement."

"And with you, sir, to have lost your kinswoman. I'm very pleased you came." The other was mumbling condolences and striving fiercely to catch hold of Fulk's right hand, buried in the sling, and Fulk pulled his fingers away with his left. "I beg your pardon."

"Philip." The taller one smiled and drew the other away. "God bless you, my lord."

"And you." Bowing, they left him.

"Byzantines," Chester said, drinking. Red wine dribbled down his chin. He stood with his feet widespread and his stomach thrown forward, like a woman with child. "They're all Byzantines." It was his word for anyone he didn't like. "Look at their clothes."

Fulk was tucking the end of the sling around his hand. "It's the present style, very French. Like the women covering their hair. So Thierry is doing well for himself." He could see Rannulf and Hugh, greeting guests—Hugh vivid and dark and Rannulf pale as ice. "I'll have to go back to the army and protect my interests."

"He makes friends easily, Thierry does." Chester smiled. "People are so easily fooled. The prince sends his sympathies. He wants you back at once."

"I'm flattered. Alain, thank you for coming."

Alain de Redvers, one of his tenants, took his good arm and bowed. "A jewel is gone from your treasure that you can never replace, my lord. What a splendid company to gather in these difficult times. You must be pleased."

Fulk bowed and said something appropriate. Alain exchanged words with Chester and rushed off—the leather of his shoes was dyed three different colors, and the turned-up toes shimmered with bells.

"Byzantine."

"What is the prince doing now?"

Chester reached out to take a jug of wine from a passing page. "Gathering everybody to go to Wallingford, having secured the west. He fights like a chessplayer. The confrontation should be interesting. The aging king, with the weight of years and experience, and the ambitious youth in all his glory."

"They confronted each other at Malmesbury and all we did was freeze. Has he agreed yet to give you Lancaster?"

"Of course." Chester loosed a peal of his harsh laughter. "He knows whom he needs."

Fulk drank ale and greeted more guests. With half the earls in England supporting him, Henry needed Chester less and less. Rannulf was coming toward him. Fulk looked up at Chester's face.

"Let us hope Prince Henry remembers his friends, my lord."

He bowed and moved off, so that Rannulf could talk to him alone. Rannulf glanced at Chester and put his back to him. "Father, Thierry is here."

"I know."

"He's upstairs, he asks if you will meet him."

Fulk looked around for a page, and seeing him look, one rushed up and took his cup and went to the table at the end of the room to fill it. Fulk said, "I'm going to Tutbury to rejoin the prince, and so is he. We will undoubtedly meet there."

"My lord—"

"You're going with me, if it please you."

Rannulf nodded. "Mother said that I should."

"Did she?" A twinge of uneasiness ran through him; even when she lay under the altar in the chapel Margaret went on. "We'll go tomorrow."

"Will you see Thierry?"

Fulk shook his head. Near the banquet table, Derby

was talking to some of his tenants, and sudden laughter boomed out. Fulk took a step toward them. "I can't, Rannulf. I don't want to." He went over toward Derby, wanting some reason to laugh.

FOUR

LEICESTER SAID, "THAT ENGI-
neer of yours, Parin, was very useful. He explained it
all in great detail to the prince, too, which kept him
entertained. God's wounds, you did get knocked around,
didn't you?"

"I understand it took them a while to put it all back
together." Fulk patted his splints. "I don't remember
the operation. Parin's a good man." He sat down on
his bed—they were quartered in Tutbury Castle, five
men to a room—and stretched his legs out. "Where's
Chester?"

"In the hall." Leicester made a quick turn around
the little room. He was tall and lean, with grizzled hair
cropped close to his head and a steep upper lip; until
his twin brother Worcester had gone on Crusade, no
one in England had been able to tell them apart.
"Stephen can't resist us now. There's no way. Derby's
come over, Warwick and Northampton are out of the
way—everybody who hasn't joined the prince is hanging back to see what happens."

Fulk lay back and folded his left arm behind his
head. They had ridden all day to get here and his
broken arm hurt. "There is Eustace. The king will certainly try to keep the throne for him, in spite of the
Pope." Eustace was King Stephen's elder son. "London
supports him, and the Earl of York and Richard Camville and Richard de Luci. And there's William d'Ypres.
I doubt—"

Somebody knocked on the door, and the squire Leicester had brought with him went to answer it. Leicester
said swiftly, "Something must be done about Eustace."
He stood back and looked at the door, and Fulk
thought, Something foul, or he wouldn't care who hears
him. Rannulf came in, with Roger behind him. Roger
stood to one side.

Throwing off his cloak, Rannulf dumped it on the
bed. His face was flushed and his eyes shone with excitement. "Everyone's here, Father, it's like Christmas.
Good evening, my lord."

Leicester smiled. "Good evening to you, my lord.
Where did you find Christmas in Tutbury in June?"

"All the people he grew up with are here," Fulk said.
"Where have you been?"

"In the town. A lot of people are staying there."
Rannulf gestured broadly.

"My lord," Roger said, "our camp is orderly, but
there's a question over booty."

Leicester muttered something under his breath. Roger
glanced at him. "There's always a problem over booty,"
Fulk said. "Who got our share?"

"They just say they didn't get enough—they were
kept out of the looting."

Leicester cleared his throat. "Someone had to stay
and guard the baggage train, Fulk. I'm sure the prince
will make amends."

"I'm sure he will."

There was another knock on the door, and Roger
went to open it. Leicester avoided Fulk's eye. Obviously
with Fulk gone they had thought it safe to rob his men.

"My lord Stafford?" A young man Fulk didn't know pushed forward between Rannulf and Roger. His eyes leaped from Leicester to Fulk.

"I'm Stafford."

"Sir, my lord the Duke of Normandy, Prince Henry, requests that you attend him at your pleasure in the great hall." He had a crisp, clipped voice and a strong Angevin accent; his clothes were marvelous. Clearly he was surprised to find Fulk half undressed. Fulk sprawled on the bed.

"You may inform the prince that I'm coming."

"If it please you, my lord, I shall wait and escort you."

"Damn it," Leicester said, "he's been wounded and he's ridden all day. Fulk, see him tomorrow."

"I'll see him tonight. I doubt he goes to bed early. You can wait if you wish, sir, but I'm slow in dressing. Rannulf, entertain this gentleman."

The Angevin drew himself up, splendid in his parti-colored coat and hose. Before he could say anything, Rannulf was pulling him toward the door, introducing himself and offering wine. Going out, the Angevin said in a sulky voice, "I should return at once to—" The door cut off his voice and the splendor of his presence. Fulk laughed.

"He's packed around with popinjays, isn't he?"

"Stinking Angevins all think they're better than we are," Leicester said. He sat down heavily; mimicking the Angevin's accent, he said, " 'Oh, England? Rather an uncivilized place, isn't it? Don't they still wear un-cured hides there?' Turns my stomach to listen to them."

"Roger, get Morgan. They're French, that's all. I understand Thierry is sleeping in the prince's armpit these days."

Morgan, Fulk's squire, came in and in silence began to lay out fresh clothes. Leicester picked his nose. "His charm is irresistible at first. I think the prince wants him more for use against you than as a boon companion, although Thierry has a collection of excellent stories."

"I've heard them all."

"My lord," Morgan said, in his soft Welsh voice, and Fulk stood up. The young man went about dressing him. Fulk looked up at the trim black head.

"How was it while I was gone, Morgan?"

"Oh—" The young man helped him into his shirt. "There wasn't much to do. I practiced a lot." And smiled his beautiful, peaceful smile.

Old Gruffyd's son, my hostage. Grown up entirely in a foreign land. Fulk said, "I'll have to hear you. You can play for me tonight."

The door swung open, and Rannulf put his head in. "Who is this fellow, anyway?" He jabbed his thumb over his shoulder; he meant the Angevin. "He's mad." His head pulled back out of sight like a turtle's, and the door closed.

Leicester gave a soft laugh. "I wonder what he's telling him. Morgan played for the prince, Fulk, you have a useful ally there."

Morgan was bent over, fixing points. Fulk laced up the front of his shirt. "I didn't know he liked music. Literature and philosophy, I thought he favored."

"Well," Leicester said, "he's a young man."

Music is for old men? Fulk sat down; Morgan put on his shoes. "I prefer love songs. Especially during long wars." His arm itched, under the bandages. He thought of the booty stolen from his men and grimaced, impatient. It was such a small thing, and yet it was like Leicester to be dishonest in small ways.

"By the by, bringing your son with you, that was a good idea," Leicester said. He stood up, and Fulk stood, and their squires brought their coats. "I like Rannulf, what I've seen of him."

"Thank you. He's pleasant company." Fulk waited until Morgan had arranged his coat over his right shoulder and hooked it and sent him after Rannulf and the Angevin. "Are you coming with us, my lord?"

Leicester raised both long hands, palms up, and laughed. "I spent the day with Prince Henry. Take your drinking elbow with you. We're supposed to discuss the march south tomorrow. I'll see you then."

"Good night."

Fulk went to the door with him, and Leicester and he talked about the weather a moment. Rannulf with his cloak and the Angevin strode toward them—the Angevin was rattling on about the intricacies of continental policy. Rannulf made a face at Fulk and shook his head slightly.

"Don't you agree, my lord," the Angevin said to Fulk, "that the natural direction of my lord the prince's interests is to push his eastern boundary to coincide with the western boundary of the empire?"

Fulk and Leicester both stared at him; the Angevin looked expectantly from one to the other. Fulk said, faintly, "Well, there is the matter of the king of France, don't you think?"

"Of little moment." The Angevin disposed of the French king with a gesture. They started down the steps toward the outer door, and in their midst the Angevin crisply detailed his plan of Henry's future.

"Already my lord rules lands greater than those of the king of France. We see in nature how as one essence grows another shrinks, and our prince's natural growth must coincide with the decline of the French Crown. But I forget that from this far corner of the world the view might be different. My lord, you should spend some time on the continent. The facts of policy have changed, it will take some while before the repercussions are felt in England."

Fulk tried to put on his cloak, and Rannulf helped him spread it over his shoulders. He caught a whiff of the stench from the midden below Tutbury's rock. "I spend a good deal of time on the continent, I am vicomte and bailiff of Bruyère in Normandy."

"Then, sir, you understand."

"More and more."

"England's a barbaric place," Leicester said. They had reached the door into the courtyard. "You must excuse us if we haven't read the same commentaries on Aristotle that you have." They went out into the open. "Fulk, I'm off. It was a pleasure to see you again, Rannulf. I hope to see you more. Good night."

"Good night."

"A charming man," the Angevin said, "but rather provincial, don't you think?"

Rannulf said, "I must ask you—"

Fulk stepped on his foot. "You'll have to make allowances for us Normans, sir, we've all grown long in the tooth dealing with small practicalities, and you know how that snuffs out one's vision of the abstract. May I ask your name and family?"

"An honor, my lord. Maurice de Marsai, at your service."

"I know your brother."

Rannulf said, "How long have you been in England, anyway?"

"Roughly a month. I'm very interested in it; this kingdom seems an excellent place for the study of primitive governance."

Rannulf choked. Fulk looked up into the sky, flecked with stars, and suppressed his laughter.

De Marsai said, "I don't know if you've had any experience with governance—"

"I have ruled the manor of Ledgefield for three years," Rannulf said coldly.

"Well. I shall have to talk to you about certain things that interest me here."

Fulk went around Rannulf, took him by the elbow, and steered him toward the gate into the far courtyard. De Marsai was only saying what all the Angevins around the prince believed—probably what the prince himself believed. Anjou and Normandy were ancient enemies. Part of the reluctance of the English barons to make the empress their queen, after her father King Henry's death, had been her second marriage to the

Count of Anjou. They walked up the steps and faced the sentries before the door into the great hall.

"If you please," de Marsai began, "I and the—"

"My lord Stafford," one of the sentries said, and stepped back and opened the door. "I'm very glad to see you, my lord."

"Thank you, Sir Richard." Fulk went through the door ahead of de Marsai and Rannulf. Immediately a servant came up to him to take his cloak. This tower was overheated and stank of wine and sweat. Through a half-open door to his right, Fulk could hear Derby's voice, laden with good humor; although he couldn't hear the words, he recognized a joke in the tone of Derby's voice, and an explosion of laughter followed. De Marsai strutted toward the door.

"Just listen to him and keep your own counsel," Fulk said to Rannulf. "Nothing he says can hurt you, but things you might say can."

"Oh, he doesn't bother me," Rannulf said in a thin voice. "I'm perfectly capable of him."

Fulk shook his head slightly and went after de Marsai toward the door. Just before he reached it, Thierry's deep voice rang out in the room beyond: "Are you sure it was a male deer, my lord?"

De Marsai flung the door wide, and Fulk followed him through it. It had been long since he had last heard Thierry's voice. Remember that nothing he can say will hurt you. They were all gathered around a table before the hearth, sprawled in their chairs, leaning on their elbows, their coats thrown off and their shirts open, and they had clearly been drinking for hours. On the left Derby sat, with Chester and two or three other barons, and on the right Thierry, and in their midst the young prince, smiling gently and very drunk. He saw Fulk at once, and his eyes moved unsteadily toward Rannulf. Above him, on the wall, hung a tapestry of King Arthur and his knights.

"Thierry," Derby shouted, "only males wear horns, isn't that so?"

More laughter. De Marsai waited for it to subside and called, "My lord, I have two more of your glum Normans here."

The last of the laughter cut off abruptly. Fulk crossed the rush-covered floor to an empty chair across the table and down from Thierry. Behind him, Rannulf said, "Good evening, my lords."

The prince lifted his hand slightly in answer. "My lord Stafford, you seem well recovered. I'm pleased to see you here." His eyes turned toward Rannulf again.

"Thank you, my lord. May I present my son, Rannulf, the lord of Ledgefield."

His scarred hands spread on the table, Thierry stared at Fulk and said nothing. Fulk watched him from the corner of his eye. While a page brought him a cup, he drew back the empty chair in front of him and sat down. Thierry looked tense, as if this meeting had come too suddenly for him. Four years had gone since Fulk had seen him clearly; Thierry's thick, curling russet hair was slightly gray, but otherwise there seemed no difference—his massive chest, his arms strapped with muscle, and his yellow eyes. Thierry seemed like a young man still, and yet he was in his forties, seven years older than Fulk.

Derby got up and came over to sit beside Fulk, and de Marsai took the chair Derby had left. After a moment's hesitation Rannulf sat down beside him, only an Angevin between him and Thierry, and Thierry smiled at him and they spoke in low voices.

Derby whispered, "There's been no mention of Thierry's outlawry since he came here. Try the wine, it's superb."

Prince Henry and Thierry were discussing the siege of Tutbury—the prince had begun talking to him, as if to make something clear to Fulk. Fulk sipped the strong red wine. "God's bones, he's drunk." Henry was talking only half as fast as usual, and when he reached for his cup he nearly dropped it.

"He holds it very well. They've been drinking all day."

"Castles," Thierry said, his voice no longer soft, "keep a man from fighting well, they keep him penned behind walls. I say, get out and fight on the flat plain, start even, and you'll see who's better."

"There speaks a man who's made the rounds of the tournaments," Derby said.

Fulk nodded. Thierry's yellow eyes grazed him, looking around the room. The wine rushed to Fulk's head. I am not ready for this.

"My lord Ledgefield," the prince said. "What do you think of this opinion of Thierry Ironhand's?"

"I agree with him most heartily, my lord," Rannulf said. "That's the only honorable way to fight, and without honor a man is not a Christian."

Derby said, "I hear Margaret talking."

"No," Fulk said. "Margaret was never so unwise."

"And yet," the prince said, "at the battle of Lincoln King Stephen came down from high ground to fight honorably and was most honorably beaten. Isn't that so? Excuse me for pursuing what may seem an obvious line of inquiry to you, my lords, but I am young and require education in these matters. My lord Chester, you were at Lincoln."

Chester swallowed a throatful of wine. "Take what you can, and worry about honor when you've won." He slouched down over his arms, folded on the table, and stared at Thierry.

"Now," the prince said softly, "we have a cunning man, endued with understanding. Somebody give me more wine." He held out his cup at random, and a page took it, gave him another, and went off. His head tilted back, the prince surveyed the men around him, and his eyes came slowly to Fulk.

"Fulk de Bruyère."

"I fought at Lincoln, my lord."

"Did you?" Henry's eyes opened innocently wide. "I was unaware of that."

"He was not," Derby whispered.

"What was the question?" Henry thumped his hand

on the table. "We have a question to argue. What was it? Oh. Which is more important, honor or winning?"

"The object of war is to win," Chester said.

"Ledgefield," Henry said. "Is that true?"

Rannulf said, "My lord, I have little experience with war."

"Oh, but surely you have some opinion on it. Such a basic thing, war. Tell us. Don't be afraid."

Thierry lifted his head. "He is young, my lord, but he is not afraid. I can vouch for his spirit."

Fulk clenched his teeth.

"The object of a war, my lord," Thierry said, "is to punish wrongdoers. God alone decides who wins and who loses, according to the merits of each, God alone."

Chester laughed. "Clearly God has had difficulty making up His mind, these past eighteen years or so."

"He had the company of most of the English baronage," Fulk said.

The Angevins all laughed, and the prince smiled sleekly. Chester grumbled a moment and burst out, "Are you accusing anyone, Stafford?"

"My lord, is placing you in the company of God Almighty an accusation?"

Derby twisted in his chair, looking for a page with wine. "Of course, Fulk rests secure in the knowledge that he supported the empress from the days of good King Henry."

"I'm just a glum Norman, my lord. Complexity bewilders me, I like to keep things simple."

"What's this?" Henry said, lisping. "Am I to believe that de Marsai's careless remark stung the Earl of Stafford?"

"My lord, a moment's reflection on the speaker assured me of the value of what he said. It was a manner of speaking."

Thierry said, "He was recently injured, my lord, and sorely bereaved. You must—"

"I don't need your apologies for me, Thierry," Fulk said.

Thierry stared at him and turned his eyes to Rannulf. "As you wish." He and Rannulf were looking at each other, and Thierry smiled a little and shrugged.

Fulk clenched his good hand into a fist. Henry was watching them avidly. When no one spoke, he gulped wine and looked around him.

"We were talking of war. My lord Derby, what is the object of war?"

Direct questions always flustered Derby; he pulled his coat sleeves down over his wrists. "Unh—I fight to protect myself, my lord—I think wars are fought to protect oneself and one's holdings."

Henry wrinkled his nose. "That's unattractive. Stafford, why do you fight?"

"Because I am a knight, my lord. My overlord commands me to fight, so I do."

"Would my vassals kept that clearly in mind. Ledgefield, we still have not had your opinion."

"My lord," Thierry said, "you have, he spoke of honor and—"

"Damn you," Fulk shouted. "Let him speak out of his own mouth."

Thierry lunged to his feet. "By God, will you shout at me?"

"If it offends you," Fulk said, and took his dagger from his belt. "You know the answer to it."

Derby was on his feet; Henry had leaned forward, smooth-faced, delighted. Chester said, "He's wounded, for God's love."

"Is that a challenge, Fulk?" Thierry cried.

"Yes, but nothing will come of it," Fulk said. "You've never yet faced me, why should you now?"

"My lord," Thierry said, and wheeled toward the prince. "You witness what provocation, all undeserved, he heaps on me."

Fulk lifted his arm in its sling and put it on the table. "You may call them provocations, I call them simple observations."

"My lord, give me your leave to—"

Henry said mildly, "Sit down, Thierry."

"I cannot stay in the company of a man who insults me without apology, my lord."

"Then go," Fulk said. "There's good wine elsewhere, and people to laugh at your jokes."

Rannulf was standing up, staring at Fulk, but Fulk gave him one look and turned his eyes back to the prince and Thierry. He could see that Henry was enjoying this; he was curious how long he'd let it continue.

"Do you give me orders?" Thierry said; he was weaving a little from drink, but his voice was properly full and outraged. "In your own lord's presence, you give me orders?"

"Suggestions," Fulk said. "Or an invitation. At any time, Thierry, I will face you over a lance, whether my right arm's broken or no."

Henry said, "Thierry, you needn't take his orders, but you should take mine. Sit."

Fulk sheathed his dagger. Thierry stood a moment, glancing around at the other men, before he slowly lowered himself into his chair. Derby sighed, and Chester, his head sunk into his shoulders like a toad's, gave a high, harsh laugh.

"You led us off the question, my lord," Henry said to Fulk. "Now I can't remember it." He smiled and knocked over his wine cup. Pages rushed to clean up the spill, but the prince ignored it, and set his elbow down in the puddle. "What was the question?"

"Honor and its place in warfare," Derby said. "Fulk, you have dodged around this long enough. Tell us."

"My lord, in war as in everything else, I do what I think will serve me best, and honor has nothing to do with it."

"Obviously," Thierry said.

"An honest answer," Henry said. "How can you tell what will serve you best, though? Eventually, the cleverest act can prove not so clever."

"I'm not a clever man, my lord. Certainly not clever

enough to outwit myself. As I said, in a manner of speaking, I'm a glum Norman."

"And a liar," Thierry said.

Henry's head struck forward like a snake's. "By God, sir, leave off. If you must interrupt me, go elsewhere. I don't need you. I don't need your comments. Get out, go, get out now."

Thierry flinched—the prince's voice had risen to a scream; the last words rolled around the room inside its stone walls, and Thierry turned pale as birch. Fulk sat back. Obviously Thierry had not met the prince's temper before. He glanced at Chester and saw him laughing.

Silent, Thierry got up and walked through silence toward the door, his shoulders rigid. No one watched him go; their eyes were fixed on the walls, they sat and waited until the door shut.

"Now," Henry said, in a normal voice. "let us proceed."

For a moment, everyone stared at him. Finally, one of the Angevins got up and took Henry's cup and went off to fill it; another of them said, "We were discussing war, my lord, if it please you."

"It does," the prince said. "Specifically, we were discussing right and wrong in war. My lord Rannulf, tell us what you think of that."

Rannulf cleared his throat. His fingers tapped nervously on the table top. "My lord, a man's first concern is the well-being of his soul, and he must judge everything he does according to that, in war as in other times." Warming to it, he leaned forward. "Aren't we always at war, my lord? With the Devil and his works?"

"God, it's a priest," Henry said, and around the table a few men laughed. Rannulf sank back again, blushing. The prince suddenly sat up straight. "Chester, my lord of Chester, my other Rannulf, start with the first premise. Is there right or wrong in war?"

Chester heaved his bulk forward and braced it up on his elbows on the table. "Is there right or wrong in anything, my lord? Those are words to command obedience, fictions, inventions to suit convenience. Are they not?"

"Splendid," the prince said, and bounced in his chair. "De Marsai, I see you bursting with the wish to speak. Answer him."

"Sir," de Marsai said, "God is certainly everywhere, we see His workings everywhere, and if God is omnipresent, so must the Devil be. My lord, if God worked not in the world, how does one explain the favor with which you, my lord, have been attended since your earliest years? Clearly, here is God bestowing gifts on His chosen."

To Derby, Fulk murmured, "I think I'd liefer hear Chester's heresies." Derby giggled. The Angevins were all murmuring agreement with de Marsai. Henry beamed; his unsteady eyes looked from face to face and saw nothing but admiration and worship. Fulk began to think of leaving.

"Remember, if you will," Henry said, "the words of Saint Augustine, that without evil there is no good. Without honor, there is no dishonor. Without law, no outlaws, like our friend Thierry Ironhand, however unjustly accused." He smiled at Fulk. "Without justice, no injustice. Fulk, you said you do what serves you. Without regard for right and wrong?"

"My lord," Fulk said, "if evil is necessary to good, and good is necessary to evil, then it behooves a man to do a little wickedness now and again, for the good of his soul. Where better than in a war, when wickedness is everywhere and good almost impossible?"

The prince cheered and clapped his hands. "Marvelous. Splendid."

"And so, my lord, I shall leave you, if you please. I rode all day, and my broken bones ache." Fulk stood up. "Thank you, gentlemen, all of you, for your pleasant conversation."

"I'll come with you," Rannulf said. He rose and bowed to the prince. "I am most honored, my lord."

"An empty phrase, if one does not believe in honor. But you do. Thank you, my lord. Stafford, you know of the council tomorrow."

"Yes, my lord. Good night." Fulk bowed and turned toward the door. Behind him, Rannulf spoke to Derby and Chester, polite and friendly, and they replied. Fulk went out into the little hall and sent one of the pages waiting there for his cloak.

"My lord," Rannulf said. "Are you feeling well?"

"Not really."

"The way you spoke to Thierry I've never heard you speak to any man," Rannulf said. He took the cloak from the page and draped it around Fulk's shoulders, and Fulk clasped it awkwardly with his left hand and started toward the door. A porter came forward to open it.

Outside, in the dark, the midden stench filled his nose and made him sick to his stomach. Rannulf said, "Thierry tried to be generous to you—at first. He meant no harm to you. I was ashamed for you, the way you spoke to him."

"If my right arm were good, I would have killed him," Fulk said. He stretched his legs, walking as fast as he could to keep Rannulf quiet. On the ramparts, torches fluttered in the wind like flags; he could still hear the voices of the men in the hall behind him.

"All he wants is your friendship, and yet you hate him so much," Rannulf said. "I don't understand."

"I see in him the same wicked man I see in me."

They had come to the door in the courtyard wall. Fulk took hold of the iron ring and pulled it open.

"How do you know he means you any harm?" Rannulf said.

"Would he be here if he did not?" Fulk shook his head. "I'm tired, Rannulf. I'm going to bed. I'll see you in the morning. Good night."

Rannulf frowned. "Good night, my lord."

Fulk went across the courtyard toward the door into the tower. A man was waiting just beyond the threshold, a candle in his hand, sheltering it from the wind with his other palm. It was Morgan; when Fulk reached him, he turned and without speaking went up the narrow stair, lighting his way.

FIVE

Rannulf said rapidly, "Did you arrange it? I wish I could go with you, I feel my duty is with you."

"Never mind your duty, you'll learn more with the prince." Fulk shifted up one step, out of the way of the men loading his gear into a wagon in the courtyard. The sun had already climbed above the castle wall; they were late. He looked for Thierry in the flocks of people inside the wall, but could not see him. "Remember that you need not answer every question put to you."

"Why is Thierry coming with you?"

"I requested it." There he came, walking toward them across the courtyard, with one of his men behind him leading two horses. One was packed with gear. Fulk said, "Anyway, the main army will be more interesting for you. The attack on Bedford especially."

"You have to take a castle, too," Rannulf said. "There is my lord Chester. What do you think of him?"

"Treacherous, and infinitely capable of cosmic explantation for it."

"Infinitely cynical, you mean."

"No." The wagon was loaded, and horses drew it rattling away. Morgan went back into the tower. "He isn't cynical at all. He's innocent. Sometimes they look the same. We're going, do you want to ride down to the camp with us?"

"Yes." Rannulf's face was bright with excitement. He rushed down the steps into the courtyard and called to his squire to bring his horse; Roger rode up from the stables, with Fulk's bay horse trailing behind him. Chester came over.

"Leaving, are you? But you've always been hasty." He laughed. "And there's my namesake. Good morning, Rannulf."

Fulk stopped on the bottom step to talk to him; the height of the step brought them nearly eye to eye. "I named him Rannulf because I like the name, Chester. I can promise that it was in spite of you."

Chester laughed again. His eyes veered toward Rannulf. "Still, one likes names because of the people that carry them."

"Well, I'm passing fond of myself, but I detest the name Fulk." Chester was wearing a belt of gold links that caught the sun. "That's a very fine belt, my lord."

"Do you really?" Rannulf said. "I like the name Fulk."

"I got it here, in Tutbury," Chester said. "Maybe you can find one on your way south. I'll watch over your heir while you're gone." He bowed elaborately to Rannulf. "Good luck, Fulk. Watch that spider of an uncle of yours." He swaggered off across the courtyard, surrounded by his hangers-on.

"He agrees with you about Thierry," Rannulf said.

Fulk's head bobbed. "Roger, we should get down to the camp."

"I don't think you want to, really," Roger said. He held Fulk's horse by the bridle while Fulk mounted. "Good morning, my lord."

"Hello, Roger," Rannulf said.

Fulk slung his leg forward over his horse's shoulder

and bent down to check his girth. "Rannulf, there's your squire."

"I see him." Rannulf plunged off across the court-yard to get his horse. Roger mounted and stretched his arms over his head.

"What's wrong in the camp?" Fulk asked.

"We were gone too long—they're lazy bastards, they go around telling each other what to do and do nothing themselves."

"We'll have a good hard march to get them in shape again."

Talking, they rode down toward the castle gate; they passed a group of men, standing and talking, and Fulk raised his hand to them. One of them called his name and stepped backward out of the group, turning toward him. Fulk stopped his horse. At first he didn't recognize the man, but when he came up to him he saw that it was William Louvel, a Norman knight.

"My lord," Louvel said. "God be with you—are you going now?"

"As soon as I can. You're with the prince, aren't you?"

"Yes. Aren't you?" Louvel scratched Fulk's horse under the jaw, and it rubbed its head against his arm.

"He's sent me off to ride his flank, and, by the way, take Sulwick Castle. Have you ever been there?"

Louvel shook his head positively. "I have never heard of it. Where is it?"

"Southeast of my castle of Bruyère-le-Forêt, in Hertford." Fulk grimaced. Through the tail of his eye he saw Rannulf coming on his chestnut horse. "Well. I'll see you again in Wallingford. Don't take it all before I get there."

With a laugh, Louvel stood back. "God support you. Good marching." He went back toward his friends, and Fulk, Rannulf, and Roger went out the gate, into the steep narrow streets of Tutbury.

"How far east of us will you be riding?" Rannulf said.

Fulk reined his horse around a hole in the road. On

either side, rows of thatched roofs descended the hill like steps. "Not far. A few days away. If the king tries to cut Henry off from Wallingford, we'll screen your flank and warn you." All the houses they had passed were empty. Fulk looked curiously in through their gaping doors. The siege had driven out all the people. He heard a muffled clanking inside one hut and bent to see through the door: a lean yellow dog was trying to turn over a broken pot. A wagon rumbled up the street, and Fulk straightened and eased his horse into line behind Roger so that it could pass them. They had to wait while another wagon worked its way around a corner. A brisk wind was blowing the midden smell out of the town.

Prince Henry intended to march straight on Bedford and seize it before he turned at last to Wallingford. It was Wallingford that had called him into England in January; King Stephen was besieging it steadily and the people had begged Prince Henry to their aid. Wallingford stood like a gate into the upper valley of the Thames, where most of the fighting of the war had gone on. Stephen had spent much of his reign trying to gain possession of it, although typically he had never pressed a siege to its conclusion. Fulk had only been there once. The heavy splints on his arm hurt him, and he tried to shift the weight.

"God's bones. They haven't even loaded the wagons." He kicked his horse into a jog down the last street to the plain. The camps of the other lords in Tutbury stretched out on either side, all boiling with action; in the center of Fulk's camp the train of wagons stood empty and waiting. Some of the men still sat around their dead fires eating bread and drinking watered wine. Fulk rode through the camp to the wagons.

"Here," Roger shouted, and rode into the middle of a circle of men not far away. "You and you, go bring those barrels here and load them on. You, go fetch the oxen. You and you—"

To Rannulf, Fulk said, "How long were we gone? They knew better before we left for Stafford." But his pleasure at the thought of leaving would not fade. The sun was already hot; he shaded his eyes to look across the camp. Roger like a high wind swept through it, and all along his wake men leaped up and ran around, gathering their gear, picking up, and bringing barrels and chests and bundles up to the wagons.

Rannulf said, "If I were you, my lord—look, is that Simon d'Ivry?"

"Yes." Simon was one of a pack of young knights surrounding Thierry, who stood head and shoulders above them all, his head bowed like a kindly tutor listening to his charges. Rannulf pulled his horse up behind Fulk's.

"I haven't seen Simon—I'll go talk to him, if you don't mind. Hello, Morgan. Father, mark you don't go before I see you again." He raced off across the camp toward Thierry, dodging the men working in his way.

Fulk grunted. The men around him were finally loading the wagons, swearing at the weight of the chests and barrels. There was little enough—salted meat, flour, kegs for water; they would have only half a dozen wagons in all. Morgan was making himself busy.

"Morgan. Find me a piece of sheepskin. Not too large."

Roger was coming back. Two teams of oxen, dragging their traces, trudged up to the first of the wagons. Fulk had always admired their way of going, never fast but never really slow, their short thick legs stamping down firmly into the dust, decisive. He rode up to watch the carters hitch them to the wagon.

"We'll make no pace with those," a knight said, and snorted.

Fulk did not reply. Prince Henry would move relatively slowly and Fulk had no wish to outride him. He was pleased that he had been commanded to ride flank. Farther to the east the forage was not so wasted, and everything he did relied on him alone. Morgan came back with a flap of sheepskin.

"My lord," Roger called. He trotted his horse up to

Fulk's; the gray's neck was blue-black with sweat. "We should be ready to leave at noon."

Morgan had climbed up onto the nearest wagon, and Fulk rōde closer to him. "I wanted to leave this morning." Morgan was rolling the hide into a fat bundle; he thrust it into Fulk's armpit to cushion the weight of the splints.

"If we leave at noon we should reach a good campground before dark." Roger slapped a mosquito on his neck. "I know we left this camp in good order."

"Thank you, Morgan. I should have left you commanding them," Fulk said to Roger. "They obey you, and they don't obey de Brise."

"Sieges are bad for discipline."

Fulk nodded. "Let de Brise and his men ride forward, when we march. Who can ride rearguard?"

"The men of Bruyère in Normandy, they're the most orderly."

Rannulf rode up, with Simon d'Ivry behind him. "Father, when are you going?"

"By noon, I think. Good morning, Sir Simon."

Simon bowed. "My lord." He was all Norman, red-faced and red-headed, already massive in the chest and shoulders; Rannulf looked like a reed beside him, although they were the same age. "My lord," Simon said, "we have a request of you— Sir Thierry Ironhand and I and my men and Sir William and Sir Rabel wish to be vanguard."

Fulk glanced at Roger. "We were just discussing that, and we had decided to put the lord of Brise in front."

"My lord, we request this honor especially."

Fulk sat still a moment, thinking of Thierry, of his yearning for glory. "Guy de Brise is a soldier of long experience. Let him ride forward for a while. We can rearrange the order of march at any time, and we doubtless will." Thierry apparently had only two of his own men with him, silent, weatherbeaten knights whose names Fulk did not know. "If you wish, Sir Simon, you may ride rearguard."

"The rearguard!" Simon flushed; his broad shoulders hunched. "My lord, if it should—"

"If you decline it, Sir Simon, at least don't expand on the topic."

"As you wish, my lord." Simon's voice was clipped. "I take my leave." He jerked his horse around and spurred away.

"Simon is very blunt," Rannulf said. "You always know what he thinks."

"He's been listening to Thierry. Here comes de Brise. Are we ready? No. God's blood. We were gone less than ten days. Rannulf, do you have wine with you?"

"No. I thought you'd bring some."

"Here." Roger held out a wineskin, and Fulk pulled the stopper out and drank. Even the wine was hot from the sun; it tasted leathery. De Brise rode up and reached for the wine.

"Excellent weather," de Brise said. "Are we taking all these wagons with us?"

Fulk nodded. "I hope you're ready to beat off outlaws. You don't know how ruined the kingdom is until you try to go anywhere on the roads. You know Rannulf, of course."

"I met him first in his cradle." De Brise shook Rannulf's hand. "Coming with us? It should be an interesting campaign."

"No, I'm going with the prince." Rannulf smiled. Something in the cast of his face suddenly reminded Fulk of Margaret, but when he tried to define it, he could not.

"Good luck," de Brise said. "And keep your own counsel, my lord."

Fulk said, "He'll learn to, soon enough."

"He'll be more comfortable than we will be, I expect. I came to find out the order of march, my lord. Although I see we have the rest of the morning to while away before we leave."

"You'll ride vanguard. How many knights do you have?"

"Twelve. How far ahead do you wish me?"

"Within hearing if either of us uses a horn. Use your judgment. Around dusk find us a suitable campsite. No need to keep running back and forth to tell me what's ahead, short of an ambush. You know the road to Bruyère le-Forêt?"

De Brise nodded; he smiled, and crow's-feet spread and deepened around his eyes. "Do you ever change the words?" To Rannulf: "Fifteen years, squire and knight, I have followed him, and ever he says the same thing." He clapped Fulk gently on the good shoulder. "Ride soft, my lord. Ride soft." He backed his horse away and rode to rejoin his men.

"I never knew you were such good friends," Rannulf said, surprised.

"He's a good man, for all he cannot command a camp." A column of knights was forming behind the wagons. "Mark what he said—these men you'll ride with are older and subtler than you."

"Yes. Is there anything I should manage for you, with the prince?"

Fulk laughed. "No. Not really. You are going with them to watch and listen, not to manage affairs. I promise you, he has given me everything I wanted of him, or I would not be here now. I want him to grow used to thinking of you as my heir. Listen."

From the castle, standing above them on its red rock, horns blasted. All the warhorses swung their heads up, ears pricked, and their wide nostrils distended. Fulk said, "You should go back, something is happening. Or someone might simply be going out and wanting a great display for it. Goodbye, Rannulf."

"Goodbye, my lord." Rannulf took Fulk's left hand and kissed it. "I shall do my best."

"God be with you. Remember to pray for your mother."

Rannulf went off toward the road up to the castle. Roger said, "We should be ready soon."

Fulk nodded. He was watching Rannulf ride up the

narrow street, into the huts that grew up the steep side of the hill below the castle. For as long as he had ruled the Honor of Bruyère, Roger had served him nine months of the year, leaving his wife and children in his brother's care. In the way that he knew the heat of the sun Fulk knew that Roger would not follow Rannulf, not as Rannulf was now. Prince Henry was little older than Rannulf, yet the great lords of England followed him without question.

"This should be good for him," he said, too loudly. "For Rannulf."

Roger was watching the men hitch another team to the wagon beside them. "By your leave, my lord, he's been too away from the world."

Margaret, longing always for the cloister. Rannulf had disappeared among the thatched roofs of the town. Fulk turned straight again and drew a deep breath.

"Let's start, move them down to the edge of the camp."

THEY LEFT TUTBURY just before noon and rode through a stretch of Needwood Forest toward the road south. In the mid-afternoon they marched out of the trees onto wasted land; once men had tilled this ground and lived on it, but now the forest was creeping out to reclaim it. Sinks of wild fen covered the lower ground. Purple vetch and speedwell and yellow charlock blossomed in the fields they rode through, patches of white yarrow, all the boisterous colors under the sun.

"We should be in the forest again by nightfall," Roger said. "Tomorrow we won't have this heat."

"Sooner than that."

The sun drenched them. On the shoulders of Fulk's horse crusty patches of dried sweat showed. He mopped his face and neck again and thrust the filthy cloth into his sling. "Look over there."

Roger stood in his stirrups. Behind them, the men-at-arms were singing a loud and bawdy song.

"It's a wall, isn't it?" Roger said.

Fulk nodded. "There must have been a castle here once. Look."

Across the top of the wall, crumbling and half-buried in weeds, a vixen and two little foxes ran; their bushy tails swished, and they vanished over the side.

"How can they wear fur in this heat?" Roger said.

"They don't have laces to take it off with."

Roger threw his head back and laughed, startled. Ahead, Fulk could see Thierry in the center of a band of young knights, talking and gesturing. What is he telling them? Stories of chivalrous doings and glory. Since Simon d'Ivry had mentioned riding vanguard a thought had simmered in his mind, and he considered it—Thierry surely knew little of actual war, he was a tournament knight, not a true fightingman. The scent of the wildflowers reached him. A yellow butterfly flew past his face, circled back, and settled tentatively on the horse's poll, between its ears.

"Roger. Send to Thierry and ask him to attend me."

Roger gave him a quick hard look and called back to Morgan.

Fulk looked off across the wasted fields. They rose steadily to a line of hills against the sky, covered with flowers in twenty different shades of yellow and blue; the mark of the plow still lay subtly on the fields, the even rippling of furrows. Once they entered the forest, the horizon would close down around them, and they would have to ride closer together, but out here they could see any enemy long before he struck. The thought of fighting stirred him, a little thrill of excitement running through him. Fighting was easy; there was no time to think. Thierry was riding toward him, bear-sized in his hauberk, his fine russet hair trailing out on the wind.

"My lord," Thierry said, cautiously, and turned to ride beside Fulk. "What is it, nephew?"

"As long as we're marching we ought to keep the peace between us, don't you think? For the sake of our purpose."

"Fulk," Thierry said, "I have never wanted anything but peace between us."

"I won't argue it."

There wasn't enough room for three horses abreast, and Roger had fallen behind. Fulk's bay snapped at Thierry's gray horse and laid its ears back. Fulk jerked on his reins. Something to say.

"Where have you been, all this while? Before you came back to England."

"In Spain, for a year. Before that, I rode to the tournaments in France." Thierry's yellow eyes looked earnestly into Fulk's. "You should go there. To France. There is such excitement and glory in the tournaments, I cannot tell you."

"We have tournaments here. Not as often. Did you do well?"

"Well enough. A good knight can make his way very well from ransoms won in tournaments."

Where is it all, then? Fulk thought, and didn't bother to ask. "I sent Alys back to her husband."

Thierry's eyes looked somewhere else. "So. Good. She was tiring of it, I think."

"Or you of her?"

"Well—" He smiled, the cheerful smile Fulk remembered from childhood. "That, too. She's a difficult thing, she always wants something, she was always after me to work some wonder for her, to win a fief and be a lord, like everyone else."

"Don't you want to be like everyone else?"

Thierry shook his head. "Of course not. Do you?"

"What do you want?"

The horses paced on, shoulder to shoulder; Fulk jiggled his near rein to keep the bay from nipping Thierry's gray horse. Thierry wet his lips.

"You know. I want Stafford and my English lands. You know they should be mine. It is Norman custom to give the younger son the English lands and the elder the Norman."

Fulk said, "Your father himself signed the testament giving them to my care. You know that. And I've held them now for seventeen years, Thierry. I won't give them up."

"I know. You are not to blame. I will not try to take them back. I can live with wanting and not having. But there is Beck. I know that Prince Henry has promised it to you, he told me he had, but it was mine, my father's legacy to me. Beck is mine."

"Serve Prince Henry and he'll give you a fief. With an heiress, there are many about."

"Beck is mine."

"You forfeited it when you were outlawed. I spent twelve years working to get it back. I won it."

"I won't fight with you."

Fulk could feel the sweat rolling down his cheek. Ahead, the trees grew thicker, pine and birch, and the road disappeared into them.

"Do you trust me, Fulk?" Thierry said, in a despairing voice.

"No."

In the field beside them, a cloud of butterflies, bright orange, rose out of the grass and circled into the air, higher than the horses, circling upward, the air vivid with their bright, quick wings.

Thierry said softly, "Nothing has changed. I have always hated you, sniveling brat you were, drippy-nosed, fawning on my father—Stafford is mine, I'll have it back, and everything else if I can, and you shall have Beck. I hate you as much as I ever did, you narrow, cold-minded little man."

Fulk smiled, his eyes between his horse's ears. "Thierry. I didn't think you'd keep it up so long, all this softness."

"I thought, for Rannulf's sake—"

"Keep Rannulf out of this." He met Thierry's eyes; the stir of excitement came back, and he leaned forward, staring into Thierry's eyes. "For hating you, God knows, I have good reason. Don't give me more."

Thierry yanked his horse around and started up toward the head of the line. Fulk swore. He booted his horse after Thierry's; they both swung out of the column into the ditch, and Thierry's gray slipped and slid on the uneven footing. Fulk pulled his horse up onto the flat ground and galloped down on Thierry. The column buckled, veering away from them. Roger shouted something.

Thierry heard Fulk coming and wheeled his horse around, and Fulk clamped his broken arm to his chest, thrust his legs down into his stirrups, and ran his big bay into Thierry's standing horse. The gray horse stumbled and went to its knees. Fulk's bay rammed its shoulder into the gray's barrel and toppled it into the ditch. Thierry rolled free. He came up running, his sword half out of the scabbard, and Fulk sawed on the reins to back his horse out of the way of Thierry's rush.

"I give you leave to go," Fulk shouted. "You don't go without my word, you do nothing without my word, Thierry, remember that." He kicked the horse at Thierry; with his arm broken he could not use a sword, but he might make the horse trample him. Thierry dodged. His hand was on his sword, but he had not drawn it—the men around them were Fulk's men. Fulk hauled his horse around and charged him again.

"My lord," a young voice cried, and Roger bellowed something. Thierry's horse had lurched to its feet, and Thierry was trying to grab its reins. Fulk ran his bay between them; the gray horse snorted, spun, and bolted out into the fields, and Thierry scrambled up out of the ditch onto the road.

The column had broken in half, and the road was clear. Fulk jumped the bay over the ditch. Thierry finally drew his sword. Fulk charged the bay at him.

"Tell me about the tournaments in France, Thierry!"

Thierry dodged, and Fulk sat back in his saddle; the bay skidded on the hard road, forelegs braced. His sword raised, Thierry darted in from the side. Fulk laid his rein against the bay's neck, and the big horse wheeled, hoofs flailing, and Thierry jumped back. They stared at each other across the blade glistening in the sun.

"Get back in the column," Fulk said. He let his reins loose.

"Do you believe—"

Roger rode up beside Fulk and handed him a clean napkin; while Fulk wiped the sweat and dirt from his face, Roger looked down over his shoulder at Thierry. Fulk's arm was hurting him. He could see no way to kill Thierry, here, without losing half his men.

"You're mad," Thierry said. He sheathed his sword with a clash of metal. Simon d'Ivry had caught his horse and brought it to him, and all the young men were clustering around him.

"Get them moving," Fulk said to Roger. He pulled off to the other side of the road. Morgan trotted up to him on his brown palfrey.

"Here. You dropped this." He held out the piece of sheepskin. While he put it back under Fulk's arm, he said, "My lord, you should not exercise your arm so much. It could mend crooked."

"Ah, you're like a mother to me."

Morgan sat back in his saddle, solemn-faced. "He might have killed you. You didn't even draw your sword."

"I couldn't. This arm—" He looked back at the column. Thierry was among his young friends, who bent toward him, solicitous. Roger had gotten them all moving again. Fulk saw the looks on the faces of the men in the line—startled, unsure. Yes. Half of them thought Thierry was in the right. A man must look after his kindred. I'll look after him, later.

"Let's go."

They rode at a jog through the field toward their place in line; thick as snowflakes, the orange butterflies danced in the air.

"MY LORD," ROGER said. "I've found something you should see."

Fulk looked back. "Why, what?"

Roger shook his head. "I don't know. Come and see."

Morgan came in the doorway behind Roger, with a bucket of water in each hand; he had already laid out their camp in the rock shell of the roofless hut and piled firewood against the wall. Fulk stood up and adjusted his arm in its sling. "Show me."

Roger started out the doorway. The sun had set while they were still making camp, and in the deepening twilight, the dozen ruined huts stood like strange animal burrows in the upper end of the meadow. Fires were already burning inside some of them, glowing on the broken walls. Under the trees that surrounded them it was already deep dark. Fireflies sparked among the trees. Fulk thought of asking if this could not wait until the morning, but Roger would have thought of that, and when he looked at Roger's face he decided that it must be serious. Whatever it was. They passed Thierry and his band of young men, camped in the rubble of a large hut, and Thierry quickly turned his back. Fulk shut his eyes a stride.

"Did you place sentries?"

Roger gave him a sharp look. "Of course, my lord."

"Then they aren't where they're supposed to be." There was nobody anywhere near the tethered horses. "They're all too loose, they need hard work and a lot of orders."

"Sieges are bad for armies," Roger said. "And Thierry does no good, they aren't sure who to follow."

"Most of them are."

"Not the younger ones."

Their feet sank into the deep floor of the forest, and they walked into the cool darkness beneath the trees. Fulk caught the aroma of wild strawberries. He stretched his legs to keep up with Roger.

"How did you come so far, to find this?"

"It isn't so far," Roger said. "Over here."

The leaves rustled under the wind over their heads. Something raced away through the bushes to Fulk's left. He followed Roger down a deer path.

"We should have brought a torch," Roger said. "Here."

He walked out into the middle of a small clearing, where an old oak had fallen, leaving a stump twice as tall as a man. In the open, it wasn't as dark as under the trees. Fulk looked around for something remarkable, and Roger nudged him toward the stump.

"Ah."

"What is it?" Roger said, excited. "Is it a god?"

Fulk made an aimless gesture with his left hand. In this light, the white stones that formed the eyes gleamed as if under the moon; a crescent of white stones made the mouth, and the nose and eyebrows had been cut into the wood with a knife. The face covered one side of the stump, a huge face, staring at him through white stones.

"It's a god," Roger said. "A pagan god."

"I don't know what it is." Someone had worked hard on this thing, carving it out. The woods sang under the evening wind; Fulk's hair prickled up.

"If we cut it down, we might bring a curse on us," Roger said.

Fulk smiled, his eyes on the stump. "I don't think so. Someone must have stayed here, some wayfarer, and had nothing else to do." He looked around for signs of a dead fire, or even other marks on the trees. There were none. "Let's go back. I'm cold."

"What should we do about it?"

"Nothing."

"You don't think the villagers made it—the people whose houses we shall sleep in?"

"God's bones. That was made within the last few months, the village has been deserted for years."

Roger walked silent beside him a few strides. Night birds sang before them and behind them. They could hear the sounds of the camp, and through the fringe of trees the campfires shone like blossoms. Roger said, "It's a god of some kind. I'm sure of it."

"Maybe."

They were afraid of it because they did not know what it was. They knew what it was, a face made of a dead tree and stones. He smelled the perfume of flowers, the scent of the open meadow, the strawberries, the tethered horses. It was lighter here. Who would have made it? Looking back, he saw the darkness spangled with lightning bugs and crossed himself.

In their hut, Morgan was kneeling on the ground, laying out the fire. Fulk sat down with his back against the wall. All across the camp, in the darkness, men walked back and forth, stood and talked, or cooked their dinners, wearing paths through the weeds around the tumbled, roofless huts. After the clearing in the forest, it was warm and friendly and familiar.

"Here," Roger said, stepping over a row of buckets to Morgan's side. "Is that how you make a fire? You should know better." He pushed Morgan aside and patiently began to teach him what Morgan had known for years. Fulk saw the look on Morgan's face and laughed.

When he had been a squire everybody had told him what to do. He remembered endless sessions with old and tedious men, who explained some point or other of warfare while the squires dozed and nodded and asked questions to prove how clever they were and threw stones at each other—he remembered being made to groom one horse three times in an afternoon, although each time there seemed no hair out of place. But he remembered that now with pleasure. It was strange.

He knew he had hated it, all of it, from the day he entered old King Henry's service as a page until the day when at last he knelt before the king and was knighted.

"Morgan?"

His hands behind his back, Morgan was watching Roger with the fire; his head rose. "My lord?"

"Do you hate being a squire?"

Roger looked up, startled, and Morgan wiggled. "My lord," he said mildly, and smiled. His eyes returned to the fire bed.

"God of angels," Roger said. "Who would not hate it?"

Fulk laughed. "Yet it's pleasant to remember it. Isn't it?"

"Oh, parts." Roger washed his hands in a bucket. "Pranks and things. And working with the horses. Learning how to fight."

"And being half-starved and beaten."

"Oh, that happens to everyone."

Squires got less food than anyone else. The older boys always stole the younger ones' rations. Fulk remembered standing for hours in the hall, waiting to serve the king and his household and the court at dinner, the smell of the food in his nose and his stomach clamped to his spine with hunger. He had always fought the older boys when they came to take his meat, until, exasperated, they held him down and beat him into one large bruise. When he was older he'd stolen from every boy weaker than he was.

"A good beating teaches a boy to accept pain," Roger said. "Here, you. Get the spits." He pushed Morgan, who raced off toward the wagons.

Fulk had always run to look busy when someone older was watching him. When nobody was around he'd done nothing. He pulled at the grass that grew between the stones of the ruined hut wall. "I am aging. I remember all that with such longing—"

Roger stretched out on the ground beside him. His

long body almost spanned the hut. "It was easier than
now."

"Oh, probably. But then we had nothing to say about
what happened to us."

"I didn't care." Roger yawned; his long arms strained
up into the air. "And of course in those days one always knew who was bad and who was good."

"The tedium of middle age. Separating trivial good
from trivial bad."

Roger laughed sleepily.

As a page, he had burned with anger to hear anything spoken against King Henry. He had swelled like
a toad with pride if the king glanced his way. He
remembered the king now as a giant—he knew that
was not so, that he remembered it so because he had
been so small himself. Past days always seem more
glorious than the present. All his childhood, he had
hung on stories of the Great King, William, thunderous,
gigantic, and part of his love of King Henry was that he
was the Great King's son.

He had taken for granted that it would go on forever, that he would be a little boy forever, carrying
dishes and candles and messages through the castles
and hunting lodges of the king.

"Did you ever hear stories of King William, when
you were little? The Great King, not Rufus."

Roger opened one eye. "Who did not? Sometimes I
wished . . ."

"What?"

Roger braced himself up on one elbow. "It's mad, I
should not say it. I used to pray that I might be magi-
cally put back into that England. You know. They all
spoke of it so well, the elders."

Morgan was stabbing pieces of rabbit onto the spits.
Fulk got up and went outside the hut to make water.
He imagined he could feel the idol in the forest, watch-
ing him. What mood is this, what fey, silly mood . . .
Talking of squires and dead kings.

Rannulf's sons, he thought, my grandsons will not
listen to stories of this reign and long to be here. Sud-

denly everything he did seemed small and useless to him. He did up his breeches and went back into the hut.

THE SKY BEYOND the wall of the hut was white with stars. Fulk lifted his head. The fire had died to ash; Roger and Morgan lay wrapped like sausages in their cloaks beside it. He had no idea how long he had slept. Somewhere, horses were moving. He had heard the drum of their hoofs through the ground, it had wakened him, and he stood up, his heart hammering. A shout rang out, and hoofs beat hard on the ground.

In the huts, in the spaces between the huts, men twitched and stuck their heads out of their blankets. Fulk fought with his tangled sling, cursing, and kicked at Morgan. "Get up! Get me my horse." He tore off the sling and threw it away. A voice rose, questioning.

"Roger."

Waking up, the men around him lifted their heads, crawled out of their blankets, and stared toward the far end of the camp. Groups of them gathered in between the huts. Morgan squirted out of his wrappings and sprinted off. Most of the camp still slept. Fulk's ears strained; what he had heard could have been the wind, and he went outside the hut and knelt and put his ear to the ground.

Far off, dim, hoofs sounded on the earth. He rose and saw Roger coming toward him.

"Follow me. Where's—good." Morgan had brought his horse at a trot through the camp, bridled but saddleless. The tall bay shook its head and snorted and looked down toward the meadow, and its ears pricked, interested.

"What is it?" a man near him cried.

Fulk scrambled up onto the wide, comfortable back of the horse and gathered his reins. "Keep them in camp," he said to Roger. "Don't let them chase anybody." He tightened his legs around the horse's barrel, and it burst into a short-strided lope, its head high.

The hoarse blast of a horn blared, and all across the camp men cried out and leaped up. Fulk's horse bolted forward. Fulk reined it down a little, and the horse neighed; he felt its ribs expand, between his knees.

Only half his men were awake. The camp was a jumble of men struggling up and calling out in sleepy voices, full of running shadows. Fulk strained to see what was happening in the meadow. Horses—he saw horses running free down there, and among them men on smaller horses. They were herding the loose stock up toward the trees. Fulk tightened his legs around the bay's barrel.

He heard de Brise shouting orders in a clear voice— "Leave your clothes, get horses—follow your lord, there." Old soldier. The men stealing their horses worked quickly to collect the horses and herd them into the trees. A knight stood in Fulk's way; someone beside him heard Fulk coming and yanked him aside.

The moonlight turned the meadow grass silver. The horse thieves saw Fulk coming and hesitated; their heads turned, one by one, like deer, and they called to one another. I have no sword, Fulk thought. He pinned his broken arm to his chest.

From his left, another horse charged down toward the thieves—Thierry, screaming like a madman, with his young knights streaming after him. Fulk kicked his horse. The thieves whirled their mounts to flee.

Thierry with his sword raised swept down on them, and they scattered before him. For a moment, alone in their midst, Thierry like a giant lashed out on all sides and cut men down like sapling trees. They did not stay to fight him, all who could fled into the trees, and Thierry with his young knights galloped whooping after them. Fulk loped his horse around behind the loose stock in the meadow and drove them back toward the camp.

Roger cantered into the meadow and helped him herd the horses together, and half a dozen other men rushed around to catch them and lead them away. One or two tried to escape, lunging and bucking in a circle of men on foot, their arms widespread. Fulk drew rein and watched a stocky chestnut stallion feint and bound neatly through a gap in the line of men surrounding him. The men swore and ran wearily after the horse, which snorted, jogged a few steps, stopped to snatch a mouthful of grass, and galloped easily out of reach.

"Who were they?" Roger said. "Did you see any of them?"

Fulk shook his head. "I don't think they were knights. Their horses were too small."

The chestnut stallion let a man come within arm's length of him and bolted away, head and tail high.

"Was anybody killed?"

"All the men at that fire, there. They were knifed in their sleep." Roger pointed to the fire bed nearest the meadow, between the place where the horses had been tethered and the first of the ruined huts.

Fulk let out his breath with a hiss. "How did they get so close? Who were the sentries here?"

"I don't know. I told Simon d'Ivry to post men all through those trees."

The chestnut was de Brise's warhorse. De Brise and fifteen other men made a circle around him and closed in, and the horse waited, tensed to leap, its eyes shining. Fulk made his muscles relax.

"He's off with Thierry, I suppose. Come along."

They rode to the edge of the meadow, and at a short lope rode all the way around that end of the meadow, along the fence of the trees. There was no one there, dead or alive—no sentries, nothing but the smell of wild strawberries. Fulk began to quake with anger and went back to the camp at a slow walk, trying to calm himself.

"Maybe they killed the sentries too," Roger said.

"If so, they took them back to be buried. There are no bodies."

Roger said nothing. A cheer rose from the camp, and Fulk turned to watch Thierry ride back, his young men parading behind him, while the men in the camp rushed down through the huts to meet them and cheered and cheered and cheered.

Fulk said, "Go tell them I would talk with them, Roger."

The big knight cantered off toward Thierry, who was trotting up to the edge of the camp. Fulk thought of Thierry's charge into the thieves—that was why the men cheered him. He made himself sit quietly on his horse until Thierry, with Simon among the young men around him, rode up and stopped in front of him.

"Well, nephew," Thierry said.

"Not so well." Fulk moved up beside him, his eyes on Simon. "You were responsible for putting sentries at this end of the camp, were you not?"

Simon's lower jaw sagged. He stared at Fulk a moment, glanced over at Thierry, and suddenly shook his head. "No. No. It was not I."

Fulk slapped him as hard as he could across the mouth. Simon reeled back in his saddle. The boys around him pulled their horses away from him and Fulk.

"When Sir Roger gives you an order it comes from me," Fulk said. He pressed his horse closer to Simon's and leaned forward, his face a hand's breadth from the young knight's. "You never fail to do what you are told to do. Four men are dead because of you."

"It was not I," Simon mumbled. "I swear on God's holy—"

"You lie," Fulk said. He pulled his horse around and rode off, past Thierry, who called to him to wait, and up to Roger.

"I won't insult you by asking if you are sure," Fulk said, and Roger glanced at Thierry and Simon and nodded.

"My lord," Simon called, in a pinched voice. "My lord, you have struck me before my friends, and I demand—"

Fulk said to Roger, "Remind him that I could as

easily have commanded his death, and if he continues to deny it I will."

"Nephew," Thierry said, "are you angry because he disobeyed you, or because he is my comrade?"

Fulk looked around and met Thierry's eyes. "A silly question, that one, uncle." He held Thierry's gaze a moment, to show he was not afraid of him, and galloped back toward the camp.

SIX

ALL THE NEXT DAY, THEY RODE through the deep forest toward Fulk's castle of Bruyère-le-Forêt. After his attack on the thieves, Thierry was the army's hero. All the young men and many of the older knights rode near him, and he kept up a chatter of stories and jokes, led them in roaring songs, and drank their wine and ate whatever they offered him. Glowering, Simon d'Ivry hung by his side.

Roger spent the morning trying to keep the column from straggling out along the road; he galloped back and forth alongside the moving army, red-faced from shouting. In the midst of it, behind Thierry, Fulk rode with Morgan beside him playing his Welsh harp and singing.

He thought there was no use in ordering the men away from Thierry. They would think it only part of his and Thierry's private feud, not an honest order. The loose discipline of the army enraged him. While Morgan's pure voice sang in his ear of ladies and wars, he brooded on ways to get rid of Thierry.

In the early afternoon, Roger rode up to him, his face coated with dust and sweat. "I cannot make them keep together. They are crowded up in front and straying off in the rear. Even de Brise is having trouble with his men."

Fulk nodded. He had been so angry so long he hardly cared about the army, he only wanted to humiliate Thierry.

"Will we stay at Bruyère tonight?" Roger said.

"Yes. I want to talk to Robert and take care of the business of the manor." Robert Molin was his bailiff at Bruyère-le-Forêt. "We'll have to camp the men in the field."

"I hope we get there."

Fulk glanced at him and went back to a plan for making Thierry the laughingstock of the army.

On either side of the road, the forest stretched away, dark and magical. The great trunks of the oaks, shrouded in vines, stood wide apart on the deep floor of the forest, but their high branches entwined, so that no light reached the ground except along the road. He could see light penetrating down to the lower canopy of leaves—broad bands of light that picked out colors in the dark and the leaves. The beauty of the forest interfered with his planning; in the middle of a problem he would catch the flicker of a squirrel's tail, the shine of a leaf unexpectedly in the sun, and all his attention would snap back, fascinated, to the forest. He remembered the face on the stump back at their last camp; for the first time he considered that a Christian had made it.

By God, he thought, Thierry is such a coward, they must see it, somehow. I can make them see it. But he knew that Thierry would use his broken arm for an excuse not to fight him.

Morgan was putting his harp away. Fulk looked over at him. "Why are you stopping?"

"You aren't listening, my lord." He laced up the case he had made for the harp and hung it on his shoulder.

"I was listening, I like to hear you play. Go on."

Morgan shook his head. "You weren't listening," he said calmly.

"None of you obeys me. I—"

He lifted his head, and his stomach knotted up. Someone had screamed, behind them, far behind. An animal, perhaps, or someone laughing. He pulled his horse out of line and galloped back along the side of the road, past the army.

The knights immediately behind him watched him in surprise. One shouted, "What is it?" Roger had seen him ride off and was following him, and Fulk left it to him to stop the column. He could see already that the men at the rear of the line were turning to ride back the way they had come, and they were drawing their swords.

"My lord," Roger shouted, behind him. Fulk waved his good arm at him impatiently; he had the reins caught in the fingertips of his right hand. The road curved to the left, ahead of him, and the whole rear third of the army was galloping back along it, past the curve. Now he heard the shouts of men fighting, and spontaneously his lungs filled with air and he shouted. He took the reins in his left hand and headed the bay along the edge of the road around the curve.

Men in the trees were shooting arrows down into the knights on the road below them. Three men were sprawled in the dust. Two loose horses galloped past him; one had an arrow in its flank. The knights in the road had their shields raised. There was no way they could fight back.

Fulk jerked his horse to a stop; he had no shield. The tail end of the column had obviously been ambushed. They were trying to ride out of the rain of arrows but the men galloping back to help them blocked the road. Arrows slithered down into their midst. Some of them were riding around in the forest, shaking their swords and trying to climb the trees after the bowmen.

"Turn around and go on," Fulk shouted. "You—

Jordan de Grace, go up the road and stop them from—"

He spurred his horse hastily up the road a little; an arrow had grazed his cheek. "Stop them from blocking the road. Get moving, you." He put his hand to his face and it came away with a great smear of blood on the palm. But he could feel nothing. Knights galloped past him up the road. One man, stripped of his hauberk, had managed to climb two thirds of the way to an archer in the high branches of an oak beside the road. The other bowmen were screaming to their companion to watch out. The knight scrambled up the last yard of trunk in a rush and before the man could turn stabbed him and threw him down. The knights in the road cheered. The bowman's body turned once in the air, bounced off a branch, and hit the road with a crunch.

"Ride off," Fulk shouted. If they took it into their minds they would stay all day to kill one more. They heard him, and covered by their shields rode after the rest of the army. Fulk dodged a volley of arrows. He waited until the last man was out of bowshot and riding up the road, and crossed to the shelter of a tree with no archer in it.

He could the men in the trees moving. They knew he was there, but they were leaving—they probably knew he had archers in the vanguard of his army, and they wanted to get out of the way. One by one they slipped down from the trees and ran off into the forest. A few of them dashed out to steal a cloak or a helmet from a fallen knight—nothing more, they were helpless on the ground, where a mounted man could run them down. They were outlaws, not King Stephen's men or men of any baron, only outlaws. They even left their dead lying in the middle of the road.

When they were gone, Fulk jogged his horse out into the road and counted the bodies. There were five of them. He caught a loose horse that was standing in the ditch and galloped up to the army, which had stopped and was waiting for him, and sent men back to get the corpses. They could be buried at Bruyère-le-Forêt.

Roger was riding up and down beside the army, shouting. Fulk reined up close enough to listen. Roger waved his arms and pointed with his whole arm down the road. "Now you have learned to ride close together, haven't you? And when you are attacked, you don't all bunch up together and stand around stupidly, do you? You take orders and clear the road so we can move along it, don't you? Answer me."

"Yes," the knights mumbled. They stirred, trying to make their lines orderly. Roger shouted some insults.

"If you're attacked from the trees, ride out of range. Are you idiots? Are you boys who have never been to a war? You're all mad. Now, ride out. Who was in command back there—de Grace? Come here, I want to talk to you. Ride out, I said."

Jordan de Grace moved out of the tangle of riders and waited, and Fulk and Roger rode down on him from opposite directions. The column of knights, in much better order than before, trotted away beside them.

"It was my fault," Jordan de Grace said, as soon as Fulk was close to him. "I know it. Don't abuse me."

"What happened?"

Morgan came up beside Fulk and straightened his sling. Jordan cleared his throat. "We were in loose order and they started to shoot—those men in the trees—and they seemed ahead of us. My hornblower was shot before he could sound the warning."

"My lord," Morgan said, "you're covered with blood."

Fulk said, "It isn't serious, let it go. Roger, did de Brise stop?"

Roger nodded. "He's close enough to hear when somebody stops. My lord, if the outlaws were ahead of Sir Jordan's men, we—"

"Must have ridden right under them," Fulk said. "I suspect they stayed well out of sight until we had passed. Keep watch on the trees. We'll change the order of riding tonight, at Bruyère."

He met Jordan's eyes. "I'll expect all my captains in the great hall at Bruyère before we eat. Now suppose we go. You keep your men together, my lord, will you?"

"I will, my lord," Jordan said. "Thank you."

Fulk grunted. His arm hurt and his throat was raw with dust. With Roger trailing after him and Morgan beside him he trotted up the road toward his place in the column. Thierry, he saw, was no longer singing and making jokes, although his friends still clung to him.

THE PORTER OF Bruyère leaned out over the gate. "Is that Roger de Nef? It is. My lord! Wait a moment." Roger had sent a messenger ahead of them, so the drawbridge was down, and they rode onto it, two by two, while the porter cranked the portcullis up. Bruyère-le-Forêt stood on a hill at the edge of the forest, looking out over the plowed ground of its manor. Inside its great wall stood another, with three towers on it; Fulk had taken advantage of King Stephen's uncertain control to build the outer wall with its double gate and dig the ditch around the top of the hill. While the teeth of the iron portcullis rose slowly into the arch of the outer gate, he studied the new wall. When the wars were over, the king would surely order all unlicensed castles to be torn down, but Fulk hoped enough of Bruyère-le-Forêt was honest that he could excuse the rest as mere additions. With the new wall and the ditch, Bruyère could withstand anything but a prolonged siege. They rode in under the portcullis.

Between the two gates there was a little paved court, with a rowan tree growing in it; in the shade of the tree Robert Molin was standing, a smile on his face, and when Fulk stopped he came up to him to greet him.

"My lord. I'm very pleased to see you again. Did you find enough room for your men? What happened to your arm?"

"I broke it. The army, save what you see, is camped between here and the village. I hope you told the villagers to keep their daughters in." Fulk dismounted and shook Robert's hand. "You look well. I'm glad. How has the spring gone for you?"

"Oh—" Robert shrugged. He was watching the knights ride through the gate into the main courtyard. "Will you come this way, my lord? The spring came and went, I hardly knew it was here. Ulf can take your horse."

Fulk gave his reins to the groom and followed Robert to the ladder up to the rampart. An old war wound had crippled him in the left leg, and he walked with a hitch of his shoulder, dragging his bad foot after him. Fulk kept his strides short. They climbed up onto the top of the inside wall and started along it toward the nearest of the three towers.

"Prince Eustace came through twice," Robert said. "Once I got enough men together to chase him, but he burned two villages and drove off their beasts. The villagers have been using our oxen to plow and I think they've planted every field they are supposed to, although I haven't been there to see. You have your uncle with you."

Fulk nodded. Thirty feet below, in the courtyard, Thierry and Simon d'Ivry stood among the chickens and the geese, peeling their saddles off their horses' backs. The other knights staying in the castle were walking their mounts around to cool them off. The kitchen maids, with bread and fruit hidden in their aprons, were strolling nearby, laughing, their cheeks red as apples.

"We met some outlaws, in the forest northwest of here," Fulk said, watching them. "Do you know anything about them?"

"Yes." Robert stopped at the door to the tower and opened it and stood aside. "Knights gone to robbery and murder. Did they attack you? I wouldn't have thought them strong enough."

"They were not. We were lax."

Fulk went into the great hall. A fire was burning here—outside, it had been warm, but indoors the chill of the coming night soaked out of the walls. The warm, dry breath of the fire drew him, and he went to stand on the hearth.

"I was sorry to hear of the death of my Lady Margaret," Robert said. "You have my sympathy and the sympathies of all your people here, my lord."

"Thank you."

"We have some guests in the castle—travelers, the Lady of Highfield and her retinue, and some knights of Lincoln. But if you would prefer not to greet them, I am sure that they would respect—"

"No. Ask them to have dinner with me. I have to talk to my captains before then. You must have matters to talk over with me, shall we do that after dinner?"

"Yes. I'm glad you came, as I said. There are instructions I must have. Do you want ale?"

"Please."

Morgan came in through the courtyard door. Fulk sat and let him pull off his boots. "I thought you expected to have wine this year—from those new vines?"

Robert gestured to a page to get them ale. "A blight killed the grapes."

"Damn this kingdom . . . unh." He wiggled his toes, freed from the narrow boots. "There's nowhere to grow good wine grapes."

"You'll like the ale."

A page brought a cup to him, and Fulk tasted it. "I do." He sipped the ale, which was thinner than Stafford's, but brighter. Morgan, with a page at his right side with a candle, was moving around the hall lighting tapers. Fulk leaned back. This hall, with the three painted shields over the hearth, the blackened oak furniture, comforted him. He finished the ale and rose.

"If you will ask my guests to dinner, Robert, I'll go to the chapel."

"I will, my lord."

"Morgan, send for me when the others get here. We'll talk later, Robert, when I am spiritually uplifted." He went out the door Morgan had come through and down the stairs to the courtyard.

Through the grille on the little window in the wooden door, he could see the twilit courtyard; the serving women were shooing the chickens down into the lower courtyard, and some of the knights who had come with Fulk were washing down their horses near the wall. They splashed each other and threw wet rags across the horses' slick backs, laughing. Fulk opened the door and went out into the late evening warmth.

Thierry and his young men were carrying buckets of water up from the well in the lower courtyard. Fulk crossed their path, and they quickly turned aside. Fulk lengthened his stride. This could not go on much longer, something would happen to break it apart. He went to the old wall and let himself through the low door into the other courtyard.

Here it was quiet; the angle of the old wall nearly cut this courtyard in half, and all the noise of the stables and the chicken coops, cowpens and pigsties lay at the far end. The chapel, a small round building, stood just before the junction of the new wall and the old. They had left the rowan trees and holly thickets standing all around it, to help keep it cool in the summer. When Fulk went in, the chapel was empty, and he shut the door behind him and walked up toward the altar.

Except for the altarcloths, the necessary gold vessels, and the gilt altar itself, he had never given anything to this chapel. Every time he came here he decided to find statues for it and commission a painter to decorate the inside walls, but nothing ever came of it. He knelt down at the altar, fixing his gaze on the Crucifix.

My Lord God, he thought, and smiled, remembering how as a child he had prayed solemnly, My Lord, this is me, Fulk. He crossed himself. Accept my prayers although I am full of wickedness, cleanse me in Your mercy.

Prayers for Margaret. He said them to the Virgin and to Margaret's favorite, Saint Anne. If she were alive she would be telling me how fine Thierry is and how much I should not hate him. He prayed for her soul and wondered all the while where it was. She had been a godly woman and was in Heaven, doubtless, singing with the angels. He could not imagine Christmas or Easter without Margaret nagging at him over policy. At the end of his prayers, he added a short prayer addressed to her, telling her that he missed her.

He confessed his sins, thinking about each and trying to feel repentant for striking Simon, trying to ride Thierry down, and plotting to kill Thierry. For that he asked no absolution because he was still contemplating it. He prayed for Rannulf, in Prince Henry's army, and for his other son, Hugh, and his daughter, Madelaine, and his grandchildren; he had to struggle to remember the names of the two new babies. Rannulf's son was Geoffrey, but Madelaine's daughter he could not recall. He had not been there for the christening, because they had been attacking Warwick Castle. Cecilia. He prayed for Cecilia and crossed himself. He liked to pray for his children and grandchildren; it gave him a feeling of confidence to think of them.

Morgan still had not come. He sat back on his heels, meditating on Christ's Passion. He preferred to think about the Last Supper rather than the Crucifixion—the example of Christ faced with betrayal was, he thought, more valuable to him. Thierry was giving him provocation to annoy a saint, and he had to make sure that what he did was not for vengeance but simply to protect himself and his family. He thought about Christ's mildness toward Judas and Judas's suicide. Too little place was made for Judas in the Church's order of things. He was absolutely necessary and in a

way his repentance had been noble. And to betray
God in the flesh was a fascinating crime. Somewhere
in the Holy Testament someone accused Judas of
thievery and of hot temper. Perhaps in some way
Christ had slighted Judas, and the betrayal had been
vengeance. To repay injury in the face of the most hor-
rible punishment was certainly noble.

To think that was clearly a sin. He confessed it and
prayed more, contemplating how each of his sins betrayed Christ as much as Judas had. He should go on
Crusade, once the wars were over. The Earl of Worcester, Leicester's twin brother, had died in the Holy
Land. I shall make a pilgrimage. If only to Rome. He
wondered if Thierry had made a pilgrimage to the
shrine of Saint James while he was in Spain.

"My lord," Morgan said, behind him. "Are you
ready?"

"I'm coming." He crossed himself again, prayed for
forgiveness for letting his mind stray during prayers,
and went out after the boy.

DE BRISE SAID, "Whatever the order,
we have to tighten up the column. Especially in the
forest."

"Yes. Exactly." Fulk sipped ale and put his cup
down. "Sir Roger and I have discussed this somewhat,
but I will do nothing without hearing your advice first,
of course. We spoke of putting you, my lord, in the
rearguard, with the archers and wagons immediately
after you, the bulk of the knights in front of them,
and Sir Thierry and his followers in the vanguard."

Thierry was lounging decoratively against the wall
near the door. He smiled and bowed his head. "We
are honored."

"But if you're attacked you are not to go chasing
anybody into the forest. You'd be ambushed within
yards of the road. Jordan?"

"My lord, could we not divide the archers and put them half in the rear and half in the front?"

Fulk looked over at Roger, who nodded.

"I think we could," Fulk said. "Godric, what do you say?"

"We'll march where you put us, my lord."

"Good. Are there more questions?"

"When shall we reach Sulwick, my lord?" de Brise said.

"In three days at the most." Fulk drank more ale. His stomach was groaning with hunger, and at the far end of the hall he could see the pages laying out trenchers and setting up tables for dinner. "Sulwick is a wooden tower surrounded by either a wall or an earthworks, lightly garrisoned, that controls the road from Suffolk to middle England. For those of you who were not present at my first council, we are ordered to take Sulwick and hold it to prevent any surprise attacks on Prince Henry while he is at Bedford. Since we have no siege equipment, we have to storm it. Otherwise we'll be held up for days or even weeks. We'll talk about that before we do it, of course, however briefly."

De Brise said, "How long will we be in the forest?"

"Another day and a half. Keep your lines tight, Guy."

Everyone laughed. De Brise joined in after he had decided that it wasn't an insult. Thierry wandered over toward Fulk. The others were talking or moving over to the table.

"Thank you for giving us the vanguard," Thierry said. "You surprise me."

"Not at all," Fulk said. "You'll have more latitude for making mistakes. Don't make any, uncle. I'll give you one warning."

Thierry laughed. He went to the door, called and waved to Jordan de Grace, and left. Immediately, the visitors came in—two or three knights and their squires, and a tall gaunt woman with three pages and two waiting women. Fulk settled back in his chair.

Smiling, Robert Molin led the lady toward him.

Fulk stood up. She towered over him; she wore her hair in the new fashion, tucked under a coif, and her gown was richly embroidered all around the hem. Her sleeves, snug at the wrist, spread out like wings back to enormous armholes. Fulk bowed over her hand.

"My Lady Rohese of Highfield, my lord," Robert said.

"Thank you. I am pleased, my lady, to give you the hospitality of Bruyère, and to be here myself to extend it."

"We are very charmed to accept it, my lord." She sat down next to him; she was bony as an old hound, but her eyes were a fresh deep blue and full of lively interest. Fulk met the knights quickly and sat down opposite her.

"I believe I knew your husband, my lady. Sir Giles Buin of Highfield."

"My second husband," she said. "Yes. I may say, my lord, that I have heard a great deal about you, none of it good, from my kinswoman Alys of Dol. I am pleased to find her judgment wrong as usual."

"Alys of Dol is your cousin?"

"Yes. I hear she spent a few days at Stafford." Her mouth drew up into a smile. "Under strange circumstances. None of us thanks you for sending her home."

"Would you have thanked me had I kept her? Where is she?"

"Now, at Collingwood Castle with her husband. I am going to take her to my home of Highfield. They refuse to send her to a convent—he says it's scarcely the place for a lady already inclined to lechery."

Fulk laughed, and the Lady Rohese clapped her hands together. "It is not an amusing subject, my lord. The condition of the convents is a shame upon us all."

"Oh, I agree, I agree." He thought that Alys would long for a convent after a while with this woman. "Shall we go to dinner, my lady?" He stood and offered her his arm, and she put her hand on it, rising.

"Yes. You have an excellent kitchen here, we had the finest saddle of lamb last night, and some very good venison and gamebirds. I approve of the way you keep your castle, my lord."

"Thank you." He refused to be irritated at her tone of voice; she was a Peverel, after all, and it was a compliment. "I'm afraid we didn't feed your cousin very well at Stafford."

"Oh, no. You did precisely right, shutting her up— thank you, Sir Joscelyn." She smiled at the knight on her left and turned back to Fulk. "She is unendurable. We are all quite ashamed of her. Oh." She picked up a strip of flesh from a carved roast on the table in front of her and popped it into her mouth.

"My lord," a page murmured, and took Fulk's cup away to fill it. All around the table, the pages and squires were serving their masters; those with nothing to do stood behind their lords' chairs. A low hum of conversation struck up. Two kitchen knaves came in, bearing enormous roasts before them, and laid them on the table to grunts of approval from the men. Another knave brought up a dish covered with a cloth.

"My lord," Robert called, from the far end of the table. "The cook made a venison stew for you, in honor of your visit."

"Did he?" Fulk took off the cloth and looked into the dish. "It smells delicious. Damn it, he must know by now that I hate mushrooms. Morgan. Take this around to the Lady Rohese and offer her some."

Roger stood up suddenly and went out the door. Morgan took the dish and carried it the short distance to the Lady Rohese, who was sitting at Fulk's right. She put her long nose down to the dish and sniffed.

"How marvelous. And I, my lord, adore mushrooms."

Morgan ladled out meat and sauce onto her plate. Another page cut slices of beef for Fulk and put a whole roast bird on his plate. Fulk drank his wine.

"Sir Joscelyn, will you—"

Roger came back in, striding long, and came straight to Fulk. Bending, he said into Fulk's ear, "My lord, don't eat the stew, the cook put no mushrooms in it."

Fulk looked quickly to see if anyone else had heard. The Lady Rohese had; she stared at him, suddenly pale, and lowered her eyes to her plate. Morgan quietly took it from her and sent another page for a clean one. Fulk raised his eyebrows.

"Someone's joke. Everyone knows I detest mushrooms. Take it away, Roger. My lady, let me offer you some lamb instead. Morgan, serve my lady. The mint sauce, too, Morgan."

Roger covered the dish of stew, took it, and went out the door. Fulk smiled at Rohese; his face felt stiff as old leather.

"How exciting," she said. "Direct from a chanson. Who would want to poison you, my lord?"

"Poison?" Sir Joscelyn said; his cheeks were stuffed with meat.

"It was a joke," Fulk said, furious. He took a huge bite of his meat, smiling at all his guests. Roger would talk to the cook, to the servants. But he knew who had done it.

"Very strange," Rohese said.

"Morgan," Fulk said, "serve those knights some of the lamb." He remembered Thierry bolting out the door. God, he thought, you see my reasons. He drank his wine with a gulp and sent the page for ale—the good wine they could serve guests was undoubtedly nearly gone.

"You have been with Prince Henry, haven't you, my lord," one of the knights on his left said. "We heard Tutbury has fallen. Is it true that Derby has joined the prince?"

Fulk swallowed a wad of gristle. "Derby was riding with the prince when I left him."

"King Stephen will attend to them," another knight said. He was older, and he hardly looked up from the chunk of meat on his plate. "Mark me, my lords, the king will make nothing of this little prince."

The others around the table craned their necks to look at him. In unison, they swiveled their eyes back toward Fulk. A page put his cup on the table.

"You'll pardon me, sir, I don't recall your name," Fulk said.

"William of Mar," the knight said, without lifting his head. He packed food into his mouth between words. "My lord is William d'Aumale, Earl of York."

Fulk sat back, and Morgan cut up the gamebird in front of him. "In my castle you may say what you please—what you believe, Sir William. I may say that I believe you slight the prince."

"All of us wonder about the prince, one way or another," the third knight said. "One wonders how much of his success is due to wise counselors."

"All the empress's success came from her brother," Rohese said suddenly. "Robert of Gloucester should have been the king."

For the first time, William of Mar lifted his head. "My lady, you don't know what you speak of."

Fulk leaned forward, angry, but cold as snow Rohese answered, without pause. "Sir William, I knew Gloucester, the empress, and the king. Gloucester was a bastard, but he was still as much the Great King's grandson as Stephen, or as Matilda was his granddaughter, for that matter. He had more of the Great King in him. Bastard or no, we should not be riding in packs for safety if Robert were the king."

"Robert is dead," the third knight said. "It's Prince Henry who concerns me. I think he's a straw knight, guided by his counselors."

"My lord," Fulk said, and spat out a mouthful of small bones. "His counselors are such as Chester, Leicester, Pembroke, and myself, with a bunch of Angevins I would say nothing of, not knowing them. Chester never gave himself good advice, and Leicester when he was King Stephen's greatest adviser lost him Normandy. I—"

"Spare yourself," Rohese said, and laughed.

"Thank you, I will. What Henry has done in this campaign is all his own, my lords, I assure you. He's hardly a stripling, without experience or learning. He may be very young, but he has fought the king of

France and rebels all through his lands. He is at least as capable as his father was."

"He's an Angevin," Sir Joscelyn said. "That family is cursed. Look at the men of the House of Anjou—Fulk le Réchin, Fulk Nerra, Geoffrey Martel—all of them living devils. Murderers, blasphemers, tyrants—"

"Well said," William of Mar cried. "Well said."

Robert Molin leaned forward. "We all have murderers and blasphemers and tyrants within our own kindred, Sir William. Don't you think?"

"I take offense at that," Rohese said. "I have none." Fulk had been chewing meat off the carcass of his gamebird; he looked up. In an undertone he said, "You're fortunate. I have a murderer, a tyrant, and a blasphemer, all in me."

Her eyes glistened. "How difficult for you."

He laughed. Sir Joscelyn was waiting for him to look up, and when he did, the knight said, "Could you support a man with such a family, my lord?"

"I am supporting him," Fulk said. "Do you support King Stephen?"

"With all my heart and soul."

Two months of the year, Fulk thought; Sir Joscelyn was obviously going home after his term of service in the king's army. "I would rather support a man whose father was Geoffrey of Anjou than the son of Stephen of Blois."

The other men stared at him, wordless. Rohese snorted.

"My lord, that isn't just. King Stephen has well proven he is not a coward."

A page transferred thick slices of lamb to Fulk's plate. Morgan moved in to cut them up. Fulk leaned sideways to let him work and said, "The Count of Blois's most famous weakness was cowardice, my lady, but it was not his only one."

Sir Joscelyn leaned back, his eyes directed toward the ceiling. "Ah, sir, but the supposed cowardice—the king's father was misinformed when he fled the Crusade, was he not? He was no coward—he went back to the Holy Land and died most bravely fighting there. I remember my father telling me of it."

Fulk ate lamb boiled in mint. The other men began comparing their own families' crusading stories to Sir Joscelyn's. Rohese turned to him. "Aren't you interested in the Crusade, my lord?"

"My father died on Crusade when I was four years old," Fulk said. "He never came back to tell me stories of Jerusalem."

"My first husband, Waleran, died in Spain," she said, approvingly.

Fulk sat back. William of Mar was gorging himself again, but Sir Joscelyn had straightened up and was reporting some great deed of his father's in the Holy Land. Fulk looked at Robert Molin and found him staring back at him. Robert lifted his eyebrows. Fulk went back to eating. The memory of the mushrooms in the stew had almost killed his appetite.

"ARE YOU GOING to marry again?" Robert Molin said. He shut the door behind the last of the guests.

"God's bones. Allow me to recover from the last. Yes, Roger, come in."

"I thought from the attentions you paid the Lady of Highfield, my lord—"

Fulk spun around. "And she is the last I would marry, that shrew, bony as a horse."

Roger was laughing; Robert dragged his bad foot over to a chair and turned it toward the fire. The dogs were growling over the bones in the corner, and he shouted at them. "I was only considering your interests, my lord. The Lady of Highfield is well endowed, and her lands align with yours—she holds Aimerie. Don't you think she's an apt choice, Sir Roger?"

"I don't know this lady," Roger said. He was trying to smother laughter. "From what I have seen, she would make an excellent wife."

"Apparently she has been, twice," Fulk said. He put his arm on the chair's. "What did you find out, Roger?"

"The mushrooms were poisonous. We fed some to an old cat, and it's dead. The cook did not put them in. He was furious, he knows you won't eat mushrooms. But the young knights had been in and out of the kitchens since we came, chasing the maids and stealing food."

"Thierry?"

"Thierry was never there. The cook knows him and says he never saw him, and I questioned some of the scullions and knaves. No. May I sit?"

"Yes, of course."

Roger sat down on a stool. "I think it must have been Simon d'Ivry. He was in the kitchen several times—one of the scullions knows him. One of the grooms saw him ride into the wood."

Fulk exhaled. "Yes. I shouldn't have hit him. I should have, actually, I'm glad I did."

"What shall we do?"

"Nothing. It didn't work." Thierry must have known it wouldn't work. Thierry had suggested it, he was sure of it.

Robert stretched his legs out. From the knee down, his left leg twisted outward. "Watch out what you eat, then, my lord."

Fulk shook his head. "I have a better idea. Morgan, go to bed, I'll get there by myself. Robert, you said you had matters to discuss with me."

"Yes, certainly." Robert hitched himself up in his chair, obviously reluctant to leave the subject of Simon's poison mushrooms. He fumbled a moment, getting his mind onto the new topic. "First of all, we are clearing the land by the river, to bring it under the plow, which is going very well."

"Good." This manor was half-covered with forest and marsh. "How much have you cleared?"

"Almost a hide. We'll plant it next year. I'm going to move serfs onto it from the south. They are sokemen there, and I trust them to work on new land so far from the castle."

Fulk nodded. The taxes of Bruyère-le-Forêt were still based on Domesday Book but the revenues had fallen steadily since Stephen took the crown; they had to bring new fields under plow every year.

"There was a writ from King Stephen's court to restore the jurisdiction over poachers in the land by the river to the abbot of Saint Mark. Shall I do it?"

"God, no. Is he after that again?"

"Oh, of course, every case I have that was once tried in his court he claims belongs to him still, but I try them anyway and he can do nothing. He has collected old men who will swear that such-and-such a case was always pleased in the abbot's court, and I have old men around who swear the opposite."

"Justice is profitable. I can deal with this at Prince Henry's court when things are more settled."

"William Malmain has an accounting of the taxes, but I can find my tally sticks if you wish."

William Malmain was Fulk's steward; he traveled from manor to manor overseeing their affairs. Fulk shook his head. "I'll catch up with William sometime."

Roger got up and went toward the back of the room. "I am having ale. May I bring you some, my lord?"

"Please." Fulk drew his feet away from the heat of the fire. "I want you to do something about the outlaws in the forest, Robert."

"I tried, all winter, my lord, but when the spring came we had so much—with the planting and the clearing of the—I'll get to it," he said hastily.

"Get to it soon."

"Thank you, Sir Roger." Robert took his ale and drank deeply. With his forefinger he wiped off the foam on his upper lip. "Now. The widow of William Eras, Constance, wishes to marry. Again. This one is a nithing knight-errant named Thomas Couctes. She is constantly at the gate beseeching me to get your permission."

"God's bones. We turned down a husband for her in the fall. What does this one offer?"

"Nothing." Robert slapped his hand down on the arm of his chair. "No land, no rank, and no way to come by either. He's worse than the last. And she has three villages and four knight's fees."

"Find her a husband. She's too young to be without one." Constance, he remembered, was Rannulf's age. "There must be poor but worthy young men around somewhere."

"Off fighting," Robert said glumly. "And making new widows, while the old ones go around with their tongues hanging down to their waists. It's a kingdom of widows." Roger was laughing; Robert gave him a stern look, and said, "You could have the best of them all, my lord, if you—"

"No. Don't speak to me of it again." Fulk glanced at Roger, who had his hand across his long face to mask his laughter. "Either of you."

"Ah, you need a wife," Roger said. "Someone to keep your bed warm."

"I am so seldom near my own bed, having a wife in it would hardly matter. Robert, tell Constance she may not marry her wandering knight. I'll find her a husband. I'll marry her to one of my Normans, she'd like that. I'm still looking for a husband for my wife's favorite waiting woman. What else?"

"A boy of the village here wishes your permission to go into the novitiate. This I recommend most heartily. He is the son of villeins, but a hermit in the marsh took him under his tutelage somewhat, and the boy is very quick and good-hearted."

"Where does he want to go?"

"They will accept him at Saint Trinity, with your permission. He'll do well."

"Send him. If he does well enough to find the monastery limiting, I can find a use for him in my chancery."

Roger said, "It sounds as if you've had a peaceful spring, Sir Robert."

"Except for Prince Eustace's raids and the outlaws. I'll deal with the outlaws, my lord."

"Nothing unusual in your courts?"

"Almost one unusual case. A man who raped and murdered a little girl."

Fulk sat up straight. "When does it—you said almost."

"The bishop said he was a clerk," Robert said.

"Ah."

"Some of the men from the village killed him. They did it in secret and hid the body. We could not discover who killed him."

Robert Molin's face was smooth as a child's; he met Fulk's eyes evenly, without blinking. Fulk lifted his ale cup. "What has the bishop to say about that?"

"He was very angry, he has excommunicated the murderers. I told him that since a court Christian would have done nothing more than degrade that man, that murderer, I found our justice superior."

"What about the excommunication?"

"After ninety days, he lifted it."

"What happened—the bishop gave his verdict and you let him go and the villagers found out?"

"Not in that order, but that."

"You should have held him. I don't blame you. I think you made a mistake, but the case was difficult. I wish you had notified me. I would have tried him if I had to come all the way from Bruyère in Normandy and try him on Christmas Day."

Robert said, "The bishop would have excommunicated you."

"Yes, he probably would have. I won't have them making small of my justice. A man is free to commit any crime these days if he can only prove he is a clerk."

"We never saw him near a church—he lived by begging and nearly drank the alehouse dry."

"I won't have you making small of my justice, either. You gave him over to the villagers and conspired with them to kill him—you are my bailiff, not the villagers."

"My lord, I—"

"Next such case, you must not go to the bishop at all. Go on."

Robert cleared his throat, glanced at Roger, and said, "Gilbert de Rys could not pay anything against his relief tax this year, but I excused him because his lands fell in Eustace's path."

"Eustace seems to have seared the earth wherever he stepped."

"He is a swine. When the archbishop refused to crown him Stephen's heir, I had them light bonfires all over the manor. I met him once, a worse man I've never encountered."

"I'll tell him so if I see him again. I need fifteen knights after the Assumption for garrison duty at Bryn Crug. Can you do it?"

"Fifteen?" Robert frowned. "I think so. I can check it tomorrow, I'll tell you before you go. Are they quiet, the Welsh?"

"I think they swallowed so much last year they can't move now for the weight of their bellies." In his mind's eye, he saw the view from Bryn Crug Castle toward the sea, the empty hills, the mist. "They're quiet, damn them."

"What of this Welsh boy, your squire?"

"Morgan? He's been with me since he could walk, he speaks no Welsh, he's a Norman. When he's knighted I'll give him land and make him my vassal. The Welsh won't have him back."

"He's a good boy, Morgan," Roger said.

"Fifteen knights." Robert frowned, thinking. "I'm trying to remember which of them hasn't paid his fee yet."

"I'll pay them if I must. See if they will pay scutage."

"Send Simon d'Ivry," Roger said.

"Ah, no." Fulk stood up. "Simon's place, I feel, is with Thierry. If that's all, I'm going to bed."

"That's all," Robert said. "Will you be here this summer to hold court?"

"I don't know. Maybe in the autumn. I'll tell you."

"What do you plan for Simon?" Roger said.

Fulk picked up a stump of candle on the table and lit it from a taper on the wall. "I'm not sure. God will guide me."

"I SHALL TELL my cousin I believe she misjudged you, my lord," Rohese was saying. "I am loathe to leave your castle—none between here and my own Highfield will offer such comforts."

"Stay as long as you like, then," Fulk said, smiling.

"You are generous." They were standing in the shade of the chapel archway; she started out into the bright morning sun, and Fulk walked along beside her. "I can only trust that you will find yourself near Highfield someday and allow me to be as gracious."

"Lady, you have repaid me amply enough with the grace of your company."

She laughed; her page ran up to open the door, and she turned toward Fulk stooping a little. "What a chivalrous gentleman you are. Alys is clearly biased."

Fulk followed her out into the main courtyard. Most of the men who had spent the night here were mounted and waiting near the gate, in the shadow of the wall. His horse stood by the gatehouse. Rohese was spending another day; he led her toward the door, talking aimlessly. The hoofs of the horses had stirred up the courtyard dust, and he could smell sweat and horses and warm metal.

"Your cousin was biased because of him," he said, seeing Thierry. "You have not met my uncle, have you?"

"No. I do not wish to, my lord. With your permission." Suddenly all angles, she strode toward the door; Fulk kept up with her, trying not to laugh. Thierry had seen them and was riding over. Fulk opened the door for Rohese, but Thierry reached them before she could go in.

"Good morning, uncle."

"Good morning," Thierry said. "My lady, good day." His helmet hung from his saddle bows, and above the massive glittering weight of his hauberk, his great head seemed as strong and fine as armor. Rohese muttered something in an icy voice.

"You should have stayed after the council for dinner," Fulk said.

"Oh." Thierry smiled; his yellow eyes widened. "I would have, my lord, but I loathe mushrooms." He reined his horse around and rode back toward the waiting lines of men.

"I am amazed at you," Rohese said. "That you allow it."

"Lady," Fulk said mildly, "I do as I wish."

She was watching Thierry; after a moment she grunted and went up the stairs into the darkness, her skirts rasping across the stone. He waved to Morgan to bring him his horse. The sun stood almost over the castle wall, and Sulwick was still far away.

SEVEN

THE ROAD LED STRAIGHT ACROSS the low hills and meadows, through ground plowed and planted, in which serfs worked bent double among the thin green stalks. Thierry and his vanguard were riding well ahead of Fulk's part of the army. Fulk could see where they were by the narrow plume of their dust. He and Roger rode just ahead of the wagons, behind a pack of archers. By mid-morning Fulk was crawling with sweat from the heat of the sun.

"What are you planning to do about Simon and Thierry?" Roger said.

"I'm still thinking about it." But he was not.

The serfs looked up when the army passed; a group of little boys ran to the side of the road to watch. Dirt covered them. Already they seemed bent and gnarled from working in the fields, their long hair shaggy and their skin seamed and inlaid with dirt. In the fields behind them the older people after a moment of watching bent over growing crops and their fingers dug into the ground, pulling out weeds.

"Thank God I was not born a serf," Morgan said, staring at the filthy boys who stared at him.

Fulk slapped at a fly buzzing around his ear. "They

122

probably thank God they weren't born the children of knights."

Roger made a face, uncertain. "You know, it seems to them that we are better off than they are, I suppose. I've never talked to a serf, beyond asking directions."

"These aren't serfs, actually. They are sokemen. Free men." The boys were trailing after them, but slower now, and from their fields their mothers' voices rose, calling them back. They turned and loped back to work. "They never have to fight," Fulk said. "If they lose their land or their harvest I have to maintain them."

"They can't get rich, either, if they don't fight," Roger said. "I suppose they have what they want."

Power, Fulk thought. They have none, except the greatest power: we do all we do for them, without them we are nothing. Ahead, the road wound down a hillside into a strip of marsh. Thierry's band of men was crossing the hill beyond. This marsh was the edge of his lands, and somewhere in the tumble of hills and marsh and forest ahead of them the lands of Sulwick began. His spine roached up with excitement.

Thierry was a tournament knight, a festival knight. Fulk thought again of how Thierry had fled Stafford at the news of Fulk's coming. Cowardice. It didn't have to be that, ignorance explained it, too—the panic of a man who did not know what to do next. Fulk strained his eyes to see Thierry's men, but they had crossed the hill ahead of them and were gone, down into the glen.

Sometime in the next day, the scouts and outriders of the men of Sulwick would find Thierry. Riding in a thin liquid skin of sweat under his hauberk, Fulk patiently thought it all out again and again, hunting down all the possible ways that Thierry might act.

IN THE MARSHES, flies and gnats and stinging insects buzzed in clouds around them. Blood seeped from punctures in the horses' necks and shoulders. The stench of the damp earth clogged up Fulk's nose and mouth, palpable as mist, so that he wondered that he breathed. With each step, his horse dragged its hoofs free of the clinging mud. They rode gratefully up onto the slopes, shrouded with thorny pine, and the insects followed them.

"Sing, Morgan."

"When I open my mouth, I breathe flies," Morgan said, but he took his harp from its case. Fulk reached out to lead his horse for him.

Roger said, "Where will we camp tonight? I haven't seen a good campground since we left Bruyère."

"There's a village ahead," Fulk said.

Morgan ran off a series of light notes. "What shall I sing, my lord?"

"Anything. The Song of the White Ship."

The slope turned abruptly sheer, and they lurched and staggered up through the light cover of pines and brush, stumbling over rocks. The drovers with the wagons began to swear in high, pleading voices. An ox lowed. Fulk swung around to watch, and saw that a wagon had jammed between two stubby trees. The oxen flung themselves into their harness, clawing at the ground with their cloven hoofs, and the trees swayed and bent. Slowly the wagon tilted upward on one side, and the oxen dragged it forward over the trees. Clouds of flies hung over their muzzles and shoulders, and their great moist noses were clogged with insects. Fulk turned forward again and rode on.

"Last night, I dreamt a doleful dream," Morgan sang, "a dream of woe and sore alarm. I dreamt I saw the old moon lying with the new moon all in her arms."

Fulk led Morgan's horse around an impenetrable thicket. Roger had gone to help pull another wagon up the slope. The ground here was covered with pine needles, soft and slippery. Roger trotted up the slope toward them.

"Is there no better way?"

"Not for Thierry. It makes no difference, we're almost to the top."

"What is he singing? Why doesn't he sing in French?"

"I think he likes the song."

Morgan sang softly to himself, while his hands played long phrases like sea waves. They reached the crest of the hill, and Fulk reined in, holding his arm in the sling out to stop the men behind him.

"Now let's see how we can get through this."

"When first he looked upon his ship," Morgan sang, "a loud laugh laughed he. When last he looked upon his ship, a tear blinded his eye."

Ahead of them lay another deep glen of thorny brush and marsh, but beyond it the land seemed to level out. Fulk sighed. "We'll have to try it. Send a man back to de Brise and tell him to wait until we have crossed, or he'll run up on us. Let's go."

They plunged down this slope, the horses bracing their forelegs against the steep drop, and the oxen trudged forward. Somewhere ahead of them, Fulk could hear the thin whir of insects' wings, and the stink of the marsh rose up to his nostrils. Morgan sang of the youth and arrogant display of the White Ship. They staggered halfway down the slope—men called back and forth, the crack of the drovers' whips resounded. Ahead of Fulk lay a rotten log, and he called back to Morgan to watch out.

"Oh, long, oh, long will the ladies sit, with their eyes turned toward the shore," Morgan sang, "waiting for their own true-loves, who will never come home any more."

The log was crawling with fur. Fulk saw it and realized it was a pelt of bees and the log their hive, and opened his mouth to yell warning, but before he could speak the bees rose in a fog and attacked him. He clamped his eyes and mouth shut and spurred his horse.

Morgan's voice broke from its song with a yell. The torrential howling of the bees surrounded Fulk; a tree swiped him, and sharp pain stabbed him on the eye, the lip, and the ear. His horse swerved suddenly and nearly threw him, and another horse ran into him from behind. Morgan was shouting to him to stop. He hauled on his reins and opened his eyes.

"Are you all right?"

"They all followed you," Morgan said, and smiled. "Listen."

Behind them, the bees were attacking everything that moved, and the oxen's base lowing rose frantically, drowning the curses of the men. Brush crackled and fell rustling to the ground. Two knights galloped down the slope past them, bounding over the rough ground. One ran into a tree and a branch swept him out of the saddle.

"God's judgment on us," Fulk said. "You brought us to this with that song." His eye, his lip, and his ear hurt in tiny, even pulses.

Morgan put his harp away and leaned out of his saddle. His fingers tugged at something in Fulk's earlobe and came away with a bee's body between them. "They die, when they sting you," he said absently.

Roger was shouting orders, above them, and the wagons rumbled down past them, the oxen bellowing and shaking their heads. Fulk bent so that Morgan could reach him; he felt the cold blade of Morgan's dagger against his skin and the pain of the stingers tearing out of his flesh.

"Your eye is swelling," Morgan said, sitting up.

"Ah." He could hardly open his right eye. His ear and his upper lip were numb and oddly cold. All over his bandaged arm, the bodies of crushed bees clung to the cloth. Some of them still fluttered their torn wings. He brushed them off. "Let's go. Keep playing."

"Do you feel well?" Morgan said kindly.

"Keep playing."

They floundered down toward the strip of glassy water at the foot of the slope, and the marsh insects, aroused and ready, rose in a swarm to feast. Morgan sang of the king's son, standing in the bow of the White Ship, who shone like the sun in its glory.

A fine black scum covered the water of the creek, and the horses would not drink it. The rocks along the stream-bed were covered with drinking bees. They struggled up the far slope through the brush.

"Were you stung?" Roger said.

"Very Biblically, on my most sinful parts."

They climbed painfully up into the dry, sweet air of the hillside.

ON INTO THE afternoon, they rode across the low hills, while before them the dust cloud of Thierry's passage hung in the air. The swellings on Fulk's face went down quickly. Just after noon, with the sun filling the sky, they rode through a little village, and they stopped to water their horses. Fulk soaked a cloth in cold well water and held it to his face. The village was tiny, only a dozen huts of splint oak branches covered with turf, and it stank of pigs. A woman there told them that Thierry had passed by before noon. Morgan spoke to her, all friendship, in his musical English, but she jerked her eyes away and ignored him. Fulk said that she probably did not understand him.

That he did not believe. They were well inside the demesne of Sulwick now, and these people knew their enemies.

Sulwick, warned of the army approaching, would certainly send out men to scout and harass. In the heat, in the dust, with his bad arm aching and itching, Fulk began to see Thierry as the enemy he pursued, and the men of Sulwick as his allies, the walls against which he drove Thierry. The hard marching of the day had dried him out and made thinking difficult. He felt shrunken in against the bone of his will, all the flesh of reason and excuse eaten up by the sun. Roger said nothing all afternoon, knowing it.

The pasturage and fields they rode through were returning quickly to the forest. Shrubs and berry bushes sprouted in a mat of tough, furry-leaved weeds. The wells were broken and filled in and there were no villages at all. Fulk could not remember that great battles had been fought here, but this same thing had happened everywhere in England during the wars, the death of the land. The forest was always waiting to reclaim it, and once the struggle to hold back the forest slackened, its vanguard attacked—these weeds, these woody little shrubs and the thickets of dense brush.

The sun slid down the western sky; Fulk strained against it, startled to find himself fighting to hold the sun in the sky. If it set they would have to camp. In this broken country he could easily command the three separate parts of the army to camp separately, but that, he knew, would be a victory for Thierry—to have survived one day alone in command would make him immeasurably stronger. He stared at the plume of dust beyond the rowans that crowned the next hill.

He prayed for help, knew he could not expect God's help for this, and prayed harder. God would understand. God had swallowed so much in the way of piety in the past twenty years that this must seem almost virtue. He shifted the sheepskin pad under his arm and only managed to jar it, and the aching pain always working in it sharpened to where he could no longer ignore it. He fell to brooding over the chance that the arm would heal crooked.

"My lord," Roger said. "Look over there—beyond Thierry's dust."

Fulk blinked. Thierry was almost directly west of them now and he had to look into the sun. The ruddy sky confused him; he could see nothing.

"Dust," Roger said.

"Oh. Yes." He scrubbed his eyes and looked again. He still could not see it. "Where is it?"

"Past him," Morgan said in his light voice. "I see it. It's more dust than Thierry's, isn't it, Sir Roger?"

"Yes," Roger said. "Shall we send to Thierry?"

Fulk nodded. "Tell him not to stop, to go straight on to Sulwick. Does he have the sense to steal a peasant to show him the way? Tell him that, too."

Roger turned and bellowed for a knight riding behind them. Fulk's mouth was dry. He strained to see the dust in the air ahead but the falling sun blotted it out. All along the horizon, the sky turned red and orange. Roger gave orders to the knight and sent him galloping west.

"Leave the wagons here," Fulk said. "De Brise can bring them. Tell the drovers that we think the vanguard is being attacked and we're going to help and they may as well wait for de Brise. Tell de Brise to come as fast as he can." He stood in his stirrups, looking up and down the line. "We'll bring the archers, if they can keep up. Tell Godric they must keep up."

Roger dropped back to give orders; Fulk rode forward to the head of the band of archers. The sun was turning blood red and its long light turned the faces around him rosy. He talked to Godric, who stood listening and rubbing his hand up and down his cased bow.

"If we can't keep up we'll wait for de Brise," Godric said. "We can move quicker on foot in this terrain than knights, my lord."

Fulk nodded. All his will was dragging him down the road, after Thierry, and his excitement drowned the pain in his arm and made his voice more clipped than usual. The archers caught it; they started off before Fulk gave them an order, but he let them go.

The knights called to him, and he drew off to one side and waved them on past him. "We'll be fighting soon—get ready. Go on." He saw how they laughed at that, and his heart jumped. Oh, yes, fighting is what we're made for. With Morgan beside him he waited until they passed. A horse galloping toward him from the rear of the column, a steady, rising pound of hoofs, made him look around, and he saw Roger. The other knights were already trotting off into the west. Fulk reined his horse around before Roger reached him and loped after them.

        OVERHEAD, THE SKY turned pink and orange and darkened to violet. Before the sun set Fulk and Roger had shouted and shoved the knights into a tight double column; they kept their horses to a short lope, one horse's length between each, up and down the rocky slopes. Thierry's dust trace had vanished into the darkness, and they had to follow his trail, cut deep and wide into the hillsides. The darkness closed down around them like a forest. The archers had fallen back, but the horses could not keep this pace for long, and they could catch up later.

"What do you think happened?" Roger shouted, riding up beside him. "Have they attacked yet?"

Fulk shook his head. He hadn't seen the other dust cloud but he was sure they would have heard something.

Morgan said, "My lord, can you use a shield and a sword both?"

"No."

They rode into the thickening darkness. The twilight was a resonant blue, strange and confusing. It was hard to see. His ears began to hurt from listening so hard, and he tried to stop, but a moment later caught himself struggling to hear. Bird calls, the sound of the wind. Somewhere a dog or a wolf howled. The road pitched down a steep slope into a well of black dark. In the cloudless sky stars were shining.

"Listen," Roger said.

He could hear nothing. The noises of the galloping column drowned all other sound. Am I to miss all the—He sucked in his breath.

Out of the darkness ahead of them came the muffled sounds of fighting, the neighing and squealing of horses, the clank of swords, and the cries of the knights. They could see nothing but the sounds were so near, right in front of them, that the men around him drew their swords. An instant later the noise faded to a distant mutter. A trick of the wind, bringing it so close. Fulk thrust his feet deep into his stirrups and shortened his reins.

"On, on," Roger shouted, in a voice like a young man's.

The knights shrieked. Their horses lengthened stride, vaulting over obstacles before them only half-sensed in the dark, straight into the black glen ahead of them.

"Bruyère, Bruyère," a voice cried, ahead of them, and the knights bellowed in answer. That was Thierry's voice. Fulk reached down to unhook his shield from his saddle, realized he would never be able to put it on, and took his reins out of the tips of his right fingers. His horse carried him over rocks and through trees, careening down the hillside in the dark. Morgan was riding beside him, with a shield on his arm, on his light mare, keeping pace with Fulk's horse.

The sounds of fighting crashed on his ears again—shrill cries and screams and the hacking of blades on metal. A horse with an empty saddle galloped up beside Roger, foam streaming from its mouth. Fulk whispered a prayer. His horse braced itself. With Morgan beside him shielding them both, he hurtled forward into the midst of the fighting.

In the dark, no one could see anything—they were fighting across a stream and up a slope, and the brush and stubby trees entangled them. They fought galloping, headed straight up the slope. No one could tell who was the friend and the enemy. A man loomed up before Fulk, headed straight for him. He saw the glint of the horses's mad eyes and the man's eyes behind the nosepiece of his helmet and set himself, filled his lungs, and shouted, "Bruyère, Bruyère." Abruptly the man before him veered off—one of his other knights. He could not see the bodies surging all around him—he heard them, he smelled them. He ran his horse into another from behind and knocked it down, and with Morgan close on his right side turned to go back.

"Keep going," Roger shouted. "Keep going—follow me!"

Fulk aimed for his voice. His horse stumbled on something and wrenched itself up onto its feet again and stepped on something that screamed. Horsemen were racing away from them, toward Sulwick, in little packs; he saw them against the sky when they topped the hill. He needed a weapon, but he knew he could not hold a lance. A horn sounded to his left, and he felt his horse shudder at the sound and his own blood tingle at it.

"Bruyère, Bruyère, over here."

He reined in, almost at the crest of the slope, and looked back. The moon was finally rising, and in its first light he could see masses of men riding back and forth over the slope, among the bushes. Roger, just behind Fulk, sounded his horn again, and the knights turned and rode up toward him. Across their saddles, they carried bodies, but only a few—in the confusion no one had killed very well. Fulk let out his breath; he did not see Thierry or any of Thierry's men.

"Make a column again," he said to Roger. "With the moon up we can see well enough."

"Where is Thierry?" Roger said.

"Ahead of us, somewhere. They all fled when we attacked." He turned to Morgan. "Carry my sword. Let's give this arm some exercise, in case the other comes out bent."

THE MOON ROSE higher, nearly full, and they rode through its pale light toward Sulwick. After the confused fighting, the knights were excited and talkative. They kept the column tight and held their horses to an even trot. Fulk left his place in the middle of the line and rode forward, looking over the men he passed. They waved to him, smiling; they were all eager to fight again.

"My lord," somebody shouted, up in front of him. "Send for the lord—look."

Fulk stood in his stirrups to see. The column broke apart, up where the man had shouted, and some of them stopped, blocking the way for those behind. High shouts rose. He galloped forward, toward the milling knights, who were watching something on the ground. Their mail glinted in the moonlight, and when they wheeled aside to let him through, the moonlight glinted on the mail of the man lying there in the grass.

"Is he ours?" a knight shouted. "Where is my lord?"

"Here," Fulk called. "Let me see."

Another knight said, "Whoever he is, he's dead."

Fulk stopped his horse and dismounted. His legs were sore and cramped from so much riding. Kneeling beside the body, he turned it over. In the vague moonlight he saw fair hair, a young, white face, wild eyes staring up past him into the sky. Not stiff yet. He just died. In the young man's chest and side there was a great wound, the links of his chain mail driven into the flesh and blood below.

"He isn't ours," Fulk said. "Where's his horse?"

Nobody had seen the horse.

"Leave him here. De Brise can bring him in the wagons, when he finds him." If he finds him. He stood up, groaning at the ache of his leg muscles. "Come along, now, straighten out this line. Get back in line and move on. You're holding us all up."

They swung their horses away, and the column trotted past, each man craning his neck to see the dead boy in the grass. Fulk gathered his reins and hauled himself stiffly into his saddle.

Roger said, "Who was he?"

"Sulwick's man."

They moved back into the column. A little way on, Fulk turned to look back. He could not see the body, but he knew where it was. The column had left it behind, and from a copse of yew nearby a long shadow slunk down toward the dead knight.

The wolves will eat him before de Brise finds him. I should have brought him with us, or stopped to bury him. His uneasy guilt at that startled him: he realized he was tired.

There was no wind. The smells of horses and men smothered the ordinary scents of the open fields; Fulk began to feel stale and filthy, encased in dirt like armor. Morgan was dozing in his saddle. Roger and Fulk passed a wineskin back and forth in silence.

"Look, over there," a man shouted, in the column in front of them.

"Another," Fulk said. He pulled his horse out of the column and galloped forward again, toward where the knights were gathering around another lump in the grass.

This lump was alive. When he reached the knights, they were laughing and holding out jugs of wine to a man who sat on the ground with his back against a tree and laughed feebly back at them. Fulk rode into their midst.

"Well, Rabel," he said. "Are you taking your leave?"

Rabel lifted his head. "My lord, I would not, but I can't find my comrades."

Fulk looked around him. "Get back in line and keep moving. Bring me a spare horse."

Reluctantly, the knights dragged their horses around and moved off. Fulk dismounted and sat down heavily beside Rabel. He still had the wineskin, and he held it out.

"No, I've had enough—it only makes me thirsty." He was pressing his hand against his leg, and when he moved it, blood, black as oil, oozed down his thigh.

"What happened?" Fulk said.

"I don't know. They attacked us. We were marching in our column and suddenly they attacked us, from all sides. We were spread out too much. We fought, I couldn't tell who I was fighting, and another band of them attacked, and we all fled—I rode away with some of the Sulwick men, I thought they were my own."

"The second band was mine," Fulk said. "Why didn't you stop and join us?"

Rabel shook his head. "He will not stop."

"Does Thierry know where he's going?"

The knight gave a hoarse laugh. "To Sulwick."

"Where is Simon? Simon d'Ivry?"

"I don't know. I haven't seen him since sundown. They attacked us at sundown. Maybe he's dead. He was with Thierry. William is dead, I think, and Miles." He shut his eyes. "Leave me here. I can find my way."

"There are wolves all through these fields. Here's a horse." Fulk stood and took the reins of a led horse from Roger. "Help me get him into the saddle."

Roger dismounted, and he and Rabel spoke softly. Fulk led his horse back into the track of the knights. They were already far ahead—he could see them riding along a ridge to the west. Walking back toward Rabel, he held the horse's bridle while Roger boosted the wounded man up onto its bare back. At the smell of blood the horse skittered nervously sideways.

"Go back the way we came," Fulk said, "De Brise is coming with the wagons. Tell him to try to catch up with us. Don't—"

He lifted his head, looking back along the trail, and the distant shout came again. "That's Godric and his archers. Good. Don't go too fast, Rabel, or you'll kill yourself. Give them warning that you're one of us. Roger, come on."

"Watch out," Rabel called. "There are Sulwick men everywhere."

Fulk and Roger mounted, and the wounded knight started back the way they had come. In tight, neat ranks, Godric's bowmen were jogging through the light brush down the last hillside. Roger said, "Did he tell you what happened to the vanguard?"

"The Sulwick men attacked them. Thierry's lost control. We'll have to gallop to catch up. Let's go."

Single file, they raced after the column of knights. In the moonlight the beaten track of the knights showed

like a long bruise on the fields. The even rhythm of
the horses' hoofs seemed loud as thunder. They rode
up onto the ridge where Fulk had seen the column
riding, and the land changed from fallow fields to
plowed ground, soft and ridged to catch the horses'
hoofs and trip them. Ahead, the column had stopped
again.

"God of angels," Roger said. "We could follow the
trail of bodies. How far are we from Sulwick?"

"Close," Fulk answered. He spurred his horse into
a flat run the last hundred yards. The knights had
seen them coming and wheeled, shouting and waving,
to welcome them back. Fulk reined in hard and stopped
his horse in their midst. Three dead men lay on the
ground before him.

"Ours," a knight said. "Miles of Bâle, Gilbert de
Brémule, and Roger Surmelch."

Fulk licked his lips. We should bury them. We can't
leave them here. He looked around at the knights and
saw them watching him expectantly. They were sure
he would do what was right. Leave them for de Brise
to find. We have to bury them.

Morgan rode up beside him. "My lord, are you—"

Fulk grabbed his arm to keep him quiet. "Listen!
Ahead." He let go of Morgan; the knights were swinging their horses toward the sound of fighting. "You
and you," Fulk said. "Bring these bodies. The rest of
you shall follow me."

He pushed forward, and they held off so that he
could go to the head of the column. Ahead of them,
someone was screaming, "Bruyère, Bruyère," and the
knights around Fulk suddenly shouted, "Bruyère," and
plunged forward.

"Roger," Fulk called. "Take half and go down
there." He waved his arm at the fields at the foot of
the long ridge. No sense waiting to see if Roger had
heard. Morgan was beside him with his shield, holding
his sheathed sword in the crook of one arm, and he
reached out with his left hand and drew it awkwardly

and sent his horse bolting along the crest of the ridge
toward the rising sounds of fighting. With yells and
shouted prayers, his army flooded down the slopes
around him.

The ridge fell off suddenly into a long steep slope
down to a meadow along a stream; Fulk braced himself and gave his horse its head, and the horse skidded
down the slope on its hocks, bouncing pebbles and
dirt along with it. In the meadow, a great ring of
knights was charging a knot of men backed up against
the stream's edge. Those were Thierry's men, that knot.
He saw Thierry among them, waving his sword over
his head. The Sulwick knights charged in, and the two
groups of horsemen merged into a single black clump
of bodies.

"God is just!"

The Sulwick men shouted that. Fulk was holding his
sword and his reins both in his left hand, the heavy
sword braced on his thigh. He shouted, "Bruyère, Bruyère, follow me." He felt his horse shift its balance,
reaching flat ground, and ahead of him, the Sulwick
men peeled away from the fighting, warned.

"Bruyère," Thierry's men cried. They were outnumbered; Thierry had less than half the men he had
started with. They threw themselves on the Sulwick
men, and the knights behind Fulk hit the level ground
and charged, roaring. The neighing of the horses and
the clash of metal swelled into a din so loud Fulk
could hear nothing. Beside him, Morgan kept his mare
shoulder to shoulder with Fulk's bay, his shield raised
to cover them both. Fulk headed toward the nearest
group of Sulwick men and dropped his reins.

Two knights leaped forward to meet him. "God is
just!" One headed for Morgan and the other for him,
and he swerved his horse hard to the right. The quick
turn put Morgan behind him and brought him head-on
to one of the knights, and he tried to make his horse
turn a little more, but the big bay would not answer
his heel. The knight raised his shield and struck at
him, and Fulk ducked out of the way and swung his

sword awkwardly left-handed. The other knight was right-handed and had shielded himself against a right-handed blow, and the edge of Fulk's sword caught him in the side and felled him. He looked around behind him and pressed his leg to the horse's side, and this time the big bay turned, and Morgan appeared on Fulk's right, white-faced behind the kite shape of the shield.

"Fall back," someone was screaming, close by. "Fall back, they are by the river, fall back!"

"On," Fulk cried; his throat was caked with dust, and he croaked, his voice no stronger than an old woman's. "On, on." There was a knight beyond Morgan, but he was answering the order to fall back, wheeling toward the river, where Roger and his men were riding at a gallop to cut him off. All the knights around Fulk were turning toward the river. They were getting away. He spurred his horse, calling to his men, his voice pleading. Morgan could not keep up and the bay horse would not slow. He chased a knight on a cream-colored horse; the knight reined down to let him draw even, and they hacked and clubbed at each other, side by side, while the horses ran blindly over the meadow.

The knight on the cream-colored horse screamed, "God is just!" and struck at Fulk's head. The weight of the sword was dragging Fulk's arm down; he could barely lift it, and every great blow hurt his arm to the shoulder. The bay was too wild to control with his legs. He felt sick to his stomach. He could see nothing but flashes of light. Abruptly the blows ended. His legs were cold. His horse slowed and stopped, and he bent over its neck and retched painfully.

"Here." Morgan said. "Let me have it. Let me have it, my lord."

Fulk loosened his fingers so that Morgan could take the sword from him, and with that hand pushed himself upright. His eyes cleared; the air felt wonderfully cool. His horse was standing to its belly in the rushing waters of the stream.

"You murderous man," Thierry said calmly. "Did you think you could run them down by yourself?"

"I thought I would have some help from you."

"You got ahead of us," Roger said. "If you hadn't stopped you would have ridden off with them."

Fulk shook his head. Morgan was washing the shoulders of his horse. "They'll go straight to Sulwick and we'll have to fight them there." He backed his horse out of the stream.

"How far is Sulwick?" Thierry said. He looked as strong and cheerful as ever. Fulk's stomach knotted itself into a huge cramp.

"I'll show you. Where are your men?"

Thierry said, "They attacked us all night long, we've been fighting since—"

"Where are the knights I gave you?" Fulk looked at Simon, behind Thierry. "Where are they?"

"Scattered," Simon said. He had a lump on his jaw, and his red hair had been plastered down by his helmet, which he held in the crook of his arm. "I don't think many are dead."

"Miles is dead," Fulk said. "We passed him, coming here. What happened? Thierry, which of them disobeyed you?"

"We obeyed him." Simon leaned forward.

"How did you lose so many?" Fulk said. "Even at night—"

"They attacked us constantly," Thierry said. "I tell you, there was nothing I could have done—"

"You lie. You gave them no chance—why didn't you keep them together?"

"You lie," Thierry said, darkening.

"No," Simon said. "He isn't lying, it's the truth. If you had kept us in our column—if you'd only stopped when—"

"It was so dark, no one could see. How could I have—how can you blame me?"

Simon raised his head; his eyes were popping with rage. "It was not dark when I begged you to stop and let Miles catch up with us, my lord. Remember?"

"You never begged me for anything. Except, perhaps, counsel."

Fulk was rubbing his stomach; he watched their intent faces. Thierry by looks and the weight he gave words had said something to Simon no one else could hear. Simon's face slackened a little.

"I thought better of you all," Fulk said. "I thought you better knights than that."

Simon's hand rose. "It was not our fault, my lord—"

"Simon," Thierry said sharply, and Simon looked unwillingly at him and dropped his eyes. Fulk shrugged.

"Roger, take half the men and form a column. Follow this stream that way—" he gestured, "—and soon enough you'll find Sulwick. Attack when my horn sounds. The rest of you, make a double column, and keep it tight together."

"Now?" Thierry said, startled. "We marched all yesterday and fought all the night, and now—"

"They won't expect us now," Fulk said. He looked up at the ridge they had ridden down from, and saw the first of the archers moving down it. "You had your opportunity to show what an excellent warrior you are, uncle. I consider it dangerous to allow you to continue. Roger, take Godric's men with you. No need to move fast. Morgan, can you find something to cushion this arm?"

Thierry looked around him, at the other knights. "I refuse this. You drive us like serfs. You are destroying us."

"Refuse," Fulk said. "Go. Don't stop when you reach the coast of England, either, but find yourself a ship and sail away."

Morgan was rolling up a wad of cloth to put under Fulk's broken arm. The knights were drawing up their columns. Thierry, with his young knights, stayed watching Fulk a moment more. Thierry swore; he turned his horse's head and rode off a little way. The young knights remained, their eyes on Fulk.

"My lord," Simon began. "It wasn't our fault, I swear it."

"Go join your column."

The young knights rode away. Morgan came up and fixed the pad under his arm. Fulk expected him to say something about Fulk's riding away from his shield in the fighting, but Morgan did not. In the eastern sky, the stars were fading, and the moon dipped down toward an edge of new light.

"KEEP THEM QUIET," Fulk said to Thierry. The dawn sky was the white of an eggshell, and on the hill above them, Sulwick Castle stood— one round tower, surrounded by an earthworks. All the knights with Fulk carried unlit torches.

On the top of the tower, from the slits of windows, the Sulwick men had undoubtedly seen Roger and his column, riding along the far bank of the stream. Occasionally, through the trees that masked this side of the hill, Fulk could see them himself. The sky brightened steadily. The birds were beginning to sing; they ceased abruptly and fluttered away when the knights rode under their trees, but everywhere else the wild clamoring of the birds grew stronger while the sun grew stronger. Fulk held up his hand and reined in his horse.

"Everybody dismount. Do you have the torches? Morgan, come here."

Morgan kicked his horse up beside Fulk's. Fulk gave him his horn.

"Stay here and wait until the sun comes up. When it's all risen, sound this."

"Why should we leave the horses?" Thierry said. "They can climb that slope."

"I'm tired of riding," Fulk said. He swung out of his saddle and took his shield from Morgan. "Come along, uncle, are you old?"

Thierry grunted and walked away. Fulk put his left arm through the straps on his shield and started up the slope. He hurt all over with an almost pleasant ache and his stomach was churning with hunger. It was impossible that it had been only one day since he had left Bruyère-le-Forêt.

He stamped up the hillside, leaning against the weight of the shield, amazed and pleased at his own strength. Everything had gone so well that it frightened him. Thierry had made a complete fool of himself and to save their own reputations all the knights he had commanded were blaming him.

Simon d'Ivry walking beside him looked grim enough to eat his armor. Like most of the men, he had caught up with Fulk; their longer legs made it hard for them to walk at his pace.

They reached the edge of the trees, and without a command they all stopped. Between them and Sulwick lay a steep, rocky knob that the earthworks crowned. Fulk sank down on one knee and stared at it, scratched idly at his beard. Sulwick was a new castle, hastily built, and no larger than a windmill, but whoever had built it had picked a good site.

"Simon," Fulk said. "Is the sun risen yet?"

"No."

"There's the gate. Do you see it? When the horn blows, Simon, run straight for it."

Simon turned to look at him, scowling. The lump on his jaw made him look more belligerent than usual. "Why should I be first, especially?"

Fulk said, "Mushrooms."

Simon's eyes widened. In the trees below them, the first ringing peal of the horn blasted. Without hesitation, Simon bounded up and bolted for the gate through the earthworks. Fulk sprinted after him.

From the foot of the hill, across the stream and well to Fulk's left, came the yells of Roger's army; the horn blared out twice more and died away. Simon was racing diagonally up the rocky slope, dropping occasionally to all fours. After the first few strides, Fulk could not keep up with him; most of the other knights passed him, running almost without effort while he strained and stumbled over the rocks.

From the tower windows, a volley of arrows flew, aimed at Roger's men. Screaming, they charged up the softer slope directly below the gate. Fulk's shield dragged at him. He saw Thierry rush past him, a handful of torches in one hand. Roger's men were scrambling up the last steep stretch to the gate. Arrows showered down on them. A man slid sideways out of his saddle, and the horses behind him vaulted the rolling body. Their harsh warcries rose: "Bruyère, Bruyère."

"Arrows," a man in front of Fulk cried out, and Fulk jerked his shield up. Light and careless as rain, arrows plinked down on his shield; he could feel the blows all along his arm.

Simon had reached the gate. Before Fulk had taken two more strides, he and another knight were climbing it, their shields hanging from their shoulders, like spiders. Fulk raced into the shelter of the earthworks and leaned against it, panting. The dirt wall rose ten feet over his head, packed hard and slick as mud. Onehanded, he could never scale it.

The archers were racing up the slope, bent over among the brush and rocks, their bows on their backs. At the edge of the cover, they knelt and strung their bows. Roger's men, in the shelter of the gate, were shouting and banging at the wood with their swords. Simon and the other knight had reached the top of the gate; an arrow struck the other knight through the chest, and he fell back into the pack of horsemen below, but Simon dropped out of sight over the gate.

"Bend down," Fulk cried. He hammered with his fist on the shoulders of the man nearest him. "Make a ladder—you, too. Jordan, Jordan, get on top of them." He swatted Jordan de Grace on the back, trying to push him faster onto the backs of the other men, bent with their hands on their knees.

"I am, I am," Jordan shouted. He scrambled up onto the two backs, got to his feet, and bent over. Fulk climbed awkwardly up onto his back.

"Not close enough. Jordan, stand up. I can hold on—stand up."

"If you were a bigger man I would give you my defiance for this." Jordan straightened up slowly, bracing himself with his hands on the wall, and Fulk put his feet on the other man's shoulders, threw his shield across the earthworks, and dragged himself up onto the flat top of the wall.

"Follow me," he shouted down to Jordan, and rolled off the wall into the compound within it; while he rolled he saw the sky stitched with arrows from the tower and from the archers in the brush outside the wall. Arrows pounded into the packed earth around him. One struck between his knees and snapped off against his thigh. He snatched up his shield and crouched behind it and ran through a hail of arrows toward Simon.

With his shield raised like a wall against the arrows, Simon was lifting off the bar that bolted the gate. He could barely lift it for the weight of it. Fulk reached him just after he had heaved the bar down and thrown the gate open to the horsemen.

Shouting, Roger's knights poured through, and in their dust, the other, horseless men. They charged the tower door. Several of them were waving lit torches. The torrent of arrows turned straight down to meet them. Fulk's archers were sweeping the top of the tower with arrows; bodies hung over the edge, and Fulk saw that the Sulwick men had left it for the shelter of the tower.

Simon was standing behind the shelter of the gate. He looked at Fulk through the corner of his eye. "I thought I put a gate between me and you, lord."

"Oh, well. I thought I'd see how you did. Are you pleased to be a hero?"

"Better than a dead coward."

Fulk hawked froth from his throat and spat it out. "I wouldn't have killed you. I wanted you to run fast. Let's go help with the burning."

"Wait. I didn't want—I didn't think you would eat the mushrooms. I was angry. You struck me."

"You gave me cause. Don't do that again. Come on."

Fulk trotted across the packed dirt of the courtyard to the tower. His men were hacking cheerfully at the wooden walls, making small piles of chips to start fires in. The thunder of the arrows on their raised shields was deafening. This side of the wooden tower was covered with arrows from the archers beyond the wall. Occasionally, an arrow slipped through the roof of shields and struck an arm, a foot, a head, and a man screamed. Inside the tower, the horses of Sulwick's knights plunged around and neighed. From the upper stories came cries of "God is just" and "God helps the righteous," and the men outside shouted back, "Bruyère."

The fires were catching. In waves, the knights drew back, their shields over their heads, while the flames lapped higher against the walls of the tower. Fulk shrank back from the heat. On the top of the tower, two men appeared, with buckets. One of them took an arrow through the throat before he reached the side and the other died while pouring the water down on the flames. It did no good; Fulk saw where the water had splashed the wood and watched the wet spot shrink and shrink and vanish from the heat before he could draw a breath.

A cry of hate and despair came from the windows above them. The arrows rattled down on them. Bright gold in the early morning sun, the fire blazed up the tower walls toward the first row of windows. The horses inside were screaming, and hoofs beat frantically against the wooden walls.

"We should save the horses," Simon muttered; his face glistened with sweat.

"Wait." Fulk drew back toward the earthworks.

Their own loose horses were galloping in a herd around the courtyard. A few of them had been struck by random arrows. Roger and another man were hack-

ing with great overhead blows of their swords at the
door to the tower, and suddenly it split open. The
arrows from the tower slackened. Roger and half a
dozen men disappeared into the burning tower and
drove horses out the narrow door—burns showed on
the flanks and sides of some of them.

"Why couldn't we force the door and capture the
tower that way?" Simon asked.

"Too dangerous."

The shower of arrows from the tower stopped entirely. From a high window a man shouted, "Give
quarter. Give quarter!"

"Quarter," Fulk shouted. "Let them out." He lowered his shield and looked around for Roger.

"Put the fires out," the man in the tower cried.

"No!"

The flames had climbed as high as the bottom row
of windows. All the horses were out; Roger was shouting to the men around him to get rope, so that they
could rescue the people in the tower. Fulk looked
around. Everything that had to be done was done, except saving their enemies. All the knights wanted to
help, to get a share in a ransom. Fulk went over to
the shade of the earthworks, lay down, and went to
sleep.

EIGHT

"HAVE YOU SEEN THE CAMP?" Roger said. "It runs out of sight up and down the river, and they have news that King Stephen himself is coming—we'll have some fighting here. It might all end here."

"You're talkative today. The marten cloak, Morgan. What's that?"

Roger went to the tent door and looked out. "I don't know. Everybody is cheering—somebody's come into the camp."

Fulk shook his sleeves out. They had reached Wallingford that afternoon and found Prince Henry and most of his army already there, furiously laying siege to Crowmarsh, the castle King Stephen had raised to help him in his own long siege of Wallingford. Fulk had left a dozen of his knights at Sulwick, along with some archers, to keep watch over the road and to build him another castle on the site of the one they had burned. He had put Simon in command. Two more bands of his knights were supposed to meet him here,

but they had not yet come from the north. De Brise
had gone back with his men, having served their two
months.

"The sun is going down," Roger said, coming back
into the middle of the tent. Fulk's baggage lay around
in heaps along the edge of the circular room, waiting
to be unpacked. Outside, the wild rush of cheering
died.

"Call my horse up."

Morgan in a fine coat of red and white and Roger
in a furred cloak stood beside the door, a little self-
consciously, to escort him out. Fulk pulled on his left
glove with his teeth. Morgan had trimmed his hair,
and the snippings had gone down his back and itched
him. He went out into the rosy light of the sunset.

Fire beds, strings of tethered horses, wagons, and
an occasional tent covered the low, flat plain as far as
the curve of the river north and the ford to the south.
In spite of the men rushing back and forth, the clumps
of men talking, the squires carrying firewood on their
backs like moving thickets, and the wagons everywhere,
the camp looked well ordered and neat. Here and
there, above a tent planted, like Fulk's, in the midst
of the camp, a standard curled in the evening wind—
Leicester's, Derby's, the White Horse of Chester, the
Bear of Hereford, Wiltshire's Black Lion. The river
ran sedately between its low banks along the edge of
the camp, past the tower and wall of Crowmarsh, past
the fortress of Wallingford, hung with pennants wel-
coming the prince.

Beyond the river lay the camp of the king's men.
They all felt it as if they breathed the knowledge in
the air. Grooms led up Fulk's horse and Roger's and
Morgan's palfrey, and they mounted.

"Bruyère," the knights camped around his tent
shouted, and they waved their arms. The cheering
spread unevenly out across the camp—half of those
yelling probably didn't know why they did it. Fulk
raised his arm in answer and started off.

Beside Fulk, Morgan carried his red banner. Roger

called orders, and the six knights escorting Fulk moved into line before and behind him. For the first time since they had left Sulwick, the horses were polished sleek and the gear of the knights shone. Roger had said they were bragging of their march to whoever would listen to them. Fulk eased his arm in its sling. They had taken off the heavy splints at Sulwick and in a few days he would be rid of even these light boards and the mass of bandages. If it healed straight he owed a statue of the Virgin to the chapel at Bruyère-le-Forêt.

"Stafford," a man shouted, when they passed. "Ho, Stafford!"

Fulk turned, smiling, and waved—that was William Louvel. He strode toward him, cutting through his camp to keep level with the horses. "You missed the plundering at Bedford, Stafford—I hear you had some good works, though."

"Bloody work in the dark," Fulk called back. "No silken coverlets such as you got. I'm glad to see you, I'll talk to you later."

"See that you do." Louvel waved and started back to his place, a great bear of a man with bear-paw hands.

"See the prince's tent," Roger said. "Oh, they say he has a leman now."

"That's the custom with young men. Except such as Morgan and my own." Rannulf had not yet come to see him, and he was angry at it.

The prince's tent was twice as large as his own, the canvas streaming silk ribbons and rosettes and scarves. A staff with a swatch of broom tied to it was stuck in the ground by the door, and above it two banners billowed heavily in the light breeze. A line of knights rode up to the door, and one dismounted; the rest rode off and the man on foot went in.

"While I am there, go find Rannulf for me," Fulk said.

Roger nodded.

They stopped before the door, and Morgan jumped

down and ran to hold the head of Fulk's horse. Before Fulk could dismount, the tent flap opened and a tall, thin man with a sour mouth came out—one of the prince's Angevins.

"Good evening, Sir Richard," Fulk said, and dismounted.

"My lord." The Angevin stood aside. Fulk went past him into the crowded, candle-lit tent.

Flanked by their pages and squires, the great barons stood or sat, rubbing up against one another. The noise reminded Fulk of the buzzing of marsh insects. With Morgan at his elbow, he crowded into the mass of bodies, nodding, smiling, saying the proper words. It was stinking hot.

"Fulk," Derby called, bulling his way through the crowd, and heads turned. "By God, sir, I'm pleased to see you. Still in the surgeon's debt, are you? Robin, lad, wine for my lord of Stafford. Good wine, from Bordeaux, Fulk. With our prince the master of Aquitaine, we can take advantage, can't we?" He rammed an elbow into Fulk's ribs and giggled. Softer, he said, "Thierry and the prince greeted each other like Mary and the Angel."

Fulk laughed. "My lord, I hear some good report of you at Bedford."

"Oh, well. I'm no soldier, Fulk. No soldier, even in my youth. Here." He took the cup from his page's hands and gave it to Fulk. "The king is coming to Wallingford. I should like to see his face when he sees who rides against him now."

The wine was the rich red wine from southern France. Fulk looked quickly around. "I haven't seen my son yet, can you see if he's here?"

"Oh, yes." Derby looked at him owlishly. "With Chester. He and Chester are the finest of friends. Rannulf hung on his sleeve all the way south. He's over in that corner now, with Thierry."

"Wonderful. This is good wine."

"Robin," Derby said to his page, "go bring the lord of Ledgefield—"

"No," Fulk said. "Let him talk to Thierry if he wishes it."

Derby's eyes sparkled. "Are you quarreling? Let me mediate."

"Not at all." Leicester's grizzled, close-cropped head appeared above the ring of bodies, and Fulk caught his eye and bowed. Leicester waved to him but went on across the room.

"When do you get rid of all this?" Derby asked. He fingered the linen sling.

"Very soon. It was a damned nuisance all the way from Tutbury, I swear to you."

"One imagines. Tell me how it went. You took Sulwick, I hear."

"Easily. But we had a day's march and a night's fighting to get there that I don't want to see again. God is my witness, my men were magnificent."

"Thierry set a proper example, I suppose."

Fulk drank wine, judging the necessary tone of voice. Not too eager to reveal Thierry's failures. "This is very fine wine."

"Aha," Derby cried, and pummeled him on the shoulder. "Tell me. I've heard such stories of his greatness in war, I want to know from your lips."

"He's a good fighter, he wants nothing for courage and skill at arms, but he has no head to command." Fulk shrugged his good shoulder. "It was my fault, I should have guessed and not asked so much of him."

"The way they talk of him, who could blame you? The way he talks of himself. So Thierry is not—"

A horn blew two notes inside the tent, piercing and loud enough to hurt Fulk's ears, and a herald bawled, "Way. Way for Henry Fitz-Empress, Duke of Normandy, Duke of Aquitaine, and Count of Anjou, rightful lord of England."

The mob quieted and pressed itself even tighter together, opening a corridor for the prince. Fulk muttered, "He announces himself so that one could scarcely miss him."

Derby laughed. His arm hooked under Fulk's good

elbow, and he dragged Fulk up through the crowd toward the front rank, where Leicester and the other earls stood. The prince went up to stand before them, between two torch-standards. The fur and velvet and silk he wore made him seem taller than he was, and less stocky. His red hair stood on end.

"My lords," he said, in a high clear voice, "I welcome you to Wallingford."

Chester was standing just beyond Leicester, but Rannulf was not with him. Fulk clenched his fist behind his back. For all I do, he still prefers Thierry. He cleared his throat, staring at the prince.

"Fulk de Bruyère of Stafford," Henry said. "I have not seen you since you left Tutbury. Did you do as we commanded you, during your march in the east?"

"My lord," Fulk said, "if I had not, I would now be on the far side of the river, with the king's men," and the barons broke out laughing. Henry, smiling, waited for that to subside.

"I should know from long dealings with you that it is an insult to ask if you accomplished what you said you would, my lord."

Fulk bowed. Behind Henry, a silk curtain divided off the rear of the tent, and he caught a glimpse of a small hand drawing it slightly aside. Roger had said that the prince had a girl with him now.

"I first came to England," Henry said, "to answer the pleas of the people of Wallingford, whom Stephen of Blois has closely besieged." He would never call Stephen the king; Fulk had already marked it. "Now I have come to that duty, and you with me. We have invested this castle of Crowmarsh, which is held by men of Stephen of Blois, and when we have taken it we shall drive away all those who would imprison Wallingford and free the people therein."

Above the small hand on the silk curtains, black curls and a soft blue eye appeared. Derby slammed his elbow into Fulk's ribs with a force that nearly lifted him off the ground.

"I know you all well enough to trust your courage

and your skill," Henry said. "I know you well enough to believe that when I tell you that Stephen of Blois himself, with an army, marches to face us here, you will strain like hounds at the leash to be commanded to attack him."

Everybody yelled.

"Tonight," Henry said, "I shall hear your advice upon what must be done to accomplish our goals: to free Wallingford from its burden of slavery, and to drive Stephen of Blois forever from this kingdom."

Everybody yelled again, but when silence fell no one spoke. Men began to cough, and there was a shuffling of feet. Henry beckoned to a page, who brought him a stool to sit on. "First, we must keep the—keep Stephen from supplying Crowmarsh from the river."

With a specific problem before them, a dozen men began to shout advice. Chester outroared them, stepped forward, and began to talk. Before Fulk could catch the drift of what he was saying, someone tugged at his sleeve, and he looked over his shoulder and saw Leicester there.

"Just for a moment," Leicester said apologetically, and bowed to Derby. He drew Fulk off to one side, clear of the crowd.

"I meant to talk to you before but Derby was there," Leicester said softly. "I have spoken this same day with men of the Bishop of Winchester, and had a letter from the Archbishop Theobald of Canterbury."

Fulk blinked stupidly. Henry of Winchester was the brother of the king, but the archbishop hated the king and had always worked against him; he could not understand why either would approach the Earl of Leicester. Abruptly he did understand, and he stiffened, excited.

"Robert. Are we to spoil the great confrontation?" He looked around to see who might be listening, but all the men around them were following the exchange between Chester and the prince. "What did they say? Winchester—what does he want?"

"What do you think? A truce between Prince Henry

and Stephen, to give them a chance to negotiate and settle the kingdom without fighting. Theobald offers his uttermost help."

Fulk shuffled his feet—he could not stand still. "All the wayward hens are coming home to roost at last. Yes. I will." He smiled up at Leicester's long, startled face.

"Good. I mean to meet secretly with Winchester tomorrow. You come with me."

Fulk nodded. He had been tuned to the long, boring rhythm of the proposed siege, and the prospect of something more interesting filled him with anticipation. "It was Winchester who gave Stephen the treasury and made him king. How fitting it should be Winchester who takes it all away from him." Winchester had also arranged the lie that freed Stephen of his oath to the old king's daughter the empress. "The prince will not like it."

"No," Leicester said. "But King Stephen will have with him all of William d'Ypres's mercenaries, York's men, Peverel's men, and his own besides, and if this army meets that one I should prefer it to be peaceful."

Fulk nodded. "When, tomorrow? Where is Winchester now?"

"He is camped down the river. We meet him at dawn. I'll send for you when I leave camp. We must be secretive, at least for the moment. Let's get back to the council." Leicester held out his hand, and Fulk shook it with his left. They forced their way separately through the crowd to the front rank.

Two barons of the west were arguing about the procedure for patrolling the ford. Prince Henry had his chin in his hand and was listening. His eyes moved to meet Fulk's, and one eyebrow rose inquisitively. Fulk patted his crotch. The prince laughed.

The girl behind the curtain had withdrawn out of sight. On either side, men argued points of war. Fulk sent Morgan to get him more wine. Massive and ugly, Chester lounged in the midst of his followers, over

near the wall of the tent. Among them was Rannulf,
with Thierry just behind him. Fulk jerked his eyes
away.

Leicester with the help of the bishops thought they
could force this truce on Henry and the king. Stephen
would never treat with the prince of his own will.
There would be arguments and insults and threats.
Henry's temper was quick enough under the calmest
circumstances. Fulk imagined a summer storm—the
thunder, the lightning, the violent wind that blew down
trees and carried off houses. In all that turmoil, he
would have plenty of chances to do some overturning
of his own. He settled down to think over his interests.

"THIERRY SAID—"

"I don't care what Thierry said."

"That you tried to have him killed in the fighting,"
Rannulf shouted. "That you put him in the front of the
fighting, like Uriah, to die."

"He didn't die."

"Do you admit it? How dare you admit it?"

Fulk knocked over a table. Wine spilled across the
dirt floor of the tent, and the jug rolled on its base
toward the wall. "Did he tell you that—"

"I have prayed for help from God for you, Father."

Fulk picked up the jug and put it carefully upright
on the ground. The air inside the tent was still and
close; he wished he could open the door to let in the
night cool. "Thierry persuaded one of my own vassals
to—"

"Sometimes I think you are possessed," Rannulf said.

"Will you be quiet and listen to me, you little prig?
Thierry set one of my own men—Simon d'Ivry, your
friend, he set to poison me. Ask Roger."

Rannulf turned his gaze toward the back of the tent.
The long march had brought out dozens of freckles all
over his face. "Sir Roger would say whatever you
wished him to."

"Ask Simon, then, if you see him again." Fulk put the table back on its feet.

"Simon is Thierry's friend. He would never lie against him."

Their eyes met. Fulk's mouth was full of a bitter taste. "No longer. Simon learned enough about Thierry to know better than to be his friend. Did Thierry tell you what——"

"No one believes it. You may spread that rumor all over the camp, but none who knows Thierry believes it."

"Aaaah."

"It's a vicious lie," Rannulf cried. "Thierry is no coward."

"I never claimed he was a coward—only that he has no skill to command. Ask any of my knights, none of them will follow him." Fulk straightened up; his face was hot. "You have the most curious loyalty—where is your loyalty to me? Why are you so loyal to Thierry and not to me?"

Rannulf's hands rose toward his face, paused, and fell back into his lap. "I'm loyal to you, my lord. I pray for you."

Fulk sat down heavily on his stool. "Well, thank you for that, at least."

"I'm loyal to you—I promised Mother I would be, at Stafford. Does that mean I must love what you do that is hateful?"

"No," Fulk said. "I'm sorry I said it, I should not have. Tell me about the march to Bedford."

Rannulf was silent a moment, his eyes on Fulk. Morgan came out of the back of the tent and mopped up the wine spilled on the floor.

"It was interesting," Rannulf said finally. "I had no idea how complicated such a thing is. The prince and I spoke together once—he's very learned, he astonishes me. Don't you think he's learned?"

"Yes." Fulk's shoulders drooped. "He's interesting to talk to. What did you talk about?"

"The laws," Rannulf said, in a wondering voice. "He

wanted to talk of philosophy and things like that, but I
know so little, I had read none of the books he mentioned. But he was interested in the customs of Ledgefield and what I know of Stafford and Bruyère-le-
Forêt and our other manors. It was fun. I didn't know
how much I knew about all that."

"Did you realize how much he knows?"

Rannulf laughed. "Of course. He never misses a
chance to tell one that."

Fulk smiled, pleased. "Did you see much of Leicester?"

"Not really. I find him rather cold—impatient, perhaps."

"Hurried. Yes, he's impatient, but not with you, he's
rather fond of you. I hear you were much in Chester's
company."

"Yes." Rannulf's head rose. "Nearly every day—he
explained to me what was going on, why certain men
commanded certain parts of the army, and other
things. He seems so—he's overwhelming, isn't he?"

"There's a great deal of him, and he never stops
talking."

"Oh, Father, even you—But you know he has a high
regard for you. Even admiration. Thank you, Morgan."

Morgan brought wine to Fulk and withdrew into
the back of the tent; a moment later his harp began
to sing.

"He's strange, Chester is. The things that happen
seem different for him, he can find strange meanings
in everything, as if—I don't understand him. Does he
hate everyone?"

"God, no. Why, what did he say?"

"Nothing. But he has such contempt for everyone.
You must know."

"I know."

"Once, when we were riding—"

Rannulf paused. He leaned forward and put his
elbows on his knees and looked at his clasped hands.
"For no reason, he started to talk, all rushed—he said
that there is no reason to life. It was heresy, I ought

not to have listened, but I—he says there is no use trying to create anything, no use in trying to do anything at all, because the more you do and the more you know the more terrible everything becomes, because knowledge is death."

"I told you he is innocent."

"It seemed sensible to me. No, not that, but the way he said it, I was haunted by it. I still am."

Fulk studied him, imagining Chester's urgent voice declaiming into Rannulf's ear, and a twinge of anger stirred in him. Stupid, insolent man—He thought of what Chester had said and his rage cooled; only Chester would think something that made further thinking impossible.

"Well?" Rannulf said. "Was he right?"

Fulk did not move. Once he had thought up long speeches to give to Rannulf, little packets of wisdom, like slabs of meat, that he could feed him. He scratched his ear, wondering where he had left them all.

"I'm not a particularly knowledgeable man, so I don't know. Nor does Chester. But I don't think it's important."

"Not important?" Rannulf stared at him, his mouth open.

Fulk shook his head, embarrassed. "Did you fight, at Bedford?"

"Holy God," Rannulf said, and snatched his cup and gulped down the wine. "I was terrified. You know I have not fought very much, and not since last autumn. I never stormed a castle. All I remember is that my ears rang for days."

"You must have done well enough or someone would have told me."

"Oh, I fought honorably. But I was so afraid. Are you afraid?"

"Everybody is, some of the time," Fulk said. "I'm very good at forgetting that I was."

"Thierry says you're afraid of nothing. Like a ferret, he says."

"Isn't that kind of Thierry."

"That's why I like him, you know. He admits that he's frightened—he prays all through battle, he says, that his courage will not fail him."

"I refuse to discuss Thierry with you."

Rannulf looked from side to side. "I should go, it's late."

"If you wish. I have to get up early."

"I hope you have prayed for God's guidance," Rannulf said stubbornly. He stood by the door, looking back. "Please."

"I do, daily. Good night."

"Good night."

LEICESTER SAID, "IT'S piercing cold," and walked forward under the trees. The coming dawn had turned the air a deep, clear blue. In the trees above their heads, birds fluttered and sang in short bursts. Fulk let his reins trail and moved away from the horses to look back down the river; he could just see the tip of the tower of Crowmarsh, over the trees and the mist. Someone was galloping toward them, on the far bank.

"Here he comes."

The galloping horsemen and the men and horses already under the trees suddenly frightened the birds. In a rushing cloud, they rose piping out of the trees and into the pale air. Their cries grew dim. Fulk and Leicester walked down to the riverbank. Fulk's hands were cold, and he pulled the ends of his fur-lined sleeves over them.

There were five riders. They came straight through the mist to the bank opposite and paused. The sun was sliding up above the horizon; the mist grew swiftly transparent. With a muffled yell, one of the riders put his horse at the smooth surface of the river. The horse yawed a moment and plunged down the bank into the water and galloped across, throwing up a spray of water on either side. The other horsemen followed; they climbed up the bank near Fulk and Leicester, their horses snorting and shaking their heads, and all the men laughing.

"My lord Leicester," one of the men called, and he rode forward, throwing back his hood. It was Henry of Winchester. Like his brother the king, he was tall and stocky, but his muscles were going all to fat now, and in his fine long hair streaks of gray showed. He reined up and dismounted, smiling.

"I brought Stafford," Leicester said, shaking the bishop's hand. "Him of them all we can trust."

"I know Fulk de Bruyère," Winchester said. He had a fine smooth smile, proper to a papal legate. "Have you told him everything?"

Fulk kissed the bishop's ring. "He has told me nothing, my lord, that I would not hear again from you. We spoke quickly and there were other men around us."

"It is simply thus," Winchester said. "The Archbishop of Canterbury and I have watched the progress of Prince Henry with both admiration and dismay. Clearly he is the only possible heir to our king Stephen; neither of the king's sons is satisfactory. We have no wish to see two such armies as the one at Wallingford and the one now approaching meet in battle. The moment is for healing wounds, not inflicting them."

He smiled, and Fulk smiled, applause for the turn of the phrase.

"Since the solution is so obvious, His Grace the archbishop and I wonder why it cannot be got without bloody battle. To this end—"

"Your pardon, my lord," Fulk said. "The solution—is it so obvious?"

"Why—" Winchester eyed him. "Clearly, King Stephen reached the throne in an ungodly fashion. Yet he is the anointed king, he cannot be uncrowned. To make things right, the lawful heir must be King Stephen's successor, and thus it will all be mended."

"You mean to let Stephen live out his life as king," Fulk said. "Prince Henry will never agree."

Leicester had been kicking at the ground; now he looked up. "Stafford, are you slow today? It is ours to see that he does agree."

"Well," Fulk said, "who is going to make the king agree?"

"The king is tired of the wars," Winchester said.

"He will never disinherit Prince Eustace. I know the younger son, William, has taken no interest in anything touching the throne, but Eustace obviously wants to rule."

"I shall deal with the king," Winchester said.

The growing light of the sun shone on Winchester's face. With each passing moment Fulk saw his features more distinctly, and he seemed to age ten years while the sun rose. Their eyes met. Fulk wasn't really looking; he was thinking of the strength and weakness of each baron and the prince, trying to judge what they would have to do to overturn the will of the prince.

"Why, yes," he said. "We can do it."

Winchester smiled broadly. "The archbishop and I will arrange the thing. You and my lord Leicester we shall leave to the prince's part of it. You shall not go unrewarded."

"I had no intention of it," Fulk said, and kept his face straight. "But that we can talk about later."

Leicester said, "The important thing now is to gain control. Nothing must be done to throw the situation out of our power. Can you keep the king away from Wallingford for a few more days?"

"Yes. He is three days distant now, he and his army, and moving slowly."

"Good." Leicester tugged at a ring on his forefinger. "I pledge you my support, my lord bishop. Here is my token on it."

The bishop took the ring. With his teeth, Fulk twisted a gold ring from his little finger, slipped it onto the tip of the forefinger of his good hand, and held it out. The bishop's fingers nipped it delicately off.

"God be with you," the bishop said. "We shall speak again very shortly. Good day."

"My lord." They bowed.

Winchester strode back to his horse and mounted. The gold flashed on his saddle, his stirrups and his reins. With a shout to his men, he rode back across the river, sitting erect as a lance in his saddle, his head thrown back. They galloped away to the west.

"The prince has grown too great, anyway," Leicester said. "We should teach him that we can overrule him, if we must."

They went back to their horses. The sun was standing just above the distant trees, and its long rays were drying up the grass and the cold, damp air. Fulk mounted; his sling got tangled, and he swore.

"Today they take this thing off me. I should lay it on the altar of the nearest church."

Leicester swung up into his saddle. "It might perform miracles. Can you talk to Chester and Derby? I shall see the others."

Fulk nodded. They started back toward the camp; both horses were rank, and kicked and shied across the short, crisp grass. All around them lay the empty, untended fields of Wallingford, seared and blackened in spots from the many battles fought here. Fulk thought of King Stephen. If he agreed to such a settlement it would be the same as admitting that he had usurped the throne, and Fulk began to wonder how Winchester could force him to accept it. He knew already what he would say to Chester and Derby.

PRINCE HENRY SAID, "Before this summer ends, by God's Passion, I shall have my vengeance for everything that Stephen of Blois has done to me and my mother."

The hot muffled air inside the tent was hard to breathe. Fulk went to the table in the back, where the cups and jugs of wine were set out. "Allow me to serve you, my lord."

"Thank you. The red wine for me." Henry twisted

around to watch Fulk, who was behind him. "How long will it take him to bring an army from London? How many men can he have? Surely most of his support is gone, the archbishop's refusing to crown his son must have . . . What can he offer them to keep them with him?"

He turned slowly forward again, following Fulk's progress from the table to the stool before him, and took one cup of wine from Fulk. He drank from it and put the cup down.

"I know nothing more than I've told you, my lord," Fulk said. He was to see Chester at sundown, but that left the whole of the late afternoon before him; he sipped his wine. "Most of the lords who followed him in the beginning of his reign have left him or are dead, but William of Ypres and his Flemings will be with him, and Stephen's own knights."

"He'll be stripped of them soon enough. What a blessing this past season has been. It must be God's will. Have you inspected Crowmarsh?"

"This morning. Derby and I rode around it."

"Good." Henry leaned forward. "Tell me what you think. I have my own opinions, of course."

"May I sit?"

"Yes. Martin, bring another stool."

The page trotted forward with a three-legged stool and set it down in front of the prince. Two other pages burst out of the back of the tent, screened off with several silk curtains, and ran giggling out the door. Henry glanced at them and turned to look back at the curtains.

"I noticed two weak points where we might be able to break the wall," Fulk said, and stopped, because the prince was not listening. He drank his wine. Henry's jawline, lightly fuzzed with red beard, tightened and relaxed, and he jerked himself straight again.

"Your pardon, my lord. What did you say?"

"That I saw two places where we might break the wall. The south gate is awkwardly placed because of the way the ground falls off there and the defenders could not easily keep it under covering fire. That is a double gate. On the river side of the castle the wall was built too close to the bank on a poor foundation and the wall is showing cracks. We could sap under it and drop the whole wall into the river very easily."

Henry's eyes never blinked; in their centers, the light from the door shone reflected. "The river side? I never thought of it. How can we attack from the middle of a river?"

"My lord, breaching a wall isn't necessarily a means of attacking through it. They would have to place so many of their men there to make certain we didn't enter through the breach that we might be able to force our way in somewhere else."

The two pages rushed in again, still giggling, and bolted into the rear of the tent, and the prince's eyes followed them. "What are they doing in there?" he said softly. The curtain was trembling all its length; streamers of sunlight colored by the red and green silk shifted across the floor.

"God's eyes," the prince said. He looked back at Fulk. "Do you think I'm mad?"

Fulk met his eyes and said nothing, but only smiled; he remembered the black-haired girl he had seen the night before.

"I am mad," the prince said. "I am. What did you say about Crowmarsh, my lord?"

"That we might sap the river wall and attack the south gate when the wall is breached. If we can place men on the wall of Wallingford opposite Crowmarsh."

"I'll have to think about that. I'm sorry if I seem— not myself. Would you bring me more wine?"

Fulk took his cup and walked around him to the table, and the prince swiveled to face him, but his eyes were on the curtain. "I thought of sending Sir Thierry your uncle to make reconnaissance to Crowmarsh, but I doubt he has the craft. What do you think?"

"My uncle is an excellent fighting man, my lord, but to my knowledge he has never laid siege to a castle."

"You laid siege to Sulwick, didn't you?"

The red wine streamed into the cup. Fulk listened to the rising musical note it made. "We stormed Sulwick, my lord." He heard a girl laugh, an arm's length away, behind the curtain.

"Someday you must tell me of that, it must have been interesting."

What does he want me to say? Fulk poured his own cup full. He could feel the prince's eyes on his back, but he knew if he looked the young man would be watching the curtain. He knows that I hate Thierry. Why did he mention him? He went around the prince with the cups and sat down again. As if he had been told, he knew that Thierry had already given the prince his own version of the march to Sulwick.

"I see you've rid yourself of your slings, though, my lord. How does your arm feel?"

"Uncertain."

"Then you won't fight in the tournament?"

Confused, Fulk set his cup on the ground between his feet. The pages came out and began to set the tent straight. "I didn't know if you had agreed to it, my lord. If it's held, I'll fight."

"Just for the few of us. I doubt there will be any danger. King—Stephen of Blois is a chivalrous man, that I know. He wouldn't attack men in their sport. It will be good exercise for us, we are all very sour from the sieges."

He seemed to talk to convince himself, and yet a moment before Fulk knew that the prince had laid some deep and subtle trap for him, talking about Thierry. His confusion rose. He said something about Stephen's known chivalry and picked up his wine.

"But you shouldn't fight if you don't feel strong."

"By then I'll be hale, my lord. It's not so weak even now."

"The tournament is in three days," Henry said. "They say they can't face another siege—before they settle down to the siege, they say, they want the tournament. I think it's mad."

"Everybody hates sieges." It was impossible to discover what Henry wanted him to say; he was floundering in a morass.

"Certainly. It's long and hard and the rewards are slight. Thierry will win the tournament. He's had so much experience. Don't you think?"

"Probably."

"Of course, nobody but you has ever actually seen him fight."

"He's a good fighter, my lord."

"Yet there are certain rumors around the camp. I—"

The curtains parted, and a black-haired girl came out, surrounded by young pages and dressed in bright green, with a gold belt and gold embroidery on her sleeves and skirt and bodice. In her hair was a garland of flowers in place of a coif. Fulk stood up; the prince stared at her as if he'd never seen her before.

"Good day, madame," he said, finally.

The girl came forward smiling; her skin was white and pink like apple blossoms, and her bright blue eyes shone. She made a deep bow before the prince, who caught her hand and bent to kiss it. Fulk backed rapidly toward the door. Over the curly red head of the prince, her brilliant blue eyes met his, bold and hard and old.

"My lord," Fulk said, and went out into the late sunshine. The memory of Red Alys of Dol rushed into his mind. It was the eyes, he thought; he could not soften the hammering of his heart, and he took his horse from the groom that brought it and rode hard toward Chester's part of the camp.

CHESTER WAS JUST sitting down to eat a dish of meat when Fulk came to see him. At his shouted orders, his servants cleared a space on the table and laid out another trencher and a cup. The table was heaped with clothes, armor, weapons, and papers; other piles of goods crowded the rest of the tent and

hid every piece of furniture in it. Fulk found a stool
under a beautiful, filthy brocaded coat and sat down
on it.

"Well," Chester said, his mouth full. "What have
you done today for the cause?" He was eating as fast
as he could put food into his mouth. Two deerhounds
prowled around him, waiting for scraps.

"I saw Prince Henry's prettiest spoil of war."

"Did you. You're very fortunate. Very fortunate indeed. He won't allow her into the presence of any
other men. I saw her, just briefly. She's charming, isn't
she? Empty-headed, of course. Damn you, villein, put
it where I can reach it."

The servant placed a roast on the table close to
Chester and went away. Fulk cut himself slabs of
meat. It felt odd to use his right arm, and he remembered once again that it had healed properly and once
again exhilaration filled him. He cut up the bloody
meat.

"And I rode around Crowmarsh," he said. "Not all
the way, of course. I had to take a boat part of the
way."

"South gate," Chester said. "It's the only way."

"I agree. I did that before I saw Henry. And before
I did my reconnaissance, I and Leicester met the Bishop
of Winchester."

Chester turned his eyes on him; his jaw champed
steadily. "What?"

"Did you know the tournament is in three days?"

"What is this about Winchester? What did he say?
Why wasn't I there?"

Fulk ate a bite. "Where is Rannulf?"

"Out. Tell me, you little swine, before I break your
neck. You know I will."

"Oh, you wouldn't." The meat was tough, and he
spat out a pad of gristle. The deerhounds lunged for it.

"Was it about the king? Of course. Is he going to
treat? No. The prince will never do it. Is that it—is it
about a settlement between them?"

"I think we can make the prince agree," Fulk said.

"You may think so. I don't. Prince Henry has come so far without it, he will go to the end without it. He's that sort."

"My sweet lord, if you can explain to me what sort Prince Henry is, I shall listen to you for once. We are to convince him that he has to treat."

"Why should he? Why wasn't I consulted in this? I was first to join him."

"You were among the first."

Chester tossed a bone down to the dogs and kicked them away. "But Leicester. Why did Winchester talk to Leicester rather than to me?"

"Leicester is a Beaumont. Don't be a fool, sir."

"If I had been born a Beaumont, I—"

"Either of us would have done far better than Leicester has. The settlement is that Stephen remain king until he dies and Prince Henry can succeed him."

"He'll never agree." Chester thrust the remains of the roast into a heap of silk drawers and pulled a meat pie toward him. "Ah." He broke the crust, absorbed, and stuck his nose close to it to catch the escaping aroma.

"He has to," Fulk said mildly. "He doesn't have enough men of his own to face King Stephen, without us and our armies."

"I should have been consulted."

"I know."

"Did you come to me first? Did you?"

"Of course. Without you, nothing succeeds." Derby had agreed to it during their boat ride that morning.

"Yes," Chester said, pleased. "Without me, you know, you could never sway the prince."

"With you, however, it is only a matter of bringing it up before him."

"You've undoubtedly messed it all up already. You and Leicester." The meat pie was hacked to pieces and devoured; vegetables swam in the last juices, and Chester speared them with his dagger and lifted the dish to his lips to drink the gravy. The dogs leaned heavily across his thigh, sniffing.

"If we have, you can tell us."

"I will," Chester said.

"Where is Rannulf?"

"Your miserable son is with your miserable uncle, and I would you consigned them both to perdition. Byzantines."

"Thierry, perhaps."

"He's back in the prince's confidence, did you know that? You're a fool, you've mishandled the entire business, letting him make himself out to be a hero, when the whole army knows he isn't."

"If the whole army knows he isn't, I haven't mishandled it."

"The prince doesn't know. Or doesn't care. You aren't eating. Here." He whacked a capon in half and gave one piece to Fulk. "I used to scare my own son into eating by telling him he'd be as small as you when he grew up—did you know that?"

"I think you've told me before."

"Your father was a small man." Chester's dagger actually paused; he stared into the dusty air. "What a man that was. Your never know him, did you?"

"He left for the Holy Land when I was a baby."

"Your grandfather loved him above his own salvation, never left off talking of him—Thierry hated him. Your father. One Christmas, I remember the old man talking of William, how brave, how noble, on and on, and Thierry—it's difficult to believe they were brothers."

"I think I'll go find Rannulf."

"Oh, aye, find Rannulf. I'll talk to Leicester tomorrow. You two will bungle this if I don't tell you how to approach it. Neither of you knows the prince."

"No," Fulk said. "Not at all." He thought of his meeting with Henry earlier that day.

"And I shall have to see Winchester. You arrange that, Fulk."

"I shall. Thank you for the share of your dinner. I hope you don't starve for want of it."

"Ah." Chester waved him violently away, and Fulk went out the door.

THE SUN WAS burning off the dawn haze, but patches of mist still clung to the ground beneath the trees, and on the river fog trailed along the quiet water. A dozen knights had already reached the field, with their squires and grooms and friends. Each of them had set himself up in a miniature camp under one of the trees that lined the field, and they were working up their horses, sorting out gear, and walking around visiting when Fulk and Rannulf and their men rode up. Roger was going to fight too, and he had brought two of his younger cousins to squire him.

"God's bones," Rannulf said. "There's none but old men here."

Fulk laughed. He steered them toward one of the few trees left unclaimed at the edge of the field. "We all know how to get good camps. Mark, we'll have enough knights out here for melees all day long, and the younger ones will wear themselves out coming in from camps back in the woods." He dismounted, stretching his right arm. "Giles. How have you been, my lord?"

Giles Constable walked over from the next tree. Behind him, his men had laid out his armor in a row on the ground; his horses were tethered to a rope stretched between two trees. Giles was naked to the waist, his square chest covered with old scars, and his nose had been broken so often it was shapeless.

"Fulk," he said. "You aren't going to fight? I saw you last covered with bandages."

"How often do we have a tournament?" Fulk pulled off his coat and threw it on the ground. Morgan was setting out his lances, his swords and his mail and helmets, on a piece of white cloth on the ground. Fulk flexed his arm. "It's stiff, but I'll account for it. How's the field?"

"Soft. It won't be bad for the first few melees, but

I won't like to ride over it this afternoon. Earn your ransoms this morning. That's your son, isn't it?"

Fulk introduced them. "Who is the herald?"

"De Tiernée. Are you fighting, sir?" to Rannulf.

"Yes, my lord."

"First tournament?" Giles looked from Rannulf to Fulk and back again.

"We had one when I was knighted, my lord. None since."

"Ah. Easy picking." Giles clouted Fulk across the shoulders. "You'll need extra ransoms to pay his off." With a guffaw, he tramped back to his camp; Fulk made an obscene gesture at his back.

"Watch out, now, he'll be after you. He's too damned old and fat to fight experienced men." Fulk swung around to watch his groom check his horse's legs. "I hate to dwell on it, but I do like that horse."

"You paid well enough for him." Rannulf stripped off his coat and shirt. "When does it start?" His voice sounded unnaturally high.

"As soon as we're ready we'll go up and put ourselves into the first melee."

The field was ringing solidly with little camps, and more groups of men rode up while he watched. A dozen men were walking over the field, staring at the ground and squinting to see the sun. Morgan held out the quilted yellow linen jacket Fulk wore under his mail. Rannulf was talking to his groom. His boy's body seemed soft and white, too slender for strength, too flexible. Fulk looked down at his own chest, seamed, like Giles, with old white scars; he was as thin as Rannulf, just as hairless. Hastily he put on his jacket.

"Let's walk the field."

Rannulf followed him out into the long meadow. Several other men strode past them; already there were paths worn into the thick, high grass. Fulk kicked at the earth.

"It's soft, as he said. The sun will dry it and they'll fight in dust this afternoon." He looked at the sun, wondering if they all did this for any reason or simply to look intelligent and experienced. Rannulf called out to someone and waved.

"Rocks here," a knight shouted, in the middle of the field. He waved gaily to everybody else. "Rocks." Fulk snorted.

The sun was brightening and growing hotter, and there was no breeze. Fulk walked down to the far end of the field, smiling and waving to the men he knew. The field was perfectly level, large enough to fight twenty to a side, and the trees around it gave them shade to rest in and watch from. He was going to enjoy this. He turned and laughed at Rannulf, who was frowning at a tuft of grass at his feet.

"Hummocky," Rannulf said. "It could trip up the horses."

"Never. Let's go, there's more than enough here now."

They walked back across the ground toward their camp. Two knights, mounted and armed, loped past them toward the end of the field, where the fighters were gathering.

"You are a fool to do this, you know," Rannulf said. "In your condition."

"My condition is one of intense anticipation. Don't talk to me as if I were the son and you the father. There's Thierry."

Thierry was in their camp, talking to Morgan; he stooped over the young man, and his winning smile flashed. All the great men in Henry's army knew of the proposed settlement with the king except Thierry, because he might tell the prince, and therefore Rannulf did not know, because Fulk was afraid he would tell Thierry. He thrust that out of his mind. Stepping across a neat pile of lances, he went up to Thierry.

"Good morning, uncle."

"Good morning, Fulk. Hello, Rannulf, are you excited?"

"I only hope I fight with honor," Rannulf said piously.

"Well," Thierry said, "no man could say more of you than that." He and Rannulf shook hands.

Fulk withdrew to the foot of the tree. Morgan brought him his hauberk and helmet. Thierry and Rannulf stood talking—Thierry's wide gestures milled the air around Rannulf's head, and Rannulf stepped back one stride, pretending to duck. They spoke a moment longer and Thierry embraced him. Fulk pulled on his hauberk, and Morgan laced up the sides. The weight of the mail on his shoulders and arms always took a moment to get used to; he walked around, swinging his arms, straining his right arm to limber up the muscles.

"Remember your honor," he said to Rannulf, when Thierry had gone. "Remember you're worth a high ransom, too, and you have to pay it, not I. Hurry and we can fight in the first melee. It's always the best."

Edwyr, his groom, led up the chestnut stallion. Fulk looked quickly for Roger and saw that he had already gone, with one of his squires. "Hurry up, Rannulf!" He was bursting with energy and excitement, like a young man's; he vaulted into his saddle, and Morgan held up his helmet.

Rannulf had been kneeling in prayer. He rose, crossing himself and stood while his squire put on his mail. Morgan brought Fulk a lance. Red and white ribbons streamed from the tip.

"Keep your back to the east, my lord," Morgan said.

Fulk tucked the lance under his arm and made the chestnut curvet. The stallion began to dance, its heavy neck arched, and he leaned forward and scratched it quickly along the base of the mane. Rannulf climbed up onto his rangy black and took his helmet and a lance, and they started at a trot across the field.

The chestnut was rank, and pulled so hard that Fulk nearly lost his seat; it tried to kick Rannulf's horse, squealed, bucked, and lunged against the bit. Fulk jerked it hard in the mouth. Derby on his giant bay cantered by, his horse's chin tucked in against its chest and spume streaming from its jaws.

Fulk said, "Remember to keep moving, and try and

stay in front on the first charge. That thing you ride will sprawl if you don't keep him together, too. Damn you, I wish you'd take that bay of mine, he'd be good for you."

"I'm very well used to this horse, and he knows me. Your horses all have bad manners."

"That's because you can't ride. They don't have bad manners for me." The chestnut leaped violently to one side, and Fulk kicked off his stirrup and spurred it hard in the ribs. Rannulf trotted along with a smug look on his face, his helmet tucked in the crook of his arm, neat as a grandmother.

De Tiernée had raised a banner at the head of the field and stood under it, leaning on a staff to ease his bad leg. "Fulk," he said, when they rode up. "I knew that was you, my lord, stuck like a burr up on that huge horse. My lord Ledgefield."

"Fulk," Chester roared, from a group of men milling around not far away. "I'll have Stafford of you today, with you just out of splints."

"Did you drink last night, Chester?" Fulk shouted.

Half the men listening laughed. One called, "Drank all night and didn't sleep, my lord. Mark the temper he's in. De Tiernée, when may we go?"

"Now," de Tiernée said, "if Stafford stays here and Ledgefield gets himself over to the other side. Twenty-two knights each."

Chester howled and clapped his hands together. "Now we'll make up for this sham of Wallingford. Go on!"

Rannulf said, "God be with you, Father," in a voice that squeaked, and galloped off toward the far end of the field. Fulk reined over to join the line next to Chester. The knights swore and horses kicked in a sudden tangle of moving bodies; abruptly the line straightened, an even rank of horsemen, their lances raised at salute.

"Damn you," Fulk said to Chester. "Learn to hold secrets, will you?"

Chester put on his helmet. His broad red face disappeared behind the iron nosepiece, and his voice sounded hollow. "Haven't you told him? Everybody else knows. Both your uncle and the prince are fighting on the far side."

"Prince Henry," Fulk said, surprised. "With none of the usual ceremony? How un-French of him."

"But romantic, of course." Chester's laughter boomed inside his helmet. "I'll take him my prisoner if I can."

Fulk grimaced. The chestnut was chewing on the bit, grinding it between its teeth so that Fulk's hair stood on end. He looked at de Tiernée, who was watching the far side of the field.

The knights there stretched from one side of the meadow to the other—it was much narrower at that end; their line had not filled in yet, but while Fulk watched horses moved up into the gaps, shifting and dancing. The field ran north and south, so that the sun shone across it, glinting on the polished chain mail and the harnesses of the horses, and from each raised lance scarves and ribbons fluttered. A few of them had painted their shields, and patches of color showed in the line, but mostly it was the gray of armor. Fulk looked back at de Tiernée, holding his breath, and when de Tiernée raised the horn to his lips he backed the chestnut up in a rush, like cocking a crossbow, and let him go.

The chestnut bolted, and an instant later the horn blasted, so that the red horse was already reaching stride while the others stood flat-footed. Half a dozen other knights had used the same trick, up and down the line, so that when Fulk shot forward into the open, he was galloping head to head with a horse four spaces away from him on either side.

Across the green meadow, a front rank of eight knights and a rearguard of fourteen charged toward them. Their shadows flew over the tall grass, and their lances fluttered with ribbons like wings. Fulk picked out a man on a brown horse, smaller than the chestnut, and veered to meet him. The space of green grass between them shrank to a ribbon. Fulk lowered his lance, set his shield, and put the red horse straight at the brown. They ran together, and all up and down the line lances cracked and shattered and men roared.

Fulk had misjudged the angle. His lance struck off center, and he braced himself to meet the other man's good strike. The lance smashed into the center of his shield and slammed him back into the cantle of his saddle, knocking the breath out of him. At the same time he felt the shock of his own lance splintering. He dropped it, the brown horse swept by him, and he hauled his chestnut around after him. The brown horse was turning slowly. The knight whirled a mace over his head, but the brown horse, leaning into its turn, was still off balance. Fulk hurled the red horse into it, and the brown stumbled to its knees.

The knight swung his mace, and Fulk ducked behind his shield and struck out awkwardly over his horse's neck. The man's shield broke in half under his blade. Lurching to its feet, the brown horse spun to put its rider into position to strike back, and he and Fulk hacked at each other, their horses circling shoulder to shoulder, while the fighting surged on around them.

Each terrific blow of the mace jarred Fulk's shield-arm to the shoulder, and his right arm, so long unused, was aching with fatigue before he'd struck four blows. But the other knight had only a tiny piece of his shield left and had to work to defend himself. Twice he nearly hit Fulk on the head with his mace. At the second one, he gave a hoarse, wordless shout, and Fulk cried, "Slow, slow," and warded off the mace with his swordblade and spurred the chestnut, which was forcing the brown horse back on its hocks.

"Ware, ware," the knight on the brown horse shouted, and Fulk hauled on his reins—a riderless horse charged down on them, and they whirled their horses out of the way to let it pass. The knight on the brown horse shouted to him, and Fulk shouted back, but two fighting knights swept into the gap between them. Fulk galloped off to find someone else.

The field was packed with fighting men. Loose horses raced aimlessly around. Some men were fighting on foot, and others were riding off and on the field. Fulk passed Chester clubbing away at a man on a wounded horse, but he saw nothing of Rannulf. He reined his horse at a hard gallop down the field, looking for him.

Abruptly, kicking up dust with every stride, Thierry on his tall gray horse charged down on him, sword drawn. Fulk gathered his reins and wheeled to meet his charge. Thierry raised his sword a little in salute, and Fulk thrust his feet into his stirrups and took a deep seat. Thierry was a veteran of this. He set the chestnut to ram the tall gray.

With a twitch of his reins, Thierry turned his horse aside, and they swept past each other. Fulk's sword struck Thierry's shield with a crack that numbed his arm to the shoulder, but Thierry's sword he turned off with one of the best parries of his life. He whirled the red horse around.

They charged together again, and this time Thierry set himself to ram Fulk. Fulk pressed his leg against the chestnut's side, and the big horse changed leads smoothly and brought him alongside Thierry. He swung early, giving Thierry plenty of room to carry off his blade on his shield, and he took Thierry's sword on his shield and held it there and hit Thierry backhand across the shoulders.

Thierry reeled in his sadle. Fulk let out a yell. He yanked the chestnut around and spurred him; the red horse charged into Thierry's gray and lifted it off its feet. Thierry bounded away into the grass and landed rolling. Fulk sent the chestnut down on him, and when Thierry staggered to his feet reined the horse down in front of him and laid the edge of his sword on Thierry's shoulder. Triumph filled him so that he could barely see.

"Well, uncle."

"Uncle," the man behind the helmet said. "I'm unsure whether it's a compliment, my lord." Prince Henry took off his helmet and smiled up at Fulk.

For a moment, Fulk could not speak. He had been certain that it was Thierry; the prince and he were much of the same build, although the prince was shorter, and the gray horse—he looked over at the horse and shook his head. Dismounting, he pulled off his helmet.

"A compliment, my lord. You know well my uncle is a master of the tournaments. You fight very well."

"High praise from you, my lord. That last feint taught me more than all my other fights combined." The prince smiled. "I won Thierry's horse from him last night at dice. Had I not seen your bandages, I should never have known you were recently wounded. Ask your ransom."

Fulk said, "Your horse and armor, my lord. The arms for me, but you may give the horse back to Thierry."

"I will, and buy him back again. He suits me well." Henry walked over to the gray horse and picked up his reins. "I wonder if we—no, there's the horn."

Fulk looked around. De Tiernée had sounded the horn, and everybody was riding or walking off the field. He shook his head. "In my youth, we fought one melee all day long. I'm pleased to have fought with you, my lord."

"I'll give you a token of it, my lord." Henry jerked off his gauntlet and took a garnet ring from his finger. "My compliments. You fight like a glum Norman, sir." And smiled.

Fulk laughed and went to his horse. Already they were organizing another melee. He mounted the chestnut, tucked the prince's ring into the palm of his glove, and cantered toward his camp. The grass of the field was torn and trampled into pulp, and dust sifted through and clouded the air. He handed his helmet to Morgan and slid down from his saddle.

"Well, Roger—Where's Rannulf?"

"Chester took him prisoner. He'll be back. What's

that?" Roger took the ring from his hand. "Very nice, my lord."

"Prince Henry." Fulk took a cup from Morgan, frosted with dew, and sipped cold water.

"Did you beat him? He brought down Derby in the first rush."

"Oh. I fought someone on a brown horse, I wonder who that was?"

"Stocky little stallion with a white blaze?"

"I don't remember the blaze."

"Leicester's son," Morgan said. "Was he good?"

"Very." Fulk spun on his heel to shout gleefully at Derby riding past. "My lord! My lord! You paid your scutage early."

Derby leaned out of his saddle. His face was smeared with dust and blood. "I softened him for you, Fulk, consider that."

In the nearby camps, heads turned. Fulk tried the garnet ring on his fingers until he found one it fit. Giles Constable was strutting toward him. "Did you fight the prince?"

"Yes, and he nearly told over me." Morgan was unlacing his hauberk, and he lifted his arms. "How did you do?"

"Oh, well enough." Giles rubbed his shapeless nose. "One only does it for the fun, after all." He sauntered back toward his camp.

Morgan pulled the hauberk off over Fulk's head. "You'll be fighting again, my lord?"

"Yes. Is Edwyr walking the—good." He watched the chestnut stallion move, with the little English groom at its head talking constantly to it. The sweat had dried in patches on the red horse's shoulders and flanks, and it stopped while he watched and scratched its head vigorously against the Englishman's side, nearly lifting Edwyr off the ground.

"Was he controllable?" Morgan said, watching.

"God's bones." Fulk stretched his right arm and shoulder. "Don't insult me."

A horn sounded, and he turned to watch the start of

the next melee. From the men watching, a shout went up; the branches of the trees around the field were studded with people, and they cheered too.

Twenty men to a side, the knights galloped together. Their lances slanted down across the dusty air, their shields rose to cover their chests, and with a crash the two lines slammed together. Right in front of Fulk, a knight in French armor took a lance dead center on his shield and shot backwards out of his saddle, hung an instant over the ground on the end of the lance, and fell head over heels. The knight who had toppled him rode him down, whooping.

All across the field, hand-to-hand fighting broke out. Metal rang like bells, and the dust rose under the horses' thrashing hoofs. A loose horse galloped out of the melee and charged neighing through a line of tethered horses.

"Morgan, I'm going to find Rannulf."

Morgan waved to him. Fulk walked along the edge of the meadow toward Chester's camp, watching the melee. The dust hung over everything in a thick cloud; from it came shouts and the crack of swords and the neighing of horses, but he could see only dim shapes twisting and lunging back and forth. A knight burst out of the cloud, grabbed a lance from his squire, and turned to fling himself back again. From the trees over Fulk's head came the cheers of women.

Rannulf was drinking a cup of Chester's ale and watching the squires pack away his armor and unsaddle his horse. He saw Fulk and looked quickly down at his feet and his ears turned pink. "Hello, my lord."

"Fulk," Chester said. "Come to reclaim your heir?"

"I'm assuming he has reclaimed himself, my lord."

A splintering crash behind him whirled him around to face the melee. Chester shouted wordlessly. Two horses were down, thrashing, only a few yards from Fulk. One of the knights had jumped clear, but the other lay half under his horse. Its wide pale belly heaved and bounced across the knight's body. Through its left foreleg the cannon bone showed, ragged-edged.

The horse struggled to stand up and fell back and the knight screamed. Chester began to swear. Two squires rushed out and with one at the horse's head and the other at its rump helped the horse to stand. On three legs, it stood trembling violently, above its rider, its whole body coated with dust and sweat and blood. Several other squires raced over to help the fallen man.

"Our Lady," Rannulf said softly.

The squires got the hurt man's arms over their shoulders and carried him away. Fulk did not recognize him and when he looked inquiringly at Chester he shrugged and turned away. The horse stood spraddle-legged, holding the broken foreleg carefully off the ground.

"A shame," Fulk said. "That's a fine horse."

Another squire came up to the horse, patted it, talked to it, and bent over the bad leg. A little pool of blood was forming under the upraised hoof. Beyond the horse the fighting surged back and forth through the screams and the dustcloud.

"Come back to camp," Fulk said to Rannulf.

"Remember you must pay me twenty marks," Chester shouted.

Fulk started back around the fighting. Rannulf walked beside him, his shoulders hunched. "You weren't hurt, were you?" Fulk said.

"No."

"What's wrong? You can still fight. I'll lend you the bay horse. What happened?"

Rannulf turned away. "He drew me out of line and knocked me down. I hardly even struck a blow. Thierry took two ransoms. Did you hear?"

"No. That's his art, he should excel at it."

"I wish I'd struck him one good blow."

"Wait until the next fight. Did you learn anything?" He pulled Rannulf out of the way of a galloping horse.

"Yes," Rannulf said. "Not what I would have wanted to know." He gave Fulk a sharp look and walked off ahead of him.

Fulk grunted, irritated; he had thought that Rannulf was outgrowing his love of poses. He followed him into the camp.

Leicester was there. He came forward and took Fulk by the arm and drew him aside. "The king's army is approaching. He'll reach Wallingford tonight. The prince wants us to go back to Crowmarsh."

"Is he going?"

"Yes. He says the tournament may go on, but some of us must go back." Leicester glanced around him. In a lower voice, he said, "The bishop will meet with Chester tomorrow morning. He says the king will agree. What do you think of it? Have we done it?"

Rannulf was watching them. Fulk moved to one side, so that Leicester's body screened him from his son. "Yes. They are all behind it, and unless someone betrays us to the prince I don't think he can deny us—we will give him the solution and force him to accept it before he can divide us up."

Leicester had not been fighting; he wore leather breeches and a linen shirt and in all the dust and noise looked like a stranger. He said, "But if he should learn of it, you think he could—"

"He won't find out." Rannulf was staring at them. "I fought your son, my lord. God is my witness, whoever trained him should be proud."

Leicester smiled. "I did. He's cool-headed enough, isn't he? And the arm on him amazes me."

"If he had a better horse—"

"Oh, he likes that horse, he says it may be slow in turning but it's stout enough to withstand any charge. You didn't beat him, did you?"

"We were separated. Tell him I enjoyed it and hope to meet him again. We should go."

"Yes. Meet me at the crossroads." Leicester waved his hand north and went off.

"What did he want?" Rannulf said. Morgan had given him cheese and bread and a cup of wine.

"The king's army is coming. He and I and the prince are going back to Wallingford. You can stay—

use my chestnut to fight, if you want, but be careful with him."

Rannulf was staring at him, his brows lowered so that they nearly met over his nose. Fulk shook his head and went off to get into his clothes, calling to Morgan to saddle up a riding horse for him.

PRINCE HENRY HAD ordered some of his men to camp on the far side of the river from Crowmarsh, near the gates of Wallingford, and Fulk and Leicester sent out scouts in pairs to patrol the road to the west. At sundown, the scouts came galloping back, shouting that they had seen the vanguard of the king's army, and Prince Henry sent to his men across the river to withdraw back into the main camp.

The tournament had ended. With the scouts still calling their news, every man in the prince's army with nothing else to do rushed to the bank of the river to watch the king ride up. They lined the north side of the river from Crowmarsh and the burned fields opposite it to the clump of trees where Fulk had met the Bishop of Winchester. Many of them stood to their hips in the water, and all of them were shouting with excitement. Fulk and the other lords rode up and down behind the long, thick mass of men, and like them watched the fields on the far side of the river.

The twilight deepened. A cool evening breeze rose out of the east. The broad plain across the river stretched empty to the trees at the horizon. On the walls of Wallingford, hundreds of people stood in the growing dark, and from the battlement of Crowmarsh Castle the king's banners stretched out on the ripening wind. The army massed along the riverbank had quieted down, enough that Fulk could hear the crickets in the fields. He turned his horse and rode east, behind the lines of his men.

"There! There!"

The hoarse shout rose and broadened, and all along

the river the army strained forward. In the dim light, the plain seemed empty as before. But all along its western and southern edge, banners and lances moved, at first among the trees, hard to see, but quickly separate; horns blew, and toward them over the flat ground rode the vanguard of the king's army.

"It's too late to fight them now," Thierry said, behind Fulk. "Tomorrow, maybe."

Fulk looked over his shoulder at him. He had not heard Thierry ride up. He was wearing a collar of filthy scarves and ribbons, prizes taken from the lances of the men he had beaten in the tournament. Fulk turned straight again.

The army had fallen quiet. There was no sound except the feeble cheering of the garrison of Crowmarsh, and, beneath that, the dim beat of hoofs. The king's vanguard scattered over the field; a troop of them loped their horses down to the river and let them drink. They stared out from behind the nosepieces of their helmets at the men massed across the narrow strip of water.

"Flemings," Fulk said. "William d'Ypres's men."

"How do you know?"

"Mark how the girths on their saddles cross."

Thierry said nothing. Fulk pulled his horse's head up and rode down the line, watching the field across it fill up with men. He felt Thierry follow him, but before he could wonder about it, horns in a wild chorus shrilled, at the far end of the king's field.

"Here he comes."

The horns blasted without pausing. The Flemings opposite Fulk twisted in their saddles to look back. All across the dark field men rode back toward the road they had come on. A little group of horsemen was galloping toward the river, coming from the road, and the Flemings gathered in a circle around them, like the shell around an egg. Banners rustled in the dark. At a hard gallop, the little group of men crossed the field to the river, a hundred yards down from Fulk, and slowed their horses and let them drink.

Rannulf rode up beside Fulk and Thierry. "The king," he said. "God grant he doesn't see me here."

"It's a little dark to recognize you, don't you think?" Fulk said, angry.

Rannulf and Thierry looked at each other. Fulk rode away from them. The king, surrounded by his officers and his earls and his Flemings, rode at a walk along the riverbank, staring through the darkness at the men across from him. Fulk spurred his horse into the midst of the knights in front of him, forcing them to part and let him through, and rode down to the edge of the water, where the king could not help but see him.

In the late twilight, the king's gray horse shone blue. He wore mail, with a white surcoat over it worked with silver, and a short cloak thrown back over his shoulders. Fulk had seen him last in chains, after the battle of Lincoln, harnessed in chains like a bull. He was surprised to find himself so eager. Not my king, he thought, which made no difference.

They rode up even with him: he saw York and—to his amazement—the Earl of Oxford, of course William d'Ypres, and the king's son, Eustace, tall and broad-shouldered as his father. They paused, and the king looked across the smooth water at Fulk and threw his head back. For a moment Fulk thought he would speak, but after a pause the king rode on. The men around Fulk burst out in excited talk.

Prince Eustace held back. "Stafford," he called. "I'll look for you, Stafford, don't run when you see me in battle." He gave a harsh laugh and cantered his horse after his father.

Fulk reined around and rode up through his men to the higher ground. Tomorrow in the morning Chester would talk to Winchester—all to make Chester feel important, because everything was settled. Winchester had arranged it all, even that they were to confront the prince tomorrow, when the prince would certainly call a council to discuss the battle to be fought with the king. "Demand of him then that he accept our agreement," Winchester had written, kingmaker to the end.

Rannulf and Thierry were talking, their horses shoulder to shoulder. After Fulk had left the tournament Rannulf had fought three times and although he had taken no one prisoner, he had not been captured again, either. Rannulf and Thierry turned and looked at him. Fulk gave them only a glance and rode away. When this was done, he would have leisure enough to deal with Thierry. The moon was rising in the east, and he put his face toward it and rode back to his camp.

"I CANNOT BELIEVE that you have come so far simply to betray me," the prince said. His square face was turning purple; his hands plucked furiously at the paper on the table before him. "I will not do it! I will not do it!"

Fulk, standing near the center of the crescent of barons facing him, noticed with a cool mind that surprised him how the prince's pale eyes shone. No one spoke. Gorgeous in blue and silver satin, in silver fox fur, the Bishop of Winchester cleared his throat but did not speak.

"Not now," Henry said. "Not now, I will not do it now—are you all traitors? Is none of you honest? By God's Passion, I will not endure it."

His nostrils flared, and his bright eyes stabbed at each of them in turn. Suddenly he leaped up from his stool and put both hands to his hair as if he meant to tear it. He stamped his foot. "No. No."

Fulk lowered his head to hide his smile. Beside him, Leicester shifted his weight from foot to foot, and beside Leicester, the bishop spoke at last.

"My lord, it is the will of your loyal men that—"

"My loyal men would bring to me no such plan as this."

"That no more blood need be shed over—"

"Hereford, my lord, do you consent to this?"

"I do, my lord," Clare of Hereford said calmly.

"Traitor."

Hereford shrugged. Winchester took a step forward. "My lord, we have all agreed to it. Even the king—"

"He is not the king. I am England's lawful king. Even you admit it in this—this—" Henry snatched up the paper and waved it at at them. But the high color was fading from his face; Fulk thought he would have to age somewhat before he could maintain such a rage for long. "You admit he is not the king."

"He is the king," Winchester said. His voice grew steadier and more confident. "He is the anointed king of England, and a man, a mere man, defies him to the peril of his soul. For our souls, we want an honorable and lawful settlement of these wars, not a conquest."

"No," Henry said, and now his face was dead white. "You cannot want a conquering king."

"My lord," Leicester said suddenly, "nor can you wish to be one. The Great King came as a conqueror, and I mark that in those circumstances lies the root of all the wickedness that has come upon us in the last twenty years—that the Great King was no lawful king, but a conqueror. Do you, my lord, wish to pass on to your heirs such a gift as that?"

"Fah," the prince said. "Do you dare speak law to me?"

Leicester stiffened. "Sir, when you are gray as I am, you might presume to speak to me of law."

The semicircle of barons clapped and called out, "Yes, yes, spoken truly," and nodded at the prince, who sat down again on his stool. His right hand clenched and opened again trembling.

"Mark you," Leicester said, in a high, stiff voice. "All our law refuses us the right to take our own vengeance—our claims we must submit to litigation, or become outlaws. What is this war against the king but your vengeance? You are not beyond the law, and we will hold you to it, now that a just settlement can be made."

"But can it be made? You, Bishop, does your brother wish to treat with me? Tell me honestly."

"He will treat with you," Winchester said firmly.

"Does he wish to?"

"His supporters wish him to. He will treat with you."

"So he is betrayed, like me."

Fulk said, "My lord, it cannot be treason to keep the law. This campaign has accomplished what we wished, to make the king realize that he must bend to the will of the kingdom."

"That is not what I wished."

The prince stared at him; Fulk met his eyes and saw in the abrupt tightening of the prince's face that he understood what Fulk intended. Henry leaned forward heavily on the table. "But my will is not to be done, obviously."

Leicester said, "The king's will is the good of the kingdom."

Henry did not answer. He looked slowly down the semicircle, from face to face, his hands knotted on the table before him. Under his fists the paper lay that Winchester, the Archbishop of Canterbury, and the earls and barons of both sides had signed and sealed. Until the prince and King Stephen signed it, the paper meant nothing, Fulk thought, and an instant later he thought that it meant far more without their signatures.

"Very well," Henry said coldly. "I shall deal with this . . . brother of yours, my lord Bishop. But I shall not trespass against my honor, not one whit, in doing so. And if this should fail, the whole of England shall know who is responsible."

The bishop bowed; all his satin crinkled softly. "It will be my object and that of Theobald of Canterbury not to fail, my lord."

"When shall I speak with him? Tomorrow?"

"Tomorrow, we believe, you ought to proclaim a truce between you—the king is willing to that, to allow us the next few months to negotiate."

"Old men's work," the prince said. "Wait. A truce. If I am not to have Wallingford—" He stood up again. "Stamford is in rebellion against me, am I to allow that to go unpunished, for the sake of this truce?"

"No, no, no." Both hands raised, the bishop smiled and bowed again. "The siege of Wallingford shall end. The truce exists merely to keep you and my lord Stephen from fighting one another. In all the kingdom there is sufficient disorder to occupy you both for several years."

"Truce," Henry said, mouthing it.

Nobody spoke. Fulk's stomach began to growl, and beside him Leicester laughed softly at it. Fulk pressed his hand against his belly.

"Go," Henry said. "I have agreed to it, have I not? What are you standing there for, staring? Go away. Leave me alone."

They rushed toward the door. For a moment no one could get out because of the mob, but at last they sorted themselves out and filed through the door into the gloom of the late afternoon. The sky was overcast; occasionally rain tapped on the roofs of the tents around them.

"Excellent," Derby said. He pumped Leicester's hand. "You spoke so powerfully, my lord—I was much moved."

"Indeed," said Winchester. "You alone won him, Robert."

The other men crowded around Leicester, stroking him with words. Winchester started toward his escort, the three knights and the clerk who waited around a small fire some way away. Fulk ran a few strides to catch up with him.

"It was not Leicester," Winchester said. "It was all of you, that you did not falter. He has a bad temper, that young man. Unattractive in a boy and vile in a king."

"He has a quick wit, too. I cannot believe that King Stephen took it all sweetly."

"Not the king. Prince Eustace. Stephen as he ages

is giving up more and more to Eustace. Who is, my lord, fully the equal of your prince."

"You don't know Henry well, I think."

"Yes. I saw Oxford with the king last night."

"I needed him there. He and de Luci are the finest of them, I think, and regard this agreement with favor. As for the others, certain of them swear they will never accept Henry as king. William Peverel and the Earl of York."

"They signed that paper," Fulk said, interested.

"So they did. I believe they hope Prince Eustace will prevent a settlement's being reached."

The chilly, wet wind blew in their faces. They had nearly reached the bishop's escort. Fulk was thinking of the means Winchester must have used to put those names on the document; he stopped, and the bishop stopped, facing him, smiling.

"Or they might hope," Fulk said, "that when the king dies, a dispute between Eustace and Henry will give them another reign to make themselves great in."

"That undoubtedly is in their minds."

"Yes. The negotiations will be of interest to me. Have you considered the more delicate matters you'll have to discuss?"

Winchester's smile widened. "I have, but you can help me define them, of course."

"For example, Henry has promised the Honor of Lancaster to the Earl of Chester, but King Stephen also has a claim to it, and he might wish it settled on one of his sons, if they are not to be princes."

"Of course." Winchester nodded. "I understand you."

"I am at your service, my lord Bishop."

"And I am equally at yours, my lord Earl."

Winchester like a cat loved secret doings; smooth as a cat, he bowed, and Fulk went with him into the midst of his knights and held his horse and kissed his ring. With all the knights and servants around them they spoke politely a moment longer, and Fulk started back across the camp toward his horse, which Roger and Morgan were holding for him at the foot of the little rise where the prince's tent stood.

Cold raindrops splashed on him; he looked into the sky and drew his cloak around his shoulders. The conversation with Winchester seemed coarse and ugly to him when he thought of it. Yet how else could men tend to their affairs, except by exchanging favor for favor? He mounted his horse without a word and rode back to his tent, his shoulders bowed to the gusts of windy rain.

RANNULF WAS STANDING outside his tent when he rode up, in its lee, talking to one of his friends. He walked over to Fulk's horse before Fulk could dismount and said harshly, "I want to talk to you, my lord."

Fulk looked down at him a moment and nodded. "If you wish." His groom stood waiting to take his horse when he got off, and Fulk waved him away. "I'll ride him down, Edwyr." To Rannulf, he said, "Get your horse and come with me."

"It's raining," Rannulf said. "Can't we—very well."

He walked around the tent to the back, where the horses were held. Fulk said to Morgan, "I'll be hungry when I get back, don't let me wait for my supper."

"No, my lord."

Edwyr had taken Roger's horse, and when Morgan started toward the tent Roger followed him. Fulk called him back, and Roger came over to him and stood by his horse's shoulder.

"I think we'll be going to Stamford next. I want to leave as soon as the truce is set. Get the men who will be going with us ready. You know who has paid this year's service."

Roger nodded. "Are you calling up others? Most of the crossbowmen are going back to Normandy."

"No. We won't need so many." Rannulf was leading his horse toward them, and he straightened up.

Rannulf mounted without saying anything, and they turned their horses and rode across the camp to the field where Fulk's horses grazed. The rain had turned to a steady drizzle. Small groups of men sat under makeshift tents filled with smoke from their fires. Fulk steered around a puddle and moved over closer to Rannulf.

"Did the prince agree to it?" Rannulf said.

"Yes."

"I wish you had told me. Everybody else knew but me. You deliberately kept it from me."

"I was afraid you'd tell Thierry, and he would tell the prince."

Rannulf gave him a sharp look. "You don't trust me at all. No more than you trust Thierry."

"I'm sorry. I should have told you." They crossed a narrow strip of marsh, rode through the willows at its edge, and came up onto the field. Under every tree, horses stood with their tails to the wind and the rain. The fires of the grooms, drovers, and prisoners glowed all around the edge of the field.

"That's just what you would do to Mother," Rannulf said. "Keep from her what you were doing. So she worked against you, and you hated her for that."

"I never hated her. She wasn't always wrong, either." He rode up to Edwyr's fire and dismounted. Rannulf looked around at the men at the fire and led his horse up in front of Fulk's, so they could talk unobserved.

Fulk yanked his girth loose. "I should have told you, as I said. I'm sorry."

"Maybe you shouldn't have. I did tell Thierry."

"What?"

Fulk had his hands on the pommel and cantle of his saddle, and he leaned on his arms and stared at Rannulf. "What did you say?"

"I told Thierry. As soon as I found out. Yesterday." Rannulf looked down, turned his back on Fulk, and pulled his saddle off his horse's back. "Chester called this siege of Wallingford a sham, remember?

When he captured me, I asked him what he had meant."

Fulk stared at his back; all the sense had flown out of his head. If Thierry had known he would surely have told the prince, and yet the prince had—Henry's fine rage when all his barons in their pompous council told him their demands, his final submission were fake, because he had known already what they would say. Chester had known that Fulk wanted it kept from Rannulf, yet Chester had—for mischief's sake, perhaps—or—Rannulf turned toward him again.

"I only did what Mother did. I shouldn't have, I know it, but if you had explained it to me I might have understood why not to tell him."

Fulk nodded, still amazed. "Yes. What has happened?"

"What do you mean?"

"Why are you so upset about it? The prince accepted the agreement, after all."

"Oh." Rannulf turned his back again and started to unbuckle his horse's bridle. "The prince has sent thirty men to take command of Sulwick, by siege if necessary. So I lost you Sulwick."

Fulk snorted. That was undoubtedly Thierry's idea. He walked around behind his horse and called to one of the knights beside the fire, who were supposed to be guarding the horses.

The knight leaped up and ran over to him. Fulk said, "You were at Sulwick, weren't you? So you know the way. Go there and tell Simon d'Ivry to withdraw all his men to Bruyère-le-Forêt and wait there for my orders."

"Yes, my lord." The knight saluted him and went off toward the horses tethered under the trees.

Rannulf was cleaning out his horse's forehoof with a stick; Fulk picked up a cloth. "Why aren't you accusing me of treason to my prince? Thierry must be." He scrubbed at the dirt on his horse's back, just behind the withers, and the horse groaned and lowered its head.

"That's what I thought yesterday," Rannulf said. "I thought it over last night. I kept thinking about what you said of loyalty."

In the trees overhead, a gust of rain rattled the leaves. Fulk shook out the cloth.

"Besides," Rannulf said. "It was only doing what Chester wanted, and he's always been our enemy. I should have thought it out first."

"Thierry has always been our enemy, too."

"No," Rannulf said. "Thierry is too stupid." He led his horse off toward the picket line in the shelter of the trees.

Fulk worked quickly over his horse's back and ran the cloth down its legs. Leicester would have to know that the prince had only allowed it to seem that the barons had forced him to the truce. That was a curious mind at work, a subtle and interesting mind. What Rannulf had said amazed him, but how he had said it amazed him more. He straightened up and stood idly stroking the horse's shoulder, thinking.

"I'll take him, my lord," Edwyr said. "He's hungry." He spoke softly to the horse in English.

"Take him," Fulk said. He stood until Edwyr had led the horse away from him, and walked over to the groom's box and threw the cloth into it. Rannulf walked up to him.

"Now we have to walk back in the rain."

"I know," Fulk said. "I'm starving."

They started down toward the marsh that separated the horse field from the camp. Fulk pulled up the hood on his cloak. The rain was blowing into their faces, and Rannulf held his hand up to shield his eyes.

"We could have talked inside," Rannulf said. "This was your idea, remember?"

"I was hoping you wouldn't come."

Rannulf laughed, fresh and clear in the evening rain.

The king's banners laid their bright reflection on the surface of the river; opposite, on this bank, Prince

Henry's barons were lined up behind him, their horses standing hipshot in the noon sun. The prince, in a blue coat and scarlet hose, stood at the very edge of the bank, with a herald and two standard bearers. Fulk leaned forward to see his face. The king's herald was shouting a list of conditions for the truce; Stephen's voice was too feeble to shout clearly over the noise of the wind and the onlookers. Fulk looked back at Leicester.

"Well?"

Leicester was pulling irritably at his horse's mane. "I don't believe it. Rannulf is mistaken. If the prince knew of what we intended the day before we told him, he would have talked to us separately and won a few of us to his side. Remember how we feared that?" He yanked two long black hairs from the horse's mane. "It was why you kept the secret from Rannulf in the—"

He lifted his head; his mouth stayed open, but no words came out, and Fulk smiled. The wind shifted suddenly and brought him the sounds of the men striking the camp before Crowmarsh. The prince and the king had already agreed to lift their siege and countersiege. The herald had stopped talking, and now Henry began to shout, in his own voice, high and firm and Angevin.

"So he made us all fools," Leicester said.

"That's what I think."

Leicester frowned at the prince. "If we reach a settlement, he is the king, and if we cannot, we will never be able to force him to anything again."

"I think we had better reach the settlement, don't you?"

"What do you think Chester meant by it?"

"I don't know."

The aldermen of Wallingford had come down to the river to listen to the arrangement of the truce; Fulk looked up at them, on the other bank but closer to the city than the king, near a clump of willows. In their best coats and caps and medals they looked scarcely less than earls.

"He's trying to butter both sides of his bread again," Leicester said. "He can always say he warned the prince. Don't you think?"

"I'm not sure. It could be only spite, that Winchester didn't talk first to him."

"Or to bedevil you and Rannulf. Or all three. He's a dangerous man. You should watch him."

Chester was down near the middle of the line of barons. Fulk did not turn to look at him. He watched the king's herald, now talking. They had settled the major conditions of the truce—the end of the sieges, the opening of negotiations, and a length of six months. Henry had just said that he meant to press his siege of Stamford. Fulk caught the last syllable of a name the king's herald spoke and clicked his tongue.

"Ipswich. He'll go chase Hugh Bigod out of the castle. See how it's all a circle."

Leicester nodded. Hugh Bigod, in the crucial days after King Henry died when Stephen seized the throne, had provided the lie that the old king on his deathbed had disinherited his daughter and named Stephen England's king.

"He won't have any trouble taking Ipswich," Leicester said. He looked to his left, and Fulk followed his eyes.

Chester was coming toward them, riding behind the line of barons, his eyes on the king. Fulk and Leicester watched him approach, saying nothing.

"Did you hear what the king has said? Our friend Hugh Bigod may finally learn to say his prayers." Chester barged into their midst, smiling, his bulging eyes cheerful.

"It was obvious," Leicester said. "Naturally the king will go to Ipswich—one need not have heard him say it."

Fulk nodded. His eyes fixed on the huge jeweled clasp that held Chester's cloak on his breast. "You seem to have been slow of thought lately, my lord Chester."

He looked into Chester's face. Chester's cheeks sagged, and the smile slid away.

"But quick to speak," Leicester said. "The sun grows hot, Fulk. Shall we find some shade?"

Fulk gigged his horse. He and Leicester rode past Chester, one on either side, and left him there alone behind them. The prince and King Stephen were shouting their farewells. All along the bank of the river, the ranks of witnesses were shifting, turning to go. Leicester reined in his horse, looking up and down the river, and Fulk brought his horse up alongside him. The bright hot sunlight bleached the sky white; the dry brown grass of the fallow fields stretched out around them on either side of the river.

With his pages and his herald riding behind him, the prince was galloping away from the water, down toward his camp. The knights and barons who had witnessed the truce followed him, in no order, a great spill of horsemen down the brown fields. Leicester reined his horse after them and started away. Fulk hung back. The aldermen of Wallingford were walking back toward the city, but even before they reached the gate it opened and the people rushed out to greet them as heroes.

NINE

"WHERE IS THIERRY?"

"With the Earl of Chester."

Fulk made a face. He was beginning to regret the luxury of snubbing Chester. He turned to look back at the column of men following him out of Prince Henry's camp. Morgan carried his banner, and Rannulf rode on his left side, although Rannulf was staying behind to go north with the prince.

"You yourself said he is stupid. Will you not keep watch on him for me?"

Rannulf said, "No, my lord. I'm not a spy."

Fulk clenched his teeth. It was hot, and the flies were buzzing around his horse's neck and ears—he carried a leafy branch to brush them away with. "Roger, when we stop tonight, send a messenger to Simon d'Ivry at Bruyère-le-Forêt and have him meet us at Stamford."

"Yes, my lord," Roger said, and between them, Rannulf, unconcerned, waved to someone in the camp.

"When we get out of the camp, send ten men to

ride vanguard. Jordan de Grace can command them. No, I want to talk to him. Someone else, you decide."

"Yes, my lord," Roger said patiently. They had reached the edge of the camp; before them lay empty meadows.

Rannulf turned toward Fulk. "Is Hugh with my uncle Pembroke at Stamford?"

"Yes. Of course."

"Tell him I think of him much, and pray for him. I'm going back, my lord. Travel well."

Fulk pulled off his glove and held his hand out, and Rannulf shook it. "I'll see you there," Fulk said. "Don't listen to that damned Chester. Or to Thierry."

"That's impossible," Rannulf said, smiling. "They both talk too much. Don't worry about me, Father." He swung his horse out of the line and rode off. Fulk watched him; he began to wish Rannulf had decided to come north with him, he was better company than Roger and Morgan. Rannulf turned once and waved, and moved toward a band of younger knights riding off in another direction.

"Do you want to talk to Jordan de Grace now, my lord?" Roger said.

"Yes."

Roger turned his horse and rode back along the column. They trotted up the easy slope ahead of them and through the fringe of trees into the fields, toward the road. Most of these fields had lain fallow since the beginning of the wars, but now that the truce was declared the haycutters were moving through them. Fulk caught a whiff of honeysuckle and sniffed harder, and the elusive scent disappeared. He thought of Chester and Thierry together and wrinkled up his nose.

"Is something wrong, my lord?" Morgan asked. He had rolled up the banner around its staff.

"Naturally."

The haymakers in the fields on either side of them raised their heads and shaded their eyes from the sun to watch the knights pass. They carried their scythes like lances over their shoulders. Jordan de Grace galloped up and drew his horse down to a walk beside Morgan, even with Fulk. Morgan held back to get out from between them.

"My lord," Jordan said.

"Sir Jordan, when were you last at Aurège?"

"Just at Easter, my lord."

Aurège Castle was the seat of the manor Jordan held of Fulk, and it stood not far from Stamford. Fulk swiped a fly off his horse's ear with his branch. "We'll probably have to resupply the army at Stamford. Where can we find provisions?"

Jordan shrugged. "Easily enough, my lord. I'll have to talk to my bailiff, but I think we can give you herds for slaughter from Aurège, and you know that there are four other manors within a day's ride of Stamford, Worcester's castle of Hautbois, and Highfield is there, and some others."

"Highfield," Fulk said. "The Lady of Highfield's manor?"

"Yes, my lord. They can supply you with meat and grain."

"Good. I'll need your help."

"You have it, my lord."

"Thank you."

Rohese's face came back into his mind. She had said she was going there, after she got Alys of Dol from her husband's home. Jordan rode along beside him, and when Roger came back they started talking, leaning forward to see around Fulk.

The thought of Alys of Dol so close to Stamford simmered in Fulk's mind. He knew he would find some way to use it. The knights behind him were singing of Alexander; in the brown fields, the scythes of the haymakers flashed in the sun.

THAT NIGHT, FULK'S men camped near the monastery of Saint Swithin, and Fulk slept in the monk's guest house, with the rest of his lords. The

monks gave them an excellent dinner of fresh vegetables and fish, soft white bread spread thick with
butter, and ale of the monks' own brewing. The abbot
himself seemed interested in the truce of Wallingford,
asking quick, shrewd questions about how it had been
arranged, and how long Fulk thought it would be
kept, and whether a settlement could be made that
Prince Eustace would abide by.

"There are those who say King Stephen is afraid of
nothing more than his own son, he will do nothing that
would impel the prince to rage at him."

"Eustace is a savage man," Fulk said, wondering
where this abbot came by all his knowledge.

"He is young," the abbot said. "There is something
cold and harsh in all our young men. These wars
have taught them nothing worthy of them, mark you,
my lord."

With Roger and Morgan, Fulk lay under a featherbed in the guest house and listened to the sounds of the
other lords in the other beds. They were all crowded
together; Morgan lay pressed against Fulk's chest and
Roger against his back.

The moonlight fell through a crack in the shutter
on the window and slanted in a thin shaft to the floor.
The noise faded away. Fulk dozed. Only half-asleep, he
thought he saw the window opened, and the hillside
and the fields blue-silver under the moon's light, many
stars in the sky, and over all a soft wind. There was a
man walking up the hill toward him, hooded so that
he could not see his face, but Fulk knew that the
stranger was coming for him and no other. Like a
waking voice in his ear, he heard his name called.

He jerked all over, as if he had stumbled, and his
eyes popped open. On either side of him, the sleeping
men stirred and went back asleep. The shutters were
closed, and only that one thin ray of moonlight lay on
the floor. Fulk put his head down again, trembling.
When he tried to remember the dream, he could recall
nothing but the moonlight and the calling of his name.

He thought, It's because I was wounded that time

in the monastery of Saint Jude, and now I am frightened
of monasteries. Suddenly he remembered that in the
dream, a man had been coming for him.

"Morgan."

"Ummm?" Morgan rolled onto his stomach and
lifted his head.

Fulk was ashamed to tell him why he had awakened
him. "Bring me a cup of water. Be quiet, Roger's
asleep."

Morgan crawled out of bed and skipped over the
cold floor to the ewer on the table beside the door.
While he poured it, he lifted one bare foot at a time
off the floor, like a peasants' dance, and he rushed
back into bed. Fulk drank the sweet, cold water and
reached over the head of the bed to put the cup down
on the floor. Morgan lay with his cheek on his arm,
watching him.

"Go to sleep."

Morgan closed his eyes obediently. Fulk put his head
down and squirmed deeper under the featherbed. The
dream still lingered on the edges of his mind, and he
was afraid to sleep, but his eyes grew heavy and he
shut them and slept.

    ALL THE NEXT day, he could not keep his
temper; the slightest thing irritated him almost beyond
bearing, and he spent the day throttling his rage. They
were riding over low, rolling ground, through open
forest and pasturage where sheep and cattle grazed. In
the later afternoon, they reached the Roman road,
camped for the night alongside it, and followed it north
all the next day. Deep in the ground as a stone river,
the road ran straight across the countryside, and fur-
leaved weeds sprouted in the cracks on its surface.

Other travelers were out, in groups of five and six
and many larger: wagons painted with scenes from
legends, peddlers and trained bears and wandering
monks, troubadours in bright, ragged clothes, beggars

and rich merchants and flocks of sheep and goats. The sight of an army riding north made them stop and stare and shout questions in broken French. Fulk stopped and talked to a merchant in an ox-drawn cart, who in spite of the heat wore a fur-lined cloak, and the man said that another army had passed them earlier that day.

Fulk asked enough questions to be sure that he meant William of Clare and his men, and not Fulk's own vanguard. The merchant was English, but he spoke French, very proud and careful of it, stumbling now and again in his pronunciation. Fulk thanked him and galloped up to his place in the line. A woman in a litter traveling in the merchant's party drew back the curtain to watch him pass.

Later the next day, they reached Stamford; low stone-colored clouds rolled across the sky, and the banners and pennons on the wall of the castle, the walls of the town, snapped in the raw wind. Pembroke, with too few men to besiege both the town and the castle, had camped on the river near the castle gate, where he could at least prevent caravans of supplies from reaching either. William of Clare, who was his nephew, was setting up his camp opposite the town's west gate. Fulk left Roger with his army and rode down into Pembroke's camp.

Three sentries hailed him before he reached the edge of the camp, and the word of his coming went on before him, so that when he rode up to the cluster of tents in the middle, Pembroke was outside waiting for him. Pembroke was one of the tallest men in England, lean as a fish, with iron-gray hair. Margaret had been his sister. He and Fulk had never been friends.

"Good day, my lord," Pembroke said. He stood at the door to his tent, stooped, as usual. "Will you come in? The weather's foul."

Fulk dismounted, and a man took his horse. "Thank you, my lord." He went past Pembroke into the tent. Pembroke came around him, under the highest part of the ceiling, where he could stand erect. He and

Fulk shook hands. Fulk had to work hard to keep
from smiling at the difference in their heights—with
his eyes level, he saw the second hook on Pembroke's
coat front.

"I have not seen you since my sister died," Pembroke said. "It was a sorrowful loss, for me as for
you."

"Thank you. I know you shall miss her sorely."

"Tell me of this truce. My nephew didn't see fit to
make anything clear to me." Pembroke sat down and
put his feet up on the table in front of him.

"Why, they have agreed to—"

Pembroke flapped his hand impatiently. "I know
that. I don't know why the prince accepted it. I see
you and Robin de Beaumont everywhere in this—
brother-in-law. What happened?"

Servants brought Fulk a canvas chair, took his
cloak, and offered him a tray of honeyed fruit. "You
see rather too meanly, Gilbert. Leicester and I had
little to do with it—all the barons together told the
prince that if he did not accept the truce we would
be much upset." He bit into an apple, and the honey
taste filled up his mouth with juice.

"I thought as much. Had I been there it would not
have happened—we should have ended it all rightly,
there at Wallingford."

Pembroke was married to a sister of Leicester's. Fulk
shrugged one shoulder. "It's all done, now. I don't
really think the kingdom needs another bleeding. I
have three hundred men, where shall I camp them?"

Pembroke tapped his fingers on his knee. "Do you
know Stamford?"

"Somewhat."

"There are three gates into the city and one into
the castle, which is on the river at this end of the city
wall. From here I can guard the castle gate, and William is watching the west gate. Unfortunately most
of the supplies enter the town through the east gate,
but none of us has men enough to guard it, so far

from the other camps—one charge would open the road again. That's my thinking—am I wrong?"

"I doubt it."

"Kindly Fulk. You may camp with William's men— he wouldn't be able to withstand a sudden attack if I were distracted and could not help him. Or take the north gate, only stay far back from it so you have space to maneuver."

"Kindly Gilbert. I'm not a squire any more." That reminded him of Hugh, his younger son.

"Have you eaten?" Pembroke said.

"Not since this morning."

"Then you'll have supper with me and William. Roger de Nef is with you, isn't he? Send a message to him to camp your men. He can do it as well as you." Pembroke raised his head and his voice. "Mahel?"

From behind a curtain, a red-headed man came, and Pembroke said, "Bear a message to Roger de Nef, whom you will find with a large band of men over beyond Lord William's camp, south of it."

Fulk considered having Roger camp his men where they were until he could attend to it himself, decided he was only angry at Pembroke, and nodded to Mahel. "Tell him to camp the army opposite the north gate of the city and report to me here afterward. Thank you."

Mahel bowed. "Yes, my lord." He went out; Pembroke was talking to his servants, who listened and bowed and murmured and lit candles and left. Fulk looked around for Hugh. He had not seen any sign of him, although he was Pembroke's squire.

"What else is of interest?" Pembroke said. "Besides that you caught the prince out and taught him what sort of men you are."

"Gilbert," Fulk said. "The prince knew what we were doing with a full day to counteract it and did nothing. We hardly forced the truce on him. Nothing else is of interest."

"Oh? How is Thierry?"

"He is coming here with Chester. Where is my son?"

"I sent him to escort William here, they'll be back before dark. He's a fine boy, he reminds me of my father."

"He should have been born a Clare."

"He should be knighted soon. He's a fine lad, and a devil of a fighter." Pembroke roared at his servants, who scurried around with ale and wine and more honeyed fruit. "How is Rannulf? Did you hear that young Harvey's dead? That makes Rannulf's wife the heiress, doesn't it?"

"She has a sister. I hadn't heard. What happened?"

"No one knows. His men say he fell dead in the forest, hunting. They brought him back across his horse, not a mark of violence on him. Here is William."

He stood, and Fulk stood. Through the door came William de Clare with Fulk's son Hugh behind him. William stopped and let out a laugh.

"What a pair you make, a broomstick and a broomstraw."

"Keep your improper thoughts in your head," Pembroke said.

Hugh came forward, bowed to Fulk, and kissed his hand. "Lord William said you were coming—I'm very glad to see you, Father, and your arm better and not twisted. My lord says I may be knighted soon. May I?"

Fulk laughed. "We'll talk about it." He put his hand on Hugh's shoulder. "If you don't stop growing you'll overtop me like Pembroke. He says good things of you. That pleases me."

"Oh, let me be knighted soon, before the wars are over."

"Perhaps, at Christmas."

Hugh let out a screech. Pembroke sat down again. "The lungs of him would make a fine bellows."

"When will the prince be here?" William asked. "Stamford's fat and much too confident—we need him to seal off all the gates and let them starve a little."

Pembroke put his feet up. "The prince will get here

when he gets here. Wait upon my lord Stafford, you lout, since he brought no squire with him."

William jumped up and took Fulk's cup to be filled. Hugh brought Pembroke a drink and set a candle down on the table near him. "How is Morgan, my lord? Didn't you bring him north?"

"He has to set up my tent. He's very well—when you're knighted, I'll knight him, too, he's old enough."

"Slight, though," Pembroke said. "If he's the Welsh boy? Yes. Not enough bone or meat for a good fighter."

"Did William tell you of our tournament? All day long, there were twelve melees. William Louvel broke his arm and one of the Angevins was almost killed."

"Strange foreign amusements. Fake wars."

"Did you fight?" Hugh said. "When did you lose your splints?"

"Four days before it. I fought—I have a new warhorse, a beauty, too. I got him from de Brise."

"Did you win? Whom did you fight? Did you beat anybody?"

"The prince. I only fought in one melee—King Stephen was on his way to Wallingford."

Pembroke was picking through a platter of tarts. "You have bone and meat in plenty, no need for all this boasting."

Fulk laughed. Hugh threw questions at him and William about the tournament, asked about Rannulf, dismissed his showing with a shrug and a careless word, and told them of a skirmish with the defenders of Stamford. The servants brought in flesh and bread; somewhere in his camp, Pembroke had ovens. Fulk spread butter from a crock onto the warm bread.

"Hugh told me that you'd broken your arm," Pembroke said suddenly. "You're fortunate it healed straight. My brother broke his twice and he looked like a man with six elbows. It's a pity how it weakens a man's swordstroke." He cuffed William. "Carve the meat."

"Gilbert, you are so courtly. Isn't he, William? All courtesy."

"God's Rood," Pembroke said. "I begin to see that Chester is right, damn him—a few less of those he calls Byzantines would serve England well." He dipped bread into the juice of the meat. "I've a thought of going to Ireland."

"Excellent," Fulk said. "When?"

"You mock," Pembroke said. "Yet I tell you that there is as much to be won in Ireland as our fore-fathers won in England when the Great King led them here. More. You might have lost that spirit, but I have not. Nor has Hugh."

"You have no lands in Normandy. It takes me the whole year just to make the circuit of my Honor. Have you made arrangements to supply the army when it gets here?"

Pembroke shook his head. He put meat into his mouth, wiped his fingers on his sleeve, and leaned back to let the servants pile up his plate again. "Since you mention it, I'll let you deal with it."

"Good. I will."

"When will the prince be here?" Hugh said.

"I don't know. He can't be more than a few days behind us, but some of the barons may not leave Wallingford for weeks."

"When he comes, will we storm the town?"

Pembroke laughed harshly. Fulk said, "I don't think so. There are easier ways to take it."

"You and Robin Leicester will find one. Hugh. The wine."

Hugh leaped up and took their cups away to fill them. Pembroke ate the rest of his meat and when a servant moved to give him more waved him away. "No. Sieges incline a man toward corpulence."

"Gilbert, your austerity humbles me."

"I hope so."

The sentry outside the tent door stuck his head in. "Sir Roger de Nef, my lord."

"Send him in." Gilbert snapped his fingers at a page, who leaped to put another plate on the table. Hugh was standing behind Pembroke, his arms folded across his chest; the boy's respect and courtesy and Pembroke's affection for him pleased Fulk deeply. He rolled a sip of wine around his mouth and spat it out.

"Disgusting French habit," Pembroke said. Roger came in, and they all stood. In between greetings, Roger told Fulk where the army was camped, and they sat down; Pembroke said, "You'll be hungry, Sir Roger —Hugh, serve him."

Hugh went promptly over to carve meat, pour wine, and even butter slices of bread. Roger said, "You've grown again, my lord, where do you mean to stop?"

"When I overtop Pembroke," Hugh said. "Will you have some of this gravy, Sir Roger? It's very salty."

Pembroke snorted. "He speaks his mind. Who is with the prince? Besides Chester and Leicester and all those."

"Giffards, Beauchamps, de Laceys, Tosnys, and Montforts."

"Will there be a tournament here?" Hugh asked.

"Pfft." Pembroke made a face. "That's nothing for such men as you and me."

Hugh's face fell, and Fulk laughed at him. "Gilbert, I shall go tomorrow to arrange for supplies. Have you made enemies of anyone in the neighborhood?"

"Practically all of them."

"I'll go with you, my lord," William said. "If I may. My men need horses."

"You won't find them here," Pembroke said. "They breed only plough stock here."

"Come along," Fulk said. "I know my vassal Jordan de Grace breeds warhorses at Aurège, north of here. I'll go there first. But I'm leaving at daybreak, and I should go to my camp and get some sleep. Roger, follow me when you've eaten."

"Thank you, my lord."

"Good night." Fulk looked at Hugh. "Good night, Hugh. See you keep your lord's trust."

"I shall, my lord."

Fulk went out into the night. Fog drifted through the camp. Occasionally, the lights of the town showed, but the rolling mist swallowed them up. He sent for his horse and stood looking toward the town. Twice he had come to Stamford to lay siege to it and neither time had it fallen. There was luck in threes. He refused to think of the work that lay before him; he was tired, and he knew it would daunt him to think of it. He pulled himself into his saddle and, with two of Pembroke's men lighting his way with torches, rode toward his camp.

THE NEXT DAY, he traveled up to Aurège Castle, the fief that Jordan held of him, and Jordan talked to his bailiff about their herds and harvests. In between arranging for two herds of cattle, one flock of sheep, and twenty swine to be sent to Stamford, Jordan sold William de Clare six horses, and Fulk talked to the bailiff about the herds and supplies of the other manors in the area. They spent the night at Aurège and rode back the next morning, with William's horses neck-roped together; when they reached Stamford, they saw that another army was camped midway between Fulk's men and the east gate of the city. From the pennants and the tents, they knew it was Leicester's.

The walls of the city were crowded with people. Fulk left Jordan and William and their knights and rode with Roger down to Leicester's camp. The sky was still overcast, and the harsh wind had strengthened. He passed a dozen men trying to put up a tent against the wind, heard their curses, and watched the tent blow down before they could stake it up. The men stood motionless a moment, staring at the heap of canvas, their shoulders bowed. But Leicester's tent was raised.

Leicester was sitting before it, staring glumly at the city. Fulk rode up; Leicester lifted his head, and his expression turned a shade brighter, but he still looked grim. Fulk dismounted.

"You're so merry, Robert. What is it—the brightly shining sun?"

"Chester is here."

"Oh."

Leicester held a straw between his fingers, and he split it lengthwise with his thumbnail and cast aside the two pieces. "He gave the prince a bad report of me—I would not have heard about it, save one of the Angevins told me."

"What has the prince said?"

"Nothing."

"And done nothing?"

"No—I know what you're thinking. The Angevin gave me to believe that Chester spoke ill of you, too."

Fulk sat down, his reins in his hands, and watched his horse crop the grass around Leicester's tent. "Untrue words in a foul mouth."

"The prince doesn't know him as we do."

Fulk was wondering why an Angevin would come bearing tales to Leicester. He dug his heel into the turf. "When will the prince be here?"

"Chester was the vanguard. The prince will arrive tomorrow."

"What exactly did Chester tell him, do you know?"

"Something about a secret treaty between us and Winchester."

"Well—I have to go to my camp. Don't worry about it until the prince gives some sign he believes it."

He stood up and put the reins over his horse's head. Leicester sat sullenly on the ground watching him. Fulk put his foot into the stirrup.

"Don't worry, Robert. Have you seen Pembroke?"

"Aaaah—" Leicester looked away.

Fulk rode through the camp toward his own. All around him, the men were building fires, taking their horses to pasture, and setting up their tents. Devil damn me, he thought. We should not have slighted

Chester, that day at Wallingford. The raw wind lashed his hair across his cheek; the first rain drops struck his hands like ice.

WITH A GREAT clamoring of cheers and hunting horns and horses neighing, Prince Henry led his army up to Stamford in the middle of the day, pitched his tents, and rode around the walls of the city, with his bright banner going before and all his barons following him. The townspeople hung over the walls and occasionally let out a cheer themselves. After the rain of the night before, the sky was a clear fresh blue and the brisk wind smelled sweet. Fulk, riding between Rannulf and Derby, could not keep from smiling.

"What are you so merry about?" Rannulf said, when they stopped so that the prince could inspect one of the gates at leisure. "See how you are left out."

"What? Oh." Fulk stood in his stirrups to see over the heads of the men before him. Prince Henry was talking to Chester and Pembroke, discussing the fortifications. The three men rode as close as a long bowshot from the gate, while the rest of the barons waited behind them. Fulk shook his head. "Are you upset? I thought Thierry was your most respected relative."

"Thierry?" Rannulf gave him a sharp look.

Prince Henry started off again, and the barons pushed and jostled, crowding after him. Leicester and Derby rode on the left, well behind the prince, surrounded by the lesser men who were their vassals. Pembroke and Chester, just behind Henry, talked together, all smiles, and Thierry rode up to them and they greeted him with exaggerated enthusiasm. Before they all had gone a dozen strides, the train behind the prince became two trains, with most of the younger men on Chester and Pembroke's side, and Leicester,

Derby, Fulk, and Rannulf and their men on the other. Fulk squinted to see what the prince was doing and saw him smiling and calling to Pembroke, pointing to the walls, his back almost constantly toward Leicester.

"Rannulf," Fulk said. "Go ride with Thierry, will you?"

"What? Why?"

"I want to see what happens."

Rannulf lingered a moment, thinking, and shrugged and galloped off across the strip of ground that separated the two parties. Long-legged and now growing into his bones, he rode well, and the bay horse he had bought from Fulk suited him well. Fulk dropped back a little so that he could see. Rannulf reached the other side, and the younger men, trailing Pembroke and Chester, drew aside, uncertain, but when they saw Thierry call and wave to Rannulf they crowded up near him and shouted to him.

Fulk laughed. His uneasiness increased, and he made himself laugh until he heard the hollow sound and stopped. Sober-faced, Roger was studying him. Fulk spurred his horse and galloped up toward Leicester. The prince was still ignoring them all on this side.

"You see," Leicester said. "It is too late. I told you."

"I don't know."

The prince was acknowledging the cheers of the people on the walls. He drew rein, and the barons fought for space around him. Fulk and Leicester managed to get close to the prince, on his left, but Chester's followers massed themselves around Henry, almost encircling him. Hugh was with Pembroke; he looked at Fulk as if he didn't see him, and Fulk could see no sign of strain on his face.

Henry spoke to Chester, gesturing toward the walls, and Chester nodded and laughed and all his men laughed and nodded although few could have heard what the prince had said. Henry's eyes flickered toward Fulk and Leicester and Derby, but he said nothing—Thierry was speaking to him, leaning forward, smooth and genial.

"Whatever happened to the black-haired girl?" Fulk said.

Leicester shrugged. "He left her in Wallingford."

Fulk put his foot up against the pommel of his saddle and buckled his shoe again, simply to look unconcerned. He heard the prince say, "Something must be done to supply us while we're here," and his back stiffened.

"My lord," Chester said, "let me do it."

"Very well, my lord."

Leicester glared at Fulk. "Speak, will you?"

Fulk shook his head. "Let Pembroke."

"My lord," Pembroke said sourly. "Stafford has already bought certain herds. I thought it was by your order or I would not have—"

"My lord Stafford," the prince said, and turned his horse so that he faced Fulk. "How reliable you are."

Fulk said nothing; before the silence could tell, the prince booted his horse forward, and they started off again across the tangled grass, past the walls of the city.

After a moment, Leicester said, "You may be right."

"You see what he does."

Leicester nodded. His face was clear, and he looked around him intently. "The weight is with us, I think."

Fulk hunched his shoulders. The Earl of Hereford had not come up from Wallingford yet, and the Earl of Wiltshire would meet them here sometime in the next few days. Hereford was a Clare and would go with Pembroke and Wiltshire would probably follow. The uneasiness swept back across Fulk's mind, and he struggled to hold it down. With everybody hanging on each sign of the prince's favor, the trick was to seem not to care.

"We need Pembroke," he said.

"Well, we shan't have him."

The prince held in his hands the power to grant or take away each man's claim to office, to lands and legacies, and the truce bound his barons as well as him, so there was no running to King Stephen in revenge. Wallingford had changed more than they had thought. He watched Rannulf riding in the midst of Chester's following, beside Thierry.

They rode back toward the prince's camp, behind Leicester's at the east gate; just outside it, the prince drew rein, and they gathered around him. Henry turned to put his back to the sun. With its light on his brilliant hair, with his scarlet cloak thrown back over his shoulders, and his gray horse gathered like a knot, he made them all quiet with a look. He waved toward Stamford.

"Here we shall prove the right of our cause," he said. "God be with us here."

He crossed himself, and everyone else did also, right arms moving in unison.

"This shall be the order of command. My lord the Earl of Pembroke commands by the river, against the castle gate, and my lord Chester shall hold the camp opposite the west gate."

Chester and Pembroke were smiling.

"My lord the Earl of Stafford shall command opposite the north gate, where his camp now is, and my lords Leicester and Derby command the east gate. I myself will order you all, by your advice."

Two by two, Fulk thought. As they boarded the Ark.

"My lord Stafford has already begun to supply us with food. Sir Thierry will be in charge of guarding the roads so that the supplies reach us."

"My lord," Fulk said, and nudged his horse forward. "The roads can best be guarded by the castles from whom the supplies come—I can give them knights to help, if they need it."

Chester and Thierry cried out together; Thierry shut

his mouth, and Chester said, "My lord, Stafford already has duties that strain even his great ability—let Thierry take some of the weight."

"No one can do everything at once, Fulk," the prince said mildly. "You must see the wisdom in what Chester says."

"If I did it with only half a mind to it, I'd still guard the roads better than Thierry—he has already proven he cannot command."

Leicester swore under his breath. Black in the face, Thierry cried out, "That is a base slander."

"Are you challenging me?" Fulk shouted. "Shall we decide it by combat, uncle?"

"Quiet," the prince said. For an instant, his face was tight, but immediately it softened into a smile. "I forgot —you'll forgive me for opening up old wounds, my lords. Rolf de Tosny will guard the roads."

In Chester's following, young Tosny raised his head and threw out his chest like a rooster, beaming.

"As you will, my lord," Fulk said, and bowed.

Henry bowed to him. "I will." His eyes gleamed; he stared at Fulk a moment longer than necessary.

Chester and Thierry were talking, low-voiced, and Pembroke turned away from them with a shrug. "So long as he is ours," he said, loudly.

"I need a herald," the prince said, "a man of high rank, to carry messages to the lords of Stamford." He looked them over calmly. "Rannulf of Ledgefield, whose side are you on?"

Rannulf had been looking down at his hands. He lifted his head toward the prince. "Yours, my lord."

Henry put his head back and laughed, and Chester and Pembroke burst out laughing. The laughter spread throughout their followers, but Fulk and Leicester stayed quiet, and their men did not laugh.

"Then," Henry said, "you shall be my herald. Come with me, Rannulf. The rest of you have my leave to go."

He turned his horse and galloped off toward his camp. Rannulf worked his way free of the crowd and rode after him, and in two bands the barons started away, glaring back and forth at each other across the widening strip of grass between them.

RANNULF TOOK MESSAGES to the aldermen of Stamford, promising them that the prince would confirm their charters and the charters of the weavers' guild, and when the sun rose the next day all the garrison had withdrawn from the walls of the town into the castle and the gates of the city stood open to the prince's army.

Henry published an order forbidding pillaging, but all during the day men from the armies outside the walls sneaked into the town and robbed, and in the night the glow of a dozen fires lit up the streets. Fulk with forty of his knights and Chester with fifty of his rode in to stop the plundering. Fulk sent Roger and ten men to chase the looters out of the area around the north gate and went down into Stamford's Jewry, where three separate fires were blazing.

Cinders and burning embers floated through the air, and the whole town smelled of fire. Most of the Jews were out wetting down the thatched roofs of their houses and shops; men carrying buckets of river water marched up and down the streets. Here and there, a rich man's house thrust its wooden roof up above the oat straw of the other houses, but these burned too; everyone suffered. Fulk led his men into an alleyway toward a burning building. Water streamed off the roofs on either side of them and dripped down on their heads and backs. A man popped out of a garden ahead of them and ran off down the alley, shouting that more pillagers were coming. Whenever they passed a house, dogs barked and charged along behind the fence and the shutters were quickly drawn.

"Down there," someone called, behind Fulk, and he looked down the street they were crossing and saw flames leaping from a house halfway along it. He swung into the street and put his horse into a lope. Black shapes dashed back and forth from the burning house to the street, carrying furniture and bundles of clothes and goods. They saw Fulk coming, dropped what they carried, and sprinted away on foot. Fulk stopped his horse in front of the house—the heat of the flames washed over him.

"It's gone," he said. The house was wrapped entirely in the fire; he could see rooms in it, furniture in it, as if the flames were the walls. "You three, gather up this—" he gestured toward the loot—"and impound it in the market-place until we can find out who owns it. Alan, find us a wagon. Let's go, the rest of you."

He started down the street after the looters, who were disappearing into an alley halfway to the cross-roads. In the firelight, he caught a glimpse of a family huddled against a wall opposite the burning house— he saw their faces, the streaming eyes of the children.

They chased the looters down the alley almost to the bank of the river, and there, they scattered, some running into other streets, and some trying to climb into the gardens around them. Fulk shouted to his men to chase them. He led three knights at a fast trot down the street to a gate into a garden where he had seen men scaling the wall, knocked hard on the gate, and told his men to break it down. In the house beyond, a woman screamed. Light appeared behind the shutters.

Fulk rode into the garden, clustered with fruit trees; it was too small to hide the looters, and they burst from their cover and tried to flee. From a window over Fulk's head, a man in a nightcap with a candle in his hand was shouting to them all to get out. Fulk ran one looter into the wall and chased him up and down it, reining his horse hard to follow the man's dodging and leaping. The looter jumped to catch the top of the wall and started to pull himself up, and Fulk rode in, slipped his arm around the man's waist, and dragged him across his saddlebows, face down.

"Who are you? What are you doing here?" the man in the window shouted; he waved his candle, and it went out, and he threw it at Fulk. Ducking back inside, he vanished. Fulk rode to the gate, where two of his men were tying up prisoners, and dumped the looter to the ground.

"Watch out!"

The man in the window had returned, with a full chamberpot, and he upended it on the heads of a knight and two looters. The knight dodged; Fulk saw the stuff splash on his shoulder, and the looter howled and clawed at his eyes. The man in the window shouted Jewish curses at them. Bending down, the knight took the looter by the hair and dragged him screaming toward the gate.

"Tie them, take them to the marketplace, and guard them. You and you." He led the remaining knight through the broken gate and loped down toward the river.

All along the wall of the castle, to their right, torches flared, and men shouted and shot random arrows. Three houses in a row were burning; the unquiet water of the river glistened with the light. A crowd stood in the street in front of them, clutching each other and whimpering. Fulk rode up between them and the fires.

"Listen to me. These are my orders to you. Go to the marketplace and wait and we will find you someplace to stay tonight. Hurry, if you stay in the street you'll be taken for looters. If anyone questions you, tell them you're under the protection of the Earl of Stafford."

A baby was whimpering, and the smaller children let out a howl at the sound of his voice, but the men grouped their families together and drove them down the street. Four more of Fulk's knights rode toward him through the crowd. A couple of the townsmen shook their fists at Fulk and cursed the knights. In the smoky, ruddy light, Fulk rode along the river street, away from the castle; there were people wandering about, and he sent two of his men to take them, if they were looting, or send them back home if they were just seeing the sights. The smoke hurt his lungs, and he kept his horse to a quick trot to get away from the fires. They turned up another street and chased half a dozen looters along it, through the dark, catching them one by one.

At the corner, eight of his knights joined him, and they turned into a street packed with Chester's men. Fulk glanced behind him. He had only a dozen men with him; the rest had gone with prisoners and booty to the marketplace. He reined in, looking for a street away from Chester.

"Stafford," a harsh voice called, and he turned forward again. Chester galloped heavily out of the tangle of his men. "This is my quarter."

"I was unaware we had divided the city," Fulk said. "How have you done?"

"Never mind that—get out of my quarter." Chester stopped beside him, their horses head to tail; his face was greasy with sweat.

"Don't make me angry, my lord. Don't bother with the river street, I've been down there. I'm going to—"

Chester crowded his horse against Fulk's. "Then go —fast."

Fulk lifted his foot, still in the stirrup, and kicked Chester's horse between the hindlegs. The horse screamed and reared up, and Fulk rode in against it and tipped Chester out of his saddle. Chester's men outnumbered his three to one and he needed some advantage. Shouting to his knights, he galloped back along the street toward the river and cut into a side street. He could hear Chester's knights charging after him. His men swore excitedly and he could hear them drawing their swords. A crossroads swept up to them, and he swerved into the street to the right, back toward the marketplace.

He was out of the Jewry; these narrow, cramped houses were the tenements of the poor, and in the middle of the dark street pigs rooted for garbage in the gutter. Fulk galloped down the side of the street, dodging the huge, lop-eared swine, waved to his men to go on, and veered off into a side street.

Midway along it, a flame licked out of a window. He swerved toward that building. Looters raced away down the alleys and through the gardens. Someone was screaming in the burning building. Bundles sailed out of a second-story window, and a man jumped after them. Before he hit the ground, he saw Fulk, and he landed running, leaving his loot behind him.

"Fire," Fulk shouted. "Fire." He had to struggle to remember the word in English. There were people in this house; he rode up to the door, bent double, and tugged at the latch, but it was fastened on the inside. It was a shop, no wider than six feet at the front, with living quarters above it. Through the door he could feel the heat of the fire.

Inside, someone was screeching for help. He backed his horse up—Chester's men were galloping down the street he had left, after his men, and he heard fighting. A woman and two children were climbing onto the wooden roof of the building from a second-story window. While he watched, another child scrambled out of the window and pulled himself nimbly over the eave. Shrieking for help, the woman ran up and down along the edge of the roof. Shingles broke off under her feet. In the next street, the fighting men ignored her.

Fulk cast around him, swearing in a monotone, and finally rode along the house until he was below the woman and her children.

"Jump—I'll catch you. Jump." He nearly forgot to speak English.

One boy promptly leaped off the roof and landed on top of him. His weight struck Fulk on the shoulder and a stray foot landed in his crotch. He gasped with the pain; dropping the boy to the ground, he raised his arms just in time to catch a little girl. She giggled and slid warmly down into his arms. The woman and her last child clung to each other and prayed in high voices; the fire glowed in the windows of the second story, beneath them, and smoke curled from the roof, and the child lifted its feet off the roof, clutching its mother.

"Jump," Fulk shouted. He glanced behind him—Chester's men and his own had gone off fighting down the next street. He held up his arms.

"I can't. I can't."

"Let him down to me. Hurry up, damn you. It's getting hot."

"I can't. I—"

"Do it," Fulk roared.

Sobbing, the woman took the child by the arms and lowered it down over the eave, kicking and screaming. Fulk could not quite reach it. "Let go. Drop him, I can—"

She let go, and he caught the child around the waist. Its arms wrapped tightly around his neck, cutting off his breath, and before he could pry its fingers loose the woman landed on top of them. The child let out a screech, and all three of them fell off the horse into the garden.

Fulk dragged himself out from under the woman and stood up. Men were running with buckets out of the buildings around them; they were wetting down the roofs of their own houses. He wiped his face on his sleeve. The two older children were squatting in the street, watching their house burn with merry eyes. The woman began to pray and sob and cross herself, and two other women from neighboring houses came up to her, threw their arms around her, and sobbed with her. Fulk walked to his horse, mounted, and rode off. Behind him, someone shouted, "Norman swine."

He came to a street where three knights were riding up and down, stopping everyone they saw. When they came up to him, he saw they were Chester's men and reined in.

"Hold," one shouted. "Hold, there, who are you?"

"Stafford," Fulk called. "Let me by."

They spurred their horses, and he whirled and galloped off down the street. They chased him as far as the crossroads, where he turned north and rode at a hard lope toward the marketplace. Loose dogs were roaming in packs; he passed twenty of them growling and fighting over something in the street. Their backs hid it from him, so that he could not see what it was. He hoped it was a pig. He could see the smoke and red light of a dozen fires in the sky. When he reached the marketplace, it was full of townspeople, wagons of plunder, and his own men, and he rode across it looking for Roger.

"Over here," Roger called, and walked toward him. Fulk rounded a wagon and reined in.

"What happened?" Roger said. "Three men came back wounded."

"Chester. I hope they killed some of his."

"We are putting people in the churches to spend the night. What shall I do with the booty?"

"Guard it until the morning. I'm going back to the camp. Don't let anybody leave this area—he has his men scattered through the town, and they're after us."

"What are you going to do?"

"Wake up our little prince. I'll send you twenty knights. If anything happens, make sure that I know." He turned his horse and jogged through the swarming marketplace toward the east gate.

"HE IS ASLEEP," the sentry said, shocked.

"Wake him up."

"If you deem it necessary, my lord." The sentry stuck his head through the door into Henry's tent and whispered to someone there. Fulk stepped back a few paces, his hands clasped behind his back, and formed words in his mind.

Voices sounded inside the tent, at first whispers, and finally a shout—the prince had lost his temper. The page came out.

"My lord." His face was white; he was only nine or ten years old. "He says he will see no one."

Fulk shoved him to one side and went into the tent.

Wrapped in a brocaded dressing gown, Henry was going back toward his bed. He spun around; there was a candle burning in the front of the tent, and Fulk could see how his face contorted.

"I said no one, Stafford," Henry shouted.

"Order Chester out of Stamford, my lord."

"Damn you—God damn you, bringing me these petty feuds of yours when I'm sleeping. Get out!"

"No."

"No—you—who are you to—Are you defying me? You petty, puffed-up little lordling, are you—Do you think you can give me orders? Do you think me your servant?"

"I'll leave when you order Chester out."

Henry swore at him, kicked over a chair, and stuck his face down close to Fulk's. "I am the king, not you."

Fulk looked him patiently in the eyes, and Henry drew back.

"I will be the king."

"Chester is attacking my men, and when I stopped to help a family in a burning house, he set upon my men, and we barely saved the family. He is not seeking looters. His knights patrol some streets, but in others and especially in the Jewry the looters do what they will, and I can't stop them because when I try I have to fight Chester. Withdraw both of us, and send Leicester in alone."

"I'll send in Leicester and Pembroke."

"That won't do. They'll fight as well. You'll have to use two men of the same party."

"There are no parties in my army—they are all faithful to me."

"That won't do either."

"I'll do it in the morning. Go away, you woke me up."

"Do it now," Fulk said.

Henry's head flew up. "Who is master here, you or I?"

"I am as angry as you are, my lord. The people of Stamford are under your power and so are the men looting them, and it is your doing that Chester thinks he can attack me."

"Get out."

"Withdraw Chester and his men."

"And leave yours there?"

"We have people and plunder in the marketplace, I can't leave them unguarded. I will turn them over to Leicester and no other, and only when Chester is gone."

Henry wrapped his dressing gown tighter around him. "I'll withdraw Chester. Get out."

"By your leave, my lord." Fulk bowed the way his sons did to irritate him and went outside. A page followed him after a moment and spoke to the sentry. Fulk lingered, being obvious. The sentry called to a nearby Angevin knight and in a voice Fulk could easily hear told him to go to Stamford and order Chester to leave.

Fulk rode over to Leicester's tent, between Henry's camp and the city. Leicester was with his clerk, writing a message; when Fulk came in and they saw it was he, they both relaxed, and Leicester moved away from the table, which he had been shielding with his body.

"I'm glad you came. I am writing to Winchester. I thought you were in Stamford—what happened?"

"I had to come ask the prince to order Chester out. Have you talked to Pembroke?"

Leicester had met with Pembroke at dinner to try and talk over their differences. He shook his head. "To no end. He was afraid I was lying. Everybody is afraid of everyone else. I trust no one but you and Derby and I'm unsure of Derby. If I knew you less well I would be unsure of you."

"Oh," Fulk said, sitting down, "I'm true as a blushing maid. What have you said to the bishop?"

"Nothing. I'm afraid to say anything for fear the

letter might be taken into the wrong places. What's wrong with Chester?"

"He attacked me. He is unsubtle."

Leicester walked up and down, punching the air with his fist. "Can we trust Derby?"

"Yes."

"I saw him speaking with Hereford today, and they spoke for a long while."

"Slight evidence against him. You know he hates Chester, because Chester took Peverel's lands and he and Peverel are cousins. My own son is Pembroke's squire."

"Is he of use to us?"

"Hugh? No. He is all Pembroke's man."

"Rannulf?"

"Rannulf will have nothing to do with any of us."

"He spends much of the day with Chester and Thierry."

"Not since we came to Stamford. Now he's friends with the Angevins. I don't know which is worse."

"How can we send this letter? Whom can we trust to carry it?"

"Give it to me. Simon d'Ivry can carry it." Simon had come that morning from Bruyère-le-Forêt.

"Simon was Thierry's man once, wasn't he?"

"Briefly. I believe in that, the contrast cannot but help me." He went over to stand behind the clerk, who was writing out the fair copy. In terms veiled as prophecy, Leicester had sketched the situation in the prince's camp; he mentioned no names at all. The clerk's pen scraped over the parchment. Fulk said, "Let me add something when you are finished."

"I'm useless in this," Leicester said. "An issue of law or a question of taxes I can deal with better than most men in this kingdom, but I have no heart for this."

Fulk said, "It is going as the prince wishes it, he may wish it different soon enough."

"You think it is all his doing."

"Not all. He fosters it."

The clerk finished and left his seat, and Fulk sat

down on the stool. Leicester said, "What are you doing?"

"In a moment, Robert."

There was a fresh-cut pen on the table; Fulk took it, dipped it in the ink, and wrote, below the closing of the letter. The sentry put his head in the door, and Leicester jumped to guard the table.

"Sir Richard de Lous, my lord."

Leicester said, in a tight voice, "Send him in."

Fulk stood up, his back to the table. De Lous was one of Henry's Angevins; he came in, bowed, and said, "My lord Leicester, my lord the Count of Anjou requires you to take such of your men as you deem sufficient to it and clear Stamford city of those looting it. He asks that you leave at once."

"I shall," Leicester said.

"Thank you, my lord." De Lous made an Angevin bow and went out.

"That will look bad," Leicester said. "To find you and me here, and the letter."

"Yes," Fulk said. He sat down and finished writing. The clerk took it and scattered sand over it and shook the paper back and forth. "But there isn't much we can do about that."

"You are so cool about all this, I envy you."

"If I weren't angry enough at Chester to kill him, I'd be as unnerved as you."

"What did you write?" Leicester sent the clerk to get a page.

"I spoke to Winchester about Chester, back at Wallingford. I was reminding him of it."

"What was it?"

"Oh, something touching the Honor of Lancaster."

Leicester stared at him. The page came in, and he sent the boy off to wake up his son and his second-in-command. When the page had gone, he said, "It is not Chester who is at the root of this. We must win Pembroke."

"We can win Pembroke by breaking Chester."

"If Prince Henry wishes it."

Fulk watched the clerk seal the letter. "Or we can break Chester by winning Pembroke, perhaps."

"Take the letter when you go. I'll take a hundred men into Stamford, and if Chester is mistaken for a looter—" He shouted for his squire and went into the back of the tent.

"It would solve many of our problems," Fulk said.

THE LOOTING WENT on, although much lessened, all the next day, and Prince Henry spoke to the leaders of the Jews and they gave him seven hundred and fifty marks as a present. Henry wanted more, but Leicester convinced him that the Jews of Stamford could give no more. Henry promised the Jews to stop the looting in the Jewry by the next morning and sent them away. He needed the money to pay for the supplies, which were coming in every day from the countryside.

After the Jews had left, Rannulf came up to Fulk and drew him to one side of the prince's tent. Fulk was pleased to find his son so much in the favor of the prince, but he said nothing for fear that Rannulf would be suspicious of his interest. All the prince's servants were packing to move into a house in the city, and the tent was filled with busy people. Rannulf said, "My lord, Chester wants to talk to you."

"I don't want to see Chester."

"My lord," Rannulf said quietly, "the prince asks you to."

"Oh," Fulk said. "Did he ask Derby to talk to Hereford, yesterday?"

Rannulf said, "He asks, that's all. If you don't wish to, don't."

"I'll talk to him." Fulk bit the inside of his cheek; a moment before, he remembered, he had been proud of Rannulf. "I'll see him on the top of that hill, south of the town on the river. The one they call the Queen's Hill, with all the birches. Tell him to come alone."

"Why there?" Rannulf gestured around him. "The prince will allow you to talk here, I'm sure."

"So no one will see us talking," Fulk said. "Everybody is very suspicious of everybody else. I'm sorry if I insulted either you or the prince."

He went to the door. Rannulf did not follow. Fulk heard him talking to one of the Angevins, and he stepped outside and sent Morgan for his horse. He did not want to meet Chester, and Rannulf's new attitude baffled him; he looked up into the clear sky and tried to think himself calm.

FROM THE QUEEN'S Hill, the countryside spread out in tawny colors, the narrow strips of the fields tracing out the curves of the low hills and hollows, the walls of Stamford picked out in rose colors by the failing sun. The wind had lulled. Fulk sat crosslegged on the ground, watching the road from the town, which ran around the foot of the hill. Behind him, his horse stamped at flies and ripped up the grass with its teeth.

Fat and red in the unclouded sky, the sun lowered to the rim of the western hills. A soft, cool wind touched Fulk's cheek. It had been blistering hot all day, and he turned his face into the wind and sighed. Down on the road, a single horse was coming. Fulk shut his eyes, and the wind cooled his eyelids.

The sounds of the city and the camp reached him, muffled by distance, enclosed in the silence of the hill and the empty fields. He saw the sun against his eyelids, blood red. The sound of hoofs reached him and grew steadily stronger. Opening his eyes, he looked toward the road, but the curve of the hill hid Chester from him. A cricket was chirruping behind him; all down the slope before him he saw them leaping, so

many that the air low over the grass was filled with
their flights. The hoofbeats drummed louder and
dropped from a canter to the even beat of a trot, and
he looked around and saw Chester riding toward him
through the birch trees.

Chester reined in and stared at him, his face all high
color. "Well, Fulk." He dismounted; he rode a black
horse with a narrow white blaze and two white stock-
ings behind, and he led it to a tree and knotted the
reins around a branch. Crickets sailed away from his
feet when he walked toward Fulk.

"It's peaceful enough here," he said, warily.

"Yes," Fulk said. "If there were a stream I would
be fishing. What do you want, Chester?"

"Not I. What Prince Henry wants." He swiped at
the crickets in the air. "You could use them for bait."
When he sat down, one of his knees cracked, louder
than the crickets. "By God, there are ants everywhere."

"You're sitting on an anthill. Move over."

Chester straightened and moved around to Fulk's
other side. The sun was half gone, as if the hills were
eating it. From their feet the shadows moved out over
the level ground.

"Prince Henry wishes us to talk out our differences,"
Chester said. "Shall we?"

The evening star shone in the sky, above the sun.
Fulk stared at it, saying, "That night in Stamford you
tried to conquer me. Since you didn't, it's easily forgotten. But you know how deep this goes, all of it, and
how far back in our families."

"There is a treaty between you and me, remember?"

"You broke it, that night in Stamford. You have
broken every bond you ever made with any man."

"Oooh. But, Fulk, you sound like a monk, or a
woman. Treaties have their use, but when the use is
past—"

"Then why bring it up?" Fulk said sharply.

"Because—" Chester tore up clumps of grass and

threw them down the hill. "If you joined me and Pembroke, all would be mended."

"You and Pembroke and Thierry?"

"Oh. Something could be done about Thierry."

"You're mad."

"Leicester and Derby and those others could not withstand the three of us, with Hereford and Wiltshire and the prince. What keeps you from joining us? What do you want?"

"I have all I want."

"Nobody has all he wants. What can you find in those men—Leicester, Derby—"

"They're my friends."

"Of them all, only you has the wit and decision to contend with us. They will follow you."

"You misjudge them. Or me."

"No." Chester flung a flowering weed down among the crickets. "You misjudge them, and yourself. Some —gaudy idea of loyalty and friendship has blinded you —these men are to be used, like oxen, to draw whatever weight they can bear, in the service of men like us. How many men do you know with the power to make of their lives what they wish?"

"None."

"I do." Chester flicked an ant off his shin. "Men like Leicester and Derby are worth only what we make them worth to us."

"I don't believe that, Chester." He wondered if Chester himself believed it and decided that he did.

"Then you don't understand yourself. You need not answer me now. When you want to join us, let me know of it, and we will discuss the terms of it." He smiled; his unwinking, bulging eyes were sleek with confidence. "Like kings."

Fulk looked away, down toward the city; the sun had gone down, and behind him, in the dusk, a nightingale began to sing. Lights showed in the city and the besieged castle. After a moment, Chester got up and went to his horse, mounted, and rode away. Where he had been sitting, the grass sprang up, leaf by leaf, hiding the gaps he had torn out.

ALL THAT NIGHT, Leicester's men battled the looters, drove them from street to street among the burning houses, the garbage, and the swine; Fulk, sitting in his tent listening to Morgan's harp, could hear occasional shouts and screams. He had tried to find Rannulf to tell him what had happened between him and Chester, so that Rannulf could report it to the prince, but Rannulf was not in the camp. Fulk thought he was with the prince.

The problem of supply would lessen when the city was quiet, because the supply masters of each army could buy in the marketplace, but the normal trade of Stamford would hardly be enough. He had not yet gone to Highfield, to ask Rohese to sell the army herds and grain, although he had thought of that, and of Red Alys of Dol, every day since he had heard how close Highfield was. There was no sense doing anything before he understood all the implications. While Morgan sang of the knight on the road, Fulk wrote out instructions to the supply masters of the army, and read letters from his steward concerning his own demesne.

His Norman lands, the seat of his family, seemed as distant and indistinct as a star; he had not been there in over a year, an extraordinary absence. Yet William Malmain his steward reported that the vicomté was quiet and the crops growing to a great harvest. The maturing yellow wine, the kind Fulk liked best, was better than usual, William wrote; since traveling ruined it; he hoped Fulk would come to Bruyère before it was all drunk up.

I'll go at Christmas. Hugh should be knighted at Bruyère, anyway. He thought, as he had before, of leaving Hugh his Norman lands, and Rannulf only the

Honor of Bruyère in England, less certain bequests
Fulk intended for the White Monks. No one man could
care for all that land anyway. That was probably
Thierry's argument. Fulk made aimless marks with his
pen along the margin of the letter he was reading.
Most of the great lords of England had lost their
Norman lands when Prince Henry's father had con-
quered Normandy from Stephen.

Stephen had given some of his barons compensa-
tion, of course, which was how Chester had come into
his claim of the Honor of Lancaster, and the Honor of
Bruyère was one of the smaller important holdings in
England, only four hundred and eight knights' fees.
Fulk drew a circle in the margin; his pen was dry, and
he dipped it again in the ink. When he had succeeded
his grandfather as lord of Stafford he had come all un-
prepared into as much as Rannulf would inherit, and
he had learned it eventually. If he split up the demesne, Hugh at least would fret for lack of things to
do.

He wrote William Malmain a letter, to tell him that
he would come to Bruyère in Normandy for Christmas
and that Hugh and Morgan would be knighted then.
William could also arrange for the commissioning of a
statute of the Virgin, for the chapel at Bruyère-le-Forêt,
from one of the woodcarvers in Rouen. He paused,
trying to remember the name of the man who had done
the work in the new church at Bruyère.

Morgan was in the middle of a verse, and Fulk
waited until it had ended. Putting down the pen, he
called, "Morgan, will you come here?"

The music stopped, and Morgan walked around
from the back of the tent to stand before his table. The
tent all around them was stacked up with packed baggage, to be moved into the city the next day.

"We are knighting Hugh, this Christmas," Fulk said.
"You should be knighted then, too."

Morgan put his hands behind his back. "No, my
lord."

"You're old enough, and you've learned enough as a squire to make you a good knight, Morgan—there isn't much more you can learn as a squire."

"I hate swords," Morgan said. "I hate shields, and fighting, and all the worse than fighting, and I will not be a knight, ever, my lord."

Amazed, Fulk stared at him, his mind empty. What the abbot of Saint Swithin had said of the children of the wars came back to him, that they had learned nothing worthy of them. Arguments boiled up in his mind, and he rejected them all. He knew Morgan would not care what other people thought of him, a man of his blood who did not become a knight.

"Whatever pleases you, Morgan."

"Thank you, my lord. You need a harp player more than a knight, anyway."

Morgan went back to his playing. Fulk watched him. He would have to get another squire, because Morgan would soon be too old for a squire. One of the candles was guttering, and he realized that he was sleepy. But he did not rise; he sat drawing in the margin of the letter until Morgan had finished the song of the knight on the road.

HE FINISHED THE letter the next morning and signed it and put it away until he could unpack his seals to seal it with; somebody shouted outside his tent, and he looked up. Morgan went outside to see what was happening, and immediately put his head in the door and said, "My lord, come out."

Fulk got up and went out into the sunshine and the bright wind. Everywhere in the camp, men were carrying their goods toward the wagons. Leicester and three other men were leading a packed horse up toward him, and when he saw Fulk Leicester booted his mount forward and dismounted.

"I'm sorry," he said, and caught Fulk by the arm. "He's dead, Fulk."

Fulk brushed past him and went to the side of the burdened horse and pulled back the covering. It was Rannulf, his head turned against the skirt of the saddle, and his hair hanging down.

Fulk stood with his arm stiffly outstretched, holding back the flap of the cloak, frozen. "No," he said. "Oh no."

"A man of mine found him in an alley in the city— he was stabbed. Come inside, Fulk."

Fulk let go of the cloak, and it fell back across Rannulf's head. "Help me," he said. He pulled blindly at the ropes that held Rannulf on the horse, and all those around him moved up and unhitched the ropes and helped him lift the body down.

Leicester said something, but Fulk could not hear it; he was weeping and a rushing sound filled his ears so that he could hear nothing. They carried Rannulf into the tent. Morgan cried out. They laid Rannulf on the ground, and Fulk knelt beside him and pulled off the cloak. Blood covered the boy's chest, and there were two deep wounds in his right side. He had not even worn mail.

"He was stabbed from behind," Fulk said. "Who?"

Leicester sent away his men. "Looters, I would think. We found him in the alley this morning, as you see him."

"What was he doing in Stamford?"

"Chester sent him in last night, apparently to carry this message to Thierry." Leicester took a scrap of canvas from his coat; there was writing on it.

"Chester sent him alone?"

"I don't know."

Fulk looked at the piece of canvas. The scribbling on it blurred so he could not read it. He said, "It's for my sins. God has stricken me for my sins."

"Will you take him to Ledgefield?"

Fulk made a small sound in his throat. Morgan had sunk down near Rannulf's head and was staring at him. "Is it too far?" Fulk said. "But Eleanor would want to bury him. His lady."

Leicester said, "I will arrange it." He got up and went to the door.

Fulk looked around. Roger came in. "My lord—" He knelt stiffly in his hauberk. "Do you need me, my lord?"

"We'll take him to Ledgefield."

"They say that Chester sent him to the city and he was killed there," Roger said.

Fulk nodded; he was staring at Rannulf's face. It looked much older. My son is dead. He could not bear to think of Margaret. Morgan went to a chest and opened it and took out a cloak lined with fur. Coming back, he unhooked the clasp of the one Rannulf was wearing. The sentry said, "My lord, my lord of Chester is here."

With Chester came Rannulf's squire, who began to help Morgan. Chester said, "Fulk, I had no idea he would go alone. He knew the city was—"

"Thank you," Fulk said mechanically, to make him stop.

"They're blaming me, all over the camp," Chester said. "Everyone liked Rannulf."

Fulk stood up. Eleanor, Rannulf's wife, with her two baby children—He thought again of Margaret. The sentry let Simon d'Ivry in, who bent down to look at Rannulf and threw a harsh glare at Chester. Fulk stared at Chester, wondering what he was doing in here, and the sentry put his head in the door and said that Thierry was outside.

"No," Fulk said, but Thierry was already through the door.

"Poor Rannulf," Thierry said, and knelt down and put his hand on the boy's wounds.

Fulk went over to Leicester and said softly, "Get them out of here, please."

Leicester spoke to the men filling the tent. Fulk went into the back, among the piles of packed baggage.

He felt hot, and he ground the heels of his hands into his eyes to stop the tears flowing.

"They're gone," Morgan said, and he turned. Even Leicester was gone. Rannulf's squire had wrapped Rannulf into the cloak. Morgan was straightening the body's legs.

"Let me," the other squire cried. "He was my master." Morgan slid back out of the way.

We should take him to Stafford, Fulk thought. And lay him under the altar where his mother lies and his great-grandfather, where I will lie. Ledgefield was closer. It's for my sins. See how I am punished. He pressed his fist to his chest.

A man of Leicester's came back, with Roger, and Roger said, "My lord, we have a litter. Is that enough?"

"Yes."

He had bled so much—his clothes were stiff with blood; if they had found him sooner, might he not have lived? He wiped his face on his sleeve. Don't think that way. I could not find him last night, he must have been in Stamford.

Hugh came in, looked at Rannulf, and came straight to Fulk. "My lord, shall I go with you? To Ledge-field."

Fulk jerked his head up. He had not thought of Hugh once. Calm, not crying, Hugh met his gaze and said, "I'm sorry. Let me go."

"I should have asked you to," Fulk said.

"Do they know who did it?"

Fulk shook his head. "Looters. Maybe we can find out." Hugh's face was all new to him, like a stranger's: my living son. "Did you see him before he died? Yesterday?"

"No. I haven't seen much of him since he came. We always fought, you know that."

So did he and I. Fulk shook his head; he felt as if he were waking up. He looked around the tent. "When will we leave?"

"Before noon," Roger said. "Morgan, get your lord some wine."

"No. I'd get drunk." Fulk stood up. "Morgan, you'll have to unpack again, I'll need clothes. We'll be gone some days, Hugh. Get ready." He walked aimlessly around the tent, and went to the door. Outside, the camp in the confusion of breaking up covered the stretch of land between him and Stamford, and he stood and watched it all blur and clear and blur before his eyes.

LEDGEFIELD CASTLE STOOD on a low round hill, baked hot and brown by the late summer sun; like Stafford, it had a gatehouse and a tower opposite each other on the wall, but it was made of gray limestone, not red rock of Stafford. They reached it in three days from Stamford, and took the body into the chapel and laid it out before the altar.

Hugh had gone on ahead of Fulk to tell Eleanor. She met them and led them into the chapel; Fulk beside her could see her hands trembling, but she neither wept nor spoke, and her pale, thin face was expressionless. She looked at Rannulf once, after he had been laid out, and turned to Fulk.

"Come inside, my lord."

She took him across the courtyard. The chickens scattered before her, clucking; the children of her household were all gathered in a quiet knot by the well. Hugh was arranging everything, she said, in a toneless voice, and took him up the stairs into the gatehouse. She passed the door into the hall and went up another flight of steps to the top room, where she slept and where her children were.

"She is asleep," she said, nodding toward the bed on the far side of the room. Fulk could see the little girl curled up on it, beside a hunting dog. It was getting dark, and Eleanor picked up a candle and lit it from one on the wall. She lifted the candle over the cradle.

All Fulk could see of the baby was its mass of dark hair and a fat little hand. Eleanor thrust her free hand out quickly to catch the wax dripping down the candle, so that it would not splash on her baby, and turned away. The light shone on her plaited yellow hair and in her pale eyes.

"I can't believe he's dead." She whimpered and moved away. "I thought I would see him once again, at least." When she walked, the bundle of keys at her belt jangled; she walked heavily, like an old woman. She was seventeen.

"Mama?" the little girl called sleepily, and the dog lifted its head and licked her face. Her nurse came out of the alcove and went over to quiet her. Fulk heard the murmur of the old woman and the child's drowsy voice and went out the door after Eleanor.

"Will you find out who did it?"

"I'll try. I don't know. They robbed him, we'll keep watch for what they took."

"Since Hugh came I looked at the babies, until you came. Just at my babies." She went down the narrow stairs, holding the candle up with one hand and her skirts with the other.

"Where is Hugh?"

"In here." On the landing before the door into the hall, she pulled at the latch, and it opened immediately from inside. Roger backed up to let them in.

"Thank you, Sir Roger," Eleanor said. She put down the candle, took a napkin edged in braided red and yellow thread and blew her nose. Her head turned toward Fulk. "Do you think it was an accident, that my husband died?"

Roger went off across the room, toward the bed in the corner. Morgan was there already, watching from the shadows, with Hugh. Fulk frowned at Eleanor. "What do you mean?"

"I have lived thus far in my life and seen nothing

that was accident," she said. "Tell me it was an accident that my husband is dead."

"He was robbed and murdered," Fulk said. With a glance, he saw that Roger was watching him intently. Chester sent him there, he thought; his heart was hammering, and he could not meet Eleanor's eyes. Chester—he shook his head. "I know what you mean. It was an accident."

All her face swollen, her eyes red behind their pale thin lashes, Eleanor faced him, exactly his height, and said, "I want my vengeance."

There was a page near the door. Fulk beckoned to him. "Go to bed, my lady."

"Rannulf is dead, I want vengeance."

The page stood beside her. Fulk said, "Light my lady to her rooms, boy. Eleanor, I have to go back to Stamford tomorrow. Whoever killed him, I will find out."

"God's curse on you if you do not." She turned stiffly, as if she were made of wood, and followed the page and his candle. From the doorway, Fulk watched her go up the stair, and after she had rounded the corner he watched the candlelight bobbing along the wall. He pulled the door shut by the iron ring of the latch.

"Do you think it was an accident?" Roger said.

Fulk crossed the room to the end where the bed was. On the hearth, there was a basin of water warming, and he sent Morgan for it. He thought, If it were no accident, then I am not guilty. "I would believe that it wasn't, if I could think who would want to kill Rannulf."

"Chester sent him there alone."

"Why should Chester kill him?" He pulled off his coat and his shirt; Morgan put the basin down in front of him, and he bent to wash his face and hands. "Chester would kill me, not Rannulf. Thierry would kill me. You just want someone to strike back at." He dried himself off and reached for his shirt again.

"Where are you going?" Morgan said. "You are tired. You should sleep."

"To the chapel," Fulk said. He put on his shirt again and took his coat over his arm. "To pray."

ELEANOR CRIED ALL through the Mass, and her daughter, terrified, clung to her and howled. Fulk could hardly keep his eyes open. He had slept a while, on the floor of the chapel, but it had not been enough. The stench of the dead man drowned the incense. The voice of the priest sounded as if it came from a great distance. They carried Rannulf down into the vault under the altar, and the clammy, sweating air woke Fulk up a little. Eleanor's sobs and the screams of the little girl and the baby reverberated around the tomb. Long before they went back up into the chapel, Fulk was shaking violently. Roger saw it and gave him his cloak.

They went up into the sunlight, the soft wind, and the blue sky. Their horses were waiting, and Roger sent the knights who had come with them to mount up. Eleanor came over, clutching the baby, with the little girl in the arms of her nurse and still screaming.

"My lord, when I spoke last night—" She bit her lip until it turned white. "I was wild, I meant no insolence."

"You are never insolent." She hadn't slept either, he could tell by her hollow eyes. "I wish I could stay longer. Is there anything I can say to comfort you?"

"My lord, you know there is not." In her arms, the baby looked up at her solemnly and yawned.

"Take your children and go to your mother. I don't want you to stay here alone."

"No," she said. "I have Ledgefield to rule, I'm a grown woman now. Be careful, my lord."

Fulk kissed her hand and her cheek and went toward his horse. He was so tired that he had to stop and gather his strength before he could step into his saddle. It had done no good, all the prayer; he had gotten neither an answer nor resignation. The ride back to Stamford seemed like a torture and the great affairs there of no more importance than the flutter of the leaves in the wind.

"Let's go," he said to Roger, and they rode at a noisy trot out the gate.

TEN

THE GOLD MEDAL OF SAINT ANNE lay in Fulk's palm. Before him, Simon twisted the ring on his little finger, as if he meant to tear his finger off. "That man of Thierry's had it—Haaken. Thierry came to him when he saw he was wearing it and they argued and Thierry took it from him. I got it later from his room. He and all his men are in one of Lincoln's houses, they don't think it odd if I go there, they know me from before, when I was Thierry's man. You know that medal is Rannulf's."

Fulk turned the medal over in his fingers. "It was Rannulf's." He drew a deep breath and held it a moment and let it out. In a soft voice, he said, "I would not have thought this of Thierry."

"My lord, let me—"

"No." Fulk stood up, took the medal, and went into the back of the room to put it into his chest. This room was large and sunny, and he could look out the windows and see the trees of the garden. He went back to Simon.

"The man who had it, before Thierry took it," he said to Simon. "Haaken. Go get him for me. Not dead."

"I can't, my lord," Simon said. "He is dead. Drowned. They took him from the river the day after I found the medal."

Fulk clicked his tongue. "Too bad. You must have frightened them. Don't go down there again, Thierry must know—No, no, go if you wish, but be careful, and keep watch on him for me. Will you?"

"My lord," Simon said, fiercely.

"Never let him go anywhere without your watching."

Simon whirled and bounded out the door. Fulk stood looking at the trees through the window; they were heavy with ripe apples.

It was proof of nothing, that the man had the medal—Fulk could think of several ways he might have come by it, and several innocent reasons why Thierry would have taken it from him. But the man was dead. Another accident. Fulk called to Morgan for his cloak and went down the stair into the hall of the house.

In the house's small courtyard, Simon was mounting his horse. He looked at Fulk, and Fulk waved him out the gate. Beyond the wall, the street was filled with people going to and from the marketplace. Because he had been at Ledgefield when they moved, he had gotten a house in the noisiest part of the town. With Morgan, he rode four streets away, to Leicester's house, where it was much quieter.

Leicester was standing in the courtyard watching a man shoe a horse; he wore leather breeches and a shirt open all down the front. The horse was fighting, and he spoke to the smith, who shouted something and laughed. Fulk dismounted and started toward him.

"Robert, let me talk to you a moment."

Leicester looked around, his hands on his belt, and raised his eyebrows. Fulk led him away from the other man.

"Chester and Thierry killed Rannulf."

With his hand on Leicester's arm he felt the other man start. "What? How do you know?"

"Simon d'Ivry found a medal of Rannulf's in Thierry's house. The man he saw wearing it was killed the next day." He paused a moment, fighting down his sense of haste; he kept his voice low. "Why would they kill Rannulf? It makes no sense."

Leicester said, "Rannulf has a son. How old?"

"Newborn."

"Aye, and if you die, and your heirs are Hugh and this baby, and Thierry makes a contest of it, who will profit?"

"None," Fulk said. "None of them."

"Chester will."

Fulk said nothing. In the corner of his eye, he saw a sudden movement, and he jumped, but it was the horse kicking out at the smith.

"You must see it."

Looking up at him, Fulk nodded; he remembered what Chester had said of using other men. "What is it in Thierry that makes him so useful a tool to everybody?"

"He's a fool. Such men are always used."

"Rannulf loved him. I—"

"Did Thierry love Rannulf? I never marked it. It's Chester who rides him now."

"They came to my tent that day, to say that—" He turned back toward his horse and took the reins and a handful of mane in his fist.

"Wait," Leicester said sharply. "The prince will not let you kill them, without suffering for it."

"Thierry is still an outlaw."

"He is in the prince's favor." Leicester took hold of the shank of Fulk's bit. The smith's hammer rang evenly, a dozen strides away. "You must have better evidence. You must try to make a case of it. I'll help you."

"No," Fulk said. "How long would that take? And it would have to go to King Stephen's court. No."

Leicester frowned. "Be careful, will you? God, you will ruin your family, if you—"

"I'm not for killing them," Fulk said. "Not yet."

"What are you going to do?"

"I don't know. Something." Fulk sawed on his reins, and the horse lifted its head out of Leicester's grip. "I'll tell you." He rode out into the street, wondering if Rannulf had known who it was that killed him.

"MY LADY," THE bailiff of Highfield said, "The Earl of Stafford is here and wishes to see you."

The Lady Rohese was sitting at her loom, in the great hall of Highfield; she rose and came smiling to meet Fulk, her tall gaunt body draped in white and dark green, and when he took her hand he felt the sharp bones and the strength of her fingers. "My lady, I'm very pleased to see you again."

"I would be more pleased to see you, my lord, if I did not know that you came to get provisions for your army. Come sit. Do you mind if I go on with my work?"

"Please."

He went around behind the loom, curious; this hall was covered with tapestry, and when he saw the work in the loom he realized that Rohese had woven it all by herself. In the center of the work on the loom was a crowned king at table, surrounded by his knights, and along the edge she had made scenes of war, of women watching, castles and feasts and hunting. The colors were bright and clear, and she had set them together well; he liked the faces especially.

"This is skillfully done," he said.

"Thank you," she said, and sat down on her stool. "I find it pleasant work. Richard, bring that chair closer."

The servant got a chair from beside the hearth and dragged it across the room. Rohese was sitting before the window, so that the light shone on what she was doing.

"As to your accusation that I'm stealing provisions—"

"I know you are not stealing them," she said. "You pay very well, I understand, and with the king's coin. But none of the manors has beasts to spare, and you take more than we can do without."

"You can buy others." Fulk sat down. "Who told you about it?"

"Durand Fitz Osbern, my neighbor to the north. He says you took one half of his cattle, and I know his calves were disappointing this spring." She snipped a thread, selected a light green one, and worked it carefully into a tree in one corner of the tapestry. "How many of my beasts do you want?"

"We need sixty cattle, hens as many as you can spare, and—" He stood up. "My lady Alys."

"I heard you had come." Alys of Dol came forward from the door. She wore a yellow gown embroidered with small blue flowers; her long red hair hung down her back in two thick braids. At Stafford her braids had been much longer. She stopped midway between the door and Fulk and looked at Rohese.

"Good day, cousin. Why did you try to keep from me that he had come?"

"I know you don't like him," Rohese said calmly. The loom creaked evenly while she worked; she was making a tree near the border, and the green rose up above the work on either side. "I didn't think you'd want to see him."

Alys gave Fulk a long, narrow look. "No. You just will not let me talk to a man. It doesn't matter who he is."

"Nonsense," Rohese said, her mouth full of threads. "You may stay if you wish, child."

"Don't call me child."

"If you persist in this discourtesy—"

"I won't." Alys sat down on a stool, facing Fulk, her hands in her lap. One of the dogs who lay near the hearth came over, and she put one hand on its head. "I promise. My lord, where is Thierry?"

Fulk sat down again. The two women exchanged glances like edges of ice rubbing together. Rohese snipped off a thread and set her scissors down with a click.

"Please, cousin," Alys said bitterly.

Rohese was searching for another color, her head bent over her basket. "I will not allow it. My lord Stafford and I were speaking of important affairs when you came in. Be quiet until we finish. You mentioned cattle and hens, my lord."

"Swine, sheep, cheese, flour. Ale or wine." He paused, in case she remembered she had not yet given him anything to quench his thirst, but she said nothing, the bobbin with its thread whipped back and forth through the moving threads.

"You sound like peddlers," Alys said, and laughed.

"And when must I have these beasts collected?" Rohese asked.

"As soon as you can. Send to me when they are counted and marked and I'll arrange to drive them to Stamford and pay you. Did Durand tell you my prices?"

"Yes. I think them good enough. I shall speak to my bailiff. How does your siege of Stamford go? I shouldn't think it would offer much difficulty to you."

Fulk watched Alys's foot wag impatiently. "No. We hold the town, and we expect the castle to fall very shortly."

"Is Thierry at Stamford?" Alys said. "Please. Tell me." Her feverish eyes darted toward Rohese and returned to Fulk.

"I told you not to—"

"You said I could ask, when you finished your business—you said I could."

Rohese put her bobbin down and looked at Fulk. "Did I?"

"I don't recall, lady."

"Oh—tell her, then, she'll hear it from someone else, if you do not."

"Thierry is at Stamford," Fulk said. "He is close to Prince Henry and in the friendship of the Earl of Chester, he is well, and he has not taken another leman."

"Stafford," Rohese said sharply. "In a handful of words you have destroyed all my work."

"You are kind, my lord," Alys said, surprised. "Have you been reconciled, you and he?"

'No. Never."

She shrugged it aside. "I should not have asked." A page came in, and she sent him down to the kitchens for honeycakes; she sat, half in the sunshine, with the creak of the loom behind her. For the first time, Fulk saw her soft and calm. She looked much younger. He knew she was plotting her way to Stamford.

"Tell me about this prince," Rohese said. "Rumor talks of nothing else. We hear that he is handsome, just and wise, and that he is a monstrous devil full of iniquities."

Fulk was thirsty; he considered asking for a drink, decided it would be discourteous, and feigned a dry cough instead. "You should meet him, my lady, and make up your own mind."

"I would—Mother of God, what a creature you must think me. Alys, will you call for a page? I have offered Stafford nothing to refresh him after riding here from Stamford. You will try some of our strawberry wine, my lord, will you not? I much prefer it to ale."

"Of course." The thought of strawberry wine alarmed him; he shifted in his chair.

"I would enjoy meeting your prince. My prince, he shall be, I understand. But I fear I would be most unwelcome in a camp of war. I wish I were a man."

"My lady wife told me several times how boring it is to be a woman."

Alys came back and sat down. "Thierry spoke lovingly of the countess. I was unhappy to hear that she died, my lord."

"But she was right that womanhood is boring," Rohese said. "I met her once, in London, I believe, but I didn't realize she and I were so much alike."

Fulk hadn't realized it either. He watched a page pour the strawberry wine—its odor was chokingly sweet. Alys was watching him, no longer soft; she had remembered to be unfriendly.

"I like being a woman," she said. "No one treats men as prettily as they treat women."

"Except women," Fulk said.

"If I were a man I would ride to Stamford to talk to this Prince Henry," Rohese said. "Ah, well, I suppose I shall meet him someday."

"Lady, you have the means to meet him now, if you wish. He loves to hunt, tell him that he may use your hunting lodge and forest and your dogs to hunt with while he is at Stamford. He would certainly come here to thank you and you could serve him dinner."

"Stafford. What a superb idea. I shall. Will you carry a letter back to him for me?"

Fulk took the cup from the page; he knew Alys's eyes were on him, suspicious. "I would be happy to." The wine was thick and sweet and almost made him retch.

"Walter," Alys said to the page. "Bring my lord Stafford some of our ale—cousin, you cannot serve men your sticky wines."

"Oh? Don't you like it?" Rohese turned toward Fulk.

"I'm sorry, my lady. No."

"What a pity. Giles detested it. My last husband. All men are alike."

Alys gave a shout of loud laughter. Rohese put her basket down and slid her stool away from the high loom. "I'll send for my clerk and write the letter now." With the keys and scissors at her waist jangling, she strode toward the door. The page Walter came back with a fresh cup and a swan's-neck ewer.

"Bring it here, Walter," Alys said, and rose. "I'll serve you, my lord. Tell me more of Thierry."

"I would rather not, my lady."

"Does he ever speak of me?"

"Once. I don't remember what he said, I'm sorry."

She poured him ale expertly, neatly, and brought it to him. When he had taken it, she picked up the strawberry wine, bending to reach it, and murmured, "Take me to Stamford."

"No." Fulk took a long drink of ale.

"I knew you would not." She held out the winecup to the page. "Walter, take this down to the kitchen."

"My lady, I cannot leave the room."

Alys threw the cup at him. "Damn you, brat, take it away, I'll twist your ears off for you, wet breeches—" She charged him, and the page skittered out of the way, his hands over his ears.

"Let him alone," Fulk said. "That's your cousin's order not to leave you alone with men. Sit down and stop behaving like an ale-wife."

"Now there's strawberry wine on the Grail tapestry," she said. "I hate it here. I cannot even ride, or walk alone in the courtyard. She never leaves me alone. You must take me to Stamford."

"No."

"I can't bear it. I'll kill myself. I'll leap off the top of the tower. You must help me escape from here."

"God's bones. Leap off the tower. Only stop screaming."

She sat down, drew her braids over her shoulders, and stared at him. "Is it true what she says? Are all women covering up their hair now, like nuns, and wearing coifs?"

"All the women in France. I think it's an ugly style, myself. You have very pretty hair."

"I shall have to find linen for a coif. I thought she was telling me so to make me cover it." She smoothed her hair back from her temples with both hands. "Why are you being so kind to me?"

"I have no reason to be otherwise. On the previous occasion, remember, I had something to gain by making you lose your temper."

"I don't believe you."

"As you wish, my lady." Rohese was coming in the door; he stood. Behind her was her clerk, a monk who was probably her confessor as well—she had many of the new habits of the continent. She sat down and motioned to the monk to sit nearby.

"Walter, bring that little table here. Brother Gervase is my confessor, my lord Stafford."

"My lord," the monk said, and made the sign of the Cross at Fulk. From his cassock, he took paper and a case of pens and ink. His fingers were ink-stained; he was very young, with a Norman accent and fine, fair hair.

"Now, write this, Gervase. 'To my lord Henry Fitz-Empress, Duke of Normandy and Count of Anjou—'" She looked inquiringly at Fulk.

"Duke of Aquitaine," Fulk said. "King of England, if you want him to love you."

"Yes." She watched the monk write. "'Greeting from Rohese, Lady of Highfield. My lord, God's blessing on you and your works. I offer you'—Is that too abrupt?"

Fulk shook his head, smiling.

"'I offer you my hunting lodge of Oakwood, my lord, if you wish to hunt, and the forest around it, which is full of game, and my packs of deerhounds and mastiffs. I am praying daily for the peace of England and the coming of her rightful king.'" She frowned.

"You lie," Alys said pleasantly.

"How can you know what my prayers are?"

"She lies," Alys said to Fulk.

"Is that sufficient? The letter." Rohese's eyes followed the monk's quick hands.

"Very good, my lady."

"It isn't grand enough—tell me more compliments to make him."

"More lies?" Alys said.

"But he has much to do, there's no need to make him struggle through too many words. Does he read?"

"Yes. He's a learned man, young as he is."

"Gervase, copy that out now, so that Stafford will have it when he leaves."

The monk mumbled something; he had written the rough draft on fouled paper, and he shuffled through the pile for a clean sheet. Fulk drank the rest of his ale.

"Do you like the ale, my lord?"

"It's excellent. I'm sure the wine is, too, lady, if I had the tongue for it."

"It is." Rohese glared at Alys. "All my friends enjoy it."

"All but one," Alys said. "How is your son, my lord?"

"Rannulf is dead, my lady."

Alys's gaze wavered and fell. "Oh," she said, so softly Fulk barely heard it. Rohese made the sign of the Cross.

"God rest his soul. And so soon after your countess died, too. I'll pray for him."

Fulk said nothing; he looked from her to Alys, who was staring at the floor and stroking the dog at her side. She looked up and caught his eyes and turned to Rohese.

"Could not Stafford have dinner with us, cousin?"

"Of course. I was assuming that you mean to stay, Stafford—it's well into the afternoon already."

"I would like to, but I have to go back to Stamford. Later, I will, I promise you."

"I shall expect it. You must come to hunt with the prince. But stay for another drink of ale."

Alys leaped up. "I'll serve you, Fulk—my lord." She smiled at him tenderly.

Rohese jerked her stool close to the loom and picked up the bobbin. "Alys, you disgrace your family."

"Oh, I'm sorry. Am I making you jealous?"

"No! Rohese's hands worked furiously. Fulk took the cup from Alys.

"Don't be vicious," he said.

"See how she blushes." Alys went back to her chair

and sat down. The monk was sanding the letter; Fulk drank the weak, pale ale, waiting for him to finish, so that he could go.

"WHAT IS SHE like, this lady of Highfield?" Prince Henry turned the letter over in his hand; he stood slouched a little so that the light of the candles fell on it.

"She is a second cousin of William Peverel's," Fulk said. He had ridden hard to Stamford, and his clothes were stained with dust and his own sweat and his horse's. "She's one of the few women I have met, though, who supported your mother the empress."

Prince Henry smiled. "Women rarely like my mother." He folded the letter and poked it into his wallet. "She must be gracious, to offer me this chance to hunt. I'll accept as soon as I can. Do you like to hunt? You must come, naturally. Sit, my lord."

Fulk sat down; Henry with a gesture sent his pages away and drew his own chair forward. "I am sorry Rannulf is dead. I liked him, I could depend on him. Is Hugh now your heir?"

"Rannulf has a son, only six months old. Geoffrey." The candles lit only a corner of the room, and in the darkness he could hear people moving around; he put his elbows on the arms of his chair. "De Bruyères die young, we get our sons early."

"We all die too young. What is this—" He looked at the letter. "Rohese. What is she like? Is she pretty?"

"Not especially. She's very French in her way of dress. She isn't young, either, she's buried two husbands and is looking for a third."

"You?" Henry sprawled back in his chair. "Are you thinking of marrying, my lord?"

Fulk shook hs head. "If I do, I'll have a young wife, and a small one, with an empty head."

Henry laughed. "The ones who can convince you that their heads are empty are the dangerous ones." He put the letter down. The candlelight fell softly on his hair and left his face in shadow. "You have met my duchess, haven't you?"

"Twice, my lord."

"What do you think of her?"

"She's beautiful, of course, and lively." Fulk heard a noise behind him and turned, and a page came up. Henry waved him off before he could speak.

"Go on, my lord."

Fulk heard the page go to the door and out again, and the door shut with a thud. "I think she has a temper like a cat's, and she won't be content with anything. She's reckless. I don't like that even in a man."

Henry shifted himself in his chair, and the light fell onto his face. He was frowning. Fulk wondered briefly why Henry was keeping him here in pleasant conversation, when obviously someone was waiting outside to see him.

"I don't know whether you are so frank from carelessness or honesty, my lord," Henry said, and called to a page to bring them wine.

"It's too much trouble to lie."

"Oh, well." Henry's face slid back into the shadows. "Chester and Leicester and Pembroke and Hereford and the bishop and whoever I have forgotten, all of them take such pains with me, then, that they must devote their lives to it, and you go to no trouble at all. Stafford, I find it rebellious in you."

"Chester would be shocked to hear you think he lies, legends of seers who go blind from the light of truth;

"All of them—they say the pious, proper things, they talk of Christian virtues with a loving air, and do the opposite, and don't seem to understand that the words mean nothing and the naked act alone is worth judging them by."

"Then judge them by the naked act, my lord, and don't listen to what they say."

"I cannot allow men to lie and lie and, because they wish to, believe what they say."

The page came with two cups of wine. Fulk took one, the gold cool to his hands, chased and figured and set with little red stones.

"Did you talk to Chester, that day?" Henry said.

Fulk nodded. "The wine will conquer England, my lord." He held a mouthful of it a moment on his tongue, swallowed it, and said, "We have never been able to grow decent wine here."

"Then it came to nothing, the talk."

"I never listen to what Chester says, I watch what he does. It took me most of my first years' ruling to learn that."

The door opened, and the page came in again, a swift patter of feet on the wooden floor. Henry said, "Tell him he must wait a little."

"My lord, it's so late, he says—"

"Tell him to wait. No, Stafford, stay." Henry gestured to the page to leave. Leaning forward, his face in the light, he said, "I find a philosopher behind that refusal to talk."

"I don't know why, my lord."

"This touches on something I've often thought of. Perhaps if we were not taught how things should be—" He lifted one hand, and the rings on his fingers flashed in the candlelight. "If we did not expect order in everything, the world would fly into chaos. You know the legends of seers who go blind from the light of truth; might the truth, the real nature of things, be so terrible that we create lies to guard our minds against it?"

Fulk savored another mouthful of wine. "You have a marvelous fondness for such philosophy."

"Argue it away, then. Convince me otherwise."

"I'll think about it. I distrust abstractions, there seems to me more convenience that truth in them. Have you read Abelard?"

"Yes. It stuns me that you have. Have you? Do you read much?"

"Characters, rulings of law, letters, such as I come on now and then. Sometimes a book comes into my hands."

"We should talk more often." Henry picked up Rohese's letter. "We shall hunt soon—I'll give you word, so that you can tell the lady of Highfield to expect us. I want to meet her." He smiled. "I'll tell you if you should marry her."

"Thank you, my lord." Fulk put down his cup, rose, and bowed. "Good night, my lord."

"Good night," the prince said. "How astonishing, that you have read Abelard. Have my page send in Pembroke."

Fulk choked back a laugh. He had been wondering who Henry wanted kept waiting. He went to the door and let himself out.

In the narrow room made by the landing of the stair, two pages and the Earl of Pembroke stood waiting; Pembroke was chewing his fingernails. He started forward.

"Fulk."

"The prince says he will see my lord Pembroke now," Fulk said to the page. "I'm sorry, Gilbert, we were talking philosophy, you must pardon us." He smiled up at Pembroke's bony face and went down the stairs. Prince Henry should not have been allowed to keep a man like the Earl of Pembroke waiting in the hall, even before he was king, but the look on Pembroke's face made him laugh, all the same.

THIERRY RODE AHEAD of Fulk into Highfield Castle, just behind the prince; it had taken them all day to ride up from Stamford, and Thierry's curly russet hair was gray with dust. Fulk looked up at the castle's gray walls, among the people gathered on the rampart on either side of the gatehouse, but he did not see Alys.

The people began to cheer. Fulk rode after Thierry into the main courtyard. The walls were hung with garlands of flowers, and the courtyard itself had been swept and all the livestock penned away. A great mass of servants awaited them. Fulk rode up toward the prince, to introduce him to Rohese, who was standing in the gatehouse door. She came forward, draped in white and red silk, and bowed to the ground.

Henry dismounted, and Fulk slid down from his saddle and ran up to him. "My Lady Rohese, my lord. My lord the Duke of Normandy."

Rohese straightened up, her hand out, and Henry bowed over it. "My lady. I am devoted to you."

"My lord," Rohese said; her voice quivered. Henry stood pressing thanks and compliments on her, her castle, and her lands. Fulk saw him glance up behind her, and looking, Fulk saw Alys on the stair above them. He looked around for Thierry.

Thierry stood talking to Pembroke, near the middle of the courtyard. He gave no sign that he had seen Alys, but of course he didn't know she was here. The servants were taking away all the horses, and a blast of hunting horns rang out.

Henry turned, looking sharply around. Rohese said, "Will you attend me, my lord?"

"With greatest pleasure, my lady."

Fulk followed them up the stair. He could imagine what had gone through Henry's mind when, in a strange castle, he heard hunting horns give a signal. Chester came after him, and he heard Thierry's voice behind him. They climbed the stairs into Rohese's great hall. It was covered with flowers, and the new tapestry hung on the wall. Three tables had been set out for the meal; three pages in matching green and white stood before a cupboard filled with cups and jars of wine and kegs of ale; on every level surface not occupied by a mass of flowers was a dish of pastry.

Rohese sat down by the hearth, with Prince Henry opposite her, leaning forward to give her his attention.

Alys lingered by the door. Fulk paused beside her. "Don't look so eager, will you?" he said softly.

She turned her shoulder on him; her eyes were fixed on the door. Fulk went over toward the hearth. The hall was filling up with people—Rohese had invited two neighboring lords and some of her tenants, and all of Henry's hunting party had come, of course. People began to chatter, and cups came rattling out of the cupboard, wine splashed into them, the pastry dishes emptied immediately, and laughter rang out.

Rohese was glowing. Fulk stood behind her—a page had brought him ale—and listened to her tell the prince exactly what was wrong with England; she was so rapt she did not see Thierry come in, and stop and speak to Alys.

Fulk watched them intently. Thierry said something, and Alys put her hand out, the palm raised, and he shook his head and bowed and went off. Alys stared after him. Fulk thought at first that she would leave, but she pulled herself up; her face looked all bones. Another man came up to her and spoke to her, and she answered him, looking over his shoulder at Thierry. Fulk looked down at Rohese and saw her still talking to the prince.

"Here is Stafford, jealous," Prince Henry said.

Rohese looked around. "Good day, my lord, I am please to see you again so soon." To the prince, she said, "My lord, I shall not keep you—you have other people to talk to. Thank you for listening to my ravings."

"Not ravings, but shrewd remarks." The prince bowed again. "Lady, we shall be friends, I think." He gave her his winning smile and went off to talk to Chester.

"He is so charming," Rohese said to Fulk. Her gaze stiffened. "That is your uncle, isn't it. I did not know that he would come."

"Yes. I should have warned you."

"What can I do? They are all spending the night—he can't, I will not allow it."

"Alys is here, but she isn't with him, is she?"

"She will find some way—"

"Rohese." He took a cup from a page and gave it to her. "How do you like our prince?"

"Oh, he loves himself well enough, and he is handsome. What a pity he is married."

Fulk laughed. "Don't pity him. I see you finished your tapestry."

"I worked on it all day long from the moment you took my message, so that it would be done. Alfred, come here, I want you to meet the Earl of Stafford."

She drew a thin young man with a wan face out of the crowd and presented him to Fulk. "Alfred is a tenant of mine."

Alfred lisped. While he and Rohese spoke of the effects of the recent rain, Fulk looked for Alys. She was talking to Simon d'Ivry, who had come with Fulk. Chester hovered nearby, attentive to her, and one of the prince's Angevin attendants waited beyond Simon to speak to her. Prince Henry was watching her steadily. Alys glanced again and again at Thierry, but he paid no notice.

"You see," Fulk said to Rohese.

"I see. Perhaps you are wiser than I."

A page held up a bowl of nuts, and Fulk took a handful and cracked a walnut in his fingers. "No. I know my uncle." He put the nutmeat in his mouth, picked out a whole walnut, and threw it at Thierry, who stood in the open by the window. Thierry jumped and put his fingers to his temple; he jerked his eyes toward Fulk. Fulk smiled at him.

"You are—irrepressible, my lord," Rohese said sharply.

"New life springs in me when I am in your company." Henry was talking to Alys, and even from a distance Fulk could see the difference in her, an artful submissiveness. "Let me look at your work, my lady," he said to Rohese. "You did all these tapestries, didn't you?"

"I did. Do you like them?"

Fulk led her around the room, commenting on the tapestries, and she leaned on him and laughed. "I see you have an interest in King Arthur," he said, looking at the Grail tapestry. The strawberry wine had stained a corner of it.

"I find those stories prettier than Charlemagne or the lives of the saints. Oh. I do think we should dine." She waved to the servant in the doorway, who went out again. "Everyone is envious of me. Did you see how the ladies looked, when I was talking to the prince?"

"Envious."

"And of you, too, giving me so much attention. Stafford, think of the rumors."

Before Fulk could think of an answer, horns blared again, and every man in the room twitched. The cook came in, carrying his ladle, at the head of a parade of servants with platters of roast meat. The watching guests let out a gasp. The aromas of beef and mutton reached Fulk's nostrils. After the first three platters came boys with great golden fish, vegetables, bread and butter. The horns blasted; four swarthy kitchen knaves in greasy aprons carried in an enormous platter, on which a roasted deer, with parchment horns and apple eyes, reclined in a lake of sauce with its head braced up.

The cook accepted the cheers and stood back and everybody went to sit down. Pages escorted the prince, Alys, Fulk, and Rohese to the high table.

"I hope you will enjoy our simple country fare," Rohese said to the prince, who sat in the high chair on her right. "We had no little time to prepare a true banquet feast."

"My lady, I have seen nothing so tempting since I left Anjou."

Alys was sitting between Rohese and Fulk, and she

wrinkled up her nose. "She has had them working for three days now." She looked at Fulk, and, against her will, at Thierry.

"He's been sorely wounded," Fulk said. "I hit him with a walnut. Simon, serve my Lady Alys first."

Simon leaned down between Alys and Rohese to put fish on Alys's plate. She said, "How do I look, my lord?"

"Very pretty."

"I haven't made a coif yet, and I will not wear one of my cousin's. Do I look too unfashionable?"

"No. I told you, you have beautiful hair. Alys, Thierry will never be jealous of me."

"Rohese will be. Are you going to marry her?"

"I am in mourning, lady. Eat your fish."

Henry was drinking soup; whenever he looked at Rohese, his eyes moved past her to Alys.

"I think you should," Alys said, judicially. "Everyone can see you like her, the way you hang on her."

"Let's talk of something else. Have you—"

"But I want to talk of this. She frets when she has no husband. She doesn't like women. I don't, either."

Rohese in her high seat reached over and cracked Alys on the head with her ring. "Don't tease Stafford."

Alys straightened away from Fulk and gave Rohese an angry look. Prince Henry laughed.

"Lady," he said. "Tease me, I enjoy it."

Alys smiled at him. "My lord, no one could ever tease you, you aren't pompous, like Stafford."

Henry laughed again; his eyes remained on Alys's sleek red hair.

ROHESE'S HOUNDS WERE tall and narrow, with narrow muzzles and dark narrow eyes; black, brindle, red, spotted, silver-gray and cream-white, they leaned against their leashes, their eyes on the forest, and their arched backs taunt with expectation. Fulk looked back at the hunting lodge in the meadow. The last of the hunters were riding down from it now, to join them.

Pembroke on his tall brown horse was walking it up and down past Fulk, his eyes on the prince and Alys. When he passed Fulk the third time he gave him a harsh look. Fulk gathered his reins and moved his horse closer to the hounds. None of them had known Alys was with them—they had left Highfield before dawn, and in the dark, cloaked and hooded, she had gone unnoticed. He was sure that Rohese didn't know she was here.

"My lord," Chester shouted. He and Thierry jogged up to the rest of the hunters. "You must pardon us for holding you back, my lord."

Henry waved to him and signed to the keeper of the hounds. The dogs were coupled in the leashes, and when they started down toward the forest, they nearly pulled their handlers off their feet. Spread out over the open slope, the horsemen followed them. Fulk drifted across to the edge of the party. The sun had not yet risen above the tree, and patches of mist clung to the ground in the shade; the grass glistened with dew, but the windless air was already uncomfortably warm. Just before they reached the forest, the crickets in the grass began their high shrilling. It would be a hot day, even in the forest.

Riding side by side, their faces turned toward each other, the prince and Alys followed close behind the hounds into the forest. Fulk eased the bow on his back. A rider loomed up beside him, and he stiffened, and his horse sensed it and shied.

"My lord." It was Simon. "Two of Thierry's men have been here since yesterday."

Fulk reined his horse back onto the trail. "Oh?" He started to look for Thierry and changed his mind. "Follow him, Simon." He rode into the forest, into the cooler air and the shade.

In the trees, the hunting party drew closer together, stirrup to stirrup. All along their path, birds and animals rustled through the underbrush, startled away, and overhead the squirrels squeaked and chattered. Chester rode just ahead of Fulk, with Pembroke, but Fulk could not see Thierry and knew he was behind him. His back tingled; he felt as if he were naked.

The dogs began to bark. "False scent," Chester cried. "It's too close." In the narrow space of the path the horses jostled back and forth, nipped, and kicked out.

"Hold your horse."

"I am—can you not hold yours?"

"Watch out, up there. Keep moving."

Ahead of the confusion, the prince and Alys disappeared around a curve in the path; Fulk caught a glimpse of her red sleeve, through the green of leaves. His horse ranged up behind Pembroke's so close Pembroke's horse skittered and pinned back its ears, and Pembroke gave him a fierce look over his shoulder. Fulk reined down. The horse fretted against his hand —he knew he was urging it, pressing it on because he wanted to get away from Thierry behind him, and he tried to relax. The dogs had quieted, only one barking now, and they rode down a steep slope toward a stream. The path widened. He moved his horse up through the crowd toward the prince. Smelling water, his horse stretched its head forward, and its ears pricked up.

Suddenly the dogs burst into their deep-throated belling; the mob of horses bounded forward, and the dogs' handlers slipped the leashes and darted into the brush. Hunting horns sounded, ringing in the trees. Two of the dogs streaked through the water and up the far slope, yelling with each stride, and the pack followed in a long stream of ears and tails and ridged backs. Fulk's horse bolted forward.

Horses jammed the ford over the stream; Fulk crossed above them, banged his knee on a tree trunk, and galloped across the slope after the ululation of the dogs. Prince Henry was charging along almost at the heels of the pack, with Alys just behind him, and

Chester racing to catch up. Fulk bent down to clear the low-hanging branches before him. The dogs veered suddenly, and the horsemen swung to follow and engulfed Fulk. With the horses galloping all around him he raced up toward the crest of the hill.

The dogs were pulling ahead of them. Their musical baying faded with distance. Close underbrush and trees slowed the horses—Prince Henry swore in a high voice. Fulk's chestnut stumbled, caught itself up, and ran up alongside Chester's horse.

Chester glanced at him. Fulk met his eyes only an instant, but Chester's hard, piercing look made him straighten up, slowing his horse. Pembroke surged up beside him, his eyes on the prince. They struggled up the last stretch of hill to the crest, through thorny bushes and clumps of rocks.

Before them lay a meadow. The pack was already halfway across it, running flat to the ground, only their slim heads visible above the high grass. The horsemen gave a single cry. At the far end of the meadow, a stag reached the trees and vanished.

In the middle of the meadow, the pack of dogs slowed, and half split off and raced in a wide curve through the grass. Fulk slowed his horse. The dogs that had left the main scent began to bay. He looked at the prince, who was racing after the first pack, but with a hoarse cry Pembroke swerved to follow the second, and Fulk pulled his horse around after him. With Pembroke a length ahead of him, he galloped across the curve of the dogs' path after them. The chestnut leaned on the bit, straining for more speed, and caught up with Pembroke's brown horse and ran head to head with it. The dogs bolted into the woods, and Fulk plowed through underbrush and thistles after them.

The dogs' wild baying led them into a narrow trail overhung with branches. Through the trees, Fulk caught a glimpse of the flying bodies of the pack; he steadied his horse. Pembroke fell behind him. A hunting horn sounded. Fulk could see nothing. The branches of the trees masked the path. He felt the horse change leads and shifted his weight in the saddle and the chestnut flung itself around a turn like a loop in the trail. A windfall loomed up before them, with young trees sprouting from its trunk. The chestnut stopped, throwing Fulk up onto its neck, cocked its ears, and jumped from a standstill. Fulk went over the windfall a foot above the saddle, hit his head on a branch, and came down into his saddle with a thump that jarred him to the teeth, his feet still in the stirrups. The chestnut bolted after the fading sound of the dogs.

The trail twisted back and forth, crossing one stream five times within a few hundred yards, and the chestnut never slackened stride. Fulk could not see more than a few steps in front of him. He gave his horse its head and hung onto his saddle. Its head aimed precisely at the sound of the dogs, the big chestnut flowed around the twists in the path. Fulk could hear riders behind him, but they were falling back.

Ahead, sunlight showed through the branches; the trail opened up into another meadow, long and narrow. Fulk gathered his reins. The note of the dogs' baying changed to shrill triumph, and he reached behind him for his bow. Back on the trail, a horn brayed.

The dogs stopped baying and began to whine.

Fulk sat back, snatching his horse to a halt. The dogs were milling around at the far end of the meadow, and between them and him were three men with longbows, their arrows nocked. He jerked the chestnut into a rear and threw himself off sidewise into the grass. The arrows sang over his head. He rolled and got to his hands and knees. Under him, the earth trembled with the hoofs of horses rushing down on him. He knew one was Thierry. The forest was only a hundred feet away, and crouched over he raced for it—he had lost his bow.

"Here," Chester shouted harshly. "Here—"

Fulk looked up and saw him charging down on him.

Chester's horse's nostrils were blood red; the bit pried its jaws apart and its bleeding tongue lolled out. For an instant Fulk could not move. He saw the great forehoofs tear up chunks of turf and fling them aside, all that weight hurtling down on him, and Chester with his bow. He dodged. The horse wheeled toward him, and he felt its steaming breath on his face. Chester was still shouting; Fulk could not hear what he said. He swerved, and the horse swerved to meet him, and Fulk stumbled and sprawled on his belly.

"Hold up," Pembroke shouted. "What's going on here?"

Fulk lay with his cheek pressed to the ground and shut his eyes, waiting for the arrow. Chester said, "He was thrown, my lord—he seems hurt."

Pembroke had no part in it, then. Fulk pushed himself up to his knees. Chester sat his black horse nearby, but he was looking at Pembroke, riding over toward them from the forest. The three bowmen were gone. Pembroke jogged his horse over to them. His lean face was expressionless, but his eyes flickered like a snake's tongue at Chester.

"Fulk. Are you hurt?"

"No," Fulk said. He got to his feet. Chester was watching him, his fist clenched on his thigh. Fulk had dirt in his mouth, and he spat it out.

"What happened?" Pembroke said.

Fulk took two running steps and leaped at Chester; Chester whirled his horse, but Fulk caught him by the belt and hung against the horse's side, and it reared and spun on its hocks. Fulk struggled to pull himself up behind Chester. Something sharp struck his hand, three hard strokes, and he fell back into the grass. Chester galloped off across the meadow. Fulk knelt in the grass and looked at his bleeding fingers, slashed to the bone.

Pembroke seized him roughly by the shoulder and turned him around. "Are you mad? Have you lost your mind? Here." He pulled out Fulk's shirt tail and cut it off with his dagger. "After the ride you led us through those trees you deserve to be thrown." He wrapped the cloth around Fulk's fingers, and it turned sodden crimson at once.

"I wasn't thrown," Fulk said. "Where's Thierry?"

"Back with the prince, I suppose. Where is the deer? Will you tell me what happened?"

"Chester tried to kill me," Fulk said. "The deer's where the dogs are."

"From what I saw you just tried to kill Chester." Pembroke pulled off his coat and took his own shirt and hacked it up for bandages. "You need a blood-letting to get this humor out of you."

"Gilbert," Fulk shouted, "he tried to kill me. He had bowmen here—" He leaped up, bandages streaming from his hands, and ran in short dashes over the grass. "Here, and here—" He kicked at the arrows in the grass. "See them? See them? They killed Rannulf—see?" He tore an arrow out of the earth and threw it at Pembroke.

Pembroke knelt, staring at him, his mouth open. Fulk's shoulders drooped; all the strength ebbed from his body, and he looked down at his wounded hands, overwhelmed. "That was why I followed you—I thought you would not—"

"Stay here." Pembroke mounted his horse and galloped across the meadow to the pack of dogs. Fulk's horse was calmly grazing along the edge of the forest, but Fulk could not find strength enough to walk over to him. He stood and wrapped the cloth around his fingers, tied knots in the bandage with his teeth, and watched the blood soak through. Chester could have killed him when Fulk jumped at him, even with Pembroke there—Chester must have panicked. Fulk thought. How fortunate I am. Pembroke trotted his horse across the meadow to Fulk's chestnut, bent from his saddle to reach its rein, and rode toward Fulk, leading the chestnut at a walk.

"It's a doe, it's been dead at least a day," Pembroke said. "We can question the gamekeepers at the lodge. Chester and Thierry must have found out we would start a deer, crossing that stream so early in the morning, and dragged the doe all across this area to split us up. It should never have worked. Prince Henry might have followed this scent—what would they have done?"

Fulk shook his head. "Called it poachers." He leaned against his horse a moment and mounted.

"You said they killed Rannulf."

"I didn't mean to. I have no proof."

"There is no proof here, either. You couldn't set it before the prince. Chester would say you were thrown from your horse and when he went to help you, you turned on him. Everybody knows you've been strange since Rannulf died."

"I'm not putting it before the prince."

Pembroke stared at him a moment. "We can't hide your hands. We have to hide the deer. If anyone found it and told the prince, anything might happen. You'll have to help me."

Fulk lifted his reins. "I forgot that the Clares have some experience with hunting accidents."

Pembroke laughed. They rode down to the deer and chased the dogs away from it; the pack had eaten away most of the deer's stomach and haunches. When they dragged it away from the place it had lain, a swarm of flies rose out of the carcass; the grass was slimed and matted down.

"We could let the dogs eat it" Pembroke said.

Fulk shook his head. "You're right—if the prince knew of it, he might suspect something." He took the deer by the foreleg, and Pembroke took it by a hind-leg, and they dragged it back into the forest. Fulk's cut hand hurt so much he could not use it, but they hauled the deer almost half a mile into the trees and walked back to their horses.

"Listen," Pembroke said.

A hunting horn sounded, far away to the north. Fulk untied his reins from the tree. "That's back toward the lodge."

Pembroke nodded. He mounted his horse and turned it toward the sound of the horn, which blasted again, twice more, and stopped. "It's the lodge's horn. Let's go."

ELEVEN

THE HORN BLEW THREE MORE blasts before they reached the lodge. When they rode out from under the trees, the noon sun clubbed them; its dazzling light made Fulk blink. Thierry and Simon d'Ivry were sitting their horses before the lodge gate, and the prince's horse stood riderless near them. Other horses were tied inside the lodge's wall.

Thierry turned and saw Fulk, and he seemed to start. Pembroke rode up past Fulk, reined in, and, smiling, said something to Thierry Fulk could not hear. Thierry did not answer; his jaw tightened. Pembroke drew his horse off to one side.

Chester and two Angevins came out of the trees and galloped up over the meadow toward them. Fulk rode over to Thierry.

"What happened?"

Thierry's yellow eyes were expressionless. "A messenger came from the Bishop of Winchester. Prince Eustace is dead."

Fulk grunted. He kicked his horse over toward Pembroke's and dismounted. One of the gamekeepers brought him a cup of tepid water, and he drank it. Pembroke was loosening his horse's girths. The bitter odor of sweat lay in the air; Fulk's nose itched from it.

"Prince Eustace is dead," Fulk said. "Did you hear it?"

Pembroke nodded. "De Lous told me. The king is willing to accept terms." He lifted his saddle up off his horse's back so that the air could get under it.

Fulk's horse scratched its head on his shoulder, and Fulk braced himself against it. Pembroke sat on his heels with his back against the lodge wall. The door into the lodge itself was closed, and the Angevin de Lous stood guard over it. Fulk draped his arm over his horse's neck, trying to look unexcited. He wondered where Alys was; her horse stood just inside the gate, chewing on the wooden wall.

"My lord," Chester cried. "Gilbert." He walked up to Pembroke and bent to whisper in his ear. Pembroke gave no sign he was listening, or that he had ever seen him come. Chester straightened; Pembroke said nothing, and after a moment looked up at Chester, impassive. Chester turned on his heel and went away.

The door of the lodge banged open, and the Angevin stepped aside. Prince Henry came out, with a stranger just behind him. He crossed the courtyard at a fast walk, arms swinging, and stopped by the gate. His face was taut and bright.

"We'll go straight back to Stamford. I'll send to Highfield and have our men go back without us. Where is my horse?"

A groom led up a fresh horse for him, and Henry mounted. Fulk climbed into his saddle. Alys had come to the door of the lodge; Henry saw her, and with his eyes on her spoke in a high, young voice to the groom, asking him the swiftest way to Stamford. Pembroke and the other lords of the hunting party were gathering behind the prince, and Fulk went to join them, but before he reached them Henry turned and beckoned to him.

"Will you take her back to Stamford?" he said. "The Lady Alys. She knows you, she is accustomed to you."

"I should not," Fulk said, "for the Lady Rohese's sake."

Henry smiled. "Oh, but for my sake, you will, won't you, Stafford." He raised his left hand a little, backed his horse, and rode around Fulk. The other lords followed him, all in a clump.

Alys was walking from the lodge to the gate. Fulk dismounted. He knew there was no need for him to go back to Stamford so quickly—Leicester was there, ahead of them all, and Leicester dealt with such things more shrewdly than Fulk. Yet he strained to go, to be there. Alys came up to him, still wearing her page's hose and coat.

"I'm sorry to burden you, my lord," she said. "I shall not hold you back. We may go whenever you wish."

Fulk looked over at Simon d'Ivry, lingering by the wall, and signed to him to bring Alys's horse. "There's no need to hurry, my lady. Nothing will happen until tomorrow, anyway."

"What does it mean? Will he be king?"

Her hair was spilling out of her cap in great red loops. Her eyes shone. Fulk said, "There was little question he would be king. The problem was when. Here's your horse, lady."

She turned, lifting her arms to take hold of her saddle. Simon held the horse's bridle, and Fulk made a cup of his hands for her knee and lifted her up onto her horse's back. Simon ran for his own horse. Fulk picked up his reins and mounted his chestnut, and before his right foot had found the stirrup, Alys was looping down the meadow, after the prince, toward Stamford.

SHE TRIED TO keep up; her hair came loose from her cap and without slowing her horse she gathered it and tucked it back up again, and she never asked to stop. But her little gelding could not match the pace of the great horses of the men, and the prince's party pulled farther ahead of them, while Fulk and Simon held their horses down so that they would not outrun her.

Finally, Fulk stopped, at the edge of a meadow full of late flowers. Alys reined down her horse angrily and cried, "You need not pause for me—can't we catch up with them?"

Fulk said, "Lady, I said there was no need to race. Leicester will handle everything."

She gave him a strange look. "Thierry will—he has never outridden me, damn him, he shall not now."

Fulk laughed. Simon was waiting nearby, looking off toward the meadow, obviously listening. Fulk leaned down from his saddle and wiped his hand across the gelding's shoulder, slick with sweat. "He won't outride you, he'll outride this jade. Come along, if you're so eager, but save your horse or we won't reach Stamford at all."

They rode on, through the edge of the forest into the fields of the manor of Highfield. All through the afternoon, they moved across the narrow strips of the serfs' corn and barley. The sun fell until it shone straight in Fulk's eyes. He saw the color gleaming on Alys's face; she had been sunburned on her nose and cheeks and chin. They followed a wide, deep trail to a village, and Fulk sent Simon to get them water and something to eat from the villagers. Alys let her reins slide through her fingers, so that her horse could graze.

"Stafford," she said. "Henry must not know of me and Thierry."

Fulk said nothing. He dismounted. The village lay in a curve of trees: a dozen two-room huts, their roofs thatched with straw. An old man had come out of one of the houses and was watching Simon approach. He seemed to be the only serf there—the others would be in the fields, of course, while the sun was up.

"Did you hear me?" Alys said.

"Lady, I think he probably knows already."

"No," she said sharply. "No. I am certain of it."

Simon spoke to the old man, who went back into his house. Chickens clucked and scratched in the dust around the huts. Through the corner of his eye, Fulk saw the door of the hut nearest him move a little, and he looked hard at it and laughed. The village was filled with people, all hidden indoors. Now that he looked he saw how each door stood a little ajar.

"What are you laughing at?" Alys said. "How can you laugh? This place is damned—how lonely it is. Where are all the people?"

Fulk shook his head, smiling down at his boots. Simon was coming back with two loaves under one arm, half a wheel of cheese under the other, and jugs in both hands. Fulk turned to Alys.

"Come down, we'll eat here."

"God in Heaven, why must we stop any longer? We can eat in the saddle."

"Lady, that style may have suited Thierry, but you'll find the prince's life a little different. Come down. Your horse can rest, too."

They ate sitting on the grass at the edge of the village, throwing crumbs to the chickens and geese that swarmed around them. It amused Fulk to watch the doors of the huts open, one by one, and empty each half a dozen people into the village. Alys ate so fast her cheeks bulged out. Simon watched her with a steady, unsmiling look. Fulk brushed the crumbs from his hands; the sun was setting.

The prince would not reach Stamford before the middle of the night. Nothing could be done until the next day, anyway. He looked at Alys, sitting cross-legged in her page's costume, with her hair coming down. She was aware of Simon's constant, adoring gaze, but she ignored it. She pulled her coat straight and pressed her hands to her cheeks.

"I am burning hot. Stafford, my skin."

"You look lovely." He got up, leaned down, and pulled her hair. "Come on, we have the whole night to ride away."

THEY REACHED STAMFORD just before dawn; the cocks in the city's gardens were crowing when Fulk left Alys in the prince's house and rode across the city to Leicester's. The sky was pale as silver but in the streets it was still dark. In front of Leicester's house, a torch burned, and when Fulk rode up to the gate, a page came out with the porter and took him straight to Leicester.

Prince Henry had called his council to meet at noon of the coming day, in the great hall of his house. None of the men who had gone to the hunt had slept more than a few hours; Fulk had not slept at all. He and Leicester had talked from the moment Fulk came into his house until they reached the prince's door. Before they were two steps into the sunlit hall, a page came to Leicester to take him to the prince. Fulk walked across the hall to the window and looked out; he and Leicester had come before anyone else.

Chester rode into the courtyard below the window, with Thierry and Wiltshire and two or three other lords of their party, dismounted, and came into the house. Talking, they strode through the door into the wide, empty hall and ranged themselves against the wall opposite Fulk. Except for the benches along the walls, there was no furniture in the room, and the fire on the hearth made it stifling hot. Derby rode in, alone, and gave his horse to a groom.

By twos and threes, the barons of the prince's council came in, and those who followed Chester and Pembroke went to Chester's side, those who followed Leicester came to Fulk's side. Derby walked up to him through the gathering crowd.

"So God has finally made His choice," Derby said,

and sighed. "And how was your hunt? What happened to your hand?"

"I cut myself. We hadn't been out more than half the morning when this news came. Here comes Hereford, now, watch."

Derby gave him a puzzled look and turned. Hereford walked into the room, with William de Clare beside him, glanced at Chester, and came over to Fulk's side. Derby swore, excited. "What happened?" he asked Fulk.

"Ssssh," Fulk said. He laid his bandaged hand on the windowsill.

He did not feel tired; strange energy filled him, but he knew that for the exhilaration of sleeplessness. Leicester had explained everything to him in loving detail—Leicester, hearing the news before anyone else, and in Stamford all the day before with the leisure to think it all out, had organized the king's terms into a bargain the prince might accept. Fulk wondered how much of his confidence was false, a sign of weariness.

Pembroke came in, and before he had come two steps into the hall a page came up to him and led him away. Chester was sitting on the bench opposite Fulk and a little more into the middle of the room, with his head back. The men around him were talking in low voices. Three Beaumonts walked in and went immediately to Fulk's side. Hereford and William de Clare greeted them coldly.

Fulk thought, It is the blood tie, because they killed Rannulf, and Rannulf was Pembroke's nephew. Margaret's son. The heat of the sunlight on his wounded hand made it throb.

Through a little door at Fulk's end of the hall, Leicester came into the room, and a startled murmur sprang up. Behind him came Prince Henry and Pembroke. Henry went forward, into the middle of the room. Most of the younger men rushed toward him, but the older men hung back, out of the heat of the crowd. Fulk stayed by the window, where there was a breeze. Leicester was looking for him, and when he

saw him, nodded and smiled. Pembroke stood beside
Leicester, his great height stooped.

"My lords," the prince said, "Eustace, the son of
Stephen of Blois, is dead, and in his bereavement the
king has offered me certain terms for the settlement of
the kingdom between us."

"He's excited," Fulk said to Derby. "He called him
the king."

"The terms are these. Stephen shall remain as England's crowned king until he dies. He will proclaim
his heir, and I shall succeed him."

The younger men all cheered. Henry lifted his hand
to silence them. In spite of the heat, he wore a coat
of white satin sewn with gold and silver thread, and his
face dripped sweat.

"To Stephen's remaining son, William, we are to give
cognizance of his claim through his wife to the Honor
of the Earl of Surrey, William de Warenne, and also
the estates that his father held before he took the
throne. That is, Boulogne and the county of Mortain,
and the English honors of Eye and Lancaster."

Fulk had been watching Chester, lounging comfortably on the far side of the room, sometimes chat-
ting to Thierry, who leaned up against the wall beside
him, one knee bent. When the prince spoke of Lancaster, Chester started up. Thierry reached out to hold
him and Chester flung off his hand and walked into
the middle of the room.

"My lord, Lancaster is mine, by your own assur-
ance."

"I am giving you the terms which Stephen has offered, my lord, no one has—"

"Give him something else, not Lancaster. Give
him—" Chester's eyes swept the opposite side of the
room. "Give him Stafford's rewards, or—"

"My lord," Henry said smoothly, "I have not yet
agreed to this. Be silent, I require advice, not a tan-
trum."

Chester stepped back; his eyes darted around the
room. All around him, the men were drawing back,

pulling away from him, pushing over to the other side of the room, and through them the low talk ran, uneasy.

"We have no leisure to consider this in," Henry said. "The terms are as reasonable as we may expect, and the king might think it too reasonable, when his mind steadies. Therefore let me put them before you without interruption, that we might come to a decision soon."

Pembroke said, "After all, the king's son has the best claim to Lancaster."

Chester turned and walked out of the hall. The prince in his even and excited voice recited the rest of the king's terms, glancing now and then at the paper that Leicester held out before him. Fulk looked out the window into the courtyard. Chester marched across it, toward his horse, and rode straight out the gate. Fulk turned back into the room, smiling.

THE BEAR ROSE up onto its hindlegs and began to pace heavily in time to the music of the pipe. All the children screamed with pleasure. The bearkeeper's boys ran around collecting money; with a look like a leer on its face, the bear pranced in a little circle. Fulk took a halfpenny from his wallet and leaned down from his horse to give it to the nearest boy.

"My lord," Morgan said. "The Lady Rohese is here."

Fulk looked where he was pointing, and saw Rohese riding toward him. He backed his horse out of the crowd of children and called to her, and she waved her hand.

"My lady," he said, when she reached him. "I didn't know you had come to Stamford."

"Stafford," she said, "I have been looking everywhere for you. You must help me with Alys. You know she is living in the prince's own house. She's mad, she won't come home, she says she's staying here. I must talk to the prince."

Fulk looked around; they were in the middle of the marketplace. "We can't talk here. Will you come back to my house?"

"I knew she ran away with him to go to the hunt," Rohese said. "But I thought she would come back. She's a disgrace, she should be whipped. What can I tell her husband?"

"Have you seen her?"

"Yes. I told you, she said she won't come home."

Fulk stopped to let a wagon full of barrels roll by. "Most people would not be so upset. This prince's grandfather made his mistresses great, and their families gained by it, too."

"It makes no difference."

Fulk led her down an alleyway, stinking of garbage, into a quieter street. She had two men with her, but no women, and he asked. "Where are you staying?"

"At my house in the city. We should go there, of course. Will you—"

A horse burst out of the alley and lunged between them. On its back, Alys looked from Rohese to Fulk and back again. "I told you not to bother him. He had nothing to do with it. If he did, I would love him for it. Go home."

Rohese said, "You are mad. You are." She wrenched her horse around and trotted off, her two men behind her. Halfway down the street, she turned and shouted, "Never come back, Alys. Never come back." Her whip rose and fell, and she bolted away.

Alys spat into the street. Fulk said, "The alewife again."

"Prince Henry's alewife, if it please you, my lord." She studied him, her hands crossed on the pommel of her saddle. "I have a message for you that will be welcome."

"What is it?"

"Tomorrow, our soon-to-be-king will announce certain charters to the people of Stamford, for which, I understand, they have given him a good deal of money. After it, he will have read a list of outlaws. Thierry Ironhand will be one of them."

She lifted her reins, watching him, and lowered them again. "Aren't you going to ask my why I told you?"

Fulk shook his head.

"Are you glad, at least?" she cried. "Are you glad at what I have done for you?"

"Oh, yes," Fulk said. "But you didn't do it for me."

She laughed, which amazed him, and sent her horse at a gallop away down the street, her braids flying. The racket of hoofs on the cobblestones followed her.

THIERRY'S HOUSE WAS at the end of a blind street, against the wall, a three-room house with a garden. In the street outside it, no noise stirred; there had been children playing with their hoops in the street but Fulk had sent them away. In the last heat of the summer, there was no wind. Fulk's shirt was stuck to his back with sweat. Beside him, Roger was drawing circles in the dust with his heel.

A horse turned into the street; it was one of Thierry's men. He galloped up to the gate of the house and started to dismount, but he saw the men waiting in the shade across from him and stopped. Cupping his hands around his mouth, he shouted, "Thierry, Thierry!"

Simon and Hugh were standing down the street from Fulk. They started across toward Thierry's house. Neither of them had drawn his sword yet. Roger moved, and Fulk put out his hand and stopped him.

Thierry looked out the window. The man on the horse called, "It's done. You are outlawed. It's finished." He looked around him and saw Simon and Hugh coming toward him, spurred his horse, and galloped away.

Hugh broke into a run, headed for the gate. Thierry's

head at the window disappeared. Roger took a step forward and Fulk put his hand on his arm.

"My lord," Roger said, pleading.

"Get his horse, and go around behind the house." He pushed himself away from the fence he had been leaning on and walked across the street to the gate.

The front door opened, and Thierry stepped out, carrying his sword in his hand. Hugh and Simon leaped forward like hunting dogs, straight for him. Fulk shouted, "Hugh—be careful—" and ran after them. Thierry dodged back behind the door and slammed it shut.

Simon and Hugh flung themselves on the door, struggling to open it. Fulk pulled Simon away. "Go around back—Roger's there, go help him. Chase him out. Go on!"

Simon raced away. Fulk went up to the door. Hugh was pulling at it, but Thierry was holding it shut. Fulk said, "Thierry, come out." He tapped Hugh on the shoulder, and Hugh stood back, panting.

Thierry said nothing, but behind the door he breathed so loud Fulk heard it. He drew his sword. Horses were coming; he looked quickly at the street and saw Pembroke and some of his men riding down it. "Thierry, come out," Fulk said, and slapped Hugh's shoulder.

Hugh grabbed the door and pulled, and it flew out of Thierry's hands. Fulk thrust his sword inside before the door was fully open. The blade nicked the doorjamb and glanced off Thierry's shoulder.

Thierry staggered back into the hall of the house. Fulk leaped after him. Before he could strike again, Hugh flew past him, screaming, "For my brother, for my brother." His sword took Thierry in the side and spun him around, into Fulk's stroke. Roger and Simon rushed up behind Thierry; Fulk wrenched his sword out of Thierry's falling body and chopped down and felt the flesh give and the bone break under the blade. Roger and Simon were clubbing at him, standing over him. Fulk stepped back. Thierry lay twisted on the floor, a great pool of blood under him. One by one, the others drew back, staring at the body.

Pembroke crashed in the door. "Is he dead?"

Hugh kicked Thierry in the side. "He's dead, my lord." He put his foot back to kick again.

"Don't," Fulk said. He pushed Hugh away. "Roger, take this and bury it." His sword was fouled with blood and brain matter, and he wiped the blade on his thigh. Turning, he saw that, at the far end of the room, there was a girl standing in the corner behind the pallet bed, her fists pressed to her breast, her head bowed as if she prayed.

EPILOGUE

OUT IN THE COURTYARD, IN THE bright November sun, groups of horses stood with their grooms, waiting; a little crowd of local people had gathered along the edge of the road. Behind him, in the darkness of the cathedral, Fulk could hear voices mumbling, winding solemn oaths and promises around the agreement between the king and the prince. Fulk folded his arms over his chest. In the shade, it was cold, a clammy cold that roughened his skin even through the layers of thick clothing.

Chester came out, looking around, gave Fulk a short nod, and went to the edge of the sunshine. Fulk straightened away from the wall he had been leaning on. Footsteps sounded in the interior dark—they were all coming out, moving up the aisle, Leicester and de Luci and Richard Camville, the king's knights, the prince's lawyers.

"God, this is tedious," Leicester said, coming up beside Fulk. "I've a thought to go home and let them work it out themselves."

Fulk said nothing. Beside Leicester, he walked down the steps into the sunlight and the gusty wind of the churchyard. None of them would dare not be here, with the king and Henry deciding each small claim and tenement and benefice in England. Passing Chester, Fulk looked covertly at him, struck again by the man's face, gray and seized with pain; it frightened him, and he jerked his eyes away.

They went to their horses and mounted. The king came from the cathedral, surrounded by his men, and rode away. The people cheered him but their voices were only a whisper compared to the shout they gave Prince Henry. The king rode slumped in his saddle, his head down.

"He is dying," Leicester said. "Prince Henry will have his throne within the year."

"Yes," Fulk said. Of them all, only Prince Henry seemed full of energy, his red hair bristling, his face flushed. Fulk lifted his reins. A familiar sluggishness dragged at him; he had often felt so, since Rannulf had died, dull and uncaring. The keen wind stung his face. Winter was coming.

Romantic Fiction

by Janette Seymour

"A boundless passion is Purity's."
—*Publishers Weekly*

_____ 81943 PURITY'S ECSTASY
over 2 million copies in print! $1.95

_____ 81036 PURITY'S PASSION $1.95

_____ 82124 PURITY'S SHAME $1.95